"Ex_____
thia_____                                            rpa-
love_____                                            ding
danger-_____ adventure."
—Booklist

"A terrific grim thriller with the romantic subplot playing a strong supporting role. The cast is powerful as the audience will feel every emotion that Andra feels, from fear for her sister to fear for her falling in love. *Finding the Lost* is a dark tale as Shannon K. Butcher paints a forbidding, gloomy landscape in which an ancient war between humanity's guardians and their nasty adversaries heats up in Nebraska."

—Alternative Worlds

"A very entertaining read ... the ending was a great cliff-hanger, and I can't wait to read the next book in this series ... a fast-paced story with great action scenes and lots of hot romance." —The Book Lush

"Butcher's paranormal reality is dark and gritty in this second Sentinel Wars installment. What makes this story so gripping is the seamlessly delivered hard-hitting action and wrenching emotions. Butcher is a major talent in the making."

—*Romantic Times*

### Burning Alive

"Starts off with nonstop action. Readers will race through the pages, only to reread the entire novel to capture every little detail ... a promising start for a new voice in urban fantasy/paranormal romance. I look forward to the next installment."
—A Romance Review (5 roses)

*continued ...*

## ALSO BY SHANNON K. BUTCHER

### NOVELS OF THE SENTINEL WARS

*Living Nightmare*
*Running Scared*
*Finding the Lost*
*Burning Alive*
*Blood Hunt*

### THE EDGE NOVELS

*Living on the Edge*

# RAZOR'S EDGE

## AN EDGE NOVEL

## SHANNON K. BUTCHER

A SIGNET ECLIPSE BOOK

SIGNET ECLIPSE
Published by New American Library, a division of
Penguin Group (USA) Inc., 375 Hudson Street,
New York, New York 10014, USA
Penguin Group (Canada), 90 Eglinton Avenue East, Suite 700, Toronto,
Ontario M4P 2Y3, Canada (a division of Pearson Penguin Canada Inc.)
Penguin Books Ltd., 80 Strand, London WC2R 0RL, England
Penguin Ireland, 25 St. Stephen's Green, Dublin 2,
Ireland (a division of Penguin Books Ltd.)
Penguin Group (Australia), 250 Camberwell Road, Camberwell, Victoria 3124,
Australia (a division of Pearson Australia Group Pty. Ltd.)
Penguin Books India Pvt. Ltd., 11 Community Centre, Panchsheel Park,
New Delhi - 110 017, India
Penguin Group (NZ), 67 Apollo Drive, Rosedale, Auckland 0632,
New Zealand (a division of Pearson New Zealand Ltd.)
Penguin Books (South Africa) (Pty.) Ltd., 24 Sturdee Avenue,
Rosebank, Johannesburg 2196, South Africa

Penguin Books Ltd., Registered Offices:
80 Strand, London WC2R 0RL, England

First published by Signet Eclipse, an imprint of New American Library,
a division of Penguin Group (USA) Inc.

First Printing, November 2011
10  9  8  7  6  5  4  3  2  1

*For Cindy Hwang, who is a truly awesome editor.*

# ACKNOWLEDGMENTS

I am blessed to have many people in my life to thank. I have a family, who is supportive of my work, even when it means they have to fend for their own food and clean underwear. I have good friends who help me keep my sanity and forget work by playing with little bits of colored glass, thread, and paper. I have beta readers who lovingly point out my endless mistakes and listen to me ramble about stories for hours on end. And I have readers who cheer me on and make me feel like a rock star. All of you touch my life and make it a sweeter place. I couldn't do this job without you. Thank you.

# Chapter One

Catching a thief was easy. Catching a thief in the act was more of a challenge—one that made Roxanne Haught's skin sizzle with eager anticipation.

The lavish retirement party was her idea, despite the fact she'd never met the guest of honor. It was the perfect trap, complete with juicy bait her target would be unable to resist.

She mingled among the well-dressed partygoers, smiling and making small talk as she passed from one cluster of people to the next, waiting for the right time to strike.

Her client, Mr. Chord, had graciously opened his home for his friend's party—something the middle-aged reclusive genius had never done before. Because of that, dozens of people had come here tonight, curious to get a peek into the executive's estate.

Roxanne cared little about the details of the hand-carved woodwork or the intricacies of the mosaic tile floor inlaid with semiprecious stone, which seemed to delight many of the people here. She'd seen it all before. She was more interested in the number of exits on each floor and the location of the information she'd been hired to guard.

The stage was set. The party was in full swing. Mr. Chord had made sure his newest employee, the unlikely named Mary Smith, knew that the plans for Chord Industries' latest invention were being kept safe on his hard drive at home, away from any possible thieves at the office. That machine had no Internet or network connection, making hacking it from a remote location impossible. No copies were being stored elsewhere, not since the last fiasco. If someone wanted that information, the only way to get it was by breaking into his home office.

He was being extra careful this time. Too bad for Mary Smith her boss suspected her of the theft and had hired Roxanne to catch her in the act.

The Kevlar designed into the bodice of Roxanne's beaded evening gown gave her little comfort. Mary looked more like the kind of woman who would prefer knives—up close, personal, and silent.

She was a small, innocent-looking woman. She had delicate, softly rounded features, like a porcelain doll. Her bright, cherry red hair was styled in an old-fashioned manner that reminded Roxanne of glamorous actresses from the 1940s. Her dress matched her flamboyant hair color and skimmed the kind of curves that made men forget their own names. If it weren't for the fact that her boss was a freaking genius, Mary probably would have continued to get away with stealing his intellectual property.

But Mr. Chord *was* a genius, and, after a bit of surveillance, Roxanne was sure he was right. Mary Smith was a thief.

Roxanne stood on the grand staircase leading to the second floor where several people mingled, both here and on the balcony above. She watched Mary laugh at something Mr. Chord said, placing her delicate hand on his chest while she batted her fake eyelashes. The redhead stared up at him in rapt attention, hanging on his every word. Her hands were quick, but Roxanne was watching carefully, expecting the woman to make a move.

Mary didn't disappoint. With a quick, graceful motion, she swiped Mr. Chord's key card from his breast pocket, palming it until it was safely in her red beaded evening bag.

Busted, but not good enough yet. Mary had to be caught

stealing the information, or no one would believe little Miss Innocent was guilty of anything more than stunning good looks.

Mary excused herself, heading toward the staircase. Roxanne turned to the nearest group of people and chatted with them as the other woman passed behind her, moving up the stairs, to the right, toward Mr. Chord's office.

Roxanne caught Mr. Chord's gaze and gave him a slight nod. Tonight, she was going to plug her client's information leak once and for all.

A smile stretched Roxanne's lips as she waited until the last flash of red skirt was gone before following Mary down the hallway. The floor plan to Mr. Chord's home was firmly in her mind. There was only one reason Mary would be headed down this hall—to reach Mr. Chord's office.

Roxanne waited a few brief seconds outside the solid wood door, giving Mary time to power up the PC and begin her illegal hacking.

The high-tech keypad controlling the office door indicated the door was securely locked. Roxanne used her key to open the lock. By the time she swung the door open, Mary was already standing, her eyes wide with innocence.

"What are you doing in here?" asked Roxanne.

"Mr. Chord asked me to look over some of his papers." She held up a key card. "See? He gave me his key."

"Liar," said Roxanne, her grin widening. "But then everything from your dyed hair to your name to that résumé you used to get hired is a lie."

Mary did a good job of sputtering in indignation and picked up her cell phone from the desk. "How dare you? I'm calling Mr. Chord right now to have security escort you out."

"Go ahead," said Roxanne, shrugging. Mary was caught, and if the sweat beading along her hairline was any indication, she knew it. The only way out was through the door behind Roxanne, or out the window, which was easily twenty feet down, thanks to the high ceilings on Mr. Chord's first floor. It was too high up to jump out the window, and there was no place in that outfit for her to hide rappelling gear.

Mary Smith was well and truly caught.

"I've been made," said Mary into the cell phone. "Heads up. Window."

Roxanne's confusion lasted for a millisecond, but even that was too long. Mary had a partner—something Roxanne had failed to uncover.

Roxanne lunged across the room to stop the woman, but before she could cross the space, Mary hurled a stapler through the window, jerked a USB drive out of the PC, and tossed it through the broken opening. Roxanne slammed into Mary, pinning her to the frame of the window. Outside, she saw a man below pick up the drive and sprint off across Mr. Chord's manicured lawn.

Sure, the data on the drive was fake, but that wasn't the point. Roxanne had been charged with catching a thief, and she'd failed to realize there were two of them.

Fury boiled up inside of her as she grabbed the dainty woman's arm to spin her around and tie her wrists with the flex cuffs she'd brought with her. Mary had other ideas.

She lashed out, slamming her pointy elbow into Roxanne's stomach. Pain flew out from that spot, driving the air from her lungs. Mary shoved away from Roxanne, but she moved only two feet before Roxanne snagged her arm and jerked her to a halt.

"You're not getting away," Roxanne snarled.

Mary's hand snapped out, striking Roxanne's forearm hard enough to break her grip, likely leaving a bruise. She reached beneath her short skirt and pulled out a slim knife. "Like hell I'm not."

Sometimes being right sucked.

Roxanne hated knives. She really did. She'd much rather be at the receiving end of a nice, fat shotgun. There was something inherently wicked about knives, something far more sinister than the effective simplicity of a revolver, or the efficiency of a semiautomatic pistol. Guns were designed to kill; knives were designed to hurt. It took a long time to die from stab wounds, unless a person were lucky enough to have an artery severed. And while Roxanne had been trained to deal with the threat, facing a shiny blade again still had the power to make her break out in a nervous sweat.

Mary stabbed forward, slicing at Roxanne's arm. The blade didn't cut her, but she was sure some of the hair on her forearm had been shaved clean. Good thing she'd brought a gun to a knife fight. It was in her evening bag, which she'd dropped on the floor by the door when Mary had shattered the window. All Roxanne had to do was get to it and the fight would be over—one way or another.

Mary kept swiping, holding Roxanne at bay as she backed up to make her exit. Roxanne made sure not to glance at her beaded bag, not wanting to give away that it was important to her. A woman cruel enough to carry a blade as her weapon of choice would not hesitate to use anything against her she could find.

"I'm leaving. Keep quiet, and I won't hurt anyone on my way out," said Mary. The wicked gleam in her dark eyes spoke differently.

"Bullshit. We both know that's a lie."

A slow, amused smile spread across Mary's mouth as she backed up a bit more. Roxanne followed her up. As she passed the desk, she picked up a heavy crystal paperweight and flung it at Mary's head.

The woman dodged, and Roxanne took the opening. She charged forward, gripping Mary's wrist and shoving it high to keep the knife away from her. She used her momentum to slam the woman into the hardwood door. Mary's head hit hard. She blinked several times as if dazed.

Roxanne didn't wait to see whether it was an act. She smashed the knife hand against the wood, over and over until the gleaming metal fell to the floor.

Mary screamed in outrage and head butted Roxanne right in the nose.

Pain flashed red behind her eyes, making them water like crazy.

Roxanne grabbed the front of the woman's dress and flung her to the floor, face-first. Mary's skin squeaked against the gleaming hardwood floor. Roxanne crashed down on top of her, driving her knee into Mary's back hard enough to make her cry out in pain. Something along Mary's back popped, but Roxanne didn't care what it was. She wrenched Mary's hands behind her and pinned them there while she fished a set of flex cuffs from her evening bag.

Mary was secured, moaning, and no longer fighting.

Time to go after the other thief.

Roxanne picked up the knife so Mary couldn't use it to free herself and dropped it into her purse. She took out her cell and dialed Mr. Chord as she raced out of the office and down to the exit nearest to where Mary's partner had been. "Mary is in your office. She might need an ambulance."

"What the hell did you do to her?"

"Not as much as I would have liked. She had a partner. I'm going after him."

Roxanne didn't wait to hear what he had to say. She raced across the lawn, but the second thief was nowhere to be seen. Behind a screen of manicured bushes, several bars had been recently cut away from one section of the iron fence surrounding Mr. Chord's property, and on the other side of that, there were dark tire marks on the street.

Roxanne had failed to catch him, which meant it was only a matter of time before a new Mary showed up to finish what the last one couldn't.

Mr. Chord was not going to be pleased.

"Mr. Chord is pissed," said Roxanne's boss, Bella Bayne, the next morning.

Bella was the owner of the Edge—the growing private security company in Dallas where Roxanne worked. They handled all kinds of needs from threat assessment to protective details to US troop support to ridding foreign countries of any number of pesky criminals—for the right price.

Roxanne's specialty was stealth security for corporate espionage cases. She made sure the bad guys didn't know who she was until it was too late and she caught them with their hands in the cookie jar. At least that *had been* her specialty. Based on Bella's scowl, she might have been demoted to cleaning the locker room toilets if she wasn't simply fired.

Roxanne really didn't want to walk away from the job she'd come to love. She had to find a way to make things right.

Bella stood to her full, impressive height. She was easily six feet tall in her combat boots, and every inch of her was sleek, sculpted muscle. Her stormy gray eyes narrowed in fury. "Where shall we start, Razor? With the fact that your client's information was stolen? Or maybe with the part where the guy who stole it got away?"

"The data was fake. I planted it. Whoever has it isn't getting anything of value."

"And now they know that, too. Mr. Chord told me how hard it was to architect that setup. Your chance to catch the thieves is gone, and he still has no idea who Mary works for or with."

Roxanne looked down and toyed with her wide cuff bracelet. "Were the police able to get her to talk?"

"Not a word. Not even to a lawyer. And now whoever is doing this knows we're onto them."

What was worse was that the police were now involved—something Mr. Chord had wanted to avoid from the beginning, which was why he hired the Edge to deal with the problem. If word got out that his designs were being stolen, his company's stock price could plummet. He might lose investors.

Roxanne had no idea about the specifics of the devices that had been stolen from him. She didn't need to know any secret information to do her job. But what she did know was that Chord Industries had contributed to several advances in the field of medicine. His machines helped people, saved lives.

Because of her, he was losing his ability to do good in the world, and that pissed Roxanne off more than her own failure.

"I'm sorry, Bella. I should have realized Mary could have a partner."

"Yes. You should have. So the question is, why didn't you?"

Roxanne considered giving her boss some lame excuse. She could come up with half a dozen that might help her cover her ass, but she couldn't do that to Bella. They were friends. Bella trusted her, and she wasn't going to screw that up by lying.

Roxanne took a deep breath and admitted what she'd hoped she wouldn't have to. "I've been distracted."

Bella crossed her arms over her chest and lifted a dark eyebrow. "Distracted? Care to elaborate on that?"

"My ex, Kurt, he's been sending guys after me, having them follow me. I thought he'd stopped a few weeks ago, but I guess I was wrong. He's not done with his games. A new man showed up yesterday, and I spent so much time losing him before I went in to do the job, I was rushed. I wasn't completely focused."

Bella's face darkened with rage, and her voice became lethally calm. "What, exactly, are these guys doing to you?"

"Nothing. They just watch me. Kurt was the jealous type, and even though we split three months ago, he apparently still hasn't managed to accept the fact that we're over."

"Give me Kurt's address. I'll go speak to him."

"No, Bella. You'd only make things worse if you confront him. I already did, and he denies everything. I know he's lying, and I told him I'd have him brought in for stalking if it happened again. I thought I'd gotten through, but either way, this is my mess. I'll be the one to clean it up."

Bella glanced at Roxanne's arm where the bruise from

last night's combat darkened her skin. "Did he hurt you, Razor?" she asked, her hands clenching to fists at her sides.

"No. It was nothing like that. He's not a bad guy. He just didn't want to let go."

"I could make him."

Roxanne had seen Bella mad. She'd seen the woman take down three armed men by herself. And she'd heard stories about that building Bella destroyed in Mexico a few months ago. But Roxanne had never seen this kind of steely, quiet rage so intense it vibrated through her entire body. She heard rumors that Bella had a dark past—one she never discussed with her employees—but seeing this kind of reaction made Roxanne wonder just what that past had been.

"I've got it covered," said Roxanne. "I'll go see him today and make sure he quits playing these games."

Bella swallowed several times before her hands unclenched and the redness in her face abated. "I won't have anyone hurting my people."

"Kurt isn't hurting me. He's just jerking me around."

"Are you protecting him?"

"No. He's an asshole for screwing with me like this, and I plan to tell him that to his face."

"I don't like the way he's treating you."

"Neither do I."

"He interfered with your work, and I can't let that slide."

"I know." Roxanne let out a long, resigned breath. She loved her job, but she knew the score. A mistake like this was too big a thing to simply ignore. "Are you going to fire me?"

Bella's mouth flattened in frustration. "I should. That would certainly appease Mr. Chord. But no, you're not fired. However, I'm not handing out any more chances, either. You blow it again, you're out. Our work is too dangerous for distractions. You need to get your personal shit straightened out before I can assign you any more jobs."

"What about finding the guy who got away?"

"The cops are involved now. They're looking into it."

"So . . . what? We just leave Mr. Chord hanging?"

"No, I'm going to offer him our services for free to calm him down, but he already said he didn't want you back. I'm sorry."

The rejection stung, but not nearly as much as her failure did. Mr. Chord was right to be mad. She let her personal life get in the way of her professional life, which was a big no-no. She knew better.

"I understand. I'll go see Kurt on his lunch break and make sure he understands that his games are over. I should be back by one."

"No. I don't want you back until you're sure you've fixed the problem for good."

Roxanne took a deep breath to keep herself from shouting at her boss. "How long is long enough to convince you?"

"As long as it takes. No less than a week."

A week? If Mr. Chord's thief had left any trail, it would definitely be cold by then. "That's more time than I'll need."

"This isn't negotiable, Razor," said Bella. "If his buddies stay away for a few days, chances are they won't come back. And there's something else, too."

"What?"

"Assholes have a tendency to escalate things when confronted. I'm not letting anything happen to you, so I'm assigning the new guy to you. Wherever you go, he goes. Got it?"

"You're giving me a babysitter?" Roxanne did shout this time, jumping to her feet in anger.

Bella strode around her glass desk and got right in Roxanne's face. "I'm giving you a badass former special operations babysitter—one I want on our team. Don't fuck that up."

Great. Now she wasn't going to be able to look into possible leads on the thief. Her babysitter would no doubt rat her out. "I don't need him, Bella."

"I think you do. And he needs you, too. While he's babysitting, you're going to explain how things work at the Edge.

He's already passed all our tests and breezed through training, but he hasn't taken on any real jobs yet. Think of this as his orientation." Bella pressed a button on her phone. "Lila, please send Tanner in."

"This isn't a good idea. I'm a horrible teacher. You need to get Riley to do the training. He's good at that kind of thing."

"Riley's good at everything, which is why he's too busy for this. You, on the other hand, happen to have some free time on your hands. Deal with it, Razor. This is happening."

Fine. Roxanne had screwed up. If this was her punishment, she'd take it like a woman, get through the next few days, and be back to her real job in no time. "Let's get this over with."

"Nice to meet you, too," said Tanner as he came in on the heels of her statement.

Bella made the introductions. "Razor, this is Tanner O'Connell."

Tanner was not what she'd expected. She'd been so upset about being saddled with a babysitter, she hadn't even considered that he might be a hot one. And he was—smokin'. Taller than Bella, even in her boots, Tanner stood with a posture that screamed complete confidence. His shoulders were wide, his back straight, and his blue eyes stayed fixed on her, unblinking. An amused grin lifted one side of his mouth and formed little crinkles at his eyes. His jeans clung to thick, long legs, and on his feet were the worn cowboy boots of a true Texan.

"Tanner, this is your new partner, Roxanne Haught. We call her Razor."

Tanner's dark brows went up at that. "Razor? Is that because you have a sharp tongue?"

"The sharpest," she replied. "You'd better beg Bella for a new trainer, or I'll skin you alive."

His gaze dropped to her mouth. "Might be worth it."

Bella grabbed each of them by one arm and pushed them toward her office door. "I see you two have a lot to talk about. Outside of my office. I have work to do."

"This is a bad idea," said Roxanne, praying for a last-minute reprieve.

Bella ignored her. "And don't think you can come back here in a few hours claiming you tried to make it work. There will be no trying today. Just doing. Got it?"

"Yes, ma'am," said Tanner. "We won't let you down."

Bella gave Tanner a stern look. "She's going to try to ditch you. Don't let it happen. Some asshole is giving her trouble, and if she gets hurt, you're fired."

All hints of amusement fled Tanner's rugged face, making his eyes turn cold. He seemed to grow a couple of inches taller and took a step closer to Roxanne. It reminded her of her best friend, Jake, who had a tendency to be a bit over-protective.

Tanner nodded. "I understand."

"Good. I'm glad that's settled. Now get out." Bella shooed them through the door and shut it behind them.

It was time to let the new kid know how things worked around here. "If I'm going to be your trainer, we have a couple of things to get straight."

"Such as?"

"I'm in charge. You do what I say, when I say."

The slightest creases formed at his eyes, but he didn't refute her order. "Is that it?"

"No. I don't want or need a babysitter. I'm going to deal with my personal problems on my own, without your interference."

"Anything else?"

Wow. He was taking that remarkably well.

"I think that covers the basics. But I reserve the right to change my mind."

He moved, somehow maneuvering her so that her back was against the wall. He nudged closer, breaking the edge of her personal space. His voice dropped to a quiet rumble that Bella's secretary, Lila, would have had trouble over-hearing from her desk a few feet away. "Then it's my turn to talk. I don't work for you. I work for Bella, which means she's the one who gets to hand out the orders, not you. So, while I'm happy to learn whatever it is you have to teach me, I'm sure as hell not going to stand around like a good little boy while you deal with your personal asshole problems when Bella specifically told me not to."

Roxanne wasn't sure what she'd expected from the seemingly good-natured man, but it wasn't that. She pulled in a breath to put him in his place, but an instant later, his thick, hot finger pressed against her lips, quieting her.

She was so shocked by the touch, she entirely forgot that she should have been upset by it. Instead, she drew in a breath scented with soap and the faintest hint of his skin.

A touch of vertigo spun inside her head, and she realized she'd forgotten to breathe. The roughness of his work-hardened finger grazed across her mouth as her lips parted slightly so she could pull in enough oxygen.

"I'm not done," he told her. "You and I are going to be working together, and I'm not going to let you do anything to screw up my chances of keeping this job. I need the work. So you and I are going to get along real nice-like and make Bella proud. Got it?"

As close as he was, she could see deep blue streaks radiating out from his pupils. The creases around his eyes were paler, as if he'd spent a lot of time in the sun, squinting. His scent reminded her of a summer drive in a convertible—warm and exhilarating with just a hint of an incoming storm.

She felt her skin heat and attributed it to her sudden flash of irritation at his high-handed ways.

Roxanne pressed her hands against his chest to push him back, but as soon as she felt the hard contours of his muscles beneath her hands, her mind stuttered for a moment before she remembered herself and finished pushing.

Tanner stepped back, his finger shiny from her lip gloss.

Roxanne pressed her lips together to fix the damage he'd done to her makeup and swore she could taste him—salt and earth and something else that made her wish for another taste just so she could figure it out.

Not that she would do that. Bella generally frowned on her coworkers tasting each other.

Roxanne cleared her throat to cover her discomfort. "I can see already that you and I are going to have problems."

"Nope," he said. "Not a single one. We're both going to do what the boss says."

No way was she letting a stranger into her personal life to help her make an ex-boyfriend back off. But he didn't have to know that. "Fine. You win. We'll meet back here after lunch and get started on your training."

By that time, she'd have dealt with Kurt and no longer have anything to hide. She'd throw herself into training Tanner, and in a few days, everything would be back to normal.

# Chapter Two

Roxanne "Razor" Haught obviously thought she was dealing with an idiot.

She was wrong.

Tanner shook his head in amusement as he followed her to the underground parking lot. She hurried out to her car, clicking over the pavement on some of the sexiest high heels he'd ever seen. The artificial overhead lighting gleamed off her perfectly styled hair, showing off several shades of golden blond that matched her wide cuff bracelet exactly. Her bare arms were subtly muscled, with a combination of strength and softness that made Tanner sweat from fighting the need to see what that felt like. The brief touch of his finger against her soft mouth was more than enough to haunt his dreams for a week. Now that he knew what her lips felt like, he was going to spend way too much time thinking about them.

Her shiny lip gloss clung to his finger, and he couldn't quite bring himself to wipe it away. He liked it there—a small reminder of a few brief, pleasant seconds that would never be repeated.

Beneath her classy slacks that hid more than they displayed, her legs were probably sexy as hell. Even though he was working with her, he couldn't help but wonder just how those legs would look if all she was wearing were those strappy leather heels.

Not that he was ever going to find out.

He'd known from the instant he saw her in her fancy clothes and sparkling jewelry that she was going to be trouble. Women with money always were, and office rumors claimed that she was rolling in it. Not only was she an only child who'd gained a substantial inheritance when her parents died a few years back; she also owned more land than was healthy for a person. Between the real estate and old oil money, Razor was set for life and then some.

She was a woman used to getting her own way, but that was about to change.

Razor slid behind the wheel of a shiny silver Mercedes and pulled out of the parking lot at the Edge. Tanner followed her, keeping his distance in the heavy lunch-hour traffic. She turned into the lot of a high-rise building and parked in a visitor's slot.

Tanner gave up his secret chase and found the first open parking spot he could, rather than lose her in the maze of the building. By the time she hit the elevators, he was right on her sexy heels.

"Why are you following me?" she asked without turning around.

"Bella told me to."

The elevator doors opened, and a small crowd of people got out, heading to lunch. Razor got in. When the doors slid shut, she turned and glared at him. "This is ridiculous. What harm can possibly come to me in broad daylight in an office building?"

"Bella seemed worried."

"Bella is overprotective."

"I noticed. Possessive, too. But so long as she's signing the paychecks, she gets to be."

Razor frowned, which only made him notice her mouth that much more. It was a nice mouth—soft, with just the barest sheen of lip gloss. In a mad corner of his mind, he wondered if it was flavored.

Tanner shoved his hand into his pocket and made sure

he'd wiped away all hints of that lip gloss from his finger before he did something stupid and tasted it.

They were working together, and that meant he needed to keep things professional between them. He knew better than to mess up his chances at the Edge by getting involved with a coworker—even one wearing flavored lip gloss.

"Is it really that simple for you?" she asked. "Bella has the money, so she gets the last word?"

"Bella hired me. Not you."

"So if I were to offer you more money to walk away, you would?"

Anger rose, flashing just below the surface. "My loyalty can't be bought."

"Seems to me as if it already has been."

The elevator doors opened and Razor strode forward, her heels clicking on the polished marble floor.

"I'm here to see Kurt," she announced as she passed the receptionist.

The young woman shot to her feet, scurrying to stop Razor from passing. "Do you have an appointment?"

Razor kept going without an answer, and as soon as the receptionist realized she could not be stopped, she scurried back around her desk and picked up the phone.

Tanner wasn't sure if she was calling this Kurt guy or security, but he wasn't about to stop and listen long enough to figure it out. Wherever Razor was going, so was he.

She opened a door on her left, walking in as if she owned the place. The man behind the desk quickly shut his laptop and stared up with a guilty look on his face.

Kurt's skin said he was nearing forty, but he had the body of a much younger man. Several pictures sat atop his desk for visitors to see, showing him rock climbing and sky-diving. There was another of him shirtless, wearing boxing gloves and dripping with sweat.

His hair had begun to gray, and he'd tanned his skin until it was a deep, crinkly brown. Even though the man was dressed in a suit and tie, Tanner could tell he was an athlete.

"This has to stop, Kurt," said Razor.

"What the hell are you doing in my office?"

"You sent another man to follow me again, didn't you?"

Kurt glanced back at Tanner, who planned on keeping his mouth shut unless things got out of hand.

"No. I've never seen this man before in my life," said Kurt.

"Not him. The skinny guy with the bad haircut."

"I have no idea what you're talking about."

Razor pulled out her phone and brought up a photo. She set it down on Kurt's desk. "Proof. Which I plan on showing the police if you don't stop sending your buddies around to follow me."

Kurt looked at the photo. "I don't know this guy. Looks like a drug addict to me."

"This isn't funny anymore. We're over. Deal with it."

"I have. As a matter of fact, I'm seeing someone else now. Not that you care."

Razor lifted one eyebrow in suspicion. "Really? What's her name?"

"Like I'm going to tell you. You'll probably go find her and act all crazy like you are with me, claiming she's trying to read your mind or something. You need help. This whole paranoid thing isn't at all becoming, so put on a tin foil hat and leave me the fuck alone."

Razor frowned and tilted her head. "You're not lying, are you?"

"No. I'm not. I got over you weeks ago. If someone is really following you—which I doubt—I have nothing to do with it."

Tanner felt a brush of air as the office door opened. He spun around and came face-to-face with a large, stone-faced security guard.

"Is there a problem here?" asked the guard.

Tanner moved so that he was between Razor and the guard.

"I think that's up to Ms. Haught," said Kurt. "What about it? Do you need an escort out?"

He hadn't called her Razor the way everyone else did. Was it because they'd been close, or because only the people she worked with used the nickname? Roxanne fit her better. It was softer and prettier. He couldn't fathom how she'd gotten the nickname.

Razor shook her head and straightened her shoulders. "No. I'm leaving. I'm sorry I bothered you."

Kurt handed over her cell phone, and the guard stepped aside for them to leave first. Of course, he rode down in the elevator with them and watched until they exited the building.

"I don't suppose you're going to tell me what that was all about, are you?" asked Tanner.

Razor shook her head in confusion, making the pale highlights in her hair catch the sun. "Apparently, there's nothing to tell. I was imagining things."

"And the photo?" he asked. "Did you imagine that, too?"

"I must have been wrong about the man in the picture following me. Or if he was, I guess it had nothing to do with Kurt. He probably just wanted to ask me out or something."

"Can I see it?"

She shrugged, drawing his attention to her bare shoulders peeking out from her sleeveless blouse. "I guess so."

Tanner took the phone from her and looked at the image. It showed a tall, thin man dressed in layers of dirty and rumpled clothing. His hair was wild, and there were dark circles beneath his eyes. "Kurt is right. He looks like a druggie. Does he associate with people like that?"

"He likes to drink, but I never saw any proof of drugs being used by him or his friends."

"Why did you think he sent this man to follow you, then?"

"Because he's the only one I knew who would do something like that. When I broke things off, he wasn't happy. He had his friends follow me. I thought he was trying to get back at me for breaking up with him by scaring me."

"Were you scared?"

"I wasn't," she said, making it sound as if she'd changed her mind.

"But you are now?"

She used the remote access fob to unlock her car doors and turned to face him, stopping in the middle of the searing pavement. She held up her hand to block out the sun and stared up at him. The wide gold bracelet on her left wrist gleamed in the sunlight. "I'm sure that whoever this guy was, I lost him yesterday. Worst-case scenario, he was checking me out as a target to mug me for drug money."

That wasn't the worst-case scenario, but then Tanner wasn't exactly going to fill in any blanks she might have in that area. He didn't want to scare her more, so he kept his mouth shut.

"He's long gone now. All I have to do is get through the next few days without a visit, and Bella will have me back working again, where I belong. Until then, I'm going to make use of my time off to get some things done that I've been putting off."

"What about my training?" asked Tanner. "You're supposed to be showing me the ropes."

She eyed him up and down. "We both know that was just an excuse Bella needed to assign me a babysitter. She wouldn't have hired you if you didn't already know what you were doing. Besides, any gaps in your training will have to be filled in while you're on a job. Sitting around and discussing things over coffee isn't going to help when you're in the field."

"Maybe, but I still plan to do what I'm told. Since that includes your participation, I'm going to have to insist that you play along as well."

"Insist?" she asked, inching closer.

He could smell her skin, warm from the sun. He pulled in a deep breath before he caught himself. Even shaded, her golden eyes caught and held the light, making them sparkle. But it was her mouth that kept pulling his attention. It had been way too long since he'd kissed a woman, and her full lips kept reminding him of exactly what he'd been missing.

Sweat broke out along his hairline, but it did little to cool his blood. "I'm afraid so."

"Here's what's going to happen," she informed him, her tone firm. "I'm going to go home. So are you. We'll meet tomorrow morning and discuss enough business to make Bella happy, and then we're done. You'll go join the brute squad, and I'll be back to my own, more delicate missions."

Delicate definitely suited her. Not that he guessed for a second that what she did wasn't dangerous. He knew it was. The bruise on her arm proved that.

"That's not what Bella wanted, and you know it."

"What I do on my time off is my business. Bella doesn't get to dictate that. Neither do you. I'll see you at the office at eight tomorrow morning. Don't be late."

With that, she turned and got in her car.

Tanner sighed and hurried to his car to follow her. Bella had warned him that Razor wasn't going to be easy to work with. She'd told him it was his job to *make* it work, and he planned to do just that.


Roxanne's new home currently looked more like a warehouse than the cottage she'd fallen in love with. Moving boxes were still piled up everywhere, turning her living room into a maze. She'd been here two months now and still hadn't had time to unpack. Of course, she wasn't home much to notice the mess, but for the next few days, it was going to be staring at her, annoying the hell out of her.

Unless she used the time to unpack. That was what a rational person would do.

Maybe it was best to call a charity and have them come and haul it all away. She didn't need any of it. All the stuff she needed was already unpacked. These boxes were simply full of memories—most of which she really didn't care to relive.

The only thing that kept her from getting rid of everything was that some of these things reminded her of Jake and the time they'd spent together as kids. He and his mom, who was the head housekeeper for Roxanne's parents, were the brightest spots in an otherwise lonely childhood. She couldn't toss those memories away with the rest. Nor could she throw away his belongings that had been left behind in his room at her parents' mansion. Most of his things had been moved to a rented storage facility, but there was no way she'd found them all. Jake was off defending the country, and she wouldn't repay him by throwing away the things that might mean something to him.

It was time to bite the bullet, sort out the good from the bad, and face the disappointments of her past. Chances were that her dismal memories weren't going to make her feel any worse than failing Mr. Chord had.

Roxanne let out a long sigh and ripped the tape off the first box.

A heavy knock sounded against her front door, and she knew without looking who it was. Tanner. He'd tailed her from Kurt's office, and it had taken her a good twenty minutes to lose him. Or so she'd thought.

She flung the door open, keeping her arm across the entrance to let Tanner know he was not welcome.

Sunshine backlit him, highlighting the breadth of his shoulders. His posture was straight and confident, telling her without words that he fully expected to get his way.

She was going to enjoy watching the mighty fall. "I thought I'd lost you."

"You did. Nice move, too, by the way. Do you have the train schedules memorized or something?"

Irritation grated along her spine. "How did you find me?"

"Bella. She wasn't pleased that you were disobeying orders."

"Bella's my boss, not my commanding officer."

Tanner shrugged, making his muscles bulge. The fact that

her gaze darted straight to that delicious masculine display served only to irritate her further.

"I was clear that I'd meet you tomorrow," she reminded him.

"You were. You just forgot the part where that's not what our boss requested, so I thought I'd come by and keep both of us from getting fired."

"I'm not worried about that."

"Maybe that's because you have more money than God. Some of us, however, have to work for a living."

Her irritation grew until it verged on anger. She hated it when people threw her money at her as if she were somehow dirty because of it. She hadn't asked to be born into a wealthy family. She hadn't asked for the loneliness she suffered, or the ridiculous expectations placed on her. She hadn't even kept most of the money after her parents died. She'd given millions away to various charitable organizations. Who the hell was he to judge her?

"Go away," she told him, not even trying to put a polite spin on it.

She started to shut the door, but he slammed his palm against it, locking his arm to hold it open. Muscles shifted under the skin of his forearm, but his posture remained relaxed. She wasn't even sure how he'd moved so fast, considering he hadn't been poised to strike.

Roxanne gave the door an experimental push, hoping he'd relent, but the wood didn't even shift.

Tanner moved forward, filling her doorway. "Please, Razor. If you work with me, I swear I'll make it worth your effort."

"Why?" she asked, her curiosity burning away some of her anger.

His jaw tightened in frustration, but he admitted, "I need this job."

"Why?"

"Does it matter?"

"It does to me. Bella said you were in the military— some badass special operations guy."

His shoulders deflated on a sigh, and guilt pinched his features. "My family needed me, so I left the service."

"That's it? They needed you, and you gave up your career?"

He frowned at her, making lines of confusion radiate out from his blue eyes. "What do you mean, is that it? I said my family needed me. You would have done the same thing."

No, she wouldn't have. In fact, she was convinced that most people wouldn't have. That he didn't seem to realize how selfless that made him gave her pause. She almost felt bad for trying to ditch him against Bella's wishes. "Why did they need you?"

His gaze shifted away, and his throat worked as if she'd made him uncomfortable. "My dad and brother died in a car accident. My sister-in-law was left with two kids and no job. No life insurance. There were lots of medical bills. I did what I could to help, but the military didn't pay that well, and it wasn't enough. My other brother—Reid—works for Bella, and he told me he'd help me get a job at the Edge if I got out. So I did."

Roxanne was left reeling at the news. She knew some families were really close and had the kind of bonds she could only imagine, but what Tanner had done was beyond generous. Then again, Reid was a good guy, too. It seemed the O'Connell brothers were deeply devoted to their family.

Tanner's mouth flattened in resignation, and until now, she hadn't noticed just how nice a mouth he had. "With the economy sucking like it does, I can't risk screwing up my chance. Bella's testing me. I'm asking you to help me make the cut. Please."

What could she say to that? If she was selfish and petty enough to send him away now, she might as well turn in her decent-human-being card and become the evil oil baroness so many people already assumed she was.

Roxanne braced herself for what she was about to do, then let go of the door and took a step back. "Come on in. We have work to do."

He unleashed a grin that should have been classified as a secret weapon. His blue eyes sparkled, and his whole face lit up. That bright gaze fixed on her, sliding down to her mouth and back again. "Thanks, Razor. You won't regret this."

Based on the way her pulse had kicked up a bit just looking at him, she was fairly certain she already did.

# Chapter Three

Roxanne's house was not what Tanner expected. It was small and simple, almost cottagelike in its appearance. It was set back from the street, secluded by trees, and while there seemed to be several acres of land, the house itself was fairly modest.

The smell of new carpet and fresh paint gave away the fact that the home had either been recently built or remodeled. Boxes were stacked everywhere, creating a wall of cardboard around the living room. A TV hung over the fireplace, and empty bookshelves lined the walls on either side. The whole place was done in bright white and pale yellow, making it seem like it had been dipped in sunlight.

Tanner sat on her couch, sipping sweet tea, listening intently as she took him through several of her recent missions, explaining some of the details that outlined standard operating procedures at the Edge.

"You'll have to file a report after each mission. It's all done online, and I'm sure Mira—our resident computer goddess—will get you set up with a password if she hasn't already. Bella hands out the assignments, and unless you've already been assigned to one of the units, she'll probably see where your proficiencies lie by testing you out on some different types of jobs."

"I know vaguely what Reid does—as much as he can

share without breaking confidentiality agreements—but what about you?"

"I'm part of the stealth protection unit. A lot of the women work there. We get hired by people who don't necessarily want others to know they're being guarded."

"Why wouldn't they want someone to know?"

"Appearances, for one. Some men think it's a blow to their manhood if they need a bodyguard. It's easier on their egos if they pretend to have a girlfriend instead. Those assignments are usually temporary and go away once an immediate threat is identified and eliminated."

"Eliminated? You kill people?"

She flinched. It was brief, but he saw a flash of revulsion shiver through her body before it passed. "We're not vigilantes, despite what people think. I'm usually assigned to corporate espionage cases. Someone thinks they have a leak, and it's my job to go in, find it, and plug it."

She'd evaded his question, but he couldn't help but smile at the image she painted. "You're like a spy."

"I suppose a little bit. It's not nearly as glamorous as it sounds. Most of the time I catch people at the photocopier or by searching e-mail records."

"So, you get an assignment and have to write a follow-up report. What about all the stuff in the middle?"

"Once you're given a job, you and anyone else on your team will create a plan of attack—how you're going to handle the problem, contingencies, contact schedules, et cetera. Bella or Payton will read through the plan, and, if they approve it, you start the job as you outlined."

"Give me an example."

"Well, in this last job I did, my plan was to draw the thief out and catch her in the act by creating a situation she couldn't resist. There was only one way for her to access the data. We were fairly sure we knew who she was, but we needed proof. I had my client throw a party in his home where the data was being stored, and all of that was outlined in my plan of attack."

"So we get to make our own decisions?"

"You'll probably be part of a team at first, so while you may have input into a plan, I doubt you'll be the lead on creating it."

"You mentioned the brute squad. What's that?"

"Just what it sounds like. While the Edge is the place to come if you don't want anyone to know you have a bodyguard, we also provide big, intimidating men like you for those who want everyone to know. Bella may start you there, or she may put you with the overseas contractors. We're guarding a film crew heading into Afghanistan in a couple of weeks. With your military background, she may put you on that team."

The idea of going back into that hot, sandy hellhole didn't thrill him, but he'd do what it took to make this job work out. His family deserved at least that much from him.

"Reid mentioned something about that. I think he's going."

"Then Bella won't assign you to the team."

Tanner hid his relief. "Why not?"

"If anything went wrong, she wouldn't want your mom to lose two sons."

Even the idea of Mom having to face the loss of another son made Tanner's blood run cold. "Do you think she cares about that kind of thing?"

Razor smiled, just a little, but it was enough to bring his attention right back to her mouth after he'd finally stopped staring at it.

"You don't know Bella very well yet, but you will. We matter to her. In fact, it was just a few months ago that she went all the way to Colombia with a couple of our men to help rescue one of her employee's friends from some drug lord who had abducted her. And Bella didn't even get paid. Payton still hasn't stopped giving her hell about that."

"Payton. That's the older man who helps run the place, right?"

"Bella lets him think so. He's like a father to her; plus

he's her primary investor. He runs in the same social circles that my parents did. Same country club, same charity balls, same number of zeros in their bank accounts."

Tanner had sensed from his first interview with Payton that he was hiding something. Maybe his net worth was it.

Razor's cell phone rang, and she answered it. "Hello?" She listened for a moment, her skin paling slightly. "Again? How bad is it?" Her slim fingers tightened on the phone. "No, I'll take care of the damage. Thanks for letting me know."

Razor hung up and looked at Tanner. She was visibly shaken, though he couldn't tell whether it was fear or anger that had driven the color from her skin.

She stood. "I think we've just about covered everything we can without actually doing the work. And I have to drop by the mausoleum."

"The mausoleum?"

"My parents' house. I'm selling it. I couldn't stand the thought of having strangers tromp around the place while I lived there, so I moved out. Besides, it was way too big for one person."

"Is something wrong?" he asked, knowing something was.

"Nothing I can't handle, but I do need to handle it, so we'll have to call it a day. If you think of any questions, write them down and we'll go over them first thing tomorrow."

Her dismissal was clear, and so casually indifferent that he couldn't stop the rise of anger forming in his gut. "You want me to leave?" he managed to ask in a calm tone.

"Yes, please. We did what Bella asked, and I have things I need to do."

"Then let me help."

"No, thank you. I have everything under control."

"You have a guy following you, and now there's some kind of damage at the place you used to live, and you think that's under control?"

"It's a vacant house in a rich neighborhood. I'm sure it's kids looking for something to cure their boredom. And we already determined that the man following me had nothing to do with my ex. It's just a coincidence."

"Did it never occur to you that whoever this guy is, he might have his own agenda?"

She propped her slender hands on her hips, looking at him with disdain. "If he did, it was probably nothing more than wanting to ask me for cash, or possibly my phone number."

"But you don't know for sure."

She smiled at him, but it was full of condescension. "Listen, Tanner. I understand that you're trying to make a good impression on Bella, but you don't need to worry. She's going to keep you. You're just the kind of devoted, obedient man she loves to work with, and as soon as she finds out about your family problems, that great big soft spot of hers will open up, and you'll be set for life."

He strained to keep his civilized mask in place, but it was slipping, and his words came out as a growl. "This has nothing to do with sucking up for a job. You need my help. I promised Bella I'd look out for you, and that's exactly what I'm going to do."

"I prefer to do this alone."

"And I prefer not to have to tail you again through Dallas traffic, but I'll do what it takes. Your call."

She squared her shoulders and glared at him. "Fine. You want to help, I'll let you help. I hope you don't mind getting dirty."

By the time they reached Roxanne's old home, the police were already there. Her real estate agent had said she'd called them, but that had been almost two hours ago. Certainly they had better things to do with their time than fuss over a single break-in.

It wasn't until she walked through the open front door and saw the damage that she realized why they were still there.

The last time the house was broken into, she hadn't finished moving out. The thief had made a mess, rifling through packed boxes and even eating a bunch of food from her refrigerator. Some of her father's clothing might have been missing, but she wasn't sure. He'd had so much. The only reason she guessed the clothes were gone was because one of the boxes she'd packed for charity was no longer full. All the drawers in the remaining furniture had been pulled out and their contents spilled onto the floor, but that mess paled in comparison to what faced her now.

There was broken glass everywhere. Every mirror in the giant living area was shattered, as well as several of the light fixtures. Doors had been ripped from their hinges. Wallpaper had been sliced and pulled away, left dangling in spiral curls. The furniture that had been left to stage the home for sale was slashed, and stuffing littered the floor. Large flaps of ruined carpet were flung back, the padding beneath torn to shreds.

Roxanne stood there in shock, unable to process the extent of the damage. She'd never loved this place, but seeing it like this was still a violation of the few fun times she'd shared here with Jake and his mom. The sheer anger displayed through the wreckage was enough to make her shake.

"Wow," said Tanner from behind her. "Someone was well and truly pissed off."

She couldn't find her voice. She stepped forward, her shoes crunching on broken glass. The pieces slid beneath her foot, upsetting her balance.

Tanner's hands caught her shoulders, steadying her. "Careful."

A man in a suit with a notebook in his hand looked up and saw them standing there. He was in his midforties, with graying hair and a slight paunch to his stomach. His tie had been loosened, and she could see the bulge of his weapon beneath his suit jacket.

He strode over to the doorway, his expression grim. "Miss Haught?"

"Yes," said Roxanne.

"I'm Detective Planar. Your real estate agent called and reported a break-in."

Roxanne nodded, still trying to absorb what had happened. A police photographer snapped a photo, and the flash made her jump.

Tanner's hand settled at the small of her back in a soothing gesture. She would have refused his offer of comfort only five minutes ago, but she couldn't bring herself to do so now.

Detective Planar glanced over at Tanner. "And you are?"

"Roxanne's coworker. I was with her when she got the call. Do they always send out a detective for break-ins?"

The detective shrugged. "In this neighborhood they do. We've searched the house, but whoever did this is long gone. It probably happened sometime last night. Your real estate agent said it was the second time. Is that right?"

She shook her head. "Last time wasn't like this. There was a mess, but nothing was . . . destroyed."

"Was your security system on?"

"Yes, unless one of the real estate agents showing the property forgot to activate it."

"We can get records from the security company, but it sounds as though you're not the only one with the code."

"No. I'm selling the house. My real estate agent has access to it, as well as any others who showed the property."

He scribbled something down on his pad. "I'll get a list from her."

"Have there been any other break-ins in the area?" asked Tanner.

The detective stared at him for a moment before answering. "None that I know of, but we're looking into it. There was a lot of rage displayed here. Any idea who might be that angry at you?"

Roxanne had irritated some of her parents' friends when she'd left her old life behind, but certainly none of them would have been angry enough for this. "Anyone who knew me well enough to be angry with me would also have known

I couldn't care less about this place. It's just a thing—one I really want out of my life."

The detective's graying brows rose at that. "You're fortunate it didn't burn down, then, or we might have a problem."

"That's not what she meant, and you know it," said Tanner. "She's the victim here."

"Of course," said Detective Planar. "I meant no insult."

"How long until you're done?" asked Roxanne. She just wanted to get this place cleaned up and have this whole situation over with.

"We're wrapping up now. Sorry to add to the mess with fingerprint dust, but we wanted to be thorough."

Her manners kicked in, and she managed to choke out, "Thank you. We'll wait outside."

She turned and left with Tanner right by her side. His hand was at her elbow, as if he expected her to fall into a faint at any moment.

"I'm fine," she told him.

"I'm not. That's a hell of a mess."

She was tempted to call a service to take care of it, but that seemed cowardly somehow, or dishonest, like she was cheating. "You don't have to stay."

"Of course I'm staying. Only an asshat would leave you to deal with that on your own. Besides, I'm not entirely convinced that whoever did this won't come back once the cops are gone."

"Great. I hadn't actually considered that until you brought it up."

"Sorry, but reality sucks. I plan on being here in case it decides to come back and bite you in the ass."

"A gentleman doesn't discuss a lady's ass."

"Right now I'm not feeling like much of a gentleman. Part of me hopes the son of a bitch comes back."

Roxanne turned and looked at him. She hadn't heard it in his voice, but she could see his anger in his face. His jaw was clenched, and a vein pounded in his temple. His mouth was drawn tight, as if he were preparing to bare his teeth. "Down, boy. No need to get worked up. Shit happens."

"Twice?"

"Coincidence," she replied, refusing to believe it was anything else.

"Just like it's a coincidence that some guy is following you?"

"One guy. And I was probably overreacting because Kurt had me followed by two of his friends a few weeks ago."

"So you're saying Kurt is connected? You need to give his name to the cops."

"No, that's not what I'm saying. I knew the two guys Kurt had tailing me right after we broke up were his friends. I recognized them. When I saw the skinny guy, I made an assumption that he was doing it again. I was wrong."

"What if you're wrong about the coincidence part? What if the skinny guy is the one who did this?"

"Then it's no different than a stranger doing it, because I don't know who the skinny guy is. Neither does Kurt. I always knew when he was lying, and he wasn't this time."

"So, the fact that your house was broken into—twice— and you have a guy following you—again—doesn't bother you at all?"

"Of course it does. I'm just not sure that one thing has anything to do with the other. Neither am I convinced that the skinny guy had some nefarious purpose. He might have just thought I was hot. It does happen."

Tanner's eyes darkened as they slid down her body and back up. "I definitely believe that."

Something inside Roxanne relaxed and heated under his gaze. She didn't normally think about the men she worked with as anything more than friends, but if Tanner kept looking at her like that, she was going to start. And that was a supremely bad idea.

She took a long step back and headed to her car. "I need to change."

"Change the subject, you mean."

"That, too. Stay if you want to stay. Go if you want to go. Either way, any discussion about my private life is now officially over."

Jordyn Stynger could barely stand. Her head pounded with the remnants of her punishment, but she had to block it out. There was no time to waste giving in to the pain.

At least it was mostly over now. The throbbing ache was nothing compared to what she'd suffered for the last three days.

She shoved the memory from her mind and forced her shaking hands to work long enough to get the car started.

Deactivating three layers of security had taken time, and she didn't have much before her mother would realize she was gone. If she couldn't get to town and back before that happened, she was going to spend a lot more than three days in the white room next time.

The idea of it made the bile rise in her throat and her hands shake even harder. A wave of dizziness swept through her, and she gripped the steering wheel tight, praying she could keep the car on the private road. If it came back all dented up, her mother would figure out what Jordyn had done.

A woman's life was at stake. Jordyn couldn't afford even a small mistake right now.

Heedless of the breakneck speed, she raced to the nearest town and parked in front of the tiny library. It had once been a house, but had been converted in the sixties. Several bikes were propped against the wall, reminding her that school was out for the summer.

Jordyn had heard that most children were allowed summer break, but having been educated by her mother, she had had no such thing as a vacation. Norma Stynger was all about discipline—a fact Jordyn would have a hard time forgetting for many weeks to come.

She wrenched the door open, feeling her muscles twinge

with the motion. She hadn't moved much in three days, and it was going to be a while before her body forgave her for it.

Cool air poured over her face, and, until now, she hadn't realized she'd forgotten to turn on the air-conditioning in the car. She'd been so focused on getting here, she hadn't noticed the growing heat inside the vehicle.

The smell of old books and coffee hit her, making her stomach heave dangerously. She came to a rocking stop, swallowing hard to keep herself from vomiting.

"Can I help you, ma'am?" came a concerned voice from behind her.

Jordyn turned and saw the woman who'd spoken. She was plump and had a kind, grandmotherly face like some of the characters Jordyn had seen on TV. Reading glasses hung on a beaded chain around her neck, and her arms were full of books. Her expression was filled with worry, making Jordyn realize she hadn't done a thing to straighten her own appearance in three days. She was probably a total wreck.

"I need to use a computer."

The librarian glanced at the only three PCs available. A kid sat at each one. "I'm sorry, but they're in use. Have a seat and I'll get you the list so you can put your name on it."

Defeat beat at Jordyn, making her head pound harder. She pulled in a deep breath and tried to keep her voice from shaking. "I can't wait. I'm in a hurry."

The older woman frowned. "Are you okay? You don't look so good. Let me call someone to check you out."

"I just need a computer for two minutes. It's important."

The woman must have taken pity on her. She lowered her voice and said, "You can use the one behind the counter, but then I have to insist that you sit down for a few minutes, okay?"

Jordyn nodded and sat. She'd agree to just about anything if it got her the Internet access she needed.

"Do you have a library card?"

"No."

"You have to have a card to use the equipment. I'll go get the paperwork from the back room. Stay right here, okay?"

Jordyn doubted that was what the woman was going to do. There was too much worry in her expression—too much suspicion. Chances were the librarian was going to the back to use a phone to call the police.

Rather than argue, Jordyn nodded and hoped she looked compliant.

As soon as the woman was out of eyesight, Jordyn bolted behind the counter to use the only available PC. The librarian had left without implementing any security procedures, leaving open the Web site she'd been using to shop for shoes.

Her e-mail program was also open.

Jordyn didn't question her good fortune or the woman's lack of caution. She used the librarian's e-mail account to send the message. She deleted all traces that the message had been sent, then hurried outside on shaking legs.

She had fifteen minutes to make a twenty-minute drive before the loophole she'd put in the security system closed and she was locked out of the compound. If she wasn't back by then, her mother would know what she'd done, and she'd be right back in the white room before the day was over.

As weak as she was, Jordyn didn't think she'd survive a second punishment.

# Chapter Four

Razor was in trouble. The fact that she couldn't seem to see it, or preferred denial didn't sit well with Tanner.

He spent the next three hours stewing while they cleaned up the carnage left behind. The more he saw, the angrier he got. There was thousands of dollars in damage, and just sweeping up the broken glass wasn't going to cut it. Much of the carpet in the house was ruined. Some of the hardwood floors were gouged, as if someone had tried to pry them up. The drywall in several rooms had been bashed in and pulled away from the studs.

Part of him was convinced this act had been motivated by revenge—the kind a pissed-off ex-boyfriend and his buddies might commit if they got drunk enough. But the rest of him questioned that. Not only had furniture and walls been destroyed, but the destruction had continued. If someone wanted to ruin a mattress, slashing it was enough. They didn't also have to gut it.

Unless they were looking for something.

Over and over, he saw signs that whoever had done this had ripped up floorboards and torn down walls in search of something.

He thought about bringing it up with Razor, but she seemed to wilt before his eyes as she moved from room to room, repairing the damage she could.

"That's enough," she finally told him, sounding defeated. "This is going to take us hours. I'm calling in a repair crew to see if they'll haul off the junk as well."

Tanner dumped a dustpan full of broken glass into the trash bin and wiped his hands off on his jeans. "Sounds like a good idea to me."

Razor looked at his jeans and frowned. A second later, she was marching across the room toward him. She now wore the workout clothes she'd had stashed in her trunk. That wide cuff bracelet was out of place next to the clinging gym shorts and tank top that showed off every feminine curve. The long length of bare legs showing nearly drove him to his knees. All dressed up in her designer clothes, she was a knockout, but dressed down like this, she was so much more alluring, because a man like Tanner felt he might have a shot.

Sure, it was a crazy notion, but there was no accounting for hormones.

"You're bleeding," she said, looking down at his legs.

Sure enough, a bit of blood was smeared across his jeans. He checked his hands and found a small cut he hadn't noticed. "It's nothing."

She took his hand in hers and turned it toward the light. Her fingers were gentle and soft against his skin. He stared at the top of her head, holding very still, letting her do what she wanted.

"I don't see any splinters," she said. "It doesn't look deep. Does it hurt?"

His voice seemed to disappear for a moment before he regained the ability to speak. "No. It's fine. I'll just wash it out."

Still holding his hand, she stared at him with the oddest look on her face. "Thank you for helping. You didn't have to do that."

Tanner shrugged, being careful not to pull away from her grip. He liked her touch—the feel of her skin on his. Sure, it was just his hand, but he was acutely aware of said hand and the warmth of her fingers against his. "I didn't mind. Besides, it beat chasing you all over town."

Her cell phone rang with an imperious chime. She let go of him and looked at the screen for a few moments, frowning in confusion. "It's from Jake, only it's not his e-mail address."

He was still mourning the loss of her touch, which made him slow to process what she'd said. "Jake?"

"My best friend. He's in the military, and I haven't heard from him in three months. The last letter I sent him was a few weeks ago. He never responded."

"Where is he stationed?"

"Afghanistan. I don't know what he does, though. He never likes to talk about it."

That meant he'd probably seen some action. Heaven knew Tanner didn't like talking about the couple of close calls he and his buddies had had over there.

He nodded to her phone. "What did he say?"

Her frown deepened until her expression was a mix of fear and skepticism. "Burn everything. They're coming."

"What?" That didn't sound good. Heedless of bad manners, Tanner stepped behind her to read the ominous text over her shoulder. All he saw was a bunch of garbled words that meant nothing. "It doesn't say anything."

"It's written in code we used when we were kids. That's how I know it must be from him even though it's not his address."

"Code?"

She turned to face him. Her cheeks turned red, but he couldn't tell if it was from embarrassment or anger. "My parents didn't like that I was friends with the hired help, so we slipped notes back and forth, hiding them in vases and the central vacuum tubes. We were worried we'd get caught, so we made up a secret code."

That short explanation hit Tanner like a blow to the stomach. Not only did it tell him that her parents had been dicks; it also made him wonder how lonely she must have been to risk angering them just so she could have a friend. But all of that he could have shrugged off. The part that really bothered him was that her friend was using that same secret code now, sending ominous messages from an e-mail address not his own. Why would he do such a thing?

"What does he mean?" asked Tanner.

"I have no idea. Maybe it's some kind of joke. He used to play pranks on me all the time when we were kids."

Tanner seriously doubted that was the case now. "Does he always write to you in code?"

"Not since we were kids."

"Could he be in trouble?"

Roxanne was standing close enough that he could smell her skin and see her bottom lip waver for a second before she controlled it. "I don't know. Maybe he told me something in his letters he shouldn't have."

"Is he the kind of man who would spill classified information?"

"Not purposefully. But if there's something in his letters to me that would get him in trouble, I need to do what he asks. He sent me a box of things a couple of months ago and asked me to store them until he got back."

"You're going to burn evidence? Do you have any idea how much trouble that could get you in?"

"I don't care. He's my best friend. I owe him at least that much." She turned and scooped her keys from the kitchen counter. "Let's go. It's going to take me some time to find his letters in all those boxes, and I want this finished tonight."

Tanner grabbed her arm before she could run off without thinking about this. "If he did something wrong, it's not your job to cover up for him."

She looked at where his fingers wrapped around her arm, right above the thick band of her bracelet. Beneath his fingers, he could feel her pulse speed.

Against his better judgment, he let his thumb slide across her wrist, grazing the smooth satin of her skin. Goose bumps rose along her arms, and Tanner had to fight the urge to rub his hands over her to warm her.

Roxanne's voice dropped to a near whisper. "I know him. If he broke the law, he didn't know he was doing it."

"Then he's not the kind of man who would ask you to become an accomplice, either. You need to slow down and think. Do you really care about him enough to go to prison for him?"

Her golden eyes flared with determination. "I love him. I'd die for him if I had to."

Whoa. Okay. So maybe they were more than just friends.

As much as that idea bothered Tanner, he didn't take the time to dwell on why. Instead, he forced himself to let go of her arm. His fingers felt chilled without the heat of her skin.

"He's a good man, right?" he asked.

"The best."

"Then that's not what he'd want for you. Think about this. Put the letters in a safety-deposit box where no one can find them, but don't destroy them. Not until you know the facts. If you burn them, you can't take it back."

"Which is why I'm doing it now, before I can talk myself out of it. Jake would never ask me for anything that wasn't necessary."

Tanner wondered if Jake knew just how precious a gift he had in Razor's unquestioning loyalty. A man could only dream of having someone with such unwavering faith in his life. Jake was one hell of a lucky man.

Tanner only hoped that Jake was worth the trouble. He had no idea what kind of a mess they were getting themselves into, but he couldn't bring himself to turn his back on Razor and walk away, even though that would have been the smartest thing do to. Heaven knew he didn't need any more complications in his life. Taking care of his family, trying to hold them together through this grief and torment, was more than enough. His brother's paycheck went almost completely to medical bills. If Tanner didn't keep this job, it was going to cause his family mountains of pain—especially Mom. He couldn't do that to her. He *had* to keep his job at the Edge and do his part to keep his family afloat.

"Just slow down," he said, stroking the inside of her arm with his thumb. He was touching her again, and he wasn't sure when that had happened. All he knew was that it felt good to have her bare skin against his. "We're jumping to a lot of conclusions here. We don't even really know what that e-mail means."

Razor pulled in a deep breath. "You're right. I need to e-mail him back and ask him what's going on."

"If he hacked into someone else's account, he's not going to get it. Could he be using an alias?"

She nodded. "I can't risk it. No one else can know he made contact with me. I need to figure this out, but I can't do that here. I need to go through his things and see if there's something I missed."

"Did you read every letter he sent?"

"Yes. Several times."

"Was there any sign of something he might want to cover up?"

"Not that I remember."

Tanner held out his hand. "Why don't you let me drive you home, and you can think about it on the way."

She hesitated for only a moment before she held out the keys. "Thanks, Tanner. I don't know why you're being so nice to me when I kept trying to blow you off."

He didn't tell her that he was only doing what any decent human being would do. He got the feeling that she'd been around too many people in her life who *weren't* decent. Instead, he winked and gave her a grin. "I'm just doing it so I can drive your Mercedes."

A hint of a smile played at her mouth, reassuring him she was tougher than she looked. "Ah. A user. I'm used to guys like you."

As sad as that statement was, he let it slide. He had to stay on her good side long enough to make sure she didn't do anything that would land her ass in prison, even if he had to steal those letters and hide them from her to make sure of it.

Brad shook his head to clear it. Everything was all jumbled up again.

He was in a car, but he didn't recognize it. A graduation cap tassel hung from the rearview mirror. A cell phone car charger dangled over the gearshift. A gym bag sat open on the floorboard of the passenger seat, revealing a pair of pink-and-white Nikes.

None of these things was his. He couldn't remember how he got here, driving down the highway at ninety miles an hour. There was a nagging sense of urgency that had his foot pressing hard on the accelerator.

This wasn't right. He didn't even know where he was.

A swell of nausea rose in his gut, and he hurriedly pulled the car off the road before he puked all over the steering wheel.

He shoved the door open and bent over, throwing up bile onto the cracked asphalt.

Waves of air shook the car as traffic passed, blasting hot wind over his sweaty face. He sat there, panting, spitting acid from his mouth and waiting for this horrible sickness to pass.

When he finally thought he was no longer in danger of puking again, he sat back in his seat and shut the door. Cool air from the vents poured out over him, driving back some of the queasiness.

He found a napkin shoved between the seats and wiped his mouth. The hand he saw was not one he recognized. It was thin, bony, pale. Small cuts dotted the back of his hands, and a splinter of reflective mirror was still lodged within one. He jerked it out, only to find more splinters running up his arms—arms also not familiar. They'd once been thick with muscle and tan from hours in the sun, but no longer.

They were skinny sticks, bruised with needle marks both old and new.

Panicked, he angled the rearview mirror and stared into it, seeing a stranger. Dark circles ringed his eyes, and his cheeks were sunken as if he hadn't eaten in weeks. A scraggly growth of beard shadowed his face—something he couldn't stand. It was against regulations.

He tried to remember how he had gotten here. The last thing he could recall was being transported to his new assignment with several of his army buddies. They'd all been recruited into some secret hush-hush type of group—the kind that was invitation only. He'd been proud to be one of the few selected and had to fight the urge to tell his family—something that was strictly forbidden.

It had been winter then. The trees had still been bare. Everything was green now, as if several months had passed without his notice.

A heavy sense of anger and loss wrapped around him. Someone had hurt him. They'd stolen his life. They'd done things to him. Made him do things.

A strangled scream of rage burst from his chest, and he pounded his fists against the steering wheel. He was going to find who'd done this to him and kill them. He was going to shatter their skulls like glass.

An image of a white rose burst inside his mind, blinding him with the intensity of the vision. He heard children screaming and saw blood splatter the rose. It trembled in pain, and that same pain detonated inside his skull, radiating down to his limbs until he was shaking with it. A woman's voice washed over him, easing the agony.

*Don't you have a job to do?* she asked inside his mind.

Brad did. He had to find the rose and pluck it. He had to bring it back for her. It was important. His life depended on it. So did the lives of his friends.

He reached for the keys to start the car, only to find that there were none. A memory popped into his mind. He'd hot-wired the car—stolen it from the mall parking lot, where he'd left his last stolen car so the woman he was following wouldn't see him.

That was right. There was a woman. She had stolen something, and it was Brad's job to get it back, even if he had to torture her to find out where she'd hidden it. And then he had to bring her back, just like he'd promised.

She was the white rose. She was the one who would be splattered in blood and shivering in pain.

# Chapter Five

Roxanne let Tanner drive her to the storage facility where she kept Jake's things for his return. A few hours ago, she wouldn't have let him come with her, but now she was glad for his company.

Seeing her childhood home destroyed had shaken her more than she was willing to admit. She had no fondness for the place, but whoever had done it had vented some dangerous rage.

She had no idea that anyone in her life hated her quite that much.

Roxanne kept trying to tell herself that it had nothing to do with her—that whoever had done it had simply seen the vacant house as an opportunity for mayhem—but there was something about it that wasn't sitting right. That level of destruction was no teenage prank. It was vengeance.

Tanner pulled into the storage facility. She'd paid extra for twenty-four-hour access, since her work schedule was often chaotic. She swiped her key to open the gate and directed Tanner to the numbered unit that housed Jake's belongings.

She unlocked the padlock and lifted the overhead door, displaying three rows of boxes and a few pieces of furniture she thought Jake might want when he finally settled down and got his own place.

"There's not much here," said Tanner.

"Jake never was much for things."

Tanner shifted a snowboard to a more stable position, propping it against the wall. They were at the back of the facility, and the evening traffic was barely audible.

"Does he talk about coming home?" asked Tanner.

"Not much. He loves what he does. He got a promotion recently and some new assignment he was really excited about. He said he couldn't tell me what it was, but that he was sure I'd be proud of him."

And she was. He was the one person in her life she thought about every single day. When she was younger, she'd hoped he'd see her as more than a baby sister, but it had never happened. Now she was glad. If they'd tried some awkward romantic relationship, it could have ruined everything.

Tanner opened a big pocketknife and slit open the tape on the first box. "Do you remember where you put the letters?"

Roxanne forced herself not to look at the gleaming blade. She'd been rattled enough today already. "Not exactly. I just labeled boxes with his name so I knew where they went. The moving company loaded everything in for me."

He pulled the flaps open but didn't look inside the box. Instead, he met her gaze. "Are you going to let me help you look?"

It was stuffy in here, even with the sun now below the horizon. The heat of the day had built up, making the whole unit and everything in it uncomfortably warm. The sooner this was over, the better. Besides, she was starting to trust Tanner just a bit. He'd helped her today when he could have just walked away or stood there, watching her do the work. "Knock yourself out."

Tanner passed her the knife, and she flinched. She hated that every time a blade moved toward her she lost control, just for a second. She'd been working for years to overcome her fear, but so far, she'd failed.

"Sorry," he said as he folded the blade shut and held it flat in his hand. "I should be more careful."

"It's not your fault. I'm just on edge."

"After seeing the mess some asshole made of your house, anyone would be."

Roxanne picked up the pocketknife and set it aside without using it. She ripped the tape off and dug into the first box.

After about fifteen minutes of searching, she finally found some of the letters and the box Jake had sent her recently, asking her to put it with his things. The box was sealed with a ton of tape, and the letter to her had been outside the box. She'd left the box sealed, thinking whatever was in there was personal or he wouldn't have bothered with all the tape. Now she was beginning to wonder if that had been the right decision.

*Burn everything.*

Did he mean this box? Or was there something she missed? Was something taken from her parents' house before she got everything moved?

Roxanne dumped out the moving box she was searching and put the letters and the sealed box inside to carry them home.

Tanner picked a box from the top of a tall stack and set it down on the concrete floor. Muscles in his back shifted beneath his shirt, and for a moment, Roxanne forgot all about Jake.

It had been a while since she'd noticed a man on the same deep level that she was noticing Tanner. Kurt had been fun and completely into her, but the chemistry had been lacking, at least on her side. Kurt was good-looking, but he was too . . . artificial. Everything about him was meticulously planned, trimmed, and groomed, down to his waxed chest.

She'd bet her trust fund that Tanner had never even considered doing the same. He was manly in a natural way and unapologetic about his testosterone. And she appreciated it more than she would have thought possible, given her oh-so-proper upbringing. Mother never would have approved of her speaking to Tanner, unless it was to give him orders about cleaning the pool. Then again, Roxanne's mother had always been a fool—one who'd had more than one affair with the hired help.

Roxanne had always wondered if her dad knew about Mom's liaisons and had suspected she wasn't his child. Maybe that was why he hadn't wanted her back when she'd been kidnapped.

Not that it mattered. That was a long time ago, and he couldn't hurt her with his casual indifference anymore. She was her own woman, and Jake was the only family she needed.

"Did you find something?" asked Tanner. A solid wood headboard was in the way of the next row of boxes, and Tanner hefted it over his head as if it weighed nothing.

It was terribly inappropriate for her to stare, but she couldn't help it. She was used to soft executives. Watching his casual display of strength was mesmerizing.

Her body heated in a way that had nothing to do with the searing confines of the storage unit. A languid softness slid through her, making time lengthen as she stared. His T-shirt stretched over his shoulders and arms, clinging to mouthwatering muscles. Her pulse kicked hard, and her mouth went dry with want.

Inconvenient, inappropriate want. They had to work together. Anything beyond friendship was frowned upon at the Edge, though if any man was worth risking her job for, it would be one built like Tanner.

Her silence stretched on, and until he gave her an expectant glance over his shoulder, she'd totally forgotten his question about whether she'd found something.

Roxanne cleared her throat and wiped sweat from her forehead. "I found some letters, but I don't know if that's all of them. I'm going to keep digging."

A shadow fell across the wide doorway as someone approached.

Roxanne assumed it was an employee checking to make sure their visit was legitimate. She wiped her dusty hands on her shorts and went to meet him.

The sky had darkened while they searched, and outside, several security lights had turned on, but they weren't as bright as the light overhead. As the man came closer, shadows moved up his body until he stood in the light spilling out from the storage unit.

As soon as his face was illuminated, Roxanne could see that it was the same man who had been following her yesterday—the man she'd photographed.

A hot wave of panic slid down her body, pinning her in place. Her heart kicked hard, thudding against her ribs. From the corner of her eye, she saw Tanner turn just as she regained her senses.

"Who are you?" she asked. "What do you want?"

"The rose and her stolen secrets."

Roxanne had no clue what he was speaking about, but his eyes were wild and bloodshot, and he was quivering from head to toe. Her first instinct was that he was high.

And he was standing between her and the gun she kept in her car.

Tanner vaulted over a box and stepped in front of her, and while she was all for equality between the genders, she knew he had a much better chance of intimidating their intruder than she did. Assuming the man had enough sense to *be* intimidated. He sure as hell didn't seem to be playing with a full deck.

"What are you doing here?" asked Tanner.

She saw the large pocketknife sitting on a box where she'd left it and inched closer to it.

The skinny man lifted his arm and revealed both needle tracks, and a gun he had hidden behind his leg. The barrel pointed right at her. "She stole from us."

Fear shot through her, making time stretch out. Colors became clearer, the light was brighter, and she swore she could smell the sour stench of vomit coming from the stranger.

"I did n—"

"Let's talk about this." Tanner cut her off, his voice calm. He raised his hands and took a step to his left, putting himself in the line of fire. "Nothing she has is worth her life. We can work this out. Tell me what she stole."

Roxanne had to clamp her lips shut to keep from proclaiming that she hadn't stolen anything. Instead of spouting her innocence, she reached over and scooped up the knife, slow and easy. The metal was cold in her hand, and her skin seemed to shrink back from touching it, but it was the best shot they had.

Using Tanner's big body for concealment, she opened the knife, locking the five-inch blade in place. Her hand shook around the metal, and she gritted her teeth in an effort to control the involuntary reaction.

"Secrets," said the man. "She stole secrets."

Roxanne kept her voice calm and stepped out most of the way from behind Tanner. She kept her right hand hidden behind his back, holding the knife steady. "I think there's some kind of mistake here. I guard secrets. I help track down people who steal them. I don't steal them myself."

The man's brow scrunched up as if he were in pain. He pressed the side of his fist against his forehead and went deathly pale. His thin body trembled. The gun wavered and drooped.

"Lies. The rose lies. She told me you would."

"Who?" asked Tanner. "Who told you that?" He took a step forward, and she could see his muscles bunch as they coiled to spring an attack.

With the gun in the way, that was a dangerous move, and if anyone was going to be risking their life, it should be Roxanne. She'd somehow gotten them into this mess. She didn't know how, but that didn't change the fact that the drugged lunatic was after her, not Tanner.

Tanner's weight shifted. She put her hand on his shoulder, letting him feel the metal of the knife, praying he'd understand her signal to hold off.

He moved to the right, slow and steady. Roxanne went left, holding the knife behind her back to hide it the best she could.

The man's head jerked up, and his eyes went wide. They glazed over in fury and he snarled at her, jerking the gun toward her again. "Stop right there. Tell me where the secrets are. I don't want to hurt the rose, but I will."

She believed him—at least the part about his being willing to hurt her. "I don't know what you're talking about."

"Lies!" he shouted, making spittle fly out from his mouth. Rage burned in his eyes and shook through his body.

"Easy," said Tanner, pulling the man's attention away from her.

The stranger turned and saw how close Tanner had come. Panic widened his eyes, and she watched his finger shift at the trigger. The tendons in his hand tightened.

He was going to shoot Tanner.

Roxanne whipped the knife out and flung it toward the man's chest, hoping her aim was decent enough to at least nick him.

The knife struck. The gun went off. Tanner dove to the side, crashing into the boxes.

Fear choked Roxanne, keeping her scream of denial inside. She lunged toward the shooter, to keep him from firing again.

She plowed into him, knocking him down. He lifted the gun to fire it at her at point-blank range.

A split second later, she saw Tanner's big cowboy boot swing through her field of vision, and the gun went flying. It clattered as it skidded across the concrete.

The stranger screamed in outrage and grabbed her by the throat, cutting off her air.

She shoved her arms between his, pushing her body up with her legs at the same time to break his grip. Tanner kicked again. This time his blow landed against the man's head. His grip went slack, and Roxanne scrambled back away from him like a crab, panting.

"Are you hurt?" asked Tanner as he flipped the man over and shoved a knee into his spine.

"I'm okay," she grated out, her voice hoarse. "You?"

"Fine. Find something to tie him up." His words were sharp, and she could hear his anger lurking just below the surface.

She found the box she'd seen earlier with Jake's clothes in it, and grabbed one of his ties. She watched Tanner secure him as she dialed 911. By the time she told the dispatcher what had happened, the stranger was starting to regain consciousness.

Tanner rolled him over, sitting on his legs to keep him pinned. Blood wet the stranger's shirt where she'd hit him with the knife, but the wound wasn't bad.

Roxanne leaned over him. "Who are you?" she demanded.

The man bared his teeth and thrashed against Tanner's hold. A dog tag slid out from his shirt.

She leaned down and picked it up. S-11-17 was stamped into the metal, but there was no name.

"We'll get our secrets back," he snarled. "We'll get our secrets, and the rose will be covered in blood, shivering with pain."

"He's out of his mind," said Tanner. "I hear sirens. Can you go meet the cops at the gate and guide them in?"

"Are you going to hurt him?" she asked.

Tanner didn't look at her, but she could hear regret radiating in his voice. "He's already broken. There's nothing more I can do to him."

Tanner waited until he was sure Razor was out of earshot before he leaned close, getting in the stranger's face. "Who were you with, soldier?" he asked. "Army? Marines?"

The man's eyes widened fractionally, giving away what Tanner had suspected after seeing the tags. He was a veteran—one that had been fucked up.

"We'll get you help, man. You can get through this."

Fear flickered across the man's face for a second before his expression hardened. "I already have help. We'll get our secrets back."

Chances were the man was delusional. His arms were covered in needle tracks, and he'd fallen a long way from the proud soldier he'd likely once been. But there was a certainty in his eyes, an absolute conviction that he was right. "We who?"

"The general—" His words cut off on a strangled cry of pain. His back arched up off the pavement, and tendons stood out in his neck.

"Easy," said Tanner. "No one's going to hurt you. We're going to get you the help you need."

It was the least he could do for a fellow soldier. Having been on the brink of breaking once himself right after his dad's and Brody's deaths, when the grief was killing him, he knew how tempting it could be to fall over the edge and let go. And while Tanner's own struggle was getting easier, there wasn't a day that went by that the grief didn't pound at him, that he didn't feel guilty for his decisions, and that he didn't think about where he'd have been now if he'd given in to the temptation to ease his suffering through artificial means.

The man passed out, going limp. Tanner flipped him over and put pressure on his wound to slow the bleeding, making sure he was still pinned in case he woke. He knew the lengths a man would go to in order to escape, and with a few screws loose, this man might do something Tanner couldn't predict.

A police cruiser showed up with another one right on its heels. Roxanne got out and pointed to where the gun lay. The officer kept Roxanne in sight, angling her away from the weapon as he moved toward Tanner.

"Is he alive?" asked the cop.

"Yeah, but he's going to need an ambulance," said Tanner.

The man spoke into the radio at his shoulder while two more officers approached. Tanner kept pressure on the wound.

The next two hours crawled by as Tanner and Roxanne

gave their statements and the soldier was taken away via ambulance. Tanner was kept separate from Roxanne, but his eyes tracked her as she moved, keeping constant tabs on her location.

She could have been killed tonight. He barely knew her, but he still felt responsible. Even if Bella hadn't assigned him babysitting duty—which he'd first thought was a waste of time—he still would have felt protective toward her. They were coworkers now, and that meant something to him.

Maybe he hadn't been out of the army long enough yet to act like a civilian, but there wasn't much he could do about that. Her life had been threatened, and, until they had the crazy soldier locked up in a nice, safe, padded room, Tanner wasn't leaving her side.

Roxanne was exhausted and starving by the time she pulled into her garage. It was after midnight, and her whole body was buzzing with the aftereffects of adrenaline.

Jake's letters and the mystery box were in her backseat, and all she wanted was for Tanner to leave so she could open it and reassure herself that the crazy ramblings of her attacker were just that.

*Burn everything. They're coming.*

Roxanne tried not to think about Jake's strange missive. It had to be some kind of prank he was playing—something they'd both laugh about when he came home for a visit.

She wasn't laughing now. She was too keyed up, too off balance, and all she wanted was some time alone to process everything.

"Thanks for your help today," she told Tanner. "You saved my life. I owe you."

"Let's hope that's one favor you never have to repay."

He got out of the car and stood there, expectantly.

She left the garage door open for Tanner to leave. "I'll meet you tomorrow at the office. Is nine good for you?"

He crossed his thick arms over his chest and gave her a disbelieving stare. "If you think I'm going to leave you after what happened tonight, you're as crazy as your attacker."

"You can't stay here."

"The hell I can't. I'll sleep propped against your front door if I have to, but there's no way in hell I'm leaving you alone."

"I'm armed. I'll be fine. Besides, he was crazy. All that stuff about my stealing something was garbage."

"And the note from your boyfriend, Jake? Was that garbage, too?"

"He's not my boyfriend, and Jake is probably just playing some kind of joke on me."

"Is he the kind of asshole that scares women for fun?"

"No. Of course not."

"Then I don't see how this could be funny to anyone." He rubbed his hand over his short hair and pulled in a deep breath as if trying to control his frustration. "Listen, until we find out what's going on, I think it would be safer if you had company. I promise not to try anything skeezy."

For some reason, hearing him say that amused her. "Skeezy?"

"You know, coming on to you, trying to accidentally see you naked in the shower—that kind of thing."

"It sounds like you've put a lot of thought into exactly what you're not going to do."

Tanner grinned. "Sue me for having a healthy imagination. But I can be a good boy. I swear."

Roxanne was too tired to argue. He was probably as hungry as she was, and he had been a huge help today even before he saved her life. "Fine."

His grin widened to a triumphant smile that made Roxanne's stomach do a slow, lazy roll. "Let me grab my bag from my car and I'll be right in."

"Are you telling me that you already packed a bag before coming here?"

Tanner shrugged. "Bella said to be ready for a few days of nonstop duty, so I am."

"Bella and I are going to have a talk when she's back in town. Not even my boss gets to dictate who spends the night at my house."

"She cares about you. And she probably figured that if you really didn't want me around, you could handle getting rid of me."

After seeing the speed and power with which he moved earlier tonight, she wasn't so sure. While she could generally handle herself in most situations, she knew better than to overestimate her combat abilities. She was good compared to an average person, but Tanner was way above average.

Badass special operations babysitter, indeed.


Nelson Bower was in trouble—the kind that could cost him his life. Everything his men did was his responsibility, and one of them had fucked up. Big-time.

He knocked on Dr. Stynger's door, knowing she'd still be awake, in spite of the late hour. He wasn't sure how she did it, but the woman slept only two or three hours a night on the nights she slept at all.

"Come," she said.

Nelson opened the door and stepped onto the plush carpet of her office. The room was dark except for the glow of the lamp on her desk. The stark white walls did little to brighten the gloomy place. Locked white file cabinets lined one wall. Along the opposite one was a white leather couch where the doctor sometimes slept. Files were stacked on one corner of her desk, and in front of her was a worn, singed leather-bound journal he'd seen many times before.

He wasn't sure exactly what was in that book, but the woman guarded it with her life.

Dr. Norma Stynger was rumored to be in her late fifties,

but she looked much younger. Bright red lipstick lined her mouth, and her pale green eyes looked almost colorless behind a dark fringe of long eyelashes. Nelson had thought she was pretty before he'd gotten to know her better.

As he entered, she closed the journal and set down her pen. She slid her reading glasses from her nose and looked up at him in expectation. "Yes?"

"One of our subjects has been taken into police custody."

Her red mouth tightened before her face once more relaxed into a regal kind of calm. "Which one?"

"Brad Evans."

She waved her hand in annoyance, showing off bright red fingernails at the end of long, bony fingers. "I don't know names. What was his number?"

Nelson had to look at his notes. "S-eleven-seventeen."

"The one we sent after the leak?"

He nodded.

"Do you know if he recovered the documents?" she asked.

"Nothing like that was listed in the police report."

Dr. Stynger stood. In her high heels, she easily met his nearly six feet in height. Skinny as a stick, she leaned forward, splaying her fingers on her desk.

Nelson backed up. He couldn't help the gut reaction to move away from this woman. He wasn't squeamish, but the things he'd seen her do were worse than anything he'd seen in his nineteen years of military service. To her, people were things, objects to be used and discarded when they ceased to serve their purpose. Even her own daughter.

Nelson was in charge of recruitment and security at the compound. The capture of one of his men had been a huge mistake he was sure she would not overlook. For all he knew, *his* usefulness to her was now at an end.

He'd rather eat a bullet than let her get her hands on him. Men who had spent time with her in the white room came out changed. Broken.

"Did he locate the woman?"

"His last report stated that she was no longer living at her previous residence. It's for sale."

"Clearly the protocol failed with him. I wish I had his body to autopsy so I could determine the root cause of the failure."

"He's not dead, ma'am."

"Pity. He's a security risk while he's still alive."

"He won't say a word," Nelson hurried to add. "He'll stick to his training."

"I don't care what he says. He'll sound like a raving lunatic and trigger the control device. I'm more concerned with physical evidence—evidence I entrusted you to find and bring back."

"I'll send another man. One who's responding better to the program, one who is more equipped to handle any obstacles that get in his way."

"Who?"

"Trevor Moss." Dr. Stynger frowned, and he hurried to add, "S-eleven-fifteen."

She shook her head. "His conditioning isn't complete. I haven't tested him yet."

"Why not let this be his test?"

She tapped her shiny red fingernail on her desk as she considered his suggestion. "Because he's not ready. He'll fail. I want this finished. We need to know where that diary is—where the woman who has it is. Bring S-eleven-sixteen in for questioning."

Nelson nodded. "Staite won't talk. That man is made of pure steel and grit. That's why I recruited him. You'll kill him before he spills his guts."

"He won't have to say a word. Jordyn will do all the talking. Bring her, too."

Nelson didn't know what the doctor was going to do to her daughter next. Whatever it was, it couldn't be worse than Jordyn's punishment for breaking compound protocol by mailing Staite's diary. She'd screamed for a whole day before her voice gave out. "She just left the infirmary a few hours ago. I'm sure she's still sleeping."

Not a flicker of emotion crossed the doctor's face. "Then wake her."

"Yes, ma'am." Nelson saluted before he turned on his heel and left. He wasn't a real general, but Dr. Stynger didn't care. She had faith in him. She'd given him a job when his own country said he wasn't good enough to serve. He owed her his loyalty, and because of that, he'd do whatever it took to make her proud.

# Chapter Six

Roxanne couldn't sleep. She'd showered, eaten, and lain down, but she couldn't stop thinking about Jake's box sitting locked in her gun safe.

Aware of Tanner sleeping down the hall on her couch, she slipped a robe on over her short summer pajamas and tiptoed to the spare bedroom. It was still stuffed full of boxes waiting to be unloaded, but she'd kept a path to her gun safe clear. She punched in the combination and pulled out the sealed shoe box.

"I was wondering how long it would take you to get to that," said Tanner from the doorway. He wore only a pair of jeans and his chest was bare, showing off just how wide his shoulders were and how beautifully he was built. Dense layers of muscle shifted beneath his skin as he leaned against the doorframe. He crossed one bare foot over the other and regarded her with a steady stare. A dark trail of hair led down below his waistband, which sat low on his hips.

Roxanne stared for too long, soaking in the sight of him. She hadn't wanted a babysitter, but the least she could do was acknowledge Bella's good taste in one.

Her skin warmed, and the bedroom suddenly felt too hot with his body filling the doorway. She had to fight the urge to strip out of her robe and let the air pull heat away from her skin. Only the fact that she wore short summer pajamas beneath held her back. She really didn't want him to think she was coming on to him by stripping down.

She had to work with this man. Getting involved with him was out of the question, no matter how much the idea appealed. If ever a man had been built to make her body melt, it was Tanner O'Connell.

"Did I wake you?" she asked.

"I'm a light sleeper."

"I'll take this back to my room and won't bother you again."

"It's no bother. I want to know what's in there, too."

"I'm sure it's no big secret. Probably just a stash of dirty magazines he didn't want me to know he had."

Tanner raised a brow in disbelief. "We both know that's not true."

"Guess we'll find out."

She took the box to the kitchen table and cut the tape open with her kitchen shears. Inside was a simple spiral notebook. Paper-clipped to the notebook was a short letter in Jake's own writing, using their childhood code.

*I'm sorry, Rox. I never meant for you to get involved, but I didn't know who else to trust.*

Roxanne looked at Tanner, hesitating to turn the page. "What if it's something horrible?"

"Like what?" His eyes were fixed on her, not the notebook. He sat still and relaxed, as if what happened next was no big deal.

"I don't know. Stolen military secrets of some kind, I guess."

Tanner leaned forward, propping his elbows on the table. Muscles in his shoulders bunched, distracting her for a precious moment.

"Is he the kind of man to commit treason?" asked Tanner.

"No. Never."

"There you go. There's nothing to be worried about. And there's one sure way to find out, rather than tearing yourself apart with curiosity."

He was right. She was stalling needlessly. Jake was a good man. Whatever was in this notebook would certainly bear that out.

Roxanne looked at Tanner and nodded. "Do you mind letting me do this alone? Jake's my friend. If this is personal, I'd rather not let anyone else see it. It's bad enough that I'm being nosy."

"Sure," he said as he stood. He placed his hand on her shoulder and gave her a quick squeeze of reassurance. "I'll be close if you need anything. Just holler."

Roxanne took a deep breath, opened the cover, and started reading.

Tanner was twisting with curiosity. He kept his distance for as long as he could, flipping through crappy late-night TV for an hour, before slipping back into the kitchen.

Razor hunched over the notebook, completely ignoring his presence.

Figuring this might take her a while, and knowing she had to be exhausted, he fired up a pot of coffee and slipped a mug onto the table beside her. He was careful to keep his eyes off what she was reading out of respect, but he was sure he'd sprained something resisting the urge to peek.

"Thank you," she said, but her voice was too unsteady for his peace of mind. Whatever she had read wasn't sitting well.

Tanner went back to the couch and sipped his own coffee as he searched in vain for something decent to watch. A few minutes later, Razor came into the living room with the notebook clutched in her shaking hand. Her skin was pale, and there was a fear in her eyes he hadn't seen even when her attacker had been choking the life from her body.

The way she wavered unsteadily on her feet made him wonder if she was going to topple at any minute.

He bounded up, took her by the arms, and eased her down onto the couch.

"This has to be some kind of joke," she whispered.

"What does?"

"This journal. It's Jake's. He started keeping one when he got his new assignment, thinking he'd use it to write a book someday about all of his adventures."

"What did it say?"

She stared at the carpet, shaking her head. "It started out fine. He talked about how excited he was for the new position, how proud he was to have been chosen. They recruited only the best."

"Recruited for what?"

"He didn't know. The man who recruited him didn't say. It was all a big secret, and he didn't find out any details until after he signed on."

"Did he mention anything about Delta Force or the Rangers?"

"No. But I think I know why."

"Why?"

"Because those groups are legitimate. The journal went through his initiation into this group, but it was really vague, as though he was being careful not to write down anything he shouldn't. There was a big gap in time with no entries. And then in the next one, his handwriting was different—sharper. The indentations he left were deeper. I could still tell it was his writing, but he was afraid."

"What did he say?"

"He talked about one of his friends who went crazy and killed himself." She sucked in a deep breath. When she let it out, Tanner could hear her fighting the urge to cry. "He said he thought it was the drugs."

"Drugs?"

"They were giving him something. They were giving it to all the men who were recruited with him. Shots every day. He said it . . . changed them. Made them sick."

A flash of the skinny soldier with track marks and a crazy gleam in his eye rushed through Tanner's mind. When he met Razor's golden gaze and saw the tears shimmering there, he knew she'd thought about that, too.

He pried the pages from her hand and set them aside. He covered her chilled fingers in his and looked her right in the eyes. "We'll get to the bottom of this, Razor. I'm sure Jake is okay."

A tear broke past her lashes and fell onto the back of his hand. "He said he was going to try to convince someone to mail this for him as proof of what was going on, but he couldn't escape. Not without his friends."

Never leave a man behind. Tanner would have felt the same way, but he didn't think saying so would make Razor feel any better. "He must have made it out with his buddies, then, because you got that e-mail today. We just have to find where he's hiding."

She swallowed, and her chin trembled. "If he made it out, he would have said he was safe. He wouldn't have just told me to burn his journal. He wouldn't have warned me they were coming. He would have come and found me himself."

"You don't know that. He could be protecting you by not making further contact."

"Or he could be in trouble. Either way, I need to find him."

Tanner didn't like the idea. While he definitely wanted to get to the bottom of what was going on, it sounded as though Jake was in serious trouble and he didn't want Razor anywhere near it. From what she'd told him about Jake, he wouldn't have wanted her to put herself at risk, either. "If you go after him, you could make things worse."

"How? From what I can tell, he's already neck-deep in trouble. He needs my help."

"Think about it. That man who attacked you—he has to be connected to all this. He said you had stolen secrets, and he was probably talking about that journal. That was why Jake warned you to burn everything. He knew you'd be at risk."

"I'm not going to burn it. It's evidence of what's going on."

"Which is why you can't keep it. For all we know, that

man wasn't alone. They could send someone else after the journal. Or after you."

Razor nodded and stood, purpose straightening her spine. "You're right. I need to hide it, or turn it in to the authorities."

"What authorities? The police? The military? The feds? We have no idea what we're dealing with." More important, they had no idea if the information she'd read would ruin her life if whoever was behind this found out exactly what she knew.

"He sent it to me for a reason."

"He also told you to burn it for a reason, but you can't destroy evidence."

"Maybe they got to him. Maybe he was scared for me."

"He should be. Until we know more, we have to assume you're in a hell of a lot of danger."

"I need to talk to Bella. She has connections. She can help me figure this out. And until then, I'll use the high-security storage vault at the Edge to keep Jake's journal safe."

That wasn't a bad idea. There were fewer places on Earth where she'd be safer than inside that building, surrounded by people who knew their way around a fight.

Tanner nodded and grabbed his shirt. "I'll drive."


"Where's Evans?" asked Jake Staite, keeping his head turned away from the cameras. He didn't know if anyone was watching them right now, but he wasn't willing to take the risk.

Over the past several weeks, it had become clear that he and the other three men recruited with him into this supposed special forces group were no longer here voluntarily. They were prisoners, and it was their duty to find a way to escape. So far, the security here seemed unbreachable, but he'd find a way out.

The weight room was one of the few places he and the others could talk. The sound of the weights banging against one another and the grunts of exertion drowned out their conversation. At least he hoped so.

The three men congregated in one corner of the room, away from the others who wore the SABER emblem on their shirts—the emblem Jake was told he'd have to earn before being sent on any missions. Those men had been here longer and were part of the establishment. Jake was also convinced they were serving as guard dogs, keeping him and the other new recruits from getting out of line.

Alan MacKenzie, Mac, kept his head down, not visibly acknowledging Jake's question. "Gone. Two days now."

Jake grabbed a fifty-pound weight and loaded it onto the bar. Trevor Moss, his bunk mate, lay on the bench, waiting for Jake to load the other side.

"Did they say where he went?" asked Moss.

"Infirmary."

"Was he sick?" asked Jake.

Mac wiped sweat from his forehead. "No more than normal."

They were all sick, and Jake was convinced it was the so-called vitamin shots that had been forced on them since they arrived. All the men took them, and it wasn't optional. He didn't know what was in that syringe, but he did know it was making him and his buddies sick.

A couple of weeks ago, he'd refused the meds. The tech hadn't fought him. He'd simply gone away. Jake thought he'd won the battle until he woke up the next morning with a new bruise on his arm.

They'd injected him in his sleep, and the only way he wouldn't have woken up when someone came into his room was if they'd drugged him. He'd never slept as hard or deeply in his life as he did here—as if someone had pulled his plug each night. And when he woke up, the grogginess that came with it was not normal.

This morning he thought he'd discovered how they were doing it, but he didn't dare say anything here for fear of one of the SABERs overhearing. He'd test his theory first.

"Have you been allowed to visit him?" asked Jake.

"They said he shouldn't be bothered."

"We're not leaving without him." Jake spotted Moss as he hefted the loaded bar. Despite having lost weight, every one of them was stronger now than when they arrived. A lot stronger.

One of the SABERs moved into their space and picked up a set of free weights. He was huge, bulging with muscle in an unnatural way.

Maybe those injections they got every day were some kind of steroids. Jake had never been hungrier in his life. He'd also never thrown up quite so much. Bulgy didn't look as though he had any trouble keeping his food down. Maybe it took a while to get used to the drugs.

Jake glanced at the other man's arm and saw needle tracks, though his weren't nearly as angry and red as Jake's were.

Bulgy went back to his SABER buddies with the weights. Moss got up and gave Jake a turn on the bench.

"Mac, see if you can wrangle a visit with Evans so we know where they're keeping him. I have a theory I'm going to test tonight."

Jake shoved the bar up, easily handling fifty more pounds than his previous record. In fact, he was holding back, pretending he was weaker than he was. So were the rest of his buddies. They didn't want the powers that be knowing how strong they'd become, hoping it would give them an edge when the time for escape finally arrived.

And they would escape. He had to believe that. Whatever this place was, whoever these people were, they were not patriots. They didn't give a shit about him or any of the other men here. With the exception of one woman he'd managed to befriend and convince to help him get word to Roxanne, everyone here had the compassion of a rattlesnake.

He feared that if he didn't get out soon, he and his friends would become just like them.

# Chapter Seven

By the time they reached the Edge's main office on the outskirts of Dallas, the sun was beginning to lighten the sky.

Jake's journal and all his letters were tucked into a shopping bag, clutched on Roxanne's lap. Her mind kept going to dark, bleak places. What if Jake needed her? What if he was hurt right now? What if he was trapped, praying she'd come save him?

What if it was already too late?

Tanner's hand slid beneath her hair, cupping the back of her neck as he drove. "Hang in there. I'm sure he's fine."

The comfort of his touch and kindness of his words sank into her, helping to drive away some of the more horrible thoughts plaguing her mind. "I hope you're right. I don't know what I'd do without him."

Sure, he wasn't around much, but he was the only family she had left. Hell, he and his mom were the only family she had ever really had, if you counted the people who truly cared about her.

She knew exactly how far her parents' love had extended—to exactly three percent of their net worth. That was the sum total of her value to them.

Roxanne shoved away the memory, refusing to let it add to her anxiety. Jake was what mattered now, not some old wound that had long ago scabbed over.

Tanner kept an eye on his mirrors, checking their backs. "Any tails?"

"I didn't see any, but I didn't see any on the way to the storage facility, either."

"Were you looking for company?"

"Not as hard as I am now—that's for sure."

Tanner parked in the private, underground lot and they took the elevator up to the main floor. The doors opened in the reception area, but most of the lights were still off.

"I don't have access to the vault, so we'll have to wait for Bella to show up. We can wait in her office."

Payton Bainbridge came around the corner from the break room, bearing a cup of steaming coffee. He wore his usual perfectly tailored suit, and despite the early hour, his tie was neatly knotted and exactly straight. While he had to be in his fifties, he still had the kind of dashing good looks that made women much younger than him take notice.

Or perhaps that had something to do with his sizable fortune.

Payton ran in the same social circles that Roxanne's parents had, but he hadn't seemed to have that same hollow spot where his soul should have been that so many of their friends did. Despite his wealth and status, Payton actually worked for a living, and that was something Roxanne couldn't help but respect.

"Razor, Tanner, what are you two doing here so early?" he asked, smiling in greeting.

"I could ask you the same thing," said Roxanne.

Payton shrugged. "Bella's away, so it falls to me to keep things going in her absence."

"Where is she?"

"Overseas on a mission. Something hush-hush, apparently." He waved a hand as if dismissing the details.

"I need to speak to her. When will she be back?"

"In a few days. Is there something I can help you with in the meantime?"

Roxanne hesitated. She didn't know Payton all that well,

but this couldn't wait. And Bella trusted him, which was going to have to be good enough. "I need to put something in the vault."

"Something belonging to one of our clients?"

"Not exactly." And then she realized a new option—one that might save Jake's life. "Actually, yes. He is a client, and I'll be paying his bill."

Payton frowned and held out his hand, indicating they should precede him. "This sounds like something we should discuss in my office. Shall we?"

Roxanne turned to Tanner and lowered her voice. "I don't know how Bella's going to feel about this. I think now would be a good time for you to disengage yourself from this whole mess. I don't want to risk your job."

He stepped in front of her and bent his knees, bowing his head until their eyes were only inches apart. "If you think I'm going to walk away after you were attacked, after finding out that your friend is in trouble, then you're crazier than the guy who thought you were a flower. We're in this together, and if that means I lose my job, then I'll find another one."

"Do you two need a moment alone?" asked Payton.

"No," said Roxanne, seeing certainty in Tanner's eyes. "I think we're ready."

The truth was, she was relieved to have him at her side. She only hoped he didn't regret his decision to stay there.

They filed into Payton's office, and he shut the door behind them. Roxanne waited until he sat behind his desk before she began.

"I have this friend, Jake Staite."

Payton nodded. "I remember him from your background check. He's in the army, right?"

Roxanne nodded and clutched the bag of letters tighter to her chest. "You have a good memory."

Payton sipped his coffee, ignoring her compliment.

"Anyway, he sent me this journal. I didn't realize that

was what it was. I was in the middle of moving, so it got packed up with the rest of his things."

"You two live together?"

"Yes."

Beside her, she saw Tanner stiffen. "You didn't tell me that."

"It's nothing romantic. Just pure practicality," Roxanne hurried to add. "We're friends. He's hardly ever home. It seemed silly for him to rent an apartment when I had that huge house all to myself. Besides, he grew up there, too."

"Ah, right," said Payton. "His mother worked for your family. I remember that now."

"She did."

"Whatever happened to her?"

"She passed away from a massive heart attack the year Jake went into the service." Grief made Roxanne's voice tight. It had been her senior year in high school. Jake was gone, and then so was the woman who had been more like a mother to her than the woman who'd given birth to her.

"I can tell you cared deeply for her. My condolences."

She swallowed down the sense of loss and forced herself to focus. She refused to let Jake leave her, too. "Thank you."

"So, can I assume that the item you're clutching in that sack is the young man's journal?"

"Yes."

"And you want to house it in our vault? You know we don't let just anything get stored there. Storage that secure demands a high premium."

"I know. There's more—just hear me out."

Payton nodded for her to continue.

"I've had the journal for weeks. I'd been moving, and it came when I was working eighty-hour weeks. I wasn't even sure Jake had meant for me to open the box."

"So why did you?"

"Yesterday, I went to my parents' estate because vandals had broken in and torn the place apart. While I was there, I got an e-mail. It was written in a code Jake and I used as kids, telling me to burn everything."

Payton set his coffee down and leaned forward, his full attention focused on her. "So, rather than doing as he asked, you read the journal."

"Yes. And I'm glad I did. I think Jake's in trouble."

"What kind of trouble?"

"He was recruited into some secret military group. After being there awhile, he started to suspect they may not even be part of the US military at all. And if they are, what they're doing has to be illegal."

"What kinds of things are they doing?"

"They're giving him drugs. He says some of the men are changing, becoming violent. One of his friends killed himself."

Even the thought of someone doing that to Jake made her want to scream. He was a good man—the best. He'd committed his life to serving his country, and now someone had tortured him. Perhaps they still were.

Tanner's hand settled on her knee as he spoke. "Razor was attacked last night at the storage facility where she kept the journal. The man was well trained. He was also out of his mind and covered in needle tracks."

Payton paled and his voice shook as he asked, "Where is that man now?"

"The police took him in. I imagine he's in a padded room by now, undergoing a psych evaluation. But he said 'they' wanted the secrets back. He may not have been alone."

"Which is why I want Jake's journal and letters locked up," said Roxanne. "It may be the only proof we have that something bad is happening to him."

Payton folded his hands, and an eerie kind of calm settled over him. "You both look tired. Why don't you get some sleep in one of the on-call rooms, and I'll lock up the journal and make a few calls."

"To whom?" she asked.

"Sloane's father is a general in the army. I'll speak to him and see if he can track down your friend. We'll locate him and make sure there's nothing to worry about."

Sloane was one of the best employees the Edge had. If her father was half as capable as she was, he was going to be a valuable asset. "And if there is?" Roxanne asked.

"No sense in borrowing trouble. Get some rest. I'm sure you're exhausted after what you've been through."

"How can I rest when Jake might be in trouble?"

Payton stood, holding out his hand for the sack. "How can you help him if you can't even stand up straight? Besides, do you have any idea where to even look for him?"

"No. Not yet."

"Then sleep. I'll do some legwork, and we'll figure out where to go from here." He gave an expectant nod toward the bag she held. "May I?"

What choice did she have? She didn't have the same connections Payton did. And if he could use them to find Jake, she had to trust him enough to let him try.

Roxanne handed him the sack, praying she wasn't making a huge mistake.

Tanner followed Roxanne to the on-call rooms and saw her safely inside one before heading to the vacant one across the hall. He turned and nearly ran smack into the uncomfortable meeting he'd been avoiding since interviewing for a position at the Edge.

Reid O'Connell, Tanner's brother, stood with his hands fisted on his hips, his feet braced apart as if expecting a fight.

Tanner wasn't going to give him the satisfaction.

He nodded in greeting. "Morning."

Reid shared the same blue eyes as all the O'Connell men. His head had been shaved a few days ago, showing the shadow of new growth. Only the long, thin scar bisecting his scalp over his left ear was left pale and glowing under the fluorescent lights—the scar Reid had earned protecting Tanner when they were kids.

The two years that separated their ages had given Tanner a serious case of hero worship for his older brother when he was a kid, but now the gap was much wider. Dad and Brody were dead, and a river of grief stood between Tanner and Reid. They were the only two men left in the family, and it had been a long time since they'd seen eye to eye.

"What are you doing here so early?" asked Reid.

"Doing my job, like Bella asked. Why are you here?"

"I have a ton of paperwork to do, but I'm leaving early for the picnic, so I'm making up the time now."

"Picnic?"

Reid simply stared at him for a moment, as if he were slow. "Millie's first birthday. Don't tell me you—"

"I didn't forget," lied Tanner.

"You're going to be there."

While his older brother's order didn't sit well, Tanner ignored his irritation. Their youngest brother was dead. Their sister-in-law had her hands full with two small children—one with serious health problems. Millie was turning one year old today, and Tanner was going to be there.

"Of course."

"You had forgotten," accused Reid. "Shit, Tanner, it's not like we have all that many parties these days. If you don't show, Mom will—"

"I'm not going to make Mom cry again." She'd done enough of that, both while he was away serving his country, and after the death of her husband and youngest son. "I said I'll be there. I don't need you—"

"Apparently you do. If I hadn't mentioned it, you would have forgotten. Just like—"

"That was different. I was in another time zone. I called her on her birthday, just not in this part of the world."

"You always have an excuse. There damn well better not be any more today."

"I said I'll be there."

Reid stared at him for a minute before finally nodding, letting it go. "Bella said you're assigned to Razor for a few days."

Tanner hesitated to confirm it, wondering how his brother could twist something so simple around and make him feel like more of an ass than he already did by forgetting Millie's party. "That's right."

Reid looked up and down the hallway, making sure they were alone. He lowered his voice, but the warning ringing in his tone was clear nonetheless. "Razor's tough, but not as tough as she thinks. And she hates working with a partner."

While he could see her resistance to teamwork, Tanner thought she'd done well when faced with danger last night. She hadn't lost her head or panicked. She'd used the weapon at her disposal and acted before it was too late. That soldier would have pulled the trigger. Had Roxanne hesitated, the O'Connell family would be mourning today instead of celebrating a birthday. "I think you might be underestimating her."

"I'm not. And you'd better not overestimate her. She's been through hell."

"You make it sound like the two of you are close." And the thought made jealousy spread out through Tanner on rotten wings.

Reid shrugged. "Not really. But there are a lot of rumors floating around about her and what happened to her when she was a kid."

"What kind of rumors?"

"I'm not going to spread gossip. If you want to know, ask her. But I can tell you that she's not tough like some of the other women Bella employs. That's why you got guard dog duty. Even Bella knows she needs a keeper."

A slow, simmering anger began to build behind Tanner's eyes. "I'm not sure if that's more judgmental or condescending. You've taken a turn toward prick since I left."

"I'm a hell of a lot more realistic than I used to be. If that hurts your feelings, so be it, but you need to know what you're dealing with. I put my neck on the line to get you this job. If you fuck it up, we could both be out—"

"I'm not going to fuck up anything. I may have been a dumb, scrawny kid when I went into the military, but I'm no longer the baby brother you remember. I don't need you to hold my hand anymore, so stop pretending the world will cease to exist without you."

Reid's jaw clenched in anger. "While you were away doing whatever the hell you felt like, I was the one taking care of the family and—"

"Doing whatever the hell I felt like? Is that what you think I was doing overseas? Lounging on a beach, drinking—"

"Might as well have been for all the good it did the family. You were on leave for only three days after the accident. I was with Mom and Karen every day. I held them while they cried. I was there when Millie was born, because Brody couldn't be. I'm the one keeping this family together, and now that you're home, it's my job to take care of you, too. If you won't take my advice, fine, but don't blame me when Razor is true to form and takes off without you."

Reid was right about having to do the heavy lifting after their dad and Brody died. Tanner had only managed to get a few days of leave. He'd had no choice but to return to the battlefield and abandon his family to deal with the loss on their own. But at least they'd had one another. All he'd had was the crushing loss of his brother and father with no one around who knew what he felt. He'd kept it hidden, secret. He'd stayed tough and shoved the grief away so he could do his job. Some days that had been all that had kept him sane. "If she does ditch me, I'll find her." Again.

"Before or after she gets herself—"

"I'm on it," said Tanner. "I don't need your help."

Reid shook his head. "I guess we'll see."

They would. Tanner would make sure he did whatever it took to handle things on his own, because, despite Tanner's never having really lived up to his dad's expectations the way Reid had and despite the chasm between them having widened over the years, Tanner still loved his brother.

Reid was carrying too much weight. Not only was Tanner determined not to add to it by fucking up; he was going to find a way to lighten his brother's load. After months of shouldering the burden alone, it was time for Reid to accept some help—whether or not he wanted it.

Payton took no chances. He locked himself in the vault and read the young man's journal from beginning to end. What he saw had to be a mistake.

Jake Staite mentioned Dr. Stynger—who was dead. Payton had killed her himself, trapping her inside that burning lab so she'd go up in flames with Dr. Leeson and all of his research.

She couldn't be alive. It had to be a coincidence—someone else with the same name.

Even as the thought entered his mind, he dismissed it. The things the young soldier described in his journal were too familiar—just like the photos of that lab Bella had destroyed in Mexico.

Payton's worst fears were being confirmed. The Threshold Project wasn't dead and buried as he and the others had wanted to believe.

He left the journal behind in the vault, then went to his office and locked the door. The security of his phone line at work was good but not as good as what he had in his basement at home. Sadly, it would have to do. He couldn't waste any time driving home.

General Robert Norwood was an early riser, and he answered his personal line on the first ring.

"We have a problem," said Payton.

"Is it Sloane?"

"No. She's fine. This has nothing to do with your daughter."

Bob let out an audible sigh of relief. "Then talk fast. I have a meeting."

"I need you to find a soldier for me. Captain Jake Slaite from Dallas, Texas."

"Why?"

"Can you please just do it? The whys aren't yet clear, but I'm hoping you can help with that."

"How soon do you need to know?"

"Yesterday."

"Hang on," said Bob. "I'll see what I can do."

Payton waited on hold for five minutes, twisting in impatience, before the general came back on the line. "He left the service in January. It was voluntary. Honorable discharge."

That made no sense. The dates in his journal were more recent than that.

"I have to say I'm surprised, though," said Bob. "He had a hell of a record. Wish I'd had a chance to talk him out of resigning."

"Are you sure he left? Do you have any kind of forwarding address?"

"What's this all about, Payton? Why the interest?"

"Are you alone?"

The general paused. "Yes."

"I have his journal. He wrote about being recruited into a secret special forces group he never named."

"He's a prime candidate for Delta Force, but he hadn't been invited yet. As far as his record is concerned, this man is now a civilian."

"He doesn't think he is. He mentioned four other men who were recruited with him, but he doesn't mention any names."

"I can check for men who left around the same time he did, but it will take some time."

"There's something else you should know," said Payton. "He described the place where he's being trained. It sounds a lot like the facilities we used to use. What if there's a connection?"

Bob stayed silent for a long time. "That's a pretty big leap."

"He talked about being given daily injections, that they were told they were vitamins, but the men were having negative side effects—aggression, depression, weight loss."

"That could be a coincidence."

"He mentioned a woman named Dr. Stynger."

"She's dead."

"Is she?"

"You told me you took care of it."

"I did. Or at least I thought I did. I never went back for the body."

"Sloppy."

"Hardly. If I'd gone back, we all would have been caught. I saved your ass that night, as well as the senator's."

"There has to be some kind of mistake," said Bob.

Payton didn't know how much more proof the man needed to see the truth. He tried to keep his voice free of irritation, but it came out clipped, anyway. "Adam Brink shows up out of nowhere, looking for people on the List. And then Bella takes those photos of that Mexican facility that looks all too familiar. Then Staite walks away from a military career and gets pumped full of drugs by a woman named Dr. Stynger? We can't chalk those things up as coincidence. We have to face this."

"Maybe Staite was on the List. He could be having flashbacks from his childhood. Delusions. He could have gone off somewhere on his own and is writing down his memories in that journal."

"That doesn't make sense, considering the police arrested another man here last night who has to be connected to Staite."

Bob snorted. "How the hell do you tie them together?"

"The man arrested last night was looking for Jake's journal, which happened to be in the possession of one of our employees. She's friends with Jake, and she's not going to let this drop. She wants to look for him."

"Was she one of ours?"

Payton knew what he was asking—if Razor had been one of the children in the Threshold Project experiments. "No. Her parents and I were friends. I never would have let that happen to her after seeing what it did to Bella."

"I want to see this journal."

"You'll have to come here. Bella's out of the country and I can't leave, especially not now."

"I'm due for a visit with Sloane, anyway. I'll fly in and meet you after dinner one night this week."

That was probably for the best. They had a lot to catch up on. Adam Brink had been a busy man these last few weeks, and neither one of them had been able to pin him down. Three more people on the List had gone missing, and, as far as Payton could tell, he and the general were the only two men who knew enough pieces of the puzzle to figure out where they might have gone.

Stopping Adam was imperative, but finding out exactly what he was doing with those people he abducted was even more important. They'd already suffered enough because of what Payton, Bob, and the others had done. The least they deserved was to live out the rest of their lives in peace, and if he had to kill Adam Brink to make it happen, then that was exactly what he'd do.

# Chapter Eight

Tanner couldn't sleep, and it had nothing to do with the strange surroundings. The room was small—just big enough for the bed and a nightstand. There were no windows, and it had to be soundproofed, based on how quiet it was inside.

Despite the quiet dark and the fatigue that made his eyes burn, he couldn't get the image of that deranged soldier out of his head.

He had to go see the man and find out if there was some way he could help. He'd been through some rough shit overseas and knew how much it could eat at a person if he let it. He also knew that it didn't have to. Whoever that man was, he deserved a chance to see what life could be like.

Tanner didn't want one more veteran sliding down into society's gutter, forgotten and ignored.

He sat up and flipped on the lamp, rubbing his eyes with the heels of his hands. He wasn't sure what exactly he could do, but he had to try something.

Tanner found Payton in his office. "I want to talk to the man who attacked Roxanne. Will you keep her here while I go to the police?"

"I already checked on him, and he's in the hospital while they treat his wounds."

"Did you talk to him?"

"No, and I can't imagine why you would want to, either, considering what he tried to do to Razor."

"He was drugged out of his mind. He may not have even known what he was doing. Maybe if they cleaned that shit out of his system, he'd make more sense."

Payton leaned back in his chair. "I'm sure the authorities have it under control."

"The authorities have no clue about the bigger picture—about how there's possibly a US soldier being held against his will."

"And you think we should tell them?"

Tanner had kept too many secrets for his government over the years—secrets that needed to be kept. He knew the potential cost of releasing information to the press. They cared about ratings and profit. Something like this was huge and could explode in a matter of hours. If Jake had been or was being held against his will, there was no way of knowing what his captors might do if they were outed on national news. He could very well get Jake killed. "No, but I do think we need to find out what he knows. Don't you?"

"Yes, which is why I pulled in some favors and asked to have a friend of mine assigned to the case. If there's anything we need to know, I'll find out from him."

"When?"

"Soon. In the meantime, I think you should stick close to Razor and make sure she doesn't decide to go running to her friend's rescue."

"She wouldn't do that, would she?" But even as he asked the question, he knew the answer. She would.

Payton smiled, but the smile didn't touch his eyes. "I see that you realize the truth now. Keep her safe."

Tanner left Payton's office at a jog, heading to the room where she was supposed to be sleeping. The door was unlocked. He didn't even hesitate. He turned the knob. If he caught her sleeping naked or something, so be it. He'd rather have her mad at him than running around alone, putting herself in the way of the next drugged lunatic.

And if he got to see her naked in the process, then that was just a grenade he'd have to fall on and take like a man. He'd already spent far too much time thinking about what Razor might look like under her clothes to pretend otherwise.

Tanner pushed the door open and peeked inside, holding his breath. The bed was empty.

Reid had been right. She'd ditched him. Again.

Son of a bitch.


Jake had just finished his workout when two of the SABERs approached. "Staite, come with us."

"What for?" asked Jake.

"Now," said the man.

Moss shifted, his stance changing slightly as if preparing to attack. Jake and his buddies were in this mess together. They'd become close over the past few weeks as it became clear that this was not some kind of exercise designed to test them. They were in real, deep trouble. And they were going to get out of it the same way they'd gotten in— together, or at least as together as they could be now that Greene had taken his own life.

Jake shook his head slightly, hoping Moss would back down. "Where are we going?"

"To see Dr. Stynger."

A little surge of excitement rushed through Jake. Jordyn Stynger had been the one person who was willing to help him. Maybe she would again.

Jordyn had mailed his journal to Roxanne. He knew there was a chance she'd be curious enough to poke her nose in his business and read it, but that was a risk he had to take. If he never got out of here, he wanted there to be some proof of what had happened here so that it wouldn't happen to anyone else.

Jake was smart and well trained. If General Bower could fool him and four men, chances were he could fool others as well. Based on the thirty-five soldiers and twelve civilians he'd counted since he'd arrived, Bower already had.

"Nice," said Jake. "It's about time we had a little eye candy around here."

"Not her," said the blond SABER. "We're seeing the head honcho. The elder Dr. Stynger. Jordyn's mom."

Jake had heard whispers about the woman, about how even General Bower jumped to obey when she summoned him.

Maybe she knew what he'd found in his room. He thought he'd covered his surprise, but there were cameras everywhere.

Apprehension slid through him until he realized there really wasn't much she could do to punish them. They were already prisoners. They were already being tortured with the drugs shoved into them every day. Besides simply killing them, she didn't have a whole lot of options left, and Jake wasn't going to be an easy man to kill.

He was escorted to a metal door that looked like all the others in this place. One of the guards knocked.

A woman's voice answered. "Come."

The door opened, revealing a sterile white room. A two-way mirror lined one wall. A metal table and chairs sat bolted in the center of the room. A skeletal woman with bright red lipstick stood in the corner. Beneath her lab coat was a simple black suit. Her bird legs stuck out from the skirt, showing off knobby knees. Her black hair was pulled back in a severe bun that seemed to stretch the skin of her face, making her age hard to determine. Forties? Fifties? Sixties? He couldn't be sure.

Jake searched for a resemblance to Jordyn, who was pretty and sweet and kind. He saw none. In fact, he had a hard time believing there could be any relation at all between her and the woman standing before them.

General Bower stood next to Dr. Stynger, glowering at him.

Jake refused to salute. The uniform Bower wore was a

lie. There was no way a man like him—a man willing to imprison and torture the men under his command—had earned those stars. The uniform Bower wore was nothing more than a costume, and Jake refused to acknowledge it.

"I'm sure you remember Dr. Norma Stynger. She's taken an interest in you."

Jake had met her only once before, and he'd been so sick at the time, he'd done little more than register her name and the fact that she was to blame for the way he felt.

Dr. Stynger smiled. "I have, indeed. I hear you are progressing well through the program."

*What program?* Jake wanted to spit those words back at the woman, but he held his tongue. The more information he could gather, the sooner he'd find a way out of this place.

"Have a seat," she offered.

"I prefer to stand." It was easier to attack from a standing position, and just being near this woman put him on edge.

General Bower glowered and shifted his weight toward Jake. That slight movement was enough of a warning to obey that Jake did so. Now was not the time to make his move. He was outnumbered four to one, and even if he did beat those odds, he couldn't leave his friends behind.

He sat down at the cold table.

Dr. Stynger moved toward him once he was seated, her high heels clicking on the tile floor. "I know what you did. What my daughter did."

Jake said nothing as he let the spike of fear shoot through him. For all he knew, this was a way for her to find out the truth. Jordyn promised she'd be careful when she agreed to help him. The last thing he'd wanted was to put her at risk. "I don't know what you're talking about."

Dr. Stynger pursed her lips in irritation. "Who is Roxanne Haught to you?"

Oh God. They knew about Rox. He couldn't let on how much that news scared him. There was no way of knowing if they'd find a way to use her against him.

Jake kept his expression calm and showed only mild curiosity. "Who?" he asked, using every bit of acting ability he had.

She sighed. "We let you keep your diary. I found it most interesting to see how your tiny mind works, but I never thought my daughter would be foolish enough to help you steal our secrets, or that she'd cover up her actions for weeks, forcing me to hear about it from my security team."

She'd read his journal? He thought he'd hidden it better than that. He'd been careful to write in it only after he'd covered the camera in his room. The split in his mattress was undetectable if one didn't know it was there. He'd never found the notebook missing, nor had there been any proof it had been so much as moved an inch. The tamper indicators he'd set had never appeared to be touched, including the one strand of long dark hair he'd stolen from the back of Jordyn's chair.

Jordyn. She'd been afraid to help him. She'd told him that if she did, it wouldn't end well for either of them. He'd been determined to use her, and battered through every resistance she'd offered. He'd bribed, he'd charmed, he'd begged. In the end, she'd caved under the pressure and done as he'd asked, sending the sealed journal to Rox.

Dr. Stynger shrugged. "Her involvement was unfortunate, but I believe she's learned her lesson."

"Did you hurt her?" he demanded, rising from his seat. "Your own daughter?"

Bower shoved him back down.

Dr. Stynger's stare was cold and direct, unblinking. Not a shred of compassion for her own flesh and blood showed through. "She paid for her involvement, but she has yet to make up for that mistake. Your diary must be found. Tell me about the woman who has it. Tell me why you had my daughter send it to her, of all people. Who is Roxanne Haught to you?"

Jake's mind raced to figure a way out of this without

sacrificing Jordyn. He wasn't sure what they'd done to her or where she was. He didn't know what she'd told them.

He had to stall while he came up with a way out of this for everyone, including Rox. "I don't know the woman. You must be mistaken."

Dr. Stynger nodded to one of the SABERs. "Bring her in."

A moment later, the blond guard hauled Jordyn through the door, his beefy hand wrapped around her arm in a crushing grip. Her long dark hair was tangled around her face. Her clothes were rumpled and dirty, as if she'd slept in them for days. Her skin was so pale that her veins showed beneath the surface. Dark crescents hung beneath her eyes, and a look of hopeless desperation haunted her face. She was barely able to stand up without the support of the blond man gripping her arm. She swayed on her feet, squinting as if the light hurt.

When her gaze met his, he could almost feel her regret. "I'm sorry, Jake."

Anger boiled to the surface, and it was all Jake could do to stay seated rather than lashing out at the older woman for whatever she'd done to her daughter. "What the hell did you do to her?"

Dr. Stynger shrugged a bony shoulder. "Nothing she didn't deserve for betraying us. She knows the rules."

"You're a fucking bitch," growled Jake.

Jordyn flinched and swallowed visibly, as if trying not to get sick.

Dr. Stynger said, "I suggest you lower your voice. My daughter has a headache."

She had a hell of a lot more than that, but Jake didn't want to make it worse, so he kept his volume in check. "You did this to her."

The doctor shook her head. "She did it to herself when she decided to listen to you. But that's not what we're here to discuss. Tell me who Roxanne Haught is."

Jake clamped his lips shut and started thinking hard. He

knew where this was going. Dr. Stynger had already done something horrible to her own daughter. He didn't doubt for a second that she'd do something else to Jordyn to force Jake to talk.

He couldn't give up Rox. He loved her. She was the only family he had left. But he couldn't let them torture Jordyn again, either.

It was time to lie.

Jake put on a show, staring at Jordyn for a long time as if thinking things over and struggling with his decision. "She's a reporter. I told her to put the journal in a safe-deposit box, to read it if anything happened to me, or if she didn't see me by Labor Day. I knew she'd print the story if she read it."

Dr. Styner didn't question his lie, but she didn't seem upset by the news, either. She turned to her daughter. "Is that true?"

"I don't know. He didn't tell me anything about her." Jordyn's voice was hoarse, as if she'd been screaming.

Jake's heart squeezed hard, pumping out another rush of anger over whatever they'd done to her. He didn't see any signs of physical damage, but there were plenty of ways to torture someone without leaving a mark. He just bet that the heartless Dr. Stynger knew them all.

The older woman's voice took on a lecturing tone. "You know how I feel about it when you lie to me. You're hardly recovered from the last time you made me punish you. Do you really need me to do it again?"

A look of horror crossed Jordyn's face. "I'm not lying. I swear."

"Hold her," ordered Dr. Stynger.

The blond guard grabbed both her arms and pinned her against his chest in a hard hug. Tears pooled in her eyes and fear made her mouth tremble.

Jake couldn't let this happen. He couldn't let them hurt her again, four-to-one odds or not.

He bounded to his feet, spinning around to take on the guard standing behind him. One hard kick to the stomach made him double over, but he wouldn't be incapacitated for long.

Jake drove his elbow into the man's neck and shoved his head down, while kicking his knee up. The sound of the man's nose breaking filled the shocked silence.

The guard tumbled to his knees, unconscious.

Jake didn't wait to celebrate his victory. He grabbed Dr. Stynger and shoved her down onto the metal table. She fought against his hold on her arms, but she was weak and scrawny and didn't stand a chance. Even the few blows she landed with her high heels didn't faze him.

General Bower pulled his weapon and aimed it at Jake's chest.

Jake flung Dr. Stynger back, plastering her against his chest to use her as a shield. "I doubt she's got enough meat on her bones to stop a bullet, but I'm willing to find out if you are."

"Lower your weapon," ordered Dr. Stynger.

"That's not how you deal with men like him, ma'am. I've got this." Bower swung his arm out until the barrel of the pistol was only inches from Jordyn's head. He looked at Jake. "Let her go."

Tears began pouring from Jordyn's eyes, but she didn't make a sound. She didn't whimper or beg her mother to tell Bower to stand down.

What kind of mother would willingly sacrifice her own child to save her life?

The woman in his grip seemed to grow colder, and his skin crawled at having to touch her. Maybe he should break her scrawny neck and rid the world of a monster.

Of course, if he did that, they'd have no leverage—no means of escape.

Jake hesitated. He didn't want to let go of his advantage, but his unlikely escape wasn't worth the life of an innocent. He needed a better plan. He needed an ally. So far, Jordyn was his only chance, and if she was gone, he and his men would rot down here in this underground prison.

Bower shifted his weight and pressed the barrel against Jordyn's temple. "I will do it." His voice was steady, sure, calm.

Jake no longer doubted it. He couldn't do this—he couldn't give up the life of a woman who had clearly suffered at least as much as he and his buddies had at the hands of Dr. Stynger.

"Let her go and I'll release the bitch," he told Bower.

"Do I look like a fool, son? You first."

With a rush of angry regret, Jake shoved Dr. Stynger away from him, making her stumble toward Bower. He caught her and steadied her on her feet.

Dr. Stynger's bun was a mess, and her red lipstick was smeared. In that moment, she looked older, more vulnerable, and Jake almost felt bad for what he'd done. Almost.

"Let her go," he ordered.

Bower nodded to the soldier, who released Jordyn.

She rubbed her arms and looked at him. Her pale gray-green eyes were luminous with tears. "I'm sorry."

The bleeding man on the floor groaned and shoved himself to his feet.

"Take the subject to the white room," ordered Dr. Stynger.

"No!" shouted Jordyn. "He let you go. You can't do that to him."

The guards grabbed Jake and shoved him through the door down the hall. He had no idea what the white room was, but he knew he wasn't going to like it.

Jordyn raced to her mother and grabbed her hands. "Please don't do this to him. I was the one who helped him. I'm the one you should punish."

Fear and anguish poured into her chest as she watched the guards take Jake away. He already had so many experimental drugs pumping through his system, there was no way to know what another might do to him.

Jordyn's mother stared down at her, unblinking and stoic. "Whether or not I do this is entirely up to you."

She didn't know what that meant, but she knew it couldn't be good. Mother was still angry over Jordyn's betrayal. "What do you mean?"

"I want to know about the woman."

Jordyn couldn't do that. Jake had trusted her with his friend's life. She couldn't stab him in the back like that. "I don't know anything."

"Very well. I'll have to find out from him, then." Mother turned and left, heading for the white room.

Jordyn was right on her heels. Her head was pounding like mad, making it hard to concentrate. The last three days she'd spent with her punishment of an artificially induced migraine and hallucinations had weakened her. Jordyn's mad dash to town to warn Roxanne Haught had taken all her strength. She was dehydrated and shaky. She hadn't been able to eat. Mother had finally allowed the pain to subside this morning, but it hadn't yet gone away completely. For three days she was sure the pain would kill her, that the monsters haunting her visions would eat her flesh, and when none of that happened, she prayed that it would—anything to end the torment.

What they were going to do to Jake in the white room was much, much worse.

By the time they got there, Jake was already strapped into a chair, straining against his bonds.

She couldn't stand to watch, and yet she couldn't bring herself to leave him alone, either. He didn't know what would happen to him. He had to be scared.

He didn't look scared. He looked furious.

Mother fetched a tray from the cabinet and pulled up a stool beside him. "Tell me who this woman really is and where she's hiding your diary, and we don't have to go through this."

"I already told you. She's a reporter. What you're doing

here is going to be revealed to the world. I can hardly wait to watch you fall."

"If that's true, you won't live long enough to see it happen. I'll have to get rid of all the evidence—including you and your friends." Mother uncovered the tray, revealing a row of syringes filled with liquid.

Terror spiked through Jordyn, pinning her in place. She couldn't even breathe. "You can't do that to him," she squeaked out.

Mother regarded her with a calm stare. "It's the only thing that won't interfere with the protocol. He left me no choice."

She tore open an alcohol wipe and disinfected his arm. His skin was already bruised and marked by needles.

"Tell me," ordered Mother.

Jake glared at her, remaining silent.

"Very well."

The needle slid into his skin. Jordyn couldn't watch. She turned away, stifling a cry of pain on his behalf. It wouldn't take long for the drug to start working on his nervous system.

Seconds later, he let out a low hiss of pain.

"I can make it stop," said Mother. "All you have to do is tell me about the woman. Who is she really? Where can I find her?"

Jake made a strangled sound, and Jordyn forced herself to look at him. She was responsible for his suffering. She knew what would happen if she was caught helping him. This was all her fault, and she couldn't simply walk away and leave him to go through this on his own.

His body bowed as much as the restraints allowed. Sweat rolled down his face and the cords in his neck stood out as she struggled within the torture.

"Tell me," said Mother, so calm and quiet, as if she weren't torturing an innocent man.

"Go. To. Hell."

Mother leaned close to his face. "There's something you should know. This is only level one. There are more. If you don't tell me what I want to know, you'll get to experience all of them."

His dark brown eyes flared wide, but it wasn't fear there—only anger. "Fuck you."

Mother's lips pursed in disapproval at his foul language. She picked up the next syringe—the one Jordyn knew would double his pain. Having lived inside pain for three long days, the fear for him was raw and wild. She couldn't let this happen. She couldn't let him kill himself.

"Stop," said Jordyn, hoping Jake would forgive her for what she was about to do. She'd been intrigued by Roxanne Haught—curious about the kind of woman who could make a man like Jake love her so deeply—and had spent some time researching her. She'd found out several things, including what had happened to her when she was younger, but none of that would interest Mother. There was only one thing she wanted to know: where to find her. "I know where Roxanne lives. She moved, but I found the new address. I'll tell you."

"No!" screamed Jake, furious accusation ringing in the single word.

Jordyn's stomach twisted, and she tried to make him understand. "I have to. She'll kill you."

His face darkened with rage. "Let her. I don't care."

Jordyn did. She cared too much. Maybe it was unfair of her to put his safety above that of his friend, but at least Roxanne had a fighting chance. Jordyn had warned her. She could run. Jake couldn't.

She looked into his eyes, watching fury and pain leap in his expression. "I'm sorry," she told him.

"Don't do this," he begged.

Mother regarded her with a steady stare. "Every second you wait is another one of torment for him."

Defeat and desperation bore down on her, stealing the

last of her strength. She had no choice. She couldn't let Jake suffer and possibly die because she had been stupid enough to help him.

If Mother found out that she'd gone out only hours ago and warned the woman, she was sure she wouldn't live through the punishment she'd suffer this time. And if she died, no one here would lift a finger to help the men who came through this facility—those who were turned from loyal, patriotic soldiers into killers who obeyed Mother's every command.

In a few weeks, Jake would be just like them. He'd turn on her, unable to do anything else. It was best if she saved him what pain she could now, because Mother would learn the identity of the woman, and she would find her. It was just a question of when.

Jordyn hung her head in defeat and recited the address she'd discovered.

"Send out the next man," Mother ordered General Bower. "Give him the address and find that diary."

"What about the woman?" he asked.

"Capture or kill. I don't care which."

Jordyn only hoped that her warning to Roxanne today would be enough to save the woman's life.

# Chapter Nine

Roxanne found Mira Sage where she always was—in the frigid, humming confines of the Edge's computer room.

"I need your help," announced Roxanne as she pushed through the door.

Mira jumped and spun around, her hand against her heart. "Geez, Razor. Don't sneak up on me like that."

"Sorry."

Mira was not like the rest of the trim, fit employees at the Edge. She was shorter than most, with a curvy, soft build. And while she wasn't likely to win any fitness competitions, she was smarter than all the rest of the employees put together.

"What do you need?" asked Mira.

Roxanne held out her cell phone. "I got an e-mail on this yesterday. I need to trace where it came from."

"Can it wait? I'm busy."

"Sorry. It's an emergency."

Mira sat down without taking the phone. "I don't need that. I'll log into the mail server and check it out."

The glow from the screen brightened Mira's green eyes as they darted over the data displayed. "Which e-mail?"

Roxanne pointed to the screen. "This one from Librarian one four one zero."

A few keystrokes later, the printer started whirring and

spat out a single page. Mira handed it to Roxanne. "Looks like the IP address belongs to a library in New Mexico."

"I hadn't expected it to be that easy to find."

"Why not?"

Roxanne wasn't about to explain that she thought it would be some secret military compound with high security. The fewer people who knew what was going on, the better. "Are you sure that the real location isn't being covered up or something? Or that this e-mail was rerouted to look like it came from here?"

Mira's brows lifted. "Pretty sure. I can look into it more if you want me to, but you'll have to tell me what I should be looking for."

"Never mind. I'm just being paranoid." Roxanne entered the library's address into her phone and tossed the paper into the shredder.

"If there's anything else you need, just let me know."

"Actually, can you give me Tanner's company phone number and e-mail address? I need to leave him a message."

Mira typed something for a few seconds. "I texted you the info. Anything else? I have a lot of work to do."

"Sorry to bother you."

"It's fine. Just try knocking next time, okay?"

Mira waited until Razor was gone, then locked the door behind her. Her hands were shaking so hard, she was sure Razor was going to notice. Thank goodness she'd been too preoccupied with her own problems to notice Mira's.

She hurried to where Clay sat slumped, hidden by a bank of servers. Blood leaked from his nose and his lip. A bruise darkened his left cheek, and there was something off about the angle of his left arm, making her think his shoulder was dislocated or maybe even broken.

"She's gone," said Mira, keeping her voice low.

"Did you say anything?" asked Clay.

His face was pale, his skin taking on a sickly ashen color

that worried the hell out of her. She kept hoping he'd get better, but over the last few weeks, the headaches and everything else seemed to be getting worse.

"No," she said, "though I have no idea why you don't want people to know you got mugged."

"It's embarrassing. I'm supposed to be able to protect myself better than that."

She grabbed a box of tissue from her desk and dabbed at his bloody nose. He winced, making her stomach turn.

She was no good with blood, which made having a friend like Clay increasingly difficult.

"I think it's broken. We need to go see Dr. Vaughn."

He shook his head slightly. "No. I told you I don't like doctors."

"Yeah, well tough patooties. I can't set a broken nose, and I'm sure not going to try to fix your shoulder."

"I'll do it myself."

"And damage your arm for life? Do you really want to lose your job?"

"Of course not," growled Clay.

"I can see you now, working in a cubicle for the rest of your life, maybe even wearing a tie."

"Enough already. I got it."

"So you'll go see Dr. Vaughn?"

"No, but I'll go to the emergency room. That way it won't end up on my work record."

It didn't have to end up on his record if he went to see Dr. Vaughn, either. If Mira had to, she'd hack into the medical records and delete them. There wasn't anything she wouldn't do for Clay, not after all the things he'd done for her. Not after the things her father had done to him.

Mira had a lot of evil to make up for when it came to Clay.

"Wherever you want to go. Let me check the security feed to make sure the coast is clear. Can you walk?"

Clay nodded, and more blood flowed from his nose. "Yeah."

She helped him to his feet. "I really wish you'd go see Dr. Vaughn. She's good. She could help you with the head-aches."

"Don't, Mira. Just let it be. The headaches aren't that bad."

She knew that was a lie. They both did. But now wasn't the time to push. That he'd agreed to go to a hospital was more than a miracle, and, right now, with him leaking blood all over the place, she was willing to take what she could get.


"Where the hell are you?" snapped Tanner as soon as he answered the phone.

Roxanne snapped right back. "Don't talk to me like that. I don't have to check in with you."

"You do until Bella says differently." She heard him let out a long breath. "Listen, Razor. I'm just worried. I went to check on you, and you were gone."

"I found a lead."

"A lead?"

"Mira's our resident computer genius, and she managed to find the place where Jake sent me that e-mail. I'm going to check it out. Want to come?"

"Absolutely. Where are you?"

"I'm headed to the back employee entrance. Meet me at my car?"

"I'm already there."

Roxanne punched the elevator call button. "How did you know?"

"I didn't. I just didn't want you leaving without me, so I parked my ass on your car."

Lucky car. She just bet he had a world-class ass under those jeans. What few glimpses she'd had of it so far were more than enough to pique her curiosity. "I need to run by my place to pick up some clothes. You?"

"I'm good."

She met him at the car. Even in the dimness of the parking garage he seemed to glow with vitality. His arms were crossed over his broad chest, making the sleeves of his T-shirt stretch to their limits over delicious muscles. He hadn't shaved, and the shadow of his beard made his cheeks look leaner and his jaw harder. His eyes settled on her, tracking her as she walked. And while his expression hadn't changed, something in his posture had. There was an awareness there, a relaxed kind of power, like that of a predator waiting to pounce.

Not that he would. He didn't seem the kind of man who lost control.

Pity.

His gaze moved up her body as she neared, and a wicked little shiver slid through her as she watched his blue eyes darken. He liked what he saw, and while she knew better than to be pleased by that, she couldn't seem to help herself.

Roxanne ripped her eyes away from his body and dug in her purse for her keys.

"Are you safe to drive?" he asked. "You didn't get much sleep last night."

"I'll sleep when I find Jake."

He said nothing about how ridiculous her statement was. She knew she might not find him today. Maybe even not tomorrow. But she needed to hold that hope close and let it comfort her, and Tanner seemed to get that.

"Where are we headed?"

"New Mexico. I put the address in my phone's GPS. I'll swing by home, and then we'll hit the road."

He paused in the act of opening the door. "I can't go. I have a birthday party I have to be at or it's my ass in a sling."

She gave him a questioning glance. "That's your call. I just thought you were all about invading my personal space."

"We can go right after."

"Sure, if you want to catch up with me, that would be

fine. You're handy to have around on the off chance that I have another lunatic try to strangle me again."

"I don't want to catch up with you. I want you to wait."

"While you go to a party? Jake needs me, Tanner."

"And my niece needs me. Or rather the rest of my family thinks so. It's her first birthday and it's a big deal."

While his commitment to his family was endearing, she wasn't about to risk Jake's life over a party that the guest of honor wouldn't even remember. "After the party, you can fly to the nearest airfield and I'll pick you up."

Tanner fell silent, his jaw clenched in frustration.

They got into her car, and she waited for the gate to lift before pulling out of the secure lot.

"Do you have a plan?" he asked.

She glanced over at him. He was too big for her sporty little car. He filled the seat, his knees precariously close to the dash. One arm was propped on the door, and the other across his lap. His shoulders were wider than the seat, forcing him to lean toward her just a bit. Cool air swept past her face, but it did little to lower her body temperature. She swore she could smell his skin with every breath she took.

Roxanne cleared her throat and focused on the road, keeping track of the cars around them. "We'll check out the area, see if anyone has seen Jake."

"Do you have a photo of him?"

She nodded. "At home. I'll bring it along."

A red truck switched lanes several cars behind her, giving her a brief glimpse of a black sedan she'd seen a few miles back. Their exit was three miles ahead, but she decided to take the next one instead.

As she veered onto the exit ramp, the black sedan passed her, speeding along the interstate.

She let out a long sigh of relief and relaxed her grip on the steering wheel.

Tanner's warm hand settled on her arm, giving her a moment of comfort. To his credit, he didn't say not to worry.

Instead, he looked over his shoulder and scanned behind them. "I think we're clear for now."

"I'm taking the back roads home. If we run into trouble, there's a gun in my glove box."

Tanner opened it, removed the weapon, released the loaded magazine, and checked it with smooth, efficient motions. "I won't risk shooting in a populated area. Stray bullets have a tendency to find the innocent."

She glanced at him, seeing a fierce tension lining his mouth and bulging in his jaw, and she wondered if he spoke from experience. "I'm not asking you to take any risks. Just know it's there if you need it."

Roxanne split her time watching the road ahead of her and behind her. When she finally pulled into her garage, her fingers were glued to her steering wheel. She unclenched them with a conscious effort, stretching her hands to ease the ache in her knuckles.

She went into the house, expecting to hear the shrill beep of her alarm, but instead, she was greeted with silence. Before she had time to process the implications of that, Tanner flung her back, onto the floor of the garage and crushed her under his bulk. His hand cradled her head, cushioning it from the hard concrete.

A heartbeat later, a thunderous boom exploded to her right. Tanner flinched and grunted.

Roxanne tried to push him up to see if he was okay, but he didn't budge.

Her heart jolted inside her chest as a rush of adrenaline poured through her. She couldn't see anything, but her nose was crushed against his shoulder, and she could smell Tanner's skin and the sharp stench of explosives. She could hear his pulse pounding and feel his hard chest press against her with every rapid breath.

He was still alive. They both were, thanks to his quick action.

The warm weight of his body left her as he pushed up. A ferocious snarl twisted his mouth. A drop of blood slid down along his cheekbone. His blue eyes were narrowed with anger, and his voice came out in cold, bitter bites. "Stay down. Don't move."

Roxanne nodded, willing to do anything for him in that moment. He'd saved her life. The least she could do was comply. Besides, her legs had gone weak, and she wasn't even sure she could stand right now.

She watched as Tanner retrieved a weapon from his bag and went into her home. The back of his shirt was bloody, and there were several holes where shrapnel had shredded the fabric. She didn't know how bad it was, but he didn't seem to be concerned.

As soon as he disappeared inside the door, Roxanne pushed herself up. Her ears still rang, especially the right one. Her elbow was abraded from the concrete floor, and her back had a bad case of rug burn. But other than a few scrapes and bruises, she was fine—shaky, but fine.

Roxanne got to her feet, staying clear of the house. She got her gun out of the glove box and tucked it into her waistband. Tanner had told her not to move, but she couldn't just lie there on the floor, doing nothing. If he ran into trouble, she needed to be ready to help.

She listened for signs of distress or some kind of struggle, but she heard none. "Tanner? You okay?"

Silence greeted her, and she was just about to go in after him when he came back. His expression was grim, made worse by the blood smearing his cheek. "Whoever did this is gone. There were no more booby traps."

Roxanne dug her feet into the floor to keep herself from running to him. He'd taken a beating, and was bleeding. It was all she could do not to reach out and try to offer some kind of comfort.

Too bad it was her fault he was in this mess.

"How did you know what was going to happen?" she asked.

"I saw the wire he used to set the trap. The light hit it just right or I wouldn't have seen it at all." That admission seemed to piss him off more.

"I didn't see anything."

"It was high. Above your line of sight. They knew you'd be focused on the knob or your security keypad."

He was right. She never would have thought to look up upon entering her home. "If you hadn't been with me, I'd be dead. Thank you."

He wiped the blood from his cheek. "Don't thank me. The fuckers ruined your house. And your safe is gone."

"My gun safe? That thing weighs a thousand pounds."

"It shows in the gouges they left in your wood floor. Sorry."

"I don't give a shit about the house. I'm worried about you. We need to get you patched up. Is it safe to go inside?"

He nodded. "I did a sweep. It looked like they were in a hurry, so they probably didn't take time to plant more than one trap."

"I bet they figured that one would be enough to take me out, because it would have been if you hadn't reacted so fast."

He shrugged and winced at the motion. "Bella ordered me to watch out for you. It's all part of the job."

"Come on. Let's see how much damage they did to you so Bella knows how loudly to scream at me for getting you hurt."

Tanner led the way inside. He was right. Her house was ruined. The area around the explosion was charred and tattered, leaving exploded bits of drywall and wooden trim in its wake. Parallel gouges in her shiny wood floor showed where they'd dragged her gun safe to the back door out onto the wooden deck. The deck railing had been ripped away and left abandoned in the grass. Tire marks were visible where their truck had dug into her manicured lawn.

She wasn't sure how they'd managed to move the thing without wheels, but they'd found a way.

At least Jake's journal was no longer in the safe. She was losing only a few guns, some cash, and a small store of ammunition.

Roxanne hoped that the time it took them to break into the safe and find out they hadn't gotten what they were after would be enough for her to find Jake.

"Go into my bathroom," she told Tanner. "I have first aid supplies in there." And there was more room to maneuver. She was still shaken from the explosion and worried she might accidentally bump into him in the smaller bathroom.

Tanner moved to strip off his shirt, but the pained look on his face had her stop him. "I'll cut it off. You won't be wearing it again, anyway."

He nodded and sat on the edge of the giant tub, facing away from her.

Roxanne had picked the tub, hoping that one day she'd have company in there. The idea of a decadent bubble bath with the hunk of her choice had always been a compelling one—one she'd spent more than a little time fantasizing about.

Now she was sure that every time she got into this tub, she'd be thinking about Tanner and the blood he'd shed to keep her safe.

With a deep breath to steady her hands, Roxanne picked up the scissors and cut the shirt away from him.

He'd bled a lot, but the damage wasn't as bad as she'd feared. With clinical detachment, she made an inventory of the cuts and scrapes. "There're some splinters of wood imbedded along your left side, but that's the worst of it."

"Good. Pull them out and let's get going."

"I think you should go see Dr. Vaughn for that. My hands aren't so steady right now."

He looked over his shoulder, his eyes bright with determination. "Those fuckers tried to kill you. Do you think I'm going to sit around in some waiting room while they get away with it?"

"I don't have anything to numb the pain. She does."

"Just do it, Roxanne. The trail is getting cold."

Her stomach heaved at the thought of hurting him, but he was right. The longer they waited, the harder it was going to be to find the men who'd done this—the men who might lead them to Jake.

Roxanne swallowed her unease and picked up the tweezers. "I'll try not to hurt you."

# Chapter Ten

She couldn't hurt him half as much as the mere thought of watching an innocent woman die could. From the instant he'd seen the triggering line, the image of Roxanne's broken, bleeding body had hovered in his mind, circling like a vulture.

He'd seen a lot of fucked-up things in his time serving overseas. He'd seen women and children being treated like animals. He'd seen entire villages wiped out, the bodies left to rot under the sun. The things people would do to one another never ceased to disgust him.

Tanner didn't like to think about those times. He preferred to dwell on the good he'd seen in people. But right now, all he wanted was to find the men responsible for trying to kill Roxanne and take them out. It wasn't rational. It wasn't his job to try, convict, and execute the guilty, but that was what he wanted.

Whoever had done this had also been willing to use a broken soldier to do their dirty work. Tanner couldn't let that stand.

A spark of pain stabbed along his ribs, dragging him out of his bleak thoughts.

"Sorry," squeaked Roxanne behind him.

"I'm fine. Keep going."

"Can you turn and lift your arm? I can't quite get that last splinter."

Tanner moved as she instructed, letting her drape his arm over her shoulder to prop it up. Her focus was completely on the task at hand, giving him the opportunity to stare at her unnoticed.

Her blond hair was mussed, making her seem more real, more human. Her golden eyes were shiny as if she were fighting back tears. All the color had fled her cheeks, leaving her too pale. Dirt smudged her jaw and marred the silky perfection of her blouse, likely from when he'd thrown her down on the garage floor.

He hadn't been gentle, but she hadn't complained. She was too practical for that, it seemed. There was no fuss, no squeamishness, as she pried bits of debris from his skin and disinfected the wounds. The only indication he had that his blood bothered her was her trembling hands and the way she held her bottom lip between her teeth in concentration.

If he'd been a second slower, she wouldn't be standing here now, fussing over him.

That thought was enough to make his blood pressure skyrocket. It had been a close call. The people who'd been here meant business. They weren't playing games. They wanted her dead.

Tanner couldn't let that happen. He also couldn't bring the shit that was following her anywhere near his family. He was going to have to call Karen and cancel. Once she got over being mad, he'd explain to her why he couldn't make it, but he didn't want her worrying about him. She'd already lost a husband. Tanner would much rather have her mad at him for being a flaky asshole than have her worried about his safety. He was already casting enough of a shadow over today's festivities.

"There," she said, releasing her bottom lip. Her teeth had left a deep dent—one he had the crazy compulsion to kiss away.

Instead, he looked down at her handiwork, seeing only clean, white bandages. "Thanks."

"I still think you should see Dr. Vaughn."

"Noted."

"You mean ignored."

He shrugged, feeling the tightness in his skin thanks to the abundance of bandages she'd applied. "I'm sure she'd say your work was more than competent. We both know time is running out."

"Let me grab a change of clothes."

"I don't want to take your car. It's too easy to spot. We can take my truck." His black truck looked like a thousand others in the city.

"That's a good idea. Check it for bombs, though. Just in case?"

"Definitely."

Tanner called his sister-in-law and told her he wasn't going to be able to make Millie's first birthday party. By the time she hung up, he could hear the tears in her voice, making him feel like the biggest asshole on the face of the planet.

There was going to be hell to pay once Reid and Mom got wind of his absence, but that was too bad. He'd take the heat when things were safer and he could talk to them face-to-face. Until then, he'd keep his distance from his family and stick to Roxanne's side.

From what he'd seen so far, she was going to need all the help she could get.

Clay was losing his mind. The blackouts were getting longer, and this time, there were more than just a few bruises left behind.

His shoulder hurt like a son of a bitch, and his chest felt as if it were on fire. His ribs had to be bruised, if they weren't cracked. His left eye was swollen, and his face ached where he'd taken a hit.

He wished like hell he could remember who or what had hit him—and why.

The ER doctor checked him out and sent him for X-rays. Clay sat on the gurney, dreading what he knew was coming next. Getting his shoulder back into place wasn't going to be any kind of fun, especially with Mira watching over him, chewing her nails in worry.

"Go back to work," he told her.

"And just leave you here?"

"It'll be hours until they're through with me. I'll call you to come pick me up when they're done."

Mira's eyes and nose were red, making him guess that she'd been crying while he'd been off getting X-rays. He hated it that he'd made her cry—again. She was like a sister to him, and he'd sooner cut off his own arm with a rusty butter knife than hurt her.

Despite his good intentions, it seemed that all he did lately was cause her worry and pain.

"I'm not leaving," she said, crossing her arms over her chest in defiance.

"It's sweet of you to abandon your beloved network for me, but I'm fine. Really."

"Have you seen anyone about the headaches?" she asked.

"Yes," he lied. "They're just stress-related. No big deal."

Her mouth flattened in frustration. "If you want to lie to me, that's one thing, but I'm really worried that you're lying to yourself, too."

"There's nothing to lie about. Everything is fine." Except for the searing pain in his body, the constant headaches and the blackouts.

*Nope. No worries here.*

"Please, Clay. Go see Dr. Vaughn. Or someone else. Maybe even a psychiatrist."

"There's nothing wrong with my head," he snarled.

Mira flinched and shrank back in her chair.

He hadn't meant to snap. She deserved better than that.

He took a deep breath and forced himself to sound calm, even though he was feeling anything but. "I'm sorry, squirt. I didn't mean to act like a dick. Please, just go back to work, and I promise we'll talk about this when I'm done here." When the pain subsided and he could stay in control better, they would talk. "I hate you having to see me in pain. I know it upsets you."

She stood and gave him a long stare. "It does more than that. Seeing you like this is killing me. If you're not willing to get help for yourself, please do it for me."

Clay wasn't making any promises. He knew she'd hold him to them, guilting him into doing something he wasn't sure he could stand. Coming to the ER for treatment was one thing—the service was rushed and impersonal. No one was going to follow up with him and invade his privacy. But if he went to see a shrink, or found a doctor who actually gave a shit about him, he'd be in trouble.

There was something wrong with him, and while he wanted it fixed, he'd find a way to fix it himself, without anyone shoving their nose into his business. He'd been on his own for a long time, and he liked it that way.

Payton approached the uniformed officer guarding Brad Evans's hospital door. After reading Jake Staite's journal, he had to know the truth. He had to know if the woman he thought he'd killed two decades ago was still alive.

Because if she was, that was a mistake he was going to have to fix. Immediately.

His skills were a bit rusty from disuse, but like riding a bike, the tricks of the trade came back to him whenever the need arose.

Brad Evans was the name of the man who'd attacked Razor at her storage unit. A friend at the police station had given him that much. From there, the rest was going to be easy.

Payton tugged at his cuffs to show off the diamond-and-gold cuff links he'd put on, and gave his Rolex an impatient glance as he neared the door. "I'm here to see my client," he informed the officer.

"Your client?"

"Brad Evans. I'm his attorney."

"I'll have to call this in."

Payton leaned one shoulder against the door. "Make whatever calls you like. I get paid by the hour. And while you're at it, tell the sheriff he left his reading glasses at the reelection fund-raiser I hosted for him last week. He can stop by and get them at his convenience."

The officer hesitated for a moment, perusing Payton's expensive suit and designer briefcase. "Go on in, but the handcuffs stay on."

"Of course," he said, as if the thought of having his client touch him was distasteful.

The officer opened the door to let Payton in and shut it behind them.

The private room was small. The window let in plenty of light, but it did not open to let in any fresh air. Or to allow anyone to escape.

In the good old days, Payton would have been able to read Brad's chart, but in this age of computers, all that useful data was stored behind password protection and encryption software.

He was going to have to get his questions answered the hard way.

"Wake up," he said, keeping his voice calm but firm.

The man's eyes opened for a moment before shutting again.

He was apparently enjoying the effects of a few narcotics.

Payton neared the side of the bed opposite to where the man's hand was cuffed to the railing. If he made a move, Payton would only need to step back to avoid any ugliness. "Brad," he said, more loudly, "we need to talk."

Brad's face was gaunt, the fluorescent lights overhead

adding to his sallow complexion. Dark circles hung below his eyes, which he cracked open with obvious effort.

"I know about the journal," said Payton.

Panic stole over the man's face, and his eyes shot open. "No. I didn't tell you. She told me not to tell anyone."

"She who?"

He pressed his lips together as if struggling to keep the words inside.

"What did she do to you?"

"Where is it? I have to bring it back."

"I'll get it for you," lied Payton. "But first you have to tell me what I want to know."

"I can't. She'll know if I say anything. She always knows."

"Who?"

The man said nothing, forcing Payton to go fishing. He searched the young man's face, hoping for no flash of recognition when he whispered the name. "Was it Dr. Stynger?"

Brad scooted back on the bed as if trying to get away from Payton. Fear blanched his face, and sweat broke out along his hairline. "She sent you, didn't she? She said she'd kill me if I failed."

It couldn't be. She couldn't be alive, and yet twice now he'd witnessed proof that he was wrong.

Payton tamped down his fury, keeping any hint of it from showing through in his expression. The troubled man shying away from him didn't deserve any more pain. Norma Stynger had clearly inflicted enough already.

"I'm not going to hurt you. I'm on your side. I won't let anyone hurt you. All you have to do is tell me what I need to know and I'll stop her."

"She can't be stopped. If you knew her, you'd know that."

Maybe Brad was right. The fact that she wasn't roasted to cinders proved that Payton had already made one grave mistake. There could be no more. "I want to help you. Please let me. Tell me where I can find her."

Brad squeezed his eyes shut. "Just go away. Before she finds you here."

"You think she'll come for you?" Payton asked, hating what he knew he had to do. "You're wrong. If you're lucky, she'll forget you even exist. If not, she'll send someone else to kill you while you sleep."

"No," whispered Brad. "She'll come for me. She'll want me back."

"And is that what you want? To go back to her? I know she hurt you. Didn't she?"

Brad shook his head, his brow furrowed in confusion. "She had no choice. We had to be ready for our mission."

"What mission?"

"Millions of lives are at stake."

It sounded like a lie meant to coerce brave young men into doing what Norma wanted. "I need to find her. Tell me where she is."

Brad's eyes lit up. "Bring me the journal and I'll take you to her."

"You're under arrest. The only place you're going is a jail cell. Let me take the journal to her myself."

"Arrest?" His gaze moved to the handcuffs. A distant look clouded his expression before melting to horror. "The rose." He shook his head as if to clear it, leaving panic behind. "It was a woman. I hurt her. Oh God."

Payton considered telling the man that Razor was fine, but there were more important things to consider than Brad's feelings. He had to find Norma and stop her—only this time he'd make sure the job was done right.

"You'll keep hurting people if you don't let me help you. Whatever Dr. Stynger did to you can be fixed," lied Payton. The honest truth was he didn't know if what had been done to him could be reversed or not. "All you have to do is trust me."

Brad's anguish shone on his face. His lips were drawn back, and his chin trembled with misery and guilt. "I don't want to hurt anyone."

"I know, son. Let me help you."

Payton would do anything in his power to see Brad Evans restored to the man he'd once been before Norma got her hands on him. He wasn't sure how much of the old Brad remained, but they'd do what they could to help him. And while they did, Brad would want for nothing. Payton would see to it personally. It was the least he could do, considering this was all his fault.

If he'd done his job twenty years ago and killed Norma, none of this would have ever happened.

Guilt for his failure weighed heavily on him, but no more so than the burden he already carried. He'd made a lot of bad decisions in his lifetime. The repercussions of those decisions would haunt him for the rest of his life. For Payton, there was no repentance. Only justice.

"I don't know where she is," said Brad. "We were underground. I don't remember how I got out or how I got here. I don't even know if the compound is in the US."

"How many people are there? How large is the facility?"

"We weren't allowed to roam, so I don't know."

"What did she do to you?"

"Dr. Stynger never touched me. She—" His words cut off abruptly and his eyes rolled back into his head. A monitor began beeping furiously.

Brad began to shake and gurgle. The door flew open and a nurse hurried in.

"You need to leave now," she said, her statement calm but unyielding.

"What's happening to him?"

"He's having a seizure. Now get out."

Two more people came in. Payton moved to the doorway where the uniformed officer stood, his eyes narrowed in suspicion. "Let them work."

"He just started shaking," said Payton, making sure the cop knew this wasn't his doing. If he was questioned, his lie about being an attorney wouldn't hold, which would raise too many questions.

He made a show of being horrified, which was an easy sell, considering that whatever Brad suffered was all his fault. "I think I'm going to be sick," he said, and sprinted down the hall toward the men's room.

Payton waited inside the restroom for an appropriate amount of time before walking out. He didn't even glance toward Brad's room. He didn't want to see a team of medical professionals walking out with the signs of failure hanging over them. For now, he wanted to pretend Brad would be fine, that he'd get the help he needed to recover, and that Norma Stynger would never again be allowed to do that to another living person.

He left through the closest exit. It wasn't anywhere near where his car was parked, but a walk in the sun felt so much better than the stale, cold hospital air.

Norma Stynger was still alive.

Not even the searing heat of the Texas sun could remove the chill of foreboding that news gave him.

"Payton? What are you doing here?" The familiar voice yanked him back to attention.

He turned and saw Mira Sage sitting on a bench a few yards away, smiling in greeting. With her soft, rounded features, she looked nothing like her father—a man Payton had once worked closely with years ago.

She cupped a soda in her hands and squinted up at him as he approached. "Visiting a friend. Why are you here? Is everything okay?"

Mira looked down. "Yeah."

"Then why are you here?"

"I'm not supposed to say."

"Mira," he chided, "you know how I feel about secrets." Or at least she knew how he felt about others keeping secrets from him. And that was the important part. If she knew half the secrets he'd kept from her, his gentle Mira would find the closest weapon and beat him with it.

"I'm not telling you, so stop prying."

"I'm not going to stop until you answer me. I know how

you feel about hospitals. There has to be a good reason for you to be here. Let me help you. Please."

"It's not me."

"Then who is it?" he asked. And then he realized. Few people would pry Mira from her comfort zone. "It's Clay, isn't it?"

She looked up at him with the most miserable expression. "I didn't tell you that. He doesn't want anyone to know he's here."

Panic shot through him for a moment before he controlled it. "Is he sick?"

"No. He got mugged, but he's too macho to admit it."

"Mugged? That's hard to believe."

"I know, right? He was probably distracted by a headache again." She clamped her hand over her mouth and mumbled behind it. "Shit. I wasn't supposed to tell you that."

Payton settled on the bench beside her to hide his concern. He didn't like it that Clay was covering things up. That could get very dangerous very fast with a man like Clay. "You know you can tell me anything, right? I only have Clay's best interests at heart. Has he gone to see Dr. Vaughn about the headaches?"

"He won't go. Hates doctors. The only reason he's here is because I don't know how to fix a dislocated shoulder. I suppose I could have Googled it, but I didn't think that would be wise."

"You're right. That's the kind of thing best left to the professionals."

"I'm thinking about getting a medical degree so I can patch him up when he's stupid."

She made it sound like this wasn't the first time this had happened, which deepened Payton's concern.

He compartmentalized his worry and gave Mira a charming smile. "And leave us? I'd hate to see you go. We'd never be able to replace you."

Mira scrunched up her nose. "I really don't like blood. I'll do it for Clay, but I won't like it."

She said it nonchalantly, as though getting a medical degree was easy. Then again, for Mira, it probably would be.

"Perhaps you should stick to what you do best and let me talk to Clay about his fear of doctors."

"You can't let him know I put you up to it."

"Of course not. I'll be very smooth. He'll never even know we talked."

"I told him Dr. Vaughn was a hot redhead. He really likes those. If that didn't work, I don't know what will."

Payton did. He wasn't sure he wanted to resort to such measures, but he would if he had to. He'd much rather manipulate Clay Marshall into getting the help he needed, because if what had been done to Clay when he was a child went bad and he turned rogue, Payton's only option would be to kill him.

# Chapter Eleven

The library in the small New Mexico town wasn't what Roxanne expected. Instead, it was an old Victorian house that had been converted for the use. From the entrance, she could see bookshelves lining what had once been a dining room and several bedrooms. The larger living area housed the checkout desk and several computer workstations, as well as a colorful rug for children's story time. A curving staircase led upstairs to another level.

Two teens sat at the computers, while the third workstation was occupied by a woman looking at online quilt patterns. A middle-aged woman in a cardigan stood behind the desk. She looked up and smiled as they came in.

Roxanne could feel Tanner at her back, close enough she could almost sense the heat coming off him. The drive here had been mostly silent as each of them took turns at the wheel while the other napped. She hadn't wanted to risk conversation and the potential turn toward any grim thoughts about Jake and what had happened to him. She had to stay focused and positive right now.

"Afternoon," greeted the librarian. "May I help you find something?"

Roxanne took the photo of Jake from her purse and laid it on the counter facing the woman. "Have you seen this man?"

The librarian frowned as she put on her reading glasses. She stared at the photo for a moment, then looked up at Roxanne. "Sorry, no. What's he done?"

"Excuse me?"

"You're not police?"

She was about to say no when Tanner stopped her with a light touch to her arm. He lowered his voice and leaned forward. "We received information that he used an e-mail account from this library to send a threatening letter."

The woman's hand flew to her chest. "We have all kinds of security software on our computers that keep people from seeing . . . unsavory things online, but I don't know if it stops people from sending e-mail."

"Do you know this e-mail address?" asked Roxanne, showing the woman her phone and the address Jake used to send the message.

"That's my e-mail address, but I assure you I never sent any threatening messages."

"We know, ma'am. This man probably hacked into your account. Do you mind if I take a look?"

"Sure. Come on around."

Tanner went behind the desk and scanned the screen. "If there was any record of the message, it's been deleted."

"Mira could find something," said Roxanne.

"That's not going to get us anywhere." He turned to the librarian. "Ma'am, have any strangers come around lately?"

"Just you. And a woman. She was here yesterday afternoon."

When the message was sent.

"What time?" asked Roxanne.

"Late afternoon, I guess. She didn't stay long, probably because she was sick."

"What do you mean?"

"She was a bit green around the gills. Swaying on her feet. I was hoping she'd let me call someone for her, but she left before I had the chance."

"What did she look like?"

"Young. Early twenties. Long dark hair that needed a good brushing. I think she was one of those goths that wear the pale makeup."

"Did she give you her name?"

"No. As I said, she didn't stay long. She drove off before I could call for help."

"Did you happen to get her license plate or see what kind of car she drove?"

"No, sorry."

Roxanne wrote down her phone number. "If you see anyone else or think of anything else, will you please call me?"

"Are you going to take my computer away for evidence?"

Tanner shook his head. "No need for that, ma'am. You've been very helpful. Thank you."

They walked back out into the heat. Disappointment fell heavy on Roxanne's shoulders, making her sluggish and tired. She'd wanted so much to hear some word about Jake—some hint that he was okay. Instead, all she got was that the message she'd thought he'd sent hadn't come from him.

Even her proof that he was alive had vanished.

Tanner's fingers threaded through hers. "Don't give up. We'll find him."

"How?"

"Does anyone else know that code?"

"Not that I know of."

"See. Jake must have told that woman what to say and given her your contact info."

"Why didn't he contact me himself?"

"Maybe he couldn't."

That's what worried her. "What if he's hurt? Or dead?"

Tanner pulled her to a stop next to his truck. He leaned close, shielding her from the searing sunlight. Pale streaks of gray shone in his blue eyes—streaks she hadn't noticed before. His lashes were long and paler than the dark hair on his head, almost as if they'd been sun bleached. There was a slight dent in his nose where it had been broken, but the imperfection only added to the rugged package he delivered.

"Don't think like that. We're going to stay positive. The fact that he was worried about you means he's still thinking clearly. That's something, right?"

"It's not enough."

"I get that, I really do, but we're going to keep doing our thing, and he's going to keep doing his. I guarantee you that a man like him will never give up fighting to get back to you."

"How can you say that? You don't even know him."

He gave her a grin and a wink. "No, but I know you. And you're worth the fight."

That put her off balance enough she forgot to worry about Jake for a moment. He had her tucked into the passenger seat before she'd realized what he'd done. As soon as he got in the truck, she said, "Nice trick with the flattery."

"Did it work?"

"It distracted me."

"Good. Hitting the reset button every once in a while is a good thing. Speaking of which, I need some food. You?"

Worry over Jake had rid her of her appetite, but she knew better than to skip too many meals. If her hands shook, she wouldn't be able to shoot straight, and if Jake was in trouble as deep as she feared, shooting straight might be the only way to get him out.


Tanner made a point of flirting with the waitress at lunch. They hadn't left town, and he was determined to find Razor some scrap of hope to carry with her. When she'd learned that it hadn't been Jake that sent the e-mail, she'd wilted before his eyes, and he wasn't going to let that happen again. At least not on his watch.

A few more days with her was all he had before she'd be

assigned a new mission and he'd be put on whatever detail
Bella deemed best. Before that happened, he needed to
find who had stolen soldiers' lives and stop them cold.

The woman waiting on their table was nearing thirty,
with fake orange hair and bright blue nails. A tattoo on her
left shoulder had once borne the name Bobby, but that had
been crossed out in barbed wire and skewered with a bloody
dagger. Whoever Bobby was, she was no longer quite so
fond of him.

She set their food down on the table and cocked her hip
toward Tanner, smiling. "Can I getcha anything else?"

Her offer for more than ketchup was crystal clear.

Tanner smiled back. "Sure can, sweet thing. This guy
owes me money. I heard he came through here. Take a look
at a photo for me?"

"Anything for you, darlin'."

Razor handed him the photo. The waitress took it, caressing his hand as she did. "Nope. Sorry. The only strangers
we get through here are truckers and crazies."

"Crazies?"

"Yeah, you know the type. Drugged out, some of them
raving about alien abduction and probing. Lots of Roswell
spillovers, I guess."

Razor punched some buttons on her phone and held it
up to the woman. "Ever see him?"

The woman squinted as she peered at the photo. "Oh,
yeah. A couple of days ago. He was some kind of gardener or
something. Asked me if I knew where to find a white rose."

Razor stilled and met Tanner's gaze. "What did you tell
him?"

"I told him what I tell them all: There's a walk-in clinic
down the street and they should really go get checked out.
Poor souls. It's the drugs, you know. We have a huge drug
problem here."

"Thanks for your help, sweet thing," said Tanner, but his
heart wasn't into the flirting. He was focused on Roxanne
and the implications of what they'd just learned.

"Let me know if there's anything else I can do." The waitress left with a wink.

"We need to check out that clinic," said Roxanne.

"We will. Eat first. We figure out our next move before we make it."

Jake's head was still pounding several hours later. Whatever they'd given him had been slow to wear off, and all he'd had to distract him from the pain was his worry for Rox and Jordyn.

He had to get out of here. That bitch Stynger had Rox's address.

*Capture or kill. I don't care which.*

The thought of either happening to Rox made Jake's blood heat, causing his pulse to beat against his skull. It was bad enough that he was in this mess; the fact that he'd inadvertently pulled Rox in along with him was unacceptable.

His bunk mate, Trevor Moss, stumbled through the doorway. "Where were you?"

"Long story," said Jake, unwilling to say anything while there was even the slightest risk that his captors would find something to use against Rox.

Moss sat on his bunk with his elbows propped on his knees, his head hanging down in exhaustion. "Bower tried to kill me today. I bitched about all the fitness shit, and he made me run until I puked, and then some."

Jake said nothing about his brain-splitting migraine. He didn't want to give anyone listening the satisfaction of his pain. "Sorry, man."

"I'm so sick of this shit," said Moss. "I didn't sign up for this. I want to see some action, or at least some fucking sunlight. Hell, I'd be happy for a thirty-mile march in full gear at this point."

Jake tossed a T-shirt over the camera in the room he shared with Moss the way he'd done dozens of time before. So far, no one had complained, but the shirt was taken down every time he woke up. He figured they still had sound and weren't too worried that there was any hope of their lab rats escaping.

Aware of possible microphone surveillance, Jake was careful with his words as he knelt on the floor. "They said it would be a couple of months before we were ready, but I think we're close to getting out of here."

Moss's head came up.

Jake glanced at the covered camera, reminding his friend they might have an audience.

Moss nodded. "When do you think the weapons training will start?"

"Hell if I know," said Jake, pointing at what he'd discovered when he'd accidentally kicked his sock under his bunk. "But it's been so long since I held a weapon, I think I've forgotten which end to point at the bad guys."

Moss crossed the room and got down on his hands and knees. Jake pointed to the small hole in the wall where some kind of nozzle poked out.

Jake got some toilet paper, wet it, and shoved it into the hole to plug it while Moss went to his side of the room and peered under his own bunk.

Moss turned around and nodded, anger twisting his face. He must have found another nozzle on his side of the room. "Yeah, I'd really like to get my hands on a weapon, too."

Jake handed him the soggy paper, hoping that they'd just plugged the means by which these assholes were drugging them at night.

"I'm going to hit the sack," said Moss. "It's been a shitty day."

With any luck at all, and without the knockout gas that had likely been shoved into their lungs every night, Jake could almost guarantee that tomorrow was going to be better. Tomorrow, they'd find a way out of this hellhole, and he'd take Jordyn and Rox somewhere that bitch Stynger couldn't find them.

\*     \*     \*

Tanner briefly considered letting his phone roll over to voice mail, but he couldn't stand to be that much of a coward.

He braced himself as he answered his older brother's call. "Hi, Reid."

"You made Karen cry."

Tanner flinched at that news. This conversation was going to get ugly, and he really didn't want Roxanne witnessing it.

He pulled the phone away from his mouth and excused himself from the table, slipping outside onto the sidewalk in front of the diner.

Heat blasted his skin but did nothing to warm him. "I know," he admitted. "I wanted to be there, but—"

"You couldn't. Bullshit, Tanner."

"It's true. I'm not even in the state."

"Story of your life. One I'm getting sick—"

"Yeah, yeah. You're sick of hearing it. Listen, Reid," said Tanner, trying to hold back his anger. "I have good reasons for skipping Millie's party today, and I'll be happy to explain them all to you, but—"

"But not now? Not over the phone? Why? Do you need more time to think up a good excuse?"

"Will you please stop with the throbbing asshole routine? It's getting old."

"Well, that's just too fucking bad. You made Karen cry. As far as I'm concerned, that makes you the asshole here."

"Razor's in trouble," said Tanner, hoping that would appease his brother enough to get him to calm down. He knew Reid had had a shitload of things to deal with since Dad died, but there was only so much slack a man could give before he ran out. Even for his brother.

Instantly, Reid's anger faded into complete attention. "What kind of trouble?"

"Things have happened. I can't go into it, but I think it's serious."

"Where are you? Are you with her? I'm coming there now."

The last thing Tanner wanted was for his brother to storm in and make things worse. Reid's temper flared too easily, and when the two of them were in a room together, things had a tendency to go to hell. Tanner didn't want to risk losing his job because he and his brother couldn't keep their personal problems personal. "No. I've got it—"

"Handled?" Reid sounded skeptical.

Irritation grated across Tanner's skin. "I may be your little brother, but I happen to have learned a few things when you weren't looking. I've got it handled."

"Fine. Whatever. But don't think this means that we're squared away. I'm not smoothing things over with Karen for you again."

"Did I ask you to?"

"You never have asked, but I always do it."

"Then stop. I'll talk to Karen when I get back. I'll take Millie out for her birthday and celebrate it then."

"Without the family." It was more than a statement. It was an accusation.

"Just because I don't do things the way you want doesn't mean I'm doing them wrong. If you could figure that out, the two of us would get along much better."

"And if you could figure out that doing things the way we always have isn't too good for you, then maybe I wouldn't have to watch so many people cry because you—"

"I didn't mean to hurt their feelings. You know that." Guilt bore down on Tanner, making him twist inside. The hamburger he just ate sat cold and hard in his gut, daring him to make a wrong move. "I'll fix it, Reid. Just give me some time."

"Do it fast, because if you make Mom cry again, I'm probably going to have to beat the hell out of you."

Maybe that would be best. Maybe once Tanner bested his older brother, Reid would see him as a man instead of as a kid. As barbaric as the notion was, it would probably work with his thick-skulled sibling. "I'd like to see you try."

# Chapter Twelve

The clinic was closed when Roxanne and Tanner arrived, despite the sign that said they should be open for another ten minutes.

Roxanne cupped her hands over the glass to ward away the glare and peered into the office. She could barely make out a TV screen on an adjacent wall.

"The TV is on. They're probably still in there doing paperwork or something," she said.

"One way to find out." Tanner rapped his knuckles on the glass.

They waited a few minutes, but no one came. He knocked again.

"I'll go peek around back," he said. "Maybe they just can't hear me knock."

"I'll go with you."

Behind the brick building was a small parking area. Two cars were still in the lot.

While Tanner knocked on the back door, Roxanne peered into the cars. One had an infant car seat in back and a rumpled set of scrubs printed with brightly colored farm animals. The other was empty of personal items.

"Still no answer," said Tanner.

Roxanne refused to let something as simple as a locked door stop her, but she was also about to break five different laws and didn't want Tanner anywhere near her criminal intent. "Okay. Go wait for me in the truck."

He crossed his thick arms over his chest. "I don't think so."

"I'll be fine," she assured him. "I'm just going to look around for a hide-a-key."

"No, you're planning to break in. I can see it on your face."

"You don't know me well enough to see anything of the sort."

He stepped forward, easing inside her personal space. She should have moved back, but she found she liked having him there, close enough that she could smell the heat coming off his skin. She tilted her head back to look him in the eye.

Shadows draped across his cheek, highlighting the angles of his face. "Don't I?" he asked. "Why don't I just stick around and we'll see who's wrong."

She couldn't very well break in with a witness, especially one she didn't want to get in trouble. "There's no other way. Our lead ends here, and I can't just stop trying. Jake needs me."

"Then we call the police and tell them what we know. In a town this small, they probably know how to reach the doctor who works here. Maybe we can go to his house."

"That will take too much time. I need to do this now."

"I won't let you break the law, because I'm not going to be the one who explains to Bella why she has to bail us out."

"Not us. Me. And I'll give you my cash card and PIN to deal with that if it happens, which it won't."

"You're damn right it won't, because we're not taking the chance. We're going to—"

From the other side of the back door came a noise. Roxanne covered Tanner's mouth to quiet him so she could hear better. "Did you hear that?"

There was a whisper of sound, barely audible over the

sound of the hot breeze. Then the door rattled as someone pushed against it from the other side. "Help."

Tanner's face went hard, and he pulled Roxanne aside. "Move away from the door!" he shouted. "I'm going to kick it open."

"What if they can't move? You might hurt them," said Roxanne. "Window."

"Right." Tanner wasted no time using a landscaping stone to bust through a nearby window. He cleared the glass away and folded his body through the opening.

Roxanne was right on his heels.

Lying in front of the back door was a young woman wearing bloody scrubs. She opened her eyes as they approached, but she didn't move.

Tanner pulled out his concealed weapon and whispered, "Stay here."

Roxanne didn't waste time arguing with him. The young woman was bleeding out. She pressed her bare hands against the bullet hole in the woman's chest. Blood seeped between her fingers.

This wasn't good enough. The pool of blood beneath the woman indicated the bullet had gone through and she was bleeding from her back as well. If Roxanne didn't do something soon, she was going to die.

Tanner came back moments later with his cell phone against his ear. "Only one of them is still alive. I unlocked the front door. Hurry." He hung up and looked at Roxanne. Whatever he saw there must have told him the whole story, because he didn't ask any stupid questions, like if the woman was going to be okay. Instead, he said, "I'll find some bandages."

Roxanne doubted that would help, but she wasn't going to turn away his offer to help.

"He shot Bill, too," whispered the woman.

"Who shot him?"

"Stranger. Sick. Drugs, I think." Her eyes fluttered shut and didn't open again.

Tanner knelt by her side, ripping open packs of sterile gauze. "The shot went through. I'm going to turn her. Keep up the pressure."

Roxanne did. As Tanner pressed the wad of gauze against the woman's back, she had to steady herself against the strength of his efforts.

Sirens blared, growing louder until she knew they had to be right outside. The sounds of men entering the clinic filtered down the hallway.

"Police!" shouted a man.

"Back here," called Tanner.

"Move away from the woman," ordered the officer.

"If we do, she'll bleed to death," said Roxanne. She glanced over her shoulder and saw a young man pointing a gun at her. Still, she didn't ease up on the pressure.

He moved so that he could see over a half wall, and his face went pale. "Oh God. Joyce." He took a step forward, then thought better of it. "The ambulance should be here in a second. Hold on."

Chaos descended on them as a swarm of people crowded the narrow hall. Roxanne gladly gave up the job of keeping Joyce's blood inside her body to the paramedics.

She moved to one of the exam rooms to wash her hands, but an older man stopped her. "Sorry, ma'am. I can't let you do that. This is a crime scene."

The blood had begun to dry, making her fingers sticky. "You're not going to make me wear her blood, are you?"

The older man's mouth flattened in distaste, making his long mustache sweep his bottom lip. Authority hung in the air around him, telling her that he was not someone to trifle with.

"Joel, collect some samples and photograph the young lady's hands, please."

Joel was in uniform, and he came over a few seconds later with a large camera. He snapped a dozen photos from various angles, then rubbed several long cotton swabs over her skin before sealing them in individual tubes.

"I'm Sheriff Bream," he said, holding out an open container of wet wipes. "How about you tell me who you are and exactly how this all happened."

"My name is Roxanne Haught. I'm looking for a friend of mine. The waitress at the diner said she'd seen a man recently who was sick, and she told him to come here. I was hoping to ask a few questions." She purposefully left out the part about being attacked by the man the waitress recognized, and even misled him into thinking that the man the waitress had seen was her missing friend.

The sheriff pulled in a deep breath and let it out, as if preparing for a challenge. "Who's your friend?"

"Jake Staite."

"Why do you think he's here?"

"I got an e-mail message from him. It was sent from your town's library."

"Who's the big guy?" asked the sheriff, nodding toward Tanner.

"Tanner O'Connell. He's helping me find Jake."

"Tell me what happened when you showed up here."

Roxanne told him exactly what had happened—how they'd knocked, saw the TV was on, and thought that they might be heard if they knocked on the back door. She left out the argument about whether or not she should break in but told him about the noise they heard and breaking the back window to get in.

"Hell of a thing," said Sheriff Bream. "If you hadn't shown up, Joyce might have died before we found her."

"She said it was a man who did this."

"That so?"

"Yes."

"Did she say who it was or what he looked like?"

"She said he was sick. I think she mentioned drugs. Don't they have a security camera here you can check?"

"We'll be looking into it," he hedged, as if unwilling to confirm or deny the existence of a camera. "In the meantime, I'd like you and your friend to come with us for a bit."

"You can't possibly think we did this," she said.

"It's routine. No need to worry. I'm sure your story will check out."

Roxanne sure as hell hoped so, because she didn't have time to waste. "Do I need to call my attorney?"

"That's up to you, ma'am. Might not be a bad idea, though."

That didn't sound good at all.


Hours later, Tanner was brought into the room where they were holding Roxanne. Red marks lined his wrists where they'd handcuffed him.

He didn't look happy about it, either.

Sheriff Bream announced, "You're both free to go. A security camera at the bank across the street caught video of a man going into the clinic's front door a couple of hours before you two. That same camera also verified your story about knocking on the front door right before the clinic's closing time."

Relief made Roxanne sag in her chair. She was exhausted, running on fumes. Hours of interrogation—as polite as it had been—had worn her down. Her worry for Jake had added to the stress until she felt stretched too thin and brittle enough to break.

Tanner moved past the uniformed female officer who had stayed in her room the whole time. Once he was at her side, she felt some of her tension ease. She wasn't sure why that was the case, or what it was about him that caused the odd phenomenon, but she was grateful for the respite.

Sheriff Bream handed them his business card. "We'd like it if you'd stay in town tonight. We'll put you up at the Hall's Bed-and-Breakfast."

"Why?" asked Tanner. "You said everything checked out."

"It did. I would just feel better knowing you were nearby in case we had any more questions."

Roxanne felt like she'd been wrung dry of information. While the officers were polite and professional, they'd been thorough—over and over again. "What else could you possibly want to know?"

"From what I can tell, at least four strangers have come through this town in two days. I'd like to know why."

"I told you why we're here. I'm looking for my friend."

"Seems to me you're not the only one looking for someone."

"What's that supposed to mean?" asked Tanner. He shifted half a step closer to Roxanne, and she couldn't help but feel the protective vibes sliding off him in waves.

The sheriff watched her face as he spoke. "Joyce woke up to say that the man who shot her told her he had to get better fast so he could find a woman named Roxanne."

Shock trickled through her, stunning her speechless for a moment. "Can I see a picture of the man?"

The sheriff nodded to the female officer, who pulled a page from a folder and handed it to Roxanne. It was a grainy image from the bank's security camera showing the profile of a man in clothing too heavy for the stifling heat. He looked to be in his thirties with a receding hairline and a nose too small for his face. She didn't recognize him.

"Do you know him?" asked the sheriff.

Roxanne shook her head. "I have no idea why he'd be looking for me. Maybe it's another Roxanne."

Bream lifted his bushy brows. "It's not exactly a common name. And I don't happen to be a big believer in coincidences. Maybe we should talk about why someone would be looking for you."

She stared right in his eyes. "You've already run my license. I'm sure you've checked into my background. Did you see anything that would make *you* look for me?"

"Money. Or this man could be tied to your kidnappers— their kid, maybe."

"Kidnappers?" asked Tanner, looking between her and the sheriff as if expecting an answer.

Roxanne wasn't going to be the one to give it to him. The shame of that whole ordeal was not something she wanted to face tonight, when she was already feeling fragile and worried.

Fortunately, the sheriff didn't answer his question, either. Instead, he continued on as if Tanner hadn't spoken. "It could be about revenge. And then there's a whole slew of things you could be hiding—things that wouldn't show up on any background search."

"I'm not hiding anything," said Roxanne. "All I want to do is find Jake and bring him home."

"We'll do what we can to help, but there's no record of his passing through. In the meantime, you two get some rest. We'll talk more tomorrow."

Roxanne opened her mouth to argue, but Tanner's hand settled at the small of her back, jolting her silent. He looked down at her. "I think that's a good idea. We're both beat."

They were escorted back to their truck and then followed an officer over to the Hall's Bed-and-Breakfast.

It was a cute place, with plenty of southwestern flare that would appeal to tourists. The rock garden in front was lit with color-changing lights that led the way to the front door. The front porch boasted several seating areas kept cool by an overhead system of tubes spraying a fine mist of water.

Roxanne barely noticed the lobby. Her eyes were burning with fatigue, and her heart was heavy with worry. She couldn't have cared less about the décor or the friendly man behind the counter. All she wanted was to go to her room, take off these bloody clothes, shower, and figure out a way to find Jake.

Maybe Mira would have some ideas about where to look next.

Tanner walked her to her door and waited while she unlocked it. The tarnished brass knob squeaked as it turned. So did the hinges.

She walked inside and set her small overnight bag on a

chair upholstered in turquoise fabric. The furnishings were old, some even antique. The dry air had caused the floor-boards to shrink, leaving gaps between the wooden slats. A small TV sat on a wall-mounted stand. Outside, a streetlight glowed bright, burning her eyes.

Roxanne drew the shades down. One of them kept sliding back up, thwarting her attempts to darken the room.

Tanner reached over her head and took the loop from her hands. He wrapped the cord around a nail that had been driven into the windowsill, presumably for that purpose.

"Thanks," she said, her voice rough from all the talking she'd been doing. At least that was what she convinced herself was causing it. Deep down, she knew it was more. She'd been fighting back tears for the last hour as her worry for Jake grew.

Tanner took her by the shoulders and turned her around. Concern lined his face and made his blue eyes brighter. His big hands held on to her, giving her more comfort than she would have liked. "Are you okay?"

His concern for her cracked her defenses, and she pulled in a shuddering breath to keep herself from tearing up. She would not cry, not in front of Tanner.

Roxanne plastered a fake smile on her face. "I'm fine. Just tired. You don't need to stay."

"I'm worried about you." He smoothed some wayward strands of hair behind her ear.

She had to resist the urge to lean into his touch, desper-ate for the comfort it brought. The casual way he invaded her space turned her brain to mush. She had to find a way to keep a professional distance, for both their sakes. "Don't worry. I'm a big girl."

A small grin lifted one side of his mouth. "Not all that big. And you were put through the wringer today."

"So were you."

"It's not my friend who's missing. I know that's hard on you. I also know we'll find him."

"How?" she asked before she realized how much that lack of faith revealed about her state of mind.

"I have some ideas. Why don't you get some sleep, and we'll talk about it in the morning."

"You're stalling, aren't you?"

He shook his head, and confidence radiated out with that single motion. "Nope. But we're both tired. And I'm really sick of having blood on my clothes."

Roxanne was, too. And the sooner she went to bed, the sooner Tanner would tell her his ideas. For now, she had hope, and that was more than she'd had when she'd walked into the room.

She wasn't sure exactly how he'd managed to turn her worry around, but she was grateful he had.

She stepped forward, and with his hands on her shoulders, she was able to press herself against his body. She hugged him tight, pressing her cheek against his hard chest and reveling in the feel of the muscles sliding under the skin of his back.

His arms wrapped around her, returning the hug.

She didn't let it last long. It felt too good for that, and anything that felt that good had to be wrong.

Roxanne pulled away, unable to meet his gaze. She walked to her door and opened it, giving him the unmistakable hint he should go.

He did, and the room suddenly felt empty and bleak without him.


Norma Stynger answered the call from one of her men stationed in the town of Dry Valley. Keeping an eye on the locals was important, and the best way to do that was to use someone no one would suspect—someone who'd lived there all his life.

S-eight-nine had been born there. He'd left to serve his country, and after a few years, Norma had been able to get her hands on him.

He'd come home to a parade, and Sheriff Bream had offered him a job working for the sheriff's office whenever he wanted it. She'd ordered him to accept the position. That had been two years ago, and S-eight-nine had become an invaluable resource.

"A doctor was murdered in town today. We have video of the man who did it, and I'm certain he's one of ours. I thought you would want to know."

Norma stifled the momentary flutter of panic that news caused. "Is he in custody?"

"No, but we're looking for him."

"Were there any witnesses?"

"Besides the camera? A nurse was also shot. She could probably identify him."

There were only a handful of subjects working in this area. Most of them did countersurveillance work, ensuring that the facility was never located by outsiders. Anyone who got too close was killed, and their body was split open and left under the sun for the animals to dispose of. It took only hours. She had to marvel at nature's efficiency.

"Take care of her," ordered Norma. "She's a threat to the project."

"Yes, ma'am. There were two other people who stumbled across the scene after our man left. Do you want me to take care of them as well?"

"Did they see him?"

"No, but there is one odd coincidence. Our man told the nurse he was looking for a woman named Roxanne. The woman here also has that name."

That was no coincidence. The odds were too slim. S-eleven-sixteen's contact was here—perhaps with the subject's diary.

A flash of panic assailed Norma before she could control it. There was no need for hysterics. The woman may have figured out where to find them, but there was no way she could know the exact location of the facility. S-eleven-sixteen didn't know, so it stood to reason that she couldn't, either. Besides, it was hidden well. Guarded. Only someone who knew the land and the security measures would have a chance at slipping by without being killed.

Still, this woman was a risk, and Norma didn't like the idea of her asking questions or raising suspicions in town. They were not going to move again because of Roxanne Haught. She wasn't worth the trouble.

"Do you know where she is?" Norma asked S-eight-nine.

"At the Hall's B and B. Second floor. They were put in the rooms on the east, the ones with the balcony."

"I'll have the general deal with them. Keep the authorities away for the rest of the night."

"Won't their deaths raise too many suspicions, ma'am?"

"I won't have them killed there. The woman may still be of some use." If S-eleven-sixteen cared for Roxanne Haught, Norma would be able to use her to verify that his induction was complete and successful. This was a rare scientific opportunity, and Norma couldn't let it slip by.

# Chapter Thirteen

Tanner could still feel the heat of Razor's slender body pressed against his as he made his way to his room next door.

He'd wanted to stay. He didn't like the idea of leaving her when she was so obviously suffering with worry for Jake. He also didn't like the idea of leaving her alone in case whoever had killed the doctor came back.

If he'd been more than a few feet away, he probably would have fought her on the issue, but he'd been in enough battles to know that sometimes falling back was the best option. He'd planted the seeds of hope tonight. After some sleep, and some time for those seeds to grow, she'd be better able to handle moving forward.

The walls were thin. He could hear the sound of water running in the shower next door. He stripped out of his bloody clothes. The shirt was ruined, but his jeans might survive. He shoved them in a plastic laundry bag and sat to wait until Roxanne was done with her shower before he would get one himself, just in case the aging B and B didn't have enough hot water for both of them to shower at the same time.

The thought shoved an image in his head of the two of them showering together and soaping each other up. He hardened in a heartbeat, his cock rising to attention at the stray thought.

*Not going to happen. Not in this lifetime.*

Tanner forced his thoughts to go in another direction as he peeled the bandages from his back, desperate to find something to distract himself. His muscles stretched at the awkward angle. His blood beat through his veins, trying to cool his skin. Even clothed in nothing more than a pair of knit boxers, he still felt overheated. Sweat beaded up along his hairline and down his spine. His hands closed into tight fists as he tried to regain control.

He wanted her. And as simple as that fact was, it came with a cargo shipload of problems, not the least of which was that they had to work together. Too bad his libido didn't care.

Soap banged against the bottom of the tub, and he tried really hard not to picture her all soapy and naked, bending over to pick it up.

Of course, trying not to think about it only made things worse. His imagination went wild, filling in all the erotic little details he hadn't had the pleasure of seeing. He'd seen her bare arms and legs when she'd thrown on her workout clothes to clean up the glass, and that alone was enough to give him wet dreams for the rest of his life. She had the kind of body that made his mouth water. Sculpted, but not hard. Sleek but curvy. And her skin was whisper soft. Covered in suds, she'd be even softer. His hands would glide so easily over her slippery skin, finding all the places that made her breath catch when he stroked them.

Tanner gritted his teeth and turned on the TV. The news was on, and an anchorwoman was talking about the economy. She was pretty, but not nearly as hot as Roxanne. Her hair was nice, falling over her shoulders in dark waves that caught the studio lighting.

Razor's hair would be dark blond right now, slicked back from her forehead by the shower. He wondered if the color was natural and if he'd ever get the opportunity to find out. He could see her doing the full spa treatment, wax and all.

Not that he'd ever have the chance to look. The only way

he was ever going to see her naked was in his dreams, which was going to be more than enough to make him uncomfortable tomorrow morning.

He knew he'd dream about her tonight. Hell, he was dreaming about her now, and he wasn't even asleep.

The water next door turned off. He made a beeline for the bathroom and took as little time as possible getting clean, ignoring the sting of soap in his cuts. The threat to her safety was real, and he sure as hell wasn't going to be caught in the shower if the bad guys came a-callin'.

The sheriff had been hiding something today. Tanner was sure of it. Maybe it was a mistress or a gambling problem, but Tanner didn't think so. Bream had been smooth, but there had been a couple of flickers of unease that didn't make sense.

Both had happened when he'd been asking questions about the strangers that had come through. It was almost as if the sheriff knew something wasn't right. The question was whether he was trying to figure out the problem or was he part of it.

One thing was for sure: Razor got a strange e-mail from the same town in which a doctor was killed by a man looking for her. That was more than coincidence, and Tanner was going to get to the bottom of it.

He might have let down his family more times than he could count, but he wasn't going to let Razor down. She needed his help, and he was going to see to it that she got it.

Tanner had finally calmed his thoughts and fallen asleep when he heard a noise that was out of place. His mind jolted into wakefulness, his body tensing to act. He lay in bed, breathing quietly, seeking out the source of that sound while his hand moved toward the gun sitting on his nightstand.

He could see nothing out of place in his room. Light from the streetlights outside filtered in around the edges of the shades, allowing him to see without trouble.

A faint scratching sound came from the balcony. It could

have been a cat or some other animal, but Tanner wasn't taking any chances.

He rose from his bed and moved on silent feet to the French doors. He lifted the edge of the curtains and peeked out.

No one was out there.

He pushed the curtain open and unlocked the door to get a better look down the long balcony that ran along the building.

From Razor's room came a clatter, as though something hard had fallen onto the floor, followed by a sharp, feminine cry of pain.

Adrenaline surged through him as a hundred different reasons for the noise flew around in his mind. None of them was good.

The balcony door was closest, so he went that way. The wooden deck was rough against his bare feet. In the few seconds it took him to reach her door, he registered the sound of crickets and the scent of heat rising from the asphalt below.

Razor's door was open. Tanner barreled through, his gun drawn and ready.

His eyes were already adjusted to the dimness, so he had no trouble seeing the wiry man who had Razor pinned on her stomach against the bed with her wrists bound. She struggled, but his knee was against her back, keeping her down. Her head was shoved into the mattress, cutting off her air and any screams she might let out. Her arms flailed and her feet kicked, trying to find some target.

The man had a syringe in his hand and was about to inject Roxanne.

The urge to shoot was nearly uncontrollable. It would have been so easy to lift his weapon and fire. But there were other people sleeping here, and the walls were way too thin.

"Stop or I will shoot," he ordered, aiming his gun for the man's back. He stepped to the right, angling himself so that any stray bullets would go into the exterior wall and not into the room where someone was sleeping.

The man froze and lifted the hand holding the syringe. Tanner followed the movement, but in doing so, he hadn't seen the intruder's intent until too late.

The man slung Razor around, whipping her up against his front as a shield. Her legs were pinned against the bed, her back bent at an extreme angle. She let out a cry of pain.

"Put the gun down or I kill her," whispered the man.

During the commotion, he'd pulled a gun and had it shoved against Razor's ribs. His other arm was around her throat, cutting off her air as he backed away toward the exit.

Her face became redder as the seconds ticked by. Her legs thrashed, and she pried at his arm with her hands, trying to free herself.

Beneath the man's mask, his dark eyes were flat and emotionless. His hands didn't shake. His voice didn't waver.

This man was a professional.

There were only a few feet separating them. If he could take the man off guard, Tanner could rush him and free Razor.

He set his gun on the floor and met her gaze, hoping she'd see his intent. He moved to stand up again, but halfway through the motion, he pounced, using his legs to propel him forward into the attacker. At the same time, Razor elbowed the man's hand holding the gun, shoving the barrel toward his body. The advantage only lasted for a second, but it was long enough to tackle both of them to the ground.

The man hit hard, letting out a whoosh of air. Tanner slammed his fist into the man's temple, but it didn't even stun him.

The gun came up. Tanner grabbed for it. He recognized the model. The safety was on the side, accessible. With one quick movement, he flipped it on to keep the weapon from firing. The man's other arm was pinned down by Roxanne, who was gasping for her first gulps of air even as she bashed the man's ribs with her elbow.

The intruder was strong—stronger than anyone Tanner could ever remember fighting. Even using two hands against his one, the man wasn't having much trouble controlling the weapon.

He aimed it at Tanner's head and pulled the trigger. Nothing happened.

A second later, Tanner felt himself flying across the room until he came to a sudden, painful stop against the dresser. Razor had regained her footing and executed a graceful spinning kick right into the man's hand.

The gun skidded across the floor, and from the angle of his fingers, Tanner was sure Razor had broken at least one of them.

Tanner picked up his weapon, but before he could aim, the man scooped up the syringe he dropped, darted out the door, and leaped over the balcony railing.

Someone knocked on the door. "Is everything all right in there?" came the elderly Mrs. Hall's voice.

Tanner ignored the woman and raced to the balcony to see if the man had survived. Not only had he lived through the long fall, but he was on his feet, running. The urge to rush after him was a pounding, hot compulsion. Only his concern for Razor held him back.

He shut and locked the door.

"We're fine," called Razor. Her voice was weak and strained, and she was out of breath. "Sorry to be so loud. We got carried away."

"Oh," said Mrs. Hall, immediately repeating the word in a tone of deeper understanding. "*Oh*. Sorry to interrupt. You two lovebirds keep it down, okay?"

"We will."


It had been a long time since Roxanne had been so afraid. She was used to being able to take care of herself, but from the moment that man's hands touched her, she knew she was outmatched.

He'd been incredibly strong, controlling her body easily, pinning her in place. She had no idea who he was, but she had a pretty good guess about what he wanted.

Jake's journal.

Tanner crouched in front of Roxanne. Propped against the bed, she was sitting on the floor, rubbing her throat in an effort to ease the ache. Her back wasn't much better, but she didn't think it was more than pulled muscles.

"Are you okay?" he asked.

She nodded, wincing at the movement. "Yeah. Just bruised, I think."

"Let me see."

He flipped on the light and brushed her hair back from her throat. He pressed gently, probing the area to check for more serious injuries.

"These men keep going for my throat."

"As lovely as it is, I wish they'd pick a different, less delicate target." Restrained anger filled his voice, but his hands were gentle.

The feel of his fingers on her skin eased some of the quaking inside her, and calmed her nerves. She focused on his face, the way his jaw was clenched and his brow was lowered in concentration and concern. His blue eyes were intent, but there was fury lurking there, just below the surface.

"I'm surprised you didn't go after him," she said.

"I couldn't leave you. Throat injuries can be serious. If there's any swelling, it could cut off your air supply."

"It's not that bad. I'll be sore tomorrow, but thanks to you, I'm still alive."

"He didn't want to kill you," said Tanner. "At least not here. He was getting ready to drug you with something when I came in—probably to keep you quiet so he could transport you."

The idea of being unconscious in that man's hands was more than she could take right now, so she forced herself to think of something else, such as the way Tanner kept stroking her arm as if to reassure her.

His fingers were warm. She hadn't realized how chilled she was until now. The frenzy of adrenaline was wearing off, leaving her feeling weak and deflated. The urge to lean forward and put herself in Tanner's arms was almost uncontrollable. She held back only because there was no time for such luxury. They had to get moving.

"Why didn't you tell Mrs. Hall to call the police?" asked Tanner.

"Because they're the only ones who know we're here. I didn't pay with a credit card. We didn't tell anyone where we were. The police are the only ones who know, so someone there must have told the wrong people."

"You've been followed before. It could be that they found you here. It's not necessarily dirty cops."

She shrugged, regretting the movement instantly. A deep ache knotted along her spine where she'd been bent too far. "Who knows? I'm not willing to accuse them of anything, but I don't trust them, either. We need to do this on our own."

"Do what?"

"Find the man who was in here tonight. Or at least find out where he came from. He'll lead us to Jake."

"That's insane. The only reason we're still alive is because he decided to leave us that way. We need to get out of here before he comes back."

"And we will. I'm in no shape for a manhunt right now. We need to find a place to hole up for a few hours."

"You need to go see a doctor."

"After what happened at the clinic today, that sounds like the worst idea ever."

He gritted his teeth so hard she swore she could hear the noise. "We're in over our heads. Whatever is going on with Jake is bigger than either of us thought. If we go in after him—assuming we can even find him—we'll get killed. Or worse."

Many of the things that fell into that "worse" category had crossed her mind when she'd been pinned facedown on the bed. She was still too close to the trauma to flippantly deny his words. "We need time to think. Let's leave here and find a safe place to stay while we figure out a plan."

He nodded. "I'd rather take you to a hospital."

"I'm fine. Really. I've been through worse than this."

His gaze shot to hers, and she realized she'd said too much. "When?"

She didn't want to talk about that time of her life. It was over, and she wanted it to stay buried in the past.

Of course, she wasn't wearing her watch or a bracelet, and if he saw the scars, he might start asking uncomfortable questions.

Roxanne crossed her arms to hide the scars. "It was a long time ago, and I'm not going to talk about it. Now, go grab your stuff, and let's get out of this place."

Ten minutes later, they left, heading straight for the highway. It was late enough that there was hardly any traffic on the roads except for truckers.

Tanner darted around them, heading east as fast as his truck would go.

Roxanne kept watch behind them, but saw nothing. Not that it meant anything. Whoever these people were, they'd found her before. They could find her again.

Until this was over, she wasn't trusting anyone except Tanner.

Fifty miles later, he pulled off and found a motel out of sight of the highway.

He came to a stop outside the front doors and turned in his seat. His shoulders were squared as if he expected a fight. "I'm only getting one room. I won't leave you alone again."

She dug in her purse and got out some cash. "You let me pay for it, and we have a deal."

"You can't go in. They'll call the cops, thinking I beat you up." He took the cash and reached behind him to retrieve his gun. He set it on the seat between them. "I won't be long. I'll be able to see you through the window the whole time."

"I'll be fine."

"You almost weren't."

"But I am. Now please go get our room so I can wash the feel of that asshole's hands off me."

He nodded and got out of the car, his long legs covering the distance in seconds. He glanced back over his shoulder. Roxanne waved him on.

His concern was comforting to her. It had been a long time since anyone had cared enough about her to worry quite so much. Granted, it had also been a long time since she'd been in trouble this deep, but she truly believed that Kurt would have ditched her at the first sign of danger. He just wasn't cut out for battle the same way that Tanner was.

Then again, there were a lot of areas in which Tanner blew Kurt out of the water. He was far better-looking. And while Kurt had kept in shape, that shape was nothing like Tanner's hard, sculpted body. In addition, Kurt had never been as aware of her as Tanner was. Kurt was more worried about what was happening in his own shallow world to take the time to care about someone else's.

Sure, Tanner had been assigned to babysit her, but she had the feeling that he would have done so even without Bella's request. He just didn't seem the type to walk away, as evidenced by his vigilant stubbornness to stay by her side.

He came out through the lobby doors, spine straight, shoulders back, walking with the kind of determination that screamed he was on a mission. She'd known confident men in her life, but never one who had the ability to impart that confidence on everyone around him. Just looking at him walk, she felt safer, more sure that they'd find Jake. It was like a magic trick, but one she so desperately needed right now.

He got into the truck and started the engine.

"There's magic in your walk," she told him.

He gave her a skeptical look. "In my . . . walk? I didn't think you'd hit your head."

She smiled and it felt good. Fear drained from her system, giving her room to breathe. "I didn't. I was just thinking that the men you worked with had to have been sorry to see you leave the military."

He shrugged. "Some of them, I suppose."

"Modesty?"

He backed into a parking spot in case they needed to make a speedy exit. "That's not exactly the kind of thing a man asks another man, you know? It's best not to think about it."

"Ah. A man who knows how to live in the moment."

"A man who knows how to deal with the situation at hand and not sweat the rest. So how about we get you settled and get an ice pack on your neck."

They got out of the truck, and after having sat for an hour, her back had tightened up to the point that standing hurt. "My back could use the ice more."

He grabbed their bags out of the back and took her arm to help her walk. And while she didn't need the help, his touch was nice.

Tanner unlocked the door and tossed their bags on the floor. "Lie down. I'll grab some ice and be right back."

Roxanne waited until he left before she dared to sit. She didn't want him to see her in pain. He was already worried enough.

He came back moments later with the bag from the ice bucket filled and tied. He wrapped it in a towel and said, "Where do you want it?"

"Between my shoulder blades. I think he pulled something when he jerked me around."

"I'm sorry. That was my fault. I pulled a gun on him and gave him no choice."

"He could have not broken into my room. I'd say that makes everything that happened after that his fault."

She rolled over slowly, but the second her face was pressed against the bed, a fast, angry panic exploded in her gut. Her heart jumped around in her chest, and her breathing became panting. Sweat formed across her skin, and all she could think about was getting off this bed—fast.

That man had been about to inject her with something. Who knew what he would have done to her after that? So soon after the ordeal, she couldn't just shrug it off, as stupid as it was.

Roxanne flipped over, making her muscles scream in protest. Her stomach heaved, and she sat up to keep from vomiting.

"Easy," said Tanner. He was holding her arms, helping her move.

"Sorry. I can't lie that way."

"Sure. No problem." There was no judgment in his voice, no condemnation for being silly. "I'll just hold the ice pack on, okay?"

She gave him an unsteady nod and took deep breaths to quiet her rioting stomach.

He sat in silence as the chill of the ice sank through her shirt. It felt good, especially on her overheated skin. The air of the motel room was stuffy and warm, as if the room had been closed for too long.

As the seconds ticked by, she began to feel more and more awkward. The rush of fear had worn off, leaving only the embarrassment of her irrational reaction. "You don't need to hold it. I'll lean against the headboard or something."

"If that's what you want. Let me grab the pillows from the other bed."

He fluffed and arranged until she was propped comfortably with the ice pack in the right place.

The silence was not her friend right now. Too much had happened, and her mind kept going over the gruesome details again and again: the dead doctor; the bleeding nurse; the deranged man who'd attacked her in Dallas; and now another attacker in New Mexico. If whoever had Jake was going to so much trouble to find her and get the journal back, there was no telling what they were doing to him.

Would they punish him for the trouble he caused, or had they already killed him for the crime?

She had to find him soon, before it was too late, assuming it wasn't already.

Roxanne cleared her throat, but her voice was still rougher than normal. "I suppose now would be as good a time as any to figure out our next move."

"I'm glad you think so. I have definite opinions on the matter."

"Oh yeah? What's your plan?"

"You go back to Dallas. We get the authorities involved. We call in favors or offer to return them in exchange for help."

His lack of confidence in her stung. "First, you can go back to Dallas anytime you want. Second, we've seen how much help the authorities have been. Third, the people who owe me favors can get me into the most exclusive country clubs, but they're not good for much else."

"What about Bella? Or Payton? He's been around long enough to rack up a few favors."

"Payton runs in the same circles my parents did. He's useless."

"He didn't seem useless to me."

"Wait until you get to know him. He has money. He's good with numbers. But I wouldn't trust him to find Jake when I'm much more capable of doing so myself."

"We're outclassed, Roxanne. If we don't admit that to ourselves, we're going to get killed, and if I do that, my brother will never forgive me."

"I suppose we could ask Reid to help. He's a decent guy."

Tanner muttered something under his breath she couldn't hear. "He's not enough."

"Okay, so maybe we ask a couple of the guys to come out and lend a hand. But we're not going to the police or the feds. I don't know who I can trust except you."

The anger in his face relaxed, and he sat down next to her on the bed. "Glad to hear I'm on the list."

"You should be glad. It's a short one. I'm a very exclusive kind of woman."

A smile flickered across his mouth. "I do have ideas that might work if we have help."

"Like what?"

"We could send them to Dry Valley and have them ask the questions we can't. We see if anyone else has seen your stalker, or the woman who sent you that e-mail warning, or Jake. Someone might know which way he went if he did pass through."

"It's worth a shot. I'll call the Edge first thing in the morning and see who's available."

He nodded his acceptance. "How's your back?"

"Cold. A little sore, but not bad. I'll get a hot shower in a few minutes and see if that helps."

Tanner smoothed her hair away from her neck. His fingers lightly traced the marks left behind.

A shiver that had nothing to do with the ice pack eased along her spine. He saw it, and his eyes darkened with a knowing look.

She hadn't had a shiver like that over a man in a long, long time—not since she'd been young and foolish and had fallen easily for a man. She hadn't known he'd only loved her money. At eighteen, she'd had no real defenses against men like that. She'd come a long way in the last ten years, and now she knew when a man was looking at her, and when he was drooling over her net worth.

Tanner was staring, but his gaze was definitely not focused on her trust fund.

His body was tense and his gaze roamed her face, returning to her mouth over and over again. His pupils had dilated, and a dark flush of lust stained his skin. She could tell that he wanted her but that he was holding back.

She covered his hand with hers, stroking his skin. She felt the ridges of a few small scars—ones he'd no doubt earned doing his duty to God and country.

Roxanne wondered what it would be like to be loved by

a man simply for who she was rather than what she could give him. Even the men who had their own wealth and prestige still had something to gain by being with her.

Tanner had never once asked her about her money. There had been no thinly veiled talk of investments or assets. He hadn't questioned her about why she was selling such a stunning home to live in her much smaller one. It simply didn't seem to matter to him.

Either that, or he was a fantastic liar.

For now, even that lie was a potent lure. She could easily pretend he was what he appeared to be and live in the moment. After the day she'd had, it was too compelling to resist.

She lifted his hand and pressed a kiss in the center of his palm.

His nostrils flared, and his jaw tightened.

She kissed him again, daring to taste his skin with just the tip of her tongue.

Tanner shifted on the bed and shut his eyes. His fingers curled down toward his palm, but he didn't pull away.

"What are you doing?" he asked.

"Thanking you for being there tonight."

"You do that with your mouth."

"I am using my mouth."

He shook his head as if trying to clear it. "I mean your words. You don't have to do this."

She tugged on his hand, and he came forward, close enough that she could loop her arms around his neck, which she did, trapping him in place. He wouldn't dare move now for fear of hurting her back. "What if I want to?"

"It's the adrenaline. Does funny things to people."

She slid her hand up the back of his head, feeling the tickle of his buzz cut along her fingers. "I'm not laughing."

"Roxanne," he said, his tone a mix of warning and pleading. "We have to work together. We can't do this."

"You called me Roxanne, not Razor like the rest of the guys. I like it—the sound of my real name rolling off your tongue. It's . . . intimate."

"I didn't mean for it to be."

"So you don't want me to kiss you?" she asked.

A low, hungry growl vibrated the air between them. It was such a primal noise, it woke up all the politically incorrect parts of her—the ones that responded to a man who knew how to be a man.

He seemed beyond words. His body was tight, the muscles in his arms straining, though whether he was holding himself back or simply angry at her question, she couldn't tell.

Time to find out.

Roxanne tugged on his neck, exerting the slightest pressure. She didn't want to force him, but she wasn't going to sit back and do nothing, either.

Sure, it was unprofessional for her to come on to him, but life was too short to worry about things like that. She'd learned that tonight as her death had seemed imminent and the list of things she still wanted to do had popped into her head.

She wanted to see Jake again. She wanted to redeem herself in Bella's eyes and catch the bad guys. She wanted a family of her own—one that cared more for people than things and status. But right now, with the specter of death so recently departed, she just wanted the basic human comfort of another person's touch. And Tanner was going to give it to her.

# Chapter Fourteen

Tanner was going to die. He was going to be split in two—the part that knew kissing Roxanne was wrong, and the much larger part that couldn't fathom the thought of not kissing her. The problem was, he knew it wouldn't stop at just a kiss. Adrenaline was one hell of a drug, and he had so much pumping through his system, he was as much animal as man.

If they started something, he wasn't sure he'd be able to stop. He wasn't sure it would even occur to him to try.

Her golden eyes dared him, and the remembered feel of her mouth on his skin only made him want more. She was so soft and beautiful. And she smelled incredible. With her staring up at him like this, with a small smile curving her lips and a naughty gleam in her eyes, he didn't know how he was going to hold back.

So he stayed where he was, propped over her with his weight braced on his arms. Her fingers stroked his head, and he could feel the heat of them sinking through his short hair.

She tugged, and despite his much greater strength, he went, unable to resist her.

Roxanne's smile widened, and she parted her lips in welcome.

Tanner forgot all about fighting her. He leaned down and did what he promised himself he would never do. He kissed her, feeling the softness of her mouth and the warmth of her breath. Desire spiked inside him, fueled by the first heady taste of her.

He tipped his head, covering her mouth more fully and taking what he needed. She was right there with him, her fingers gripping his shoulders and holding him close as if she feared his moving away.

Not a fucking chance. Now that he'd had a taste, he knew exactly what he'd been missing.

They fit together well, their bodies lining up as if they were a matched set. He covered her, pressing her down, pulling pillows out from under her as she went, until she was flat on her back. The ice pack flew and hit the floor with a squishy sound. It gave him pause, but he was too busy kissing her to figure out why.

His tongue swept across her lip, dipping into her mouth for a taste. She was sweet and intoxicating, and she went straight to his head. Her fingernails dug into his back, and she let out a throaty moan of pleasure.

If he didn't get his mouth off hers soon, he was going to end up fucking her.

The thought should have stopped him cold, but, instead, it inflamed him, putting powerful images into his head. He could see her long, tanned legs wrapped around his hips as he drove into her, and he could hear her cries of release as he took her with his mouth.

"Yes," she whispered against his lips.

His cock throbbed inside his jeans. His skin was overheating beneath his clothes. He needed to be naked and then strip her down so they could feel each other's skin. Just the thought of cupping her naked breasts, of suckling her nipples, was nearly enough to make him come.

Tanner clamped down on his control long enough to make room between their bodies for his hand. He found the hem of her T-shirt and slid his hand beneath, spanning her stomach. Her belly fluttered under his touch, and she made a noise of approval that spurred him on.

She was so soft here, so smooth. The curve of her waist fit his palm just right and urged him to go higher and see if the rest of her fit, too.

Roxanne nibbled at his bottom lip and then licked away the sting. He'd never kissed a woman who showed as much enthusiasm as she did. Every little noise, every fluid motion of her body urged him on, calling to him on a deep level that had never before been touched.

He wasn't sure if he should like it quite as much as he did, but there was no space to worry about that now. She filled his senses—her scent, the sight of her flushed body, the taste of her eager mouth and all those wicked little sounds she made—every bit of her sang to him, driving away all control.

His hand inched up, giving her time to refuse his advances. As enthusiastic as she seemed to be with him, it was his duty as a decent human being not to rush her.

It took all of his willpower, but rather than finishing the too-long journey to her breast, he slid his hand around her body to caress her back.

She wasn't wearing a bra. No strap barred his path. They'd been in such a rush to leave the B and B, and she'd been dressed for bed, it made perfect sense, but it still shocked him to be greeted by smooth, bare skin.

Roxanne's mouth left his and wandered lower, kissing a path to his neck. Her hands cupped his ass, holding him still while she ground herself against his erection. His toes curled in his boots, and it was all he could do not to crush her against him. Her talented tongue drew circles on his throat, and spikes of pleasure radiated out into his limbs. He sucked in a deep breath and held it. His arms tightened around her, and he threaded his fingers through her hair to hold her in place.

Suddenly, she let out a gasp of pain and went stiff in his arms.

Tanner let up on the pressure and looked around for the source of her pain. No one was in the room. They were alone. Then he realized his grip was hurting her back—the one some asshole had injured less than two hours ago.

Remorse doused his lust, allowing him to think clearly again for the first time since his mouth had touched hers.

"I'm sorry," he said, rolling carefully away so as not to hurt her more.

She rolled right on top of him, straddling his hips. Her mouth was a bit swollen and a deep, sexy pink. Her hair was mussed and her nipples beaded up against her T-shirt, taunting him with what he'd missed. "I'm not. But this might work better if I'm on top."

Tanner closed his eyes to block out the sight of her, but that only made his other senses that much sharper. He could feel the heat between her thighs soaking through his jeans, right against his throbbing cock. Every breath she took rocked her slightly against him, but it wasn't nearly enough. The scent of her skin and her heightened arousal filled the air. The taste of her was still on his tongue, tempting him to take more.

"We can't do this. You're hurt. We're partners. It's wrong."

"To hell with wrong. Right is what feels good."

"That's easy to say now. Tomorrow, not so much. Please stop."

She let out a long, heavy sigh and dismounted his body. He instantly grew cold, and his skin prickled at the loss of contact with hers.

"You're right," she said. "I won't push you again."


Roxanne refused to feel guilty for what she'd done. Or hadn't done. Then again, if she had slept with Tanner, she might have had reason to feel guilty. As it was, she simply felt foolish for trying to seduce a man like him. Not only was he too hot for words, but he also had a noble streak a mile wide. And she now had proof that he didn't want her for her money, because if he had, he would have done whatever she asked in order to get to it. Part of her respected him even more for turning her away, but the unsatisfied part of her was throwing a tantrum and stomping its feet in a petulant display.

She'd really wanted to lose herself in something good for a while, and Tanner was definitely that. He was better than the men she normally dated, perhaps enough better that he was out of her league. Still, she'd never been one not to try for something she wanted.

No guts, no orgasm.

She sighed into the shower spray, letting out all that pent-up frustration. The heat eased the cramped muscles in her back, but probably not as much as the languid aftermath of sex would have. Or a set of big, strong hands to rub away the ache.

Of course, if she got a certain set of big, strong hands on her, she probably wouldn't want to stop there. It was best to suck it up and deal with the pain on her own. Whatever suffering she endured was worth it if she found Jake. And she would. No job, no man, and no series of thugs would stop her from finding Jake and bringing him home.

Tanner felt like he'd just missed the last bus to Disneyland. Disappointment weighed him down, but he tried to give himself a pep talk.

Stopping had been right. Not fun, but right. They both still had their jobs. He was thinking with his brain, instead of with his cock.

If someone had come for them when she'd been in his arms, he probably wouldn't have even noticed. That wasn't exactly the kind of behavior that saved lives. He knew better.

And yet he still felt cheated.

He checked the locks and peered through the blinds to see if there was any sign of trouble. No new cars had arrived. No vehicles sat on the road within sight. He didn't have that feeling of being watched, which had saved his ass more times than he could count.

All was well. He was just horny—and going to stay that way.

Tanner fixed the pillows and refilled the ice pack so it was ready for Roxanne when she came out of the shower.

Not Roxanne. Razor. He had to think of her as Razor, no matter how much he loved the idea that she thought his saying her real name was intimate.

Remembering the ibuprofen he'd asked for at the front desk, he dug the packet out of his pocket and set it on her bedside table.

The water turned off. He checked his e-mail on his phone, trying not to think of her naked, rubbing lotion into her skin or doing whatever it was she did to make herself so soft.

Karen had sent him pictures from Millie's party. The little moppet was grinning, her mouth covered in blue frosting from her first birthday cake.

He wished like hell that his little brother and father had been there to see the family's newest addition turn one.

Tanner tried to swallow back his grief, but sometimes it was harder than others. He should have been there in Brody's place. Not that he could ever take the place of a real father in Millie's life, but he'd sincerely intended to be the best uncle any kid had ever had.

And yet he'd missed the big day.

Maybe Reid was right. Maybe he never would be able to balance his work and his family. It had been easy when he'd been in the army. He was either at home, one hundred percent invested in being with his family, or he was at work, one hundred percent focused on the job. Splitting his attention was something he'd never done before. What if he couldn't?

Roxanne came out of the bathroom, a cloud of steam trailing behind her. She was dressed in a sloppy T-shirt that fell to midthigh. He couldn't tell if she had shorts on under that shirt, and he wasn't sure which option to root for.

She'd dried her hair and wore it in two low pigtails, which he found adorable. Her skin was rosy from the hot water, and without her makeup and fancy clothes, she looked vulnerable.

Tanner found himself heading toward her before he thought better of it. He stopped in his tracks. If he touched her again, he might forget his good intentions.

He shoved his hands into his pockets. "There's some ibuprofen for you if you want it. Or I could run to get you something else."

"Thanks, that's perfect."

"You should try to get some sleep."

"What are you going to do?"

"I saw a vending machine at the corner. I'm going to get something to eat. Want anything?"

She wrinkled her nose. "I think I've risked my life enough tonight. But I wouldn't mind some water."

He nodded and left the room. The night air was warm. Bugs swarmed around the lights leading down the building. He stopped and listened, but he heard nothing more than the songs of crickets and the hum of the vending machines.

He stood outside the door, breathing fresh air and trying to focus. He could almost feel Roxanne at his back, her presence calling to him. Never before had a woman had quite such a strong effect on him, and as far as he was concerned, it was a case of shitty timing.

If he lost this job, there weren't exactly a whole ton of other opportunities out there—at least not ones that paid as well as the Edge did. Helping his family crawl their way out of debt would go a long way toward Karen and the kids getting their lives back on track. And getting Reid to cut him a break.

They'd never gotten along well, but there had been a time when they could sit in the same room and not be uncomfortable. Mom picked up on every little expression and prolonged silence. She always knew when they were at odds, and right now, with her dealing with the death of a husband and a son all at once, she deserved not to have her two living sons at each other's throats.

Tanner had to find a way to make things right with Reid, and the only thing he could think to do was to make him proud on the job. That, at least, was something he knew how to do.

He squared his shoulders, feeling renewed purpose. He was going to help Roxanne find Jake and get him home safe and sound, because if he didn't, he knew she wouldn't stop looking for her friend. And that could very well get her killed.

Once that was done and Roxanne was back at home, he was going to make it his personal quest in life to find those responsible for the death and pain that had been caused and make sure they met justice head-on.

Jake woke at the sound of his door opening. He'd been waiting for it, ready to pretend he was asleep like a good little drugged-up boy.

He didn't want to give away what he and Moss had done—plugging the tubes—knowing they would need that element of surprise when they finally did break out of this place.

He kept his breathing steady and even, his eyes relaxed and mostly closed. He watched through the narrow slit, gathering information he could use to help them escape so he could warn Rox.

A man in a white lab coat wheeled a small cart through the door, its wheels squeaking as it moved. A battery-operated desk lamp glowed atop the cart, but Jake couldn't see what else the cart held.

Even though he and Moss had never discussed any plan, he must have come to the same conclusion Jake had—that they didn't want to show their cards yet—and was playing possum.

The lab tech went to Jake's bed first. He knotted a thick

rubber tube around Jake's biceps and drew blood. Next, he jabbed Jake again; only this time, it was to give him something that burned going in.

Almost instantly, Jake's head began to spin and a boiling wave of nausea hit him. He swallowed, trying not to throw up and give himself away.

The tech propped Jake on his side by shoving his pillow behind him to keep him from rolling over. At least if he puked now, he wouldn't choke on it.

Sweat broke out along his forehead, and a buzzing filled his ears. Time seemed to stretch out as the tech went through the same routine with Moss.

Finally, the squeak of metal wheels began again, and the tech left, shutting the door behind him.

Moss bolted to the toilet, retching. The sound made Jake's stomach heave, but Jake made it only as far as the trash can.

After the worst had passed, Jake sat back on his heels and looked at Moss. He was sweating and shaking so hard, Jake could see it with only the minimal light from under the door brightening their room.

They shared a look of suffering but didn't say a word. No one could know they were awake and coherent, or they might figure out that they'd plugged the nozzles that piped gas into the room.

Jake quietly knotted the trash bag to contain the stench of bile, then rinsed his mouth before stumbling to Moss's side.

"Cover me," he whispered as quietly as he could.

Moss shook his head furiously, mouthing the word *no*.

Jake couldn't argue with him. He had to find Jordyn and convince her to help them get out of this place.

He put his hand on Moss's shoulder, hoping it would reassure him. Jake couldn't just sit here and do nothing. They had to find a means of escape, and Jordyn was their best hope.

He slipped out of the room on bare feet. Wearing only a

T-shirt and boxers, he felt naked. He was used to having plenty of protective gear strapped to his body when he went on a mission, but he'd fight naked if that was what it took to get the fuck out of here.

Jake followed the hall, keeping careful watch behind him for the lab tech with the cart. Cameras silently watched his progress, but he prayed that no one was monitoring them at this hour. Eventually, there would be hell to pay for what he was doing, but there was no help for it. If the cost of freedom was another trip to the white room, so be it. He'd find a way to survive.

His stomach rebelled at the thought, but he swallowed down his fear and kept moving.

On silent feet, he made his way toward what he suspected was the section that housed the personal quarters for the staff. He'd spent days trying to map out the place in his head, but there were simply too many areas he'd never been allowed to wander. The one thing he could tell was that rather than a block of space carved out of the earth, they'd dug tunnels that branched off in several directions.

If he'd been designing the facility, he would have put all the eggheads' barracks together so that they could talk shop and be safely away from the soldiers. He also would have put them near the labs and away from that torture room so their rest wasn't interrupted by inconvenient screams.

After a couple of wrong turns, he came to a hallway lined with doors. Nameplates had been slid into aluminum holders, identifying who was inside.

It was neat, functional, and efficient—just like so many of the scientists he'd met here. He bet they never thought that one of the lab rats would be able to slip out at night and go exploring when they were supposed to be fast asleep.

The next nameplate read J. STYNGER. Jackpot.

He turned the handle, hoping to get lucky and find the door unlocked. It wasn't. Of course.

Jake knocked softly. He wasn't sure she'd hear it over the pounding of his heart, but he didn't dare make any more noise.

A bubble of tinted plastic hung from the ceiling at the end of the hall. There was a camera inside, and he was sure he could feel it watching his every move.

Behind the door, he heard a shuffling sound, then the click of a lock sliding free. The door opened a couple of inches.

Jake didn't wait to give her the chance to slam it shut and raise the alarm. He pushed the door open, taking control of her body as he moved forward. She was too shocked to fight him.

He pinned Jordyn's wrists behind her back with one hand and covered her mouth with the other. He kicked the door shut behind him and said in a low voice, "I'm not going to hurt you."

Her pale green eyes were wide with fear, telling him she didn't believe him.

Jake couldn't let himself care about that right now, so he steeled himself and used his body to walk her backward until they were in her bathroom.

He let go of her wrists long enough to turn on the faucet. "Is there a camera in here?" he asked her.

Her mouth moved against his palm as she shook her head.

"Are you going to scream?"

Again, she shook her head.

Jake moved his hand, but kept it close in case she was lying. He'd pinned her hips against the sink with his, preventing her from slipping away.

"I'm sorry," she told him. "I know she's your friend, but I couldn't let Mother do that to you. I had to tell her what she wanted to hear."

"You shouldn't have caved. I'm tough enough to take a little pain."

Jordyn paled until her already-pale skin went nearly

transparent. He could see her veins below the surface, pounding in time with her frantic heartbeat. "You don't know her. You don't know what she would have done. I do."

Jake wasn't going to argue with her about the past. He didn't have time. They needed a plan. "I have to get out of here. Find Rox and warn her."

"I already did."

"What?"

"I used your code and sent her a message. I'm sure she'll think it's you."

"How do you know about the code?"

"The letter you wrote her—the one I mailed with the journal. You wrote it in that code. It wasn't hard to figure out."

Considering he'd been ten when he and Rox had created it, that wasn't hard to believe. "What did you tell her?"

"To burn everything. That people were coming for her."

Jake prayed that was enough to do the job, but knowing Rox, it would only make her more curious. Still, Jordyn had tried, and that was worth something. "Thank you."

Her pale eyes slid to the floor, and she shifted uncomfortably at his gratitude. "I wish I could have done more. She's still in danger. Mother won't stop until she gets what she wants, and if your friend burned the journal as I directed her to, Mother may never believe it's really gone."

"We need to get out of here. Now. Tonight. We'll get help and shut this place down, freeing everyone."

"I can't. I don't like what Mother does, but she has no choice. The end is coming, and we have to be ready."

Jake was stunned silent for a moment. "The end? What are you talking about?"

"The end of the world. The big war." Her statement was casual, as if everyone knew about it.

"I don't know what you're talking about."

She frowned at him as if he were the one not making sense. "They didn't tell you, did they?"

"Who didn't tell me what?"

"The government tries to hide it, but they know the end is coming. That's why we're down here, working so hard every day. If we don't have an army ready, the rest of the world will kill us all. We have to be ready to fight. We can't let all those people be killed."

Things were starting to make a bit more sense now. Jordyn didn't seem the kind of person to ignore the suffering and violation of rights going on around her—unless she thought she had no choice.

"Is that what your mother told you?"

"Yes. Her ways are cruel sometimes, but she's doing what must be done."

"She's lying to you. She's doing these things because she's a heartless bitch."

Jordyn flinched as if he'd hit her.

Jake lowered his voice, searching for patience. If he could convince Jordyn that she was being fed a load of bullshit, she'd help him escape. He knew she would. "Listen. I'm sure the things she's told you are scary as hell, but they're lies. Have your friends ever talked about the end of the world like it's a foregone conclusion?"

"My friends are all down here, working with me and trying to save humanity."

Great. This entire facility was filled with nut-jobs. "What about when you were a kid? Did your teachers ever talk about it?"

"Mother was my teacher."

Of course she was. Nothing like brainwashing a kid from the crib to get her to believe you.

"Then let's get out there and look for the truth. I'll take you to talk to people who can answer your questions."

"You make it sound as though I'm a kid who's confused. I'm not. I've talked to people online—people who know the truth."

Jake barely stifled the urge to roll his eyes. "Of course you can find some idiot online who thinks the end of the world is coming. You can also find idiots online who think the Earth is hollow. That doesn't make it true."

The light in her eyes winked out as if she'd drawn the shutters closed. He felt her pulling away at his insults when what he'd wanted to do was get her to help him.

"You should go," she said. "If they find you here, you won't like what happens."

"They're going to find out. There are too many cameras around for them not to. I'm surprised the cavalry hasn't already come to save you."

"Then you should leave."

"I've already committed the crime. I came here hoping you'd help me and my friends escape."

"I can't. I'm sorry. I've already done everything I can to help your friend. That's all I can offer."

"We need to get out of here."

"I can't go anywhere."

"You can't stay here. Your mother is a fucking monster."

"My place is here. Please try to understand that. I do what I can to . . . mitigate the things Mother does. I have to stay."

He couldn't listen to any more. He grabbed her arms, struggling to keep his grip light enough not to hurt her. He wanted to shake her and knock some sense into her, but he worried that if he made the wrong move, she'd stop listening to him. "Why did you help me mail my journal? You had to know that the authorities would find it and shut this place down. You'll be held as accountable as the rest of them."

"No one will ever find us. We move around. We hide. We've been doing it for years, and no one's ever found us. If I don't stay, who will stop her from doing the truly horrible things?"

"You don't think what she's done so far is horrible?"

Jordyn's gaze slid to the floor. "I've seen worse."

This whole mess had grown far beyond what he'd thought was at stake. Sure, Rox was in trouble, and he and his buddies were in even worse trouble, but it was more than that. If he didn't stop Dr. Stynger, more men would be fooled into coming here. More men would be drugged and tortured—or worse, if Jordyn was to be believed.

Jake couldn't let that happen.

"Just ask yourself this," he said. "What if you're wrong? What if you have a better chance of stopping her from the outside?"

He saw a flicker of indecision cross her face. "I don't. There are too many other locations where they could go, and I know how to find only a few of them."

"Are you sure she's not exaggerating? She holds people against their will. She tortured me, and if I'm not mistaken, you as well. How big a leap is it to think she'd lie, too?"

Jordyn turned her back on him. "You need to go. Now. Or I'm going to raise the alarm."

"Please, just consider what I said. That's all I ask. Just think about it." All he had to do was plant the seeds of doubt in her mind. She was smart. She'd figure the rest out herself.

At least he hoped she would.

"Go!" she commanded .

Jake backed away, feeling defeated. "I'm leaving. In fact I'm leaving this whole place. With or without your help."

Jordyn heard the door to her quarters shut.

Her legs sagged beneath her, going weak. She sank down to the toilet and cradled her head in her hands.

What if he was right? What if Mother was lying? It certainly wouldn't have been the worst thing she'd done.

Then again, what if she wasn't? And what if Jordyn's only chance to help was to stay where she was?

She didn't know what to believe. The one thing she did know was that if she lost what little control she had, countless innocent lives would be destroyed.

There were no simple answers. But she did know for sure

that if Jake was caught roaming the halls, his punishment would be severe.

There wasn't much she could do to help him, but she had to try something. She logged in to the security system and began deleting stored images from the camera feeds as fast as she could.

# Chapter Fifteen

Roxanne woke suddenly. Fear spurted through her system before she had time to register what had caused her to wake. For a moment, she couldn't remember where she was. It was dark and cold.

A noise—that was what had woken her.

"Easy," came Tanner's low, reassuring voice. "It's just me. I'm sorry I woke you."

"It's okay. I'm a light sleeper." The alarm clock said she'd been asleep for only an hour, but now that adrenaline had flooded her body, she wasn't sure she could go back to sleep. Besides, the dreams she'd been having weren't much fun. She kept reliving the episode at the clinic, but this time the nurse was dead, too, and Jake had been in one of the exam rooms, bleeding out onto the floor. Roxanne hadn't been able to save him. He'd died while she watched, begging her to help.

Suffice it to say, she was not enjoying her subconscious's effort to work through her worry, guilt, and fear.

She fumbled to find her bottled water and gulped some down. Her throat ached as she swallowed, and it probably didn't look any better than it felt.

Tanner flipped on the bathroom light, and it cast a yellow glow over the right side of his body. He was shirtless, and his jeans had been unbuttoned, displaying ridges of muscle that angled beneath his low waistband.

She blinked her eyes, letting them adjust to the light. A slow, warm heaviness began to build in her abdomen, driving away some of the lingering effects of her startle.

If she kept staring, she was going to start thinking about their kiss, and if she did that, she was going to embarrass herself by trying to get another. As needy and desperate as she was beginning to feel, she certainly didn't want to *look* like she was needy and desperate. It wasn't at all becoming.

Roxanne threw the covers back so she could get up. Cold air hit her bare legs. "It's freezing in here."

His gaze slid up her legs, and he shoved his hands in his pockets. "Sorry. The air conditioner has only two settings—arctic and off."

"Doesn't matter. We should get moving, anyway."

"There's no rush. No one is at the Edge yet, and you haven't had enough sleep."

"Did you sleep?"

His response was a shrug.

"What does that mean? You did sleep or you didn't?"

"I dozed."

"Why don't you doze some more while I call Payton. He's an early riser. And if he's not up yet, I really don't mind waking him."

"Or I could call Reid. It wouldn't be the first time I woke him up at crazy o'clock."

"We'll call both of them. We need all the help we can get."

"And then we'll go find breakfast."

She smiled at that. Tanner was always hungry. "It's a wonder you're not fat."

"Fast metabolism."

"I can only wish."

"It's really not as great as you might think. We were cut off from our supply lines once, out scouting in a small group. We got pinned down for three days with no food, unable to even move enough to hunt for lizards or anything, and I can tell you that the guy with the fast metabolism is the first one to starve."

The thought of him suffering like that gave her pause. She had never once been in a position where there was no food—not even when she'd been held hostage. Hunger wasn't something she ever had to face. She tried to imagine what it must have been like—how desperate he must have felt.

She reached up and touched the side of his face. "I'm so sorry."

He swallowed and stared down at her mouth. "It's no big deal. But I am really happy to be back in the land of the Big Mac."

"And we're happy to have you home."

She was standing too close. His eyes had dark blue rays jutting out from his pupils, which were swallowed up by black as he continued to stare. The short stubble under her fingers tickled her skin.

She wasn't supposed to touch him. They were keeping their distance now. Staying professional. She didn't fondle the faces of the men she worked with.

With a strenuous force of will, Roxanne stepped back and let her hand fall. She fled and hid in the bathroom, praying her heart would slow and her body would stop trembling.

Tanner O'Connell was a potent package, and she kept being pulled in by him. Knowing what he'd suffered was only going to make it that much harder to keep her hands to herself. Nobility was a prize worth more than gems or precious metals. It couldn't be bought, but it was within her reach, beckoning her to grab hold and never let go.

She shoved aside the ridiculous notion and dialed Payton. He answered on the second ring, his voice clear and alert.

"Good morning, Razor. You're up early."

"Or late, depending on how you look at it. Is Bella back yet?"

"Not for another three days. I'm afraid you're stuck with me."

"I was wondering if you had any manpower you could spare," she said.

"Where are you? Is this about that journal?"

"It is. We're in New Mexico. We've run into some trouble. I need help."

"Of course. You're willing to pay our usual rates, I'm sure."

Payton cared more about profit than any man she knew. Of course, it was because of him that the Edge had the money to cover Bella's expenses. "You know that's not a problem. But I need people I can trust. Tanner wants to call in Reid. I think our best bet is to find a couple of men who can pass as good ol' boys in a small town."

"Gage Dallas fits that profile."

"But he's not much of a talker. I need someone who can chat up the locals and find out if any strangers matching Jake's description have passed through."

"Why not do it yourself?"

"We tried. We ended up in police custody, and I'm not too sure just how friendly local law enforcement is to our cause."

"Were you charged with anything?"

"Not yet. Two medical professionals were attacked. They have Tanner and me on camera going in well after the attack took place. They also have the guy who did it on video. I don't think it will be a problem, or I would have already called my attorney."

"But news spreads fast in a small town. And no one is going to trust you now."

"Exactly," said Roxanne.

"Clay is on call. I'll send him and Gage to meet you. Will that suffice?"

"Add Reid's time onto my bill, too. He'll probably come without getting paid, since he's Tanner's brother, but he shouldn't have to."

"I'm not so sure he'd come. Tanner and Reid aren't exactly close."

"No?"

"No. Not that it's any of my affair."

Which was rich for *I know juicy gossip that I'm not going to tell you.*

"I'll let them sort that out," she said, refusing to get nosy. She was dying to know more about Tanner, even if it wasn't something sterling and noble. She craved information, but she wasn't willing to talk behind his back. If he wanted her to know, he'd tell her. Right after she asked.


Payton breathed deeply, struggling to still his internal panic. His training kept him calm on the outside, but inside, he was boiling with anxiety.

Razor's life was at stake. So were the lives of several others—people he had sworn to protect. But he couldn't stand by and do nothing. He had to know the truth. He had to know if the entries in that journal were the deranged ravings of a lunatic, or solid proof that what he'd felt in his gut was true.

The Threshold Project wasn't dead. It wasn't buried under a mountain of top secret documents—those he hadn't destroyed himself. The research had started again. Maybe it had a different name, and maybe they were using grown men instead of children, but the results were still the same. People were going to die, their lives would be destroyed, their families torn apart.

And what about the original subjects? The List had been destroyed, or so they'd thought, but he still remembered the names of the people he'd hurt.

He couldn't let it happen again.

Sending Gage and Clay helped ease some of his concern. Even with Clay's injuries, he would be an asset. Both men were deadly. Both would protect Razor with their lives. Both of them would know where to look for signs of human experimentation, since they'd both been subjected to the same thing. Neither one remembered, but the knowledge was in them, buried deep and hidden under layers of security.

Maybe something they'd see would strike a chord and they'd find whoever was doing this and stop them fast.

Then again, maybe seeing that same thing would break away some of those layers, leaving them closer to remembering the truth. If that happened, not only would his cover be blown, but chances were neither of them would live through it.

Payton considered going into hiding for one brief, cowardly moment. He had enough money to live out his life in peace. He could find a beach somewhere and be served fruity drinks by busty women until the day he died.

But if he did, what would happen to those kids? They needed him here, watching over them, keeping them safe from themselves. Keeping the world safe from them.

So far, only one of the kids on the List had turned rogue. He'd killed seven women before Payton had found him. Those seven deaths were on Payton's head, like so many others. The only thing he could ever do to make up for all the evil he'd caused was to stay where he was, where he could do the most good, and watch over his kids.

With that in mind, the panic eased, and he lifted the phone from its cradle to call the men.


Nelson Bower stifled the urge to cower as he entered Dr. Stynger's office.

Her head rose from the worn journal and she stared at him in expectation. Her bright red lipstick was the only vivid color in the room, and he found himself staring, unable to look away from her bloodred mouth.

He swallowed his unease and forced himself to speak. "There was an incident last night. One of the subjects got out of his room."

"How is that possible? They all should have been sleeping."

Nelson shrugged. "I don't know how it happened, but I'm dealing with the guard responsible for not stopping it while it was happening."

"Where is the subject now?"

"Training."

"At least he didn't get out of the facility. That would have been unfortunate."

"He doesn't know that we know. I thought you might want to deal with his punishment."

"Which one?"

"Jake Staite," he said, before remembering she didn't care for names. "S-eleven-sixteen."

Dr. Stynger shook her head, bringing attention to just how scrawny her neck really was. It would be so easy to break. Nelson wondered why he feared her as much as he did.

Maybe because he'd seen what she could do with those drugs of hers. He checked every day for needle marks, making sure she wasn't slipping him anything when he slept.

"He's proving to be more difficult than the rest. He's not afraid of pain, and he's not responding fast enough to our protocol."

She'd had him kill the last man who hadn't performed to her expectations, and while he'd do what he must, he didn't relish the idea of snuffing out Jake's life. The man had promise. "Maybe he just needs more time. He fits the profile. It's not like you want a bunch of pansies in your ranks."

"I can't allow him to be destroyed until his diary is back in our possession. We may need him for bait."

"So, what do we do with him? We can't let him run around the halls at night."

"I'll move him to the next phase early."

"I thought you said that was dangerous."

"It can be, but his lack of obedience is even more dangerous—to all of us. The investors are coming, and I can't show any signs of weakness."

"Yes, ma'am." Nelson pulled in a deep breath. "There's one more thing."

Dr. Stynger sighed in impatience. "I'm busy, General. Spit it out."

"Some of the camera footage from last night is gone. Deleted. There is a five-minute block of time during which we weren't able to follow his actions."

"It was Jordyn," she stated, disappointment clear in her tone. "She seems to have a soft spot for the subject."

"What do you want me to do to her?"

"I'm her mother. I'll deal with her myself."


Jake shoved down his food, forcing himself to eat it. He didn't know how long it would stay down, but he had to try to keep his strength.

Moss was paler today and as green around the gills as Jake probably was.

They sat at the breakfast table with Mac, the fourth spot where Evans usually sat glaringly empty. He still hadn't been released from the infirmary, if that was even where he was being held.

Moss told Mac about the tubes they'd discovered and what had happened last night. After Jake had slipped back into their quarters, another man had come through a while later. He'd taken their blood pressure and temperature, and he had removed the T-shirt from the camera.

At least that explained that mystery.

"So, they're drugging us to sleep every night?" asked Mac, keeping his voice low and his mouth full of food to obscure their conversation for anyone who might be watching.

"Looks like it," said Moss. "I don't know how many more nights I can fake sleeping through that."

"I think we should unplug the tubes until we're ready to go. It'll reduce our chances of getting caught."

"And when will that be?" asked Mac. "Evans is still missing. I won't leave without him."

Jake glanced at Moss. His cheeks were more sunken today, and the circles under his eyes were darker. They were running out of time. "What if he's already out?"

"You mean dead, like Greene."

It had crossed his mind. "If we don't act soon, none of us is going to make it out. You know we'll come back for him—bust this whole place wide open and reveal it for what it is."

Mac shook his head. "Whatever happened to 'never leave a fallen man behind'?"

"We don't know if he's fallen. What I do know is that we need to escape so we can come back with reinforcements and free him, too."

"Let me request a visit again. If they won't let me see him, then we'll act."

"Okay. We'll decide on our plan at dinner."

One of the SABER goons came to their table. His biceps bulged against the fabric of his uniform. The red band on his left arm identified him as one of the elite here in the compound. "Jake Staite, come with me."

"Where are you taking me?" asked Jake.

The man said nothing; he simply waited for Jake to obey.

"Tell us where he's going, or he's not going anywhere," said Moss, rising to his feet.

Now was not the time for a confrontation. If Moss got locked in a cell somewhere, getting out of here was going to be much, much harder.

Jake lifted his hands to his friend to ward him away. "I'll be fine."

"You don't know that." Moss didn't say anything about last night's escapades, but his intense gaze spoke volumes. He was worried.

So was Jake. "I'll see you soon," he said, praying it wasn't a lie.

*    *    *

Roxanne and Tanner met the men from the Edge at a motel a few miles away. They pulled up in a huge RV that was plastered with NRA bumper stickers. The one next to the side door read INSURED BY SMITH AND WESSON.

She grinned as she came out to meet them, hopping up into the back of the RV with Tanner right on her heels. "Nice ride, guys."

"We aim to please, little lady," said Clay, tipping his cowboy hat.

He was tall and slim, filling out his jeans better than most men on the planet. His features were a bit gaunt, as if he could use a few extra meals. Roxanne bet there was a line of women ready and willing to provide. All he had to do was ask.

Even so, she'd never seen him with a woman, or heard him talk about dating. She wasn't sure if it was because he was being professional, or if he just didn't date. The latter seemed an impossible notion, but stranger things had happened.

He had two black eyes that brought out the intense amber color of his irises. He sported a fresh cut on his cheek held closed with Steri-Strips, another cut on his lip, and several of his knuckles were bruised and split open.

"What happened to you?" she asked.

"Bar fight. I got into one so I'd blend in, just for you, Razor."

She smiled at him. "I think that's the nicest thing a man's ever done for me."

Tanner shifted a small step closer, and she swore she could feel more than hear a low rumble coming from his chest.

Reid got up from the passenger seat. "If my brother hasn't been treating you right, Razor, just let me know." There was no smile on his face or sign that he was joking. Instead, he gave Tanner a level stare of warning.

The brothers' eyes were exactly the same brilliant blue color, and both men had the same rough, handsome features. Tanner's were leaner and more defined, whereas Reid's were more blunt, but as they stood near each other like this, the family resemblance was unmistakable.

"Of course he's treating me well," she said, looping her fingers over Tanner's arm to solidify her defense. "Stop acting like an overbearing brother. Tanner has been fantastic. He's a great addition to the company."

Reid's gaze fell to where her hand touched Tanner, and his expression tightened. He shook his head in disgust, and Roxanne was sure he had the wrong idea about what had passed between them.

Or maybe he didn't. Maybe he knew they'd kissed, and that was enough to elicit such a look of disapproval.

Roxanne refused to worry about what Reid thought. She had bigger problems.

Gage had been driving. He stood but stayed behind the others, keeping his distance. She could barely see his eyes beneath the shadowed rim of his cowboy hat. They were the same color as the faded denim jeans he wore. A short growth of stubble covered his jaw, adding another layer of unrepentant male onto the total testosterone-laden package. He tipped his hat in greeting, but he said nothing.

"I don't know how to thank you three for coming," she said.

Clay pointed in back to where a small table was bolted to the floor. "Have a seat and fill us in."

While Roxanne had never had need for one of the Edge's Mobile Command Centers—MCCs—she'd been in them before during her training. The space was cramped, stuffed full of computer and communications equipment. It contained a small kitchen and an even smaller bathroom.

She slid into the booth. Tanner squeezed in beside her. His hard body lined up alongside hers, warming her from knee to shoulder. She tried not to squirm and rub herself against him, but the urge to do so was driving her crazy. The only thing that kept her in check was Reid's watchful gaze.

This was so ridiculous. She was a grown woman, not

some infatuated teen. She shouldn't have been so easily excited to simply be this close to a man. Not that he was just any man. He was way beyond the average, filling her sense and raising her awareness whenever he was near.

Clay and Reid crammed their big bodies in the other side of the booth, and Gage stood nearby, his hips propped against the only counter in the tiny kitchen.

"I don't know how much Payton told you, so I'll start from the beginning." She told them about Jake and the journal he'd sent. She explained how he thought he'd been recruited into a legit military unit, but then discovered that he'd been tricked. She included the attacks, as well as the part about the dead doctor and wounded nurse. The only thing she left out was that blistering kiss that still had the power to make her break out in a sweat.

Tanner shifted beside her, as if he were remembering the same thing.

"So all we know is that the person who sent me the e-mail warning was in that town, the same town where the doctor was killed by a man looking for me. The same town where I was attacked in my sleep. Whatever is going on has to be nearby, making me think that Jake is, too."

Reid nodded. "I agree. But there's not a whole lot of anything out here. How do we find him?"

"He said he was in an underground facility of some kind. It could be the basement of a building, or it could be the whole thing is underground."

"They'll be guarding the place," said Clay. "Snipers, surveillance systems, perimeter guards. We could look for those."

"Spiral search pattern? Grid?" asked Gage.

Tanner shook his head. "There's too much ground to cover. Every day that passes is another one that Razor is in danger. We need to find him fast."

"Did he give you any other clues?" asked Reid. "Smells? Sounds? Passing trains, that kind of thing?"

She thought about it. "I can't remember any, but I'll ask

Payton to check the journal again, in case I missed something. I was pretty upset when I read it."

"I'll have Mira pull up some satellite images of the area," said Clay. "Maybe we'll see something that doesn't belong."

"In the meantime," said Tanner, "we'd like you three to go to Dry Valley and snoop around. Avoid law enforcement, since they're a bit twitchy over strangers right now."

"Cover story?" asked Gage.

"You're supposed to meet your hunting buddy for some kind of shooting tournament."

Reid nodded. "That'll work. Do you have a photo of the guy?"

"It's in my purse."

"Let me have that, too. I'll see if Mira can mock up some photos of the four of us. Tanner, we'll need you to stand in for Jake so Mira has a head to cut off."

Tanner smirked. "Whatever you need."


The four men posed in front of the RV-turned-MCC for Roxanne to photograph them.

Tanner could feel his brother waiting for a moment to pounce, and decided it was better to just get it over with than to wonder when he'd strike.

Gage and Clay had gone inside the MCC to work on some details, and Roxanne was on the phone with Payton. Tanner walked around outside to the back of the vehicle to find some privacy, just in case Reid needed to yell. He really didn't want an audience for this.

He hadn't even stopped walking when his brother hit him with, "You slept with her, didn't you?"

Tanner turned around, counting to five before he responded. Reid could make his temper flare like no one else, and it didn't serve the mission, or help Roxanne, for him to give in to the temptation to shout. "I wanted to. I didn't. Don't ask me about it again."

"She's into you. I can tell by the way she looks at you, by

the way she stands closer to you than anyone else. She wants—"

No way was Tanner going to let Roxanne's reputation get called into question. "Maybe she just trusts me. We've been working together. I saved her life. More than once. Maybe you should thank me for that, rather than slinging accusations."

"This wouldn't be the first time your dick hampered your judgment. Remember—"

"Lisa is nothing like Roxanne. And I was sixteen at the time. She didn't want you. Get over it, already."

Reid stepped in close, getting right in Tanner's face. He lowered his voice. "Do you have any idea how close Mom is to losing the house? If you fuck up this job, you'll—"

"I'm not going to fuck anything up. Just back off and treat me like an—"

"Starting acting like an adult and I will."

"What the hell more do you want from me? I quit the military. I came home. I'm working where you want me to work, living where you want me to live, giving Mom nearly my entire paycheck. What more could I possibly do to appease you?"

"You could have taken Dad fishing. *You could have died instead of Brody.*"

The life seemed to drain out of Tanner's body. He went cold and started shaking. How many times had he screamed at himself for not having been the one with Dad that day? He was a better driver than Brody. Maybe he could have avoided the drunk who just had to make that cell call on the highway.

After all, it had been his turn to take Dad on the annual trip. He should have been the one to die, not Brody. And now Millie and Lyle were going to grow up without a father because he'd put his duty to his country over his duty to his family.

"I'm sorry," said Reid, scrubbing his hand over his face. "I shouldn't have said that. I didn't mean it."

"You did. But that's okay. I don't blame you. I know you and Brody were tight."

Reid's eyes teared up, and he blinked fast to keep those tears from falling. "I miss him."

"Me, too."

Reid cleared his throat and wiped his eyes. "We should head back. I don't want to leave all the work to the others."

Tanner nodded, wishing he felt he could safely hug his brother, but he knew better. Reid stayed mad a long time, and now that he knew his brother had thought the same things Tanner had, it was clear that the gap between them wasn't going to shrink anytime soon.

Grief sucked, and Reid had to deal with it in his own way, in his own time, just as Tanner was doing. He just hoped that when his brother was done dealing, the two of them would still be on speaking terms.

He turned to find Roxanne standing there, looking stunned.

"This is a private conversation, Razor," said Reid.

Her face turned pink. "Sorry. I didn't mean to eavesdrop." She turned and fled, slipping into her motel room.

"Well, shit," muttered Reid as he stalked off. Tanner stood there watching both of them walk away. He couldn't bring himself to follow either of them. He couldn't take Reid's anger, and he couldn't face Razor with the weight of his guilt crushing him.

He stayed outside and shoved his damn emotions into a box so he could do what he needed to do. He'd deal with his baggage later—much, much later.

Roxanne leaned against the motel door, letting the cool air wash over her. She hadn't meant to overhear Tanner's conversation with his brother, but now that she had, she couldn't get the image out of her head.

Reid had apologized for his remark, but she'd seen what it had done to Tanner. There was so much guilt between them, so much anger and grief.

She ached to go after Tanner and hug him. Not that he'd want that from her. He had his pride, and she didn't want to take that from him—not on top of everything else he'd suffered.

Roxanne briefly considered having a talk with Reid. What he'd said was way out of line, even for a grieving man. Then again, what kind of anger would spew from her mouth if something happened to Jake?

All she would do was make things worse if she interfered, so she'd keep her mouth shut and leave their family problems to people in their family.

She had enough problems of her own to worry about.

# Chapter Sixteen

Gage, Clay, and Reid had spent the rest of the day poking around Dry Valley while Tanner and Roxanne stayed behind in the RV. Used as a mobile command center, the vehicle was equipped with all the communications equipment they'd need to talk to both the men on the ground, as well as staying in touch with Mira back in Dallas.

Tanner turned off the microphones that transmitted to the receivers in the men's ears so they wouldn't be distracted by any chatter back in the MCC. He and Roxanne could hear the men talk, but little else could be heard through the earpieces.

Roxanne's head drooped into her hands, and she seemed to wilt in defeat. "No one seems to know anything."

"Give them time. It's a small town. Someone will have seen something."

"What if Jake was never there?"

"Have a little faith. Reid's good at his job."

She was only two feet away. The cramped confines of the RV practically had them sitting in each other's laps. Not that he would have minded having Roxanne on his lap.

That was the problem.

He could smell her skin and the herbal shampoo she'd used. It reminded him all too much about last night and how far he'd let things go before putting on the brakes.

He could have let things go further. He could be sitting here right now, knowing exactly how she sounded when she climaxed. His curiosity and his regret at not taking what she'd so willingly offered were driving him mad.

Sure, he still had his honor, but right now, with her sitting so close, suffering, all he really wanted was to pull her in his arms and make them both forget everything else.

*You could have died instead of Brody.*

He'd never forget the look of devastation on his brother's face as he'd uttered those words. Reid had claimed he hadn't meant it, but Tanner knew otherwise.

Roxanne sniffed, pulling him out of his bleak thoughts. Her face was hidden, and he had the distinct impression she was crying.

"You okay?" he asked, his voice tight with his own emotional baggage.

She sucked in a long, deep breath and plastered a too-bright smile on her face as she looked up. "Yeah. Just frustrated."

"We'll find him," said Tanner.

"Or we could let them find us."

"What do you mean?"

"You said yourself that they weren't trying to kill me. The man who broke into my room probably wanted to take me to wherever they're hiding Jake. Maybe I should let them do it."

Just the thought of her putting herself into that kind of danger made outrage and anger swell inside him. "I won't let you do that," he growled.

One of her blond eyebrows lifted in challenge. "You won't *let* me? Did you seriously just say that?"

"You heard me. It's stupid and risky. You have no idea what would happen to you if you put yourself in their hands; nor do you know if it would even help us find Jake. Or that you'd live through it."

"True, but I also know it's my call. Not yours."

No. Tanner couldn't let it happen. If he had to knock her

out and sling her over his shoulder like a caveman and lock
her in a room at the Edge until Bella could talk some sense
into her, he would. Even if it meant she never spoke to him
again. "Don't push me on this, Razor. You won't like what
happens."

"I'm not going to push you at all. I'm simply going to do
what I see fit. With or without your approval."

This was getting them nowhere fast. He couldn't put
himself at odds with her and still expect her to trust him.
And he needed her to trust him—at least enough to keep
him in the loop on what she planned to do.

If she was foolish enough to walk willingly into a trap, he
had to at least be there when it sprang.

It was time to use diplomacy. "We need to give the men
more time."

"They've been in town all day. How many more days do
you think Jake has?"

"He's tough and well trained. He'll survive until we find
him."

Reid's voice came over the speakers. "The VFW was a
bust. No one there's seen him, and we nearly didn't escape
the gravitational well of conversation. I've never heard men
talk more than those old-timers."

Tanner flipped the microphone on as he watched Roxanne's reaction to the news. "Did they say anything of use?"

"Nothing much," said Clay. "They've seen a few strangers around town, but that's not much to go on in a town so
close to a major highway."

Reid spoke again. "One of them is convinced there's
something strange going on southwest of here. Of course, he
thinks it's aliens, so I'm not sure how valid his claims are."

"He wasn't lying," said Gage, his low, quiet voice rough
with disuse.

"I'm sure he believes every word he says," said Reid.
"That doesn't make it true."

Roxanne's body seemed to sag in defeat. Tanner placed
a reassuring hand above her knee, realizing his mistake too

late. The slender strength of her thigh beneath his palm made him want to stroke higher, or to delve beneath the fabric of her jeans so he could feel her bare skin. He remembered how soft she'd been, how fast she'd responded to his touch. He remembered all the little sounds she'd made, and how her mouth had moved against his.

Desire hit him hard and fast, making sweat break out along his spine. His hand tingled and heat slid up his body as his cock hardened painfully against his fly.

Tanner shifted in his seat, trying to ease the ache, but all it did was make him look twitchy.

"We've got one more place to hit," said Clay. "There's a bar on the north side of town that is apparently the one and only source of nightlife in this area. We'll go there and see what we can dig up."

"Do you want us to come get you?" asked Roxanne.

"No. Stay put. We're going to walk over. It's not that far. We'll see you in a bit."

Tanner flipped the switch controlling the microphone and turned down the volume on the speakers. He didn't want Roxanne hearing them talk about anything that might upset her more.

"It's going to be another dead end," she said. Defeat rang hollow in her voice, and a hint of grieving made her eyes glisten with tears.

She was spiraling down fast, losing hope. Hopeless people were desperate people, and Tanner couldn't let her become desperate. She'd do something foolish and get herself killed.

"Stop it," he ordered her. "We are going to find him. We are going to save him. And if you can't stay positive, then you need to go back to the Edge and let me finish the job without you."

That got her spine straightened out. She shot up from her chair, fury darkening her cheeks. Her blond hair framed her face, and the waning sunlight flowing through the pale curtain over the window made it glow like a fiery halo.

She loomed over him, shoving her finger hard against his chest. "If you think I'm backing off, you've lost your mind. This is *my* mission. *My* friend. We'll do things *my* way."

Roxanne looked like some kind of ferocious goddess in her anger. She radiated power, and her possessive talk only served to heighten the lust Tanner kept trying to fight off. Her lips were pulled back in a feral snarl, and all he could think about was kissing them again.

He stood, crowding her in the small space. The fact that she had to look up to him did nothing to diminish her ire. She was still radiating the power of her fear, worry, and determination with every beat of her heart.

Tanner took the hand she'd jammed against his chest and flattened her fingers with his palm until they were splayed over his heart. His body was buzzing with energy, his blood pounding hot and hard through his veins. He could no longer hear the men chatting over the sound of his own pulse.

Her fingers curled slightly, digging into his muscles.

He stepped closer, closing the space between them and holding her elbow so she couldn't easily back up. Not that there was anywhere to go. "As long as doing things your way doesn't get us killed, I'm game."

"Do you think I don't know what I'm doing? That I don't know how to run a mission?"

"No, I think you're emotionally compromised. I think you're understandably upset."

She blinked and spoke in a whisper. "I can't lose him, Tanner. He's all the family I have left."

His heart squeezed, shoving out a wave of grief for his brother and dad. He'd lost so much, but not nearly as much as Roxanne had. He didn't know how long it would be until he could think of them without pain. Right now, that kind of miracle seemed impossible. He wasn't sure how she'd made it through her grief alone. At least Tanner and the rest of his family had one another to work through their loss. "You're not going to lose him. I won't let it happen."

One side of her mouth lifted in a half smile. "I almost believe you."

"That's because I'm right. I'm not going to make you go through the kind of grief Reid and I've had to suffer."

She closed the remaining few inches between them and laid her head on his shoulder. Her arm snaked around his waist, and she gave him a tight hug. "I'm so sorry you lost them. I can only imagine how hard it must be for you to keep going every day."

It was easier with her around. He didn't understand why that was—whether she distracted him or kept him busy enough that he didn't have time to think about it, or if there was simply something magical about her that drove away all the bad stuff. Either way, he was grateful for the bubble of comfort she provided.

Tanner wrapped his arms around her and hugged her back. He didn't want her to pull away just yet, so he cupped the back of her head to hold her in place while he steadied his pounding heart.

His whole body rejoiced at her nearness, his skin heating and tingling wherever she touched. Her scent filled his head, shoving out all rational thought. He knew he shouldn't be this close to her; he just couldn't remember or care why.

Her fingers stroked his chest. Her breath tickled his neck. Her breasts cushioned his ribs as his breathing sped up.

He felt her head shift slightly, rubbing his fingertips against her scalp. A second later, her lips brushed his neck, the touch so light he wasn't even sure it had really happened. She probably hadn't meant to do it. It was just an accident created by the ill-timed movements of their breathing.

Tanner held his breath, praying for a repeat of the accident. His body was rigid, his muscles tense.

Nothing happened—no more strokes of her mouth on his skin.

Disappointment roared inside him, and only then did he

realize how much he had wanted her touch. He knew he shouldn't, but the why seemed inconsequential in the face of so much need. He could never want something that was bad for him as much as he wanted Roxanne.

She pulled her head away, and he had to fight the urge to force her to stay right where she was. He liked her here, plastered against him, close enough he could feel her breathing and know she was safe. But in the end, he couldn't hold her captive, so he moved his hand, letting her silky hair slide between his fingers.

Instead of stepping away as he'd expected, Roxanne tilted her head back and looked at him. Her eyes had darkened to a rich hammered bronze, and her glossy lips were parted in invitation. Her gaze scoured his face, but she said nothing. She simply looked at him with some kind of longing he couldn't translate. Was it for him? For Jake's return? He couldn't tell, so he kept staring, trying to puzzle it out.

What if she did want him? They'd already decided that their being together was a bad idea. But right now, that decision seemed like the mistake.

Tanner didn't dare move. He felt trapped between what he wanted and what he knew was right. His noble intentions were swiftly fading as each second ticked by.

She licked her lips, drawing attention to her glossy mouth. He gritted his teeth until his molars ached from the force of his restraint.

"I want to kiss you," she admitted, "but I promised myself I wouldn't make a move on you again."

He thought that was a seriously fucked-up idea. "Why?"

"You made it clear you didn't want me."

"Never. I've wanted you from the moment I saw you."

A slight smile curved one side of her mouth, and that crooked smile nearly drove him to his knees. If it hadn't been for the fact that he'd take her down, he wouldn't have been able to find the strength to stay standing. "Maybe. But you're trying to be good. Do the right thing. Unfortunately, my impulse control isn't so well developed. If you don't let me go, I'm afraid I'm going to ruin all those good intentions of yours."

That sounded like a fine idea to him. Who needed good intentions when he had Roxanne in his arms, sweet and eager?

He couldn't shed the heat building inside him. His breathing sped and his heart was struggling to cool his blood, but it wasn't working.

She was so fucking pretty. So soft. And her mouth was begging for his. She didn't know he'd killed his brother. She looked at him like he was a hero, not a failure, and he liked it. She made him forget all the bad stuff. When he looked at her, his whole world shimmered with warmth.

Warning bells were gonging in his head, but he didn't give a shit. He knew it was against the rules to get involved with her, but they could be careful. No one would have to know. After the hell he'd been through, he deserved something good in his life. Didn't he?

She seemed to think so, and right now, that was enough for him.

Tanner lowered his head until their mouths met. He felt the moist slide of her lip gloss as she opened to his kiss. Her whole body seemed to melt in his arms, and she let out a soft, womanly sigh of pleasure.

Her arms tightened around his neck as her kisses became more greedy and desperate. His tongue swept inside her mouth, and, instantly, her taste filled his head, shoving all rational thoughts away. She was so sweet, like vanilla. They moved perfectly together, anticipating the motions of the other as they struggled to get closer.

The MCC was cramped, with barely any room to move, but he had to find enough space to feel what he'd denied himself last night.

Tanner put his hands on her ass and lifted her from the floor. She wrapped her legs around his hips as he carried her back to the small kitchen. All the windows were covered. The doors were locked. No one could see in. They were alone, and no one was going to stop him from taking what she wanted to give.

He set her down on top of the table and started kissing his way south. She flung her head back, baring her slender neck to his mouth.

Bruises lined her throat. A dark, feral rage bubbled inside him, and he had to tamp it down for fear of scaring her. Instead of going hunting for the asshole who'd hurt her, he gently kissed each one of those bruises, silently willing away her pain—not that she seemed to be feeling any pain now.

She was breathing hard. Her face was flushed. Her fingers were working the buttons on her shirt, undoing them to make way for him. He loved it that she wasn't at all shy, but threw herself into the moment with abandon. A woman like that went straight to a man's head.

As soon as the buttons were free, she stripped the shirt off and tossed it behind her. Between kisses, he caught a glimpse of her white lace bra and the way it lifted her breasts toward him, as if offering him a treat.

Tanner groaned at the sight. He stared down and traced one finger along the edge of the lace, watching as her nipples beaded up against the thin fabric. She shivered at his touch. He slid his finger beneath the strap and eased it down over her shoulder.

His mouth followed in the bra's wake as he dragged the lace across her nipple, baring her breast completely. As much as he wanted to move slowly, her noises of encouragement were driving him on, spurring him to take more and more.

He palmed her breast, lifting it to his watering mouth. Her skin was so soft here, so smooth and feminine. She fit in his hand just right, making him wonder how well the rest of them would fit. The thought drove him wild, and he covered her nipple with his mouth, licking and sucking to see what she liked best.

The scent of her skin filled his head, mixed with a heady dose of arousal. He'd been with her like this only twice, but he knew without a doubt that he'd always remember the way she smelled right now, so sweet and hungry for him.

He sucked harder, drawing a low moan of pleasure from her mouth. She hooked her ankles around his hips and pulled him closer, until he was settled between her thighs, feeling the heat of her mound sinking through their clothing.

His cock surged toward her, eager to be free of all the fabric. He wanted to feel her naked skin, slick from her arousal, sliding against him.

Her hands gripped his shirt, tugging it up. He let go of her nipple long enough to strip out of the garment, then bared her other breast to his mouth. Her eager noises of appreciation told him she liked what he was doing. No way was he stopping now.

Roxanne's fingers moved between them, stroking his erection through his jeans.

Lights exploded behind his eyes, and he had to dig deep for the self-control it took to stop himself from losing it right there. He hadn't been with a woman in months—too long for him to have the kind of patience he needed to play it cool. He was running hot, dying for more of her, while drowning in what he'd already experienced. She overwhelmed him, filling his senses and stimulating him to the point of insanity.

"I need you," she whispered as her fingers tugged at the waistband of his jeans. The button popped open easily. The zipper slid down. A second later, her silky fingers were on him, stroking down his cock.

He groaned at her breast, and her hand tightened.

"Now, Tanner." There was no hesitation in her voice. No question. Just the demanding confidence of a woman who knew what she wanted.

Tanner thanked God that he was the object of that want. He wasn't going to fuck it up by losing control before he'd had the chance to give her what she needed.

He tugged her hand from his pants and pushed her back

until she was lying on the table. It was bolted to the floor, nice and secure. He could drive hard and deep inside her and not worry about any furniture malfunctions.

He wasted no time undoing her jeans. He slid them and her panties from her slim legs, knocking her shoes off as he went. His hands were poised at his waistband, ready to shuck his own jeans, when he caught sight of her. His whole world went still.

Muted sunshine from the setting sun flowed in through the RV's curtains, casting golden swaths of light across her skin. Slender muscles lent a feminine strength to her body that left him speechless. Strong but delicate, she was a woman to be cherished for her rareness. And she wanted *him*.

Tanner couldn't stop himself from touching her. He splayed his hand across her stomach, feeling the muscles beneath his palm flutter in reaction to his touch. Goose bumps rose on her skin. Her nipples were red and puckered from his mouth, and a pink flush spread out over her chest and shoulders.

His hand slid down, reveling in the feel of her skin against his. What little hair she had covering her mound was dark blond, and with her legs wrapped around him like this, she couldn't hide the shiny proof of her arousal.

He cupped her there, feeling her wet heat against the heel of his hand. His fingers slid between her labia until he found her engorged clit. He barely brushed it, but the touch was enough to make her arch her back off the table and suck in a breath.

She was so responsive, so sensitive. He couldn't help but do it again and watch as her lips parted on a heavy sigh.

She looked up at him, her golden eyes half-lidded and luminous with desire. He'd never had a woman look at him like that before—with such utter need. "Now, Tanner. Please."

He couldn't deny her—not when she looked at him like that. He wanted to give her the world.

Tanner shucked his jeans, and the condom from his pocket went on in seconds.

She sat up, looped her arms around his neck, and kissed him as if he were the only man on Earth. He lifted her up enough to align their bodies and then let her sink down. The moment her tight heat slid around the head of his cock, he was lost.

Her sweet sigh of pleasure reassured him even as it drove him further out of control. Sharp fingernails bit into his shoulders, setting his nerve endings ablaze. His entire spine was on fire as he laid her down on the table and set a hard, fast pace.

He didn't want this to end, but he wasn't going to last long, not with her mouth on his, and her sexy little cries filling his ears. His usual stamina was AWOL.

Tanner forced himself to slow the pace and stood upright. She tried to follow him, but he pressed one hand between her breasts, pinning her to the table.

Roxanne opened her mouth to say something, but he didn't want to talk—not now, not when he was so close to the edge. Words were beyond him.

He covered her lips with his finger. She sucked it into her mouth and gave him the most wicked, knowing stare.

A wave of lust hit him so hard, his heart nearly exploded from the pressure. Sweat cooled his back. He grabbed her hips and pulled them to the edge of the table, which drove his cock deep inside her, locking them together.

She gasped, and her eyes fluttered closed in pleasure. Her body went languid as her arms sprawled over her head and her back arched. She made one slow, undulating rotation of her hips, which Tanner felt all the way to his toes.

He wasn't going to survive this. She was going to kill him with pleasure.

He couldn't bring himself to care what happened to him, so long as he got to hear her climax, to feel her pulse around him as he sent her spinning.

Roxanne tugged at her nipples while he thrust inside her. She kept her gaze fixed on him, telling him she wasn't thinking about anyone else—just him.

Her sexy show turned him on, and he took mental notes, watching how she pleasured herself so that he could do it the way she liked next time.

If there was a next time.

The unwelcome thought was cast aside. It had no place between them—not now.

A searing wave of sensation trickled down his spine, and he stopped midstroke, waiting for it to pass. Roxanne apparently wasn't willing to be patient. Her hips bucked and her breathing sped until she was panting. She grabbed his arms and held on tight while she ground herself against him.

A dark red flush and a light sheen of perspiration covered her chest and face. Her nipples stood at attention. He had to taste them again.

Tanner leaned over her, gathering her in his arms to bring her close. The heat of her skin amplified his own until he was sure he'd combust on the spot. The need to come coiled inside him, shoving him higher with every stroke of their bodies.

He licked her nipple, tasting the salt of her skin and smelling her rising desire. She let out as sharp whimper and dug her fingernails into his scalp. He felt the first fluttering contractions around his cock and heard her pull in a deep breath.

She let it out in a harsh cry of pleasure, her body thrashing against his as she climaxed.

His body's reaction was immediate and violent. A searing wave of sensation exploded through his body, blinding him with the force of it. He roared in response, unable to control the hard, frantic thrust of his hips against hers as he came. The power of his orgasm choked the breath from his body as his semen pumped from his cock in time with the pulses of her climax.

If he hadn't been in such good shape, sex with Roxanne probably would have killed him. As it was, it left him sprawled on the floor of the MCC, gasping for breath. She was on top of him, limp and boneless. Small aftershocks shook her body and fluttered around his cock.

He was still inside her, and in no hurry to leave, but that wasn't safe for her. Condoms could leak, though he was still hard enough that the thing was on tight. Rather than risk it, he disengaged their bodies and settled her against his chest.

Slowly, their breathing returned to normal, and their skin cooled. He stroked her hair, floating in the calm after the storm.

Roxanne pushed herself up and hovered over him. Her hair was a mess and her makeup was smudged. There was a bit of beard burn on her chin and even more on her breasts.

He was going to have to shave before he made her come again.

The thought gave him pause. There were no guarantees of a repeat performance. And while what they'd done was perfectly legal, it was against company policy.

Her golden eyes scoured his face. "You're already regretting it, aren't you?"

Regret was not the right word. He could never regret something as perfect and explosive as what they'd just shared. But his family had to come first for once. And right now, his family needed him to keep this job.

"We both know the two of us will never be more than a good time in the sack. Now that we've gotten the lust out of our systems, we'll be able to focus on getting Jake home."

She flinched, but covered it quickly. "You're right," she said as she pushed herself to her feet and turned her back. "The itch is scratched. Time to move on."

That wasn't exactly what he'd meant, but the reality was the same. He just wished the thought of never holding her again didn't bother him half as much as it did.


Roxanne gathered her clothes and hid in the minuscule bathroom to dress.

She felt discarded. Not used—she'd wanted Tanner as much as he'd wanted her, maybe more—but she'd been set aside. Dismissed.

Not that she blamed him for being curt. He'd been clear to her from the start that he didn't want to mix business with pleasure. She'd all but thrown herself at him, and she had gotten exactly what she deserved.

Along with the most mind-blowing orgasm of her life. Her head was still swimming, and she was sure her pulse would never again return to normal.

All in all, the risk had been worth the reward. She was satisfied, and her curiosity was appeased.

The problem was, now that she knew what it was like to be with Tanner, there was no doubt in her mind she'd want more.

Oh, well. It wouldn't be the first thing in her life she'd wanted and not been able to have. Despite her wealth, that list was too long to count. The important things in life couldn't be purchased with any amount of money.

She guessed that meant she wasn't all that important. She'd been worth only three percent to her own flesh and blood. Her own parents hadn't been willing to pay a penny more for her safe return, and because of them, she was literally scarred for life.

Shame burned her cheeks. She checked the mirror and did her best to repair her hair and makeup. There were obvious signs of their tryst: her swollen lips, a red mark on her chin where his stubble had rubbed her as they'd kissed, and a hickey on her neck that could possibly be mistaken for one more bruise. But the real sign was in her eyes. They seemed darker, as if the knowledge of what she'd lost before she could ever really have it lurked there for everyone to see.

She wasn't going to let anyone, including herself, feel sorry for her. If her eyes were too expressive, she'd buy a pair of fucking sunglasses. It was time to get over her own personal drama and focus on Jake. He was out there, he needed her, and she was going to tear down heaven and earth to find him.

# Chapter Seventeen

The hair on the back of Clay's neck stood on end. Someone was watching him, and it wasn't the sweet young blonde with the perky tits that was setting off his radar.

Reid was at the pool table, chatting up a couple of divorcées. Gage was playing poker at a table in the back room. Clay sat at the bar, nursing a beer and making nice with the bartender. He waited until the bartender was busy at the other end of the bar before he spoke. "I think we have company."

"Fold," said Gage.

"Eight ball, corner pocket. Then I have to go," said Reid to the ladies.

A burly man in his early twenties sat down on the stool next to Clay. His back was straight, and he moved like a man who knew his way around a fight. His wide jaw was clean-shaven, and his hair was military short. He wore a T-shirt and jeans, but rather than the ubiquitous cowboy boots the rest of the town wore, this man had combat boots on his big feet.

"I hear you're looking for a friend," said the man.

"That's right. Our buddy Jake. Have you seen him?"

The man looked around before responding. "Maybe. What's he look like?"

Clay pulled a photo from his shirt pocket and slid it across the polished wood. "Seen him?"

"Yeah. Maybe a week ago. He was sick."

"What's your name?" asked Clay.

"Hemmer."

Clay held his hand out to the man. "Good to meet you, Hemmer. I'm Clay."

Hemmer nearly crushed the bones in Clay's hand, but Clay had the distinct impression that he hadn't meant to do it. There was no look of challenge in his eyes, no hint of insecurity. In fact, there was nothing in Hemmer's dark eyes at all. He looked . . . empty.

A flash of memory slammed into Clay, making his brain spin. There was an older man in a white room. Clay knew him. Trusted him. A kid sat on the edge of a narrow bed, staring off into space with that same blank look Hemmer wore.

It was then that Clay realized he was a kid, too. The man in front of him had done that to the boy. He'd turned him into a doll—he could move and talk, but there was nothing inside anymore.

And the man wanted to do it to Clay, too.

Reality whirled back around and caught him hard. He gripped the edge of the bar to keep from toppling off his stool. His sore shoulder burned with the strain. Sweat beaded up along his brow, and he was sure he was going to puke up his beer all over the floor.

From the corner of his eye, he saw Gage stand from the poker table and start toward him. "Hang on. I'm coming."

Reid extracted himself from the ladies and headed his way, too.

Clay swallowed and cleared his throat. "Whew. One too many, I guess."

"That stuff isn't good for you."

*No shit, Sherlock.* "So, where did you see Jake?"

"An abandoned ranch outside of town."

"What the hell was he doing there?"

Hemmer shrugged. "Didn't ask."

Reid had walked up during the last exchange. "What were you doing there?"

"A woman."

A flimsy story made even thinner by the lack of lust or gloating in his voice.

Gage took the stool on the other side of Hemmer—the one nearer the exit.

"Can you tell us how to get there?" asked Reid.

"I can show you."

Of course he could. "Lead the way."

"I'm going to stay for another round. I'll catch up with you later," said Reid. Once Clay and Gage were out of earshot, Reid's voice came through his comm unit. "It's a trap."

Clay waited for Hemmer to pass through the exit before he turned back to look at Reid. "I know, but it's the best lead we've got."


Tanner had just pulled up his jeans when he heard his brother's angry voice echoing over the speakers. "Tanner! *Fuck.* Where are you?"

He scrambled to the communications station and flipped on the microphone. "I'm here. What's up?"

"Where the hell have you been?" Reid sounded out of breath.

No way was Tanner going to tell his brother that he'd lost his mind and had sex with Roxanne. "What's going on?"

"Clay and Gage are walking into some kind of trap. We need backup. Now, before I lose them."

"Where are you?"

"Outside the bar. Heading north. On foot."

Roxanne came out of the bathroom in time to hear Reid. Without hesitation, she slipped into the chair and started flipping switches. One of the monitors came on and displayed a map. Red dots glowed on the map, and next to each one was a numerical ID.

She looked up at Tanner. "Drive." Into the microphone, she said, "We're coming for you, Reid. I see your location. Clay's and Gage's, too. They're wearing their tags."

Tanner got behind the wheel and started the engine. The sun was down, and the sky was a brilliant display of pinks and oranges. He gunned the engine, driving as fast as he dared in something so unwieldy.

"Left up ahead," said Roxanne. "Seventh Street."

Tanner turned, following her directions. "How did you find them?"

"Mira put trackers in our ID tags. They don't work over long distances, but there's a receiver here that can track them."

They'd looked like normal dog tags to him, except for the information displayed. Instead of his name stamped into the metal, there was a bar code—one he hadn't been able to see until Mira showed him the tag under UV light. To the naked eye, the thing looked like just a blank tag. And even if someone did find the bar code on the tag, she said they'd have to be able to cross-reference that ID with a secure database in order to find out any personal information.

At the time, Tanner had thought her measures had been overkill. Now he wasn't so sure.

Roxanne came to the front. "Right two blocks ahead and you should see him."

He took a hard right and saw his brother running up ahead. They pulled over, and Reid hopped inside. He was sweating, and his chest surged with each speedy breath. "They're in a black SUV."

"Are you okay?" asked Roxanne.

"Fine, Razor. Just follow them. Something's up."

"Sure thing. I'll go monitor the map."

"Why did they go if they knew it was a trap?" asked Tanner.

Reid angled the vent toward his face, so Tanner turned up the fan to help him cool off. "It was the first lead we'd had all day. I'm sure they figured it was our only shot at finding Jake."

"They've hit the highway," said Roxanne. "We're going to lose them if we don't pick up the pace."

Tanner gunned the engine. "Which way?"

"West."

He could feel Reid's glare hitting the side of his face. He didn't have to look to know his brother was pissed. "Where the hell were you?"

"Here. We never left the MCC."

"You also weren't monitoring comms. Were the two of you—"

"I'm not going to talk about this with you."

"Fuck," spat Reid. "You did it, didn't you? After all my warnings, after all I went through to get you this job, you went and broke the rules your first week out."

"I'm not going to talk about it. What I do is my—"

"It's my business, too. I put my reputation on the line for you. I promised Bella you'd be a good addition to the team. I can't believe you went and fucked—"

Rage rose up inside Tanner's chest, making his voice right. "Stop right there. You can bitch at me all you want later, but not now. Focus on the job."

"I lost them," said Roxanne. "The signal faded."

Reid scrubbed his face with his hands but fell silent.

Tanner took the entrance ramp toward the west and began a steady acceleration. "This beast won't go much faster."

"I'll keep looking. Maybe we'll pick up something."

"Call Mira," said Tanner. "If she has trackers in our tags, chances are she has them on our phones, too."

Reid pulled his phone from his pocket. "I'll do it."

"Never mind. They're back again," Roxanne called out. "Take the next exit."

It was flat out here, and the lumbering MCC was going to be easy to spot. "I don't want to get too close."

"They're still moving, but the speeds are slow. Maybe they're looking for something."

"Or on a gravel road. There's nothing out here."

Tanner took the next exit and stopped at the end of the ramp.

"Left," said Roxanne. "But go slow. They're not far. Less than half a mile."

He turned off the headlights. The sun had set, but it wasn't completely dark yet. There was just enough gray light left in the western sky to allow him to see. But that wasn't going to last long, and there were no streetlights out this far. He couldn't even see a single security light on a house or barn. It was just a wide stretch of blackness.

After a few more minutes, Roxanne said, "They stopped."

"How far?"

"Quarter mile to our east."

"We should go in on foot," said Reid.

Tanner turned the MCC around in case they needed to get out fast and pulled it off the road. He didn't dare go far for fear the vehicle could get stuck in the ravine running alongside the gravel road.

Roxanne was in the back, digging through cabinets. A small pile of gear sat on the table where he'd taken her only a short while ago.

He couldn't regret it—not something as mind-shattering as what they'd shared. But he did regret what that decision was going to do to his life. Reid was furious. Bella was going to fire him and maybe Roxanne, too. His mom was going to be so disappointed.

For a moment, he considered going back into the service. Life there made sense to him. He had a job, a purpose. And he was damn good at it. Here, in the civilian world, things were much more complicated and messy.

"There are only two pairs of NVGs," said Roxanne.

Before Tanner could think through the consequences of his words, he said, "You should stay here where it's safer."

Her face darkened, and her eyes blazed with fury. Heedless of Reid's attention, she shoved Tanner back against the wall, her finger hard against his chest. Her voice was low, but the anger vibrating through her tone was unmistakable. "If you think you're going to start telling me what to do just because I had your dick in me, think again."

"I'll stay," said Reid, his voice cold. "Mira sent me satellite images of the area. I can guide you."

Tanner gave his brother a look of silent thanks. Reid could have made the situation worse, but instead had chosen to defuse it. Tanner had no idea why.

"Fine," snapped Roxanne. "We leave as soon as you're geared up. I'll be waiting." She grabbed a few items from the table, snatched up her go-bag, and stomped out the door.

"This is why Bella has a policy," said Reid.

"Thanks for stepping in. I saw things spiraling out of control there for a second."

Reid stared at him for a long moment. "If ever there was a woman worth breaking the rules for, Razor would be her."

Jealousy fluttered through Tanner before he could control it. "Do you have a thing for her?"

"No, I just get it. That's all. You're a fucking bonehead for screwing her, but I get why you would want to."

Tanner strapped on a tactical vest. "It won't happen again."

Reid grunted. "Not if you keep opening your mouth, it won't. Of course, if Bella fires you, there would be no reason not to pursue Razor for real."

The thought stopped him cold. His hands froze on the NVGs.

He wanted her. Even now, after having been with her so recently, he was ready for another round. He liked her. As angry as she was now, it would pass. What remained was a dedicated woman who would stop at nothing to see her friend safe, a woman who cared for others and put their needs above her own.

But could there be more between them than chemistry?

He'd never been with the same woman for very long. Maybe he wasn't capable of that type of relationship. And if he wasn't, he sure as hell didn't want to find out and hurt Roxanne in the bargain. Then again, maybe his caring about her enough to protect her from that meant there could be something more between them.

"She's waiting," said Reid. "Get your shit together and get out there."

Tanner was emotionally stunted. That was the only explanation for why he was standing around like an idiot at the very thought of a relationship. It would be best if he just stuck to business and kept his dick in his pants for the rest of this mission. After that, he'd have plenty of time to wallow in his own emotional immaturity while he searched for a new job.

The tactical gear felt good on his body. Right. This was the world that made sense to him. The only thing missing was his rifle. The one he had now would do the job, but it wasn't his. He didn't know its quirks. It hadn't saved his life.

Tanner slid the earpiece in place and went outside. Roxanne was strapped in, ready to go. Her pale hair was pulled back, covered by a clinging knit cap. She'd smeared greasepaint on her face and changed out her leather sandals for a sturdy pair of boots.

The transformation was amazing. Gone was the classy socialite, and standing in front of him was a warrior. Part of him was shocked at the change, but mostly he was turned on. He'd always loved strong women, and she was looking like the stuff of fantasies. "Wow. You look . . . different."

"Save it. Come here." She rubbed her finger in some black paint and smoothed it across his skin.

As platonic as the touch was, he still felt it to the soles of his feet.

He hadn't had enough of her—not yet. Not even close. Even though he'd told himself he wouldn't touch her again, part of his mind was already searching for a way to seduce her. It didn't matter that he knew better. The only thing that mattered was the list of things he still wanted to do with her, to her.

"There," she said, stepping back to admire her work. "That should do it. You ready?"

He nodded, not trusting his voice.

"Reid, can you hear us?" she asked.

"Affirmative."

"Good. We're moving in now."

Tanner didn't dare ask her if he could go first; he simply moved out, setting a pace she'd have a hard time outdoing. They followed the gravel road up a slight rise. Heat rose from the crushed rock under their feet, bringing with it the scent of dust and sunshine.

"You should be close," came Reid's voice in his ear.

Tanner stopped to survey the area. He kept his voice quiet. "There's a building ahead. Looks like an old barn."

Roxanne stopped next to him. "I see one man on the south wall."

"We'll skirt around and get another view from the back."

"I'm not hearing anything through Gage's and Clay's comms," said Reid. "We're in range, so that's not a great sign. You need to hurry."

Tanner followed the lay of the land, using the brush and rocks to keep them out of sight. Roxanne was right on his heels, moving like a silent shadow behind him. They cleared the north side of the building and saw no other guards.

There was a door on this side. Without knowing what was on the other side, he was definitely not going to let Roxanne go in there.

"I'll go in that way. Cover me." He left before she had time to argue.

Her whispered reply promised payback. "You play dirty."

"I'm not playing at all."

Tanner moved fast over the open ground, his rifle ready. He stopped at the door and listened.

His heart was pounding, but he had plenty of practice filtering it out so he could hear other sounds. There were two men talking in low voices. He couldn't tell what they were saying, or if they were Gage and Clay, or other men. They didn't sound upset or afraid. It was more like a conversation over dinner, given the casual ease with which they spoke.

Tanner put his hand on the doorknob and turned it slowly, testing to see whether it was locked. It wasn't.

He crouched and opened the door just a crack. Light from inside blasted through his NVGs. He shoved them up and blinked while his eyes readjusted. The voices were louder now, but he couldn't tell if they were strangers, or if one of them could be Gage. The man had barely said ten words since they'd met, and Tanner didn't have a good feel for his voice.

"We should have knocked them out," said the first man.

"Relax. Reinforcements are on the way. We can hold two men for ten fucking minutes."

"They could get out."

"With what? I stripped the room clean. There's nothing in there but dust."

Man one's voice wavered with fear. "You know what she'll do to us if we fail, man."

"Pussy," muttered the second man. "Go check on them again if it makes you feel better. Just shut the fuck up about it."

Tanner tested his vision. It wasn't perfect, but he could see clearly enough now to make out the general layout of the room. The floor was concrete. The roof and walls were supported by steel I-beams. The walls themselves didn't appear to be much of an obstacle, but getting through them would make too much noise.

One guard was visible, sitting on a folding chair with his feet propped on a second chair. He had a rifle at his side and was dressed for battle.

Tanner changed his angle, looking for the second man and scanning the room for more. On the extreme right end of his line of sight, he could barely see the heels and back of another man in a camouflaged uniform.

That was where they were keeping the men.

He silently closed the door and backed up a few feet. In a slight whisper, he said, "I found them. They're locked in a room, but we're on a clock. Reinforcements come in ten minutes."

"What's your plan?" asked Reid in his ear.

Roxanne spoke up. "We need to keep them alive for questioning."

"That's going to complicate things," said Reid.

"She's right. These aren't enemy combatants." Yet. If they started firing, that would be a different story. "They're wearing body armor. That should make things less risky if we have to open fire."

"I have a tranq gun. We'll toss in a flash-bang. Then I'll hit them while you go after Clay and Gage."

"I saw only two, but can you take out two of them before they start shooting? You'll have to hit them in an unarmored area, too."

"Do you have a better idea?" she asked.

Not one that would get them out of here in less than nine minutes. "Move in, and don't forget we have a guard on the south side of the building."

"I'll bring the MCC closer and take care of him," said Reid. "You two get the men out."

"And a hostage," said Roxanne. Her voice became arctic and took on a tone he'd never heard her use before. "One of them is going to tell us where Jake is."

"Let's hope they know," said Reid. "I'm moving now. Give me two minutes to get into position."

Tanner felt her presence a second before she was at his side. In the midst of the smears of black paint her eyes blazed with golden determination. The set of her jaw was as hard and cold as her voice had been.

He put a hand on her shoulder, trying to offer her some reassurance. Her eyelids fell shut, and she drew in a breath as if collecting herself. When she looked at him again, she was all business. "Where are they?"

"West wall, about twenty feet from this corner."

She nodded.

He reached for her NVGs and lifted them. "The lights are on inside."

She pulled out a flash-bang grenade. "Where's the best place to toss this?"

"They're seated in folding chairs a few feet from the southeast corner."

She offered him the grenade. "Will you do the honors? You know where they are."

"Sure."

Tanner wanted to say more. He wanted to tell her to be careful, but he was certain that wasn't what she wanted to hear right now. She probably wouldn't thank him for doing anything to ruin her focus, so instead, he kept his mouth shut.

Reid's whisper piped into their ears. "I'm in place. I have a bead on the guard."

"Tranqs only," said Roxanne.

"Sorry, Razor. You took the only gun. I'll keep him pinned down and try not to hit anything important. That's all I can do."

"Fine. Wait for the bang." She nodded to Tanner.

He pulled the pin and eased the door open again, this time wide enough for his arm to pass through. He gave the grenade a good toss, releasing the spoon, then shut the door fast.

*Boom.*

Tanner shoved the door wide and went through first to keep any rounds from hitting Roxanne. He heard the clatter of metal on concrete as a weapon hit the floor. The men were yelling, their voices echoing off the metal walls.

Outside, a series of shots went off. Another exploded inside, and he had to fight to keep from turning around to see if Roxanne had been hit.

Their best chance of survival was getting their allies free to fight with them.

Tanner raced across the floor toward the only door along that wall. It was locked.

"Back away," he roared. He waited only a moment before firing a series of rounds through the wood near the lock.

Behind him, more shots were fired. His blood pressure skyrocketed. "Roxanne?"

"I'm busy!"

Her voice flowed over him like cool water. She was still alive.

Tanner kicked the door, and the wood splintered. He kicked again. The lock held, but the chunk of wood connected to it separated from the rest, and the door flew open.

"About fucking time," said Clay.

Gage said nothing, but he grabbed Tanner's knife from its sheath as Tanner passed to help Roxanne.

Smoke obscured his vision of the far side of the room, but he could hear movement. She gasped in pain, and Tanner's world narrowed down to that single, horrific sound. He was in the smoke, his rifle ready. He didn't give a shit that he had no nonlethal ammunition. Whoever had hurt her deserved to die.

A weapon fired. In his ear, he heard a hard exhalation of air that was almost a scream, cut off short. It had come from Roxanne.

Fear exploded behind his eyes. She'd been hit. He knew it. He could feel it.

"Roxanne!"

Smoke billowed in the air, dissipating too slowly for him to see. He charged toward where he thought she was, keeping low.

He saw her boot—too small to be a man's. It wasn't moving.

Another boot came into view. Someone was standing over her.

Rage took over, pouring through his body. No one was going to hurt his Roxanne. Ever.

Tanner charged, flinging himself at the man. His rifle hit first, clashing with the man's weapon. Tanner let his go and slammed his fist, targeting a head he couldn't see. His fist hit something hard. His knuckles split open.

They fell backward under Tanner's momentum. He reached for his knife only to find the sheath empty. His rifle was locked in place between them, and the only weapons he had now were his fists.

The men hit the ground hard. There was the sickening sound of bone hitting concrete. Tanner slugged him again, and this time, his head snapped to the side. He was out cold.

Tanner shoved himself up, crawling under the smoke. "Roxanne!"

"I've got her," said Gage.

"Go!" yelled Clay.

There she was, limp in another man's arms.

There were no real thoughts running through Tanner's head, just surges of instinct. He had to get Roxanne out, get himself out. He pushed to his feet and ran. His eyes never left her boots, which flopped limply over Gage's arm.

Headlights bobbed over the uneven ground. It was the MCC.

They piled in, sloshing around as Reid turned the RV way too fast.

"We may have company," he said. "I wounded the guard, but not enough to keep him from reporting back."

Gage set Roxanne down on the floor. Clay crowded beside him. Tanner couldn't see her. He grabbed Clay's arm and jerked him back to make room.

"Geez, Tanner. It's not like I was—"

"Back the hell off," he barked. "She's mine."

"Dude. Do *not* let her hear you say that."

Tanner didn't care what she heard him say, so long as she woke up and heard something. He didn't see any obvious signs of blood. There was a smudged spot in the paint on her jaw. She could have been punched, but he wouldn't know until he wiped the paint away.

Her chest rose and fell, and that was the only thing that

kept him breathing himself. If anything had happened to her . . .

Reid said something Tanner didn't catch—something about a prisoner.

"He's secure," said Gage.

"Which way are they coming from?" asked Reid.

The buzzing of his brother's voice inside his head irritated him. They were taking too damn much, distracting him. He had to figure out what the hell was wrong with Roxanne.

He pulled the small earpiece out of his ear and tossed it aside.

Tanner patted the uninjured side of her face. "Wake up, honey. We have to go find Jake."

Her eyes fluttered open. "Jake?"

Relief bore down on him, making his hands shake. "Where does it hurt?"

"Side." Her voice was weak and hard to hear over the noise of the straining engine.

Tanner unfastened the straps of her vest. As he moved her arm, he saw the hole a bullet had made.

His heart stopped beating. Two inches lower, and the bullet would have gone below her body armor. And even though it hadn't—even though the Kevlar had done its job and kept her safe—the alternative was now in his head. He could see her bleeding and writhing in pain.

She was so fragile. As tough as she was, her life was still so tenuous. She could have easily lost it tonight.

But rather than tell her that, he kept his mouth shut and continued his search for other injuries. He removed the vest and pushed her shirt up, shielding her from the other men with his body. There was a bruise on her waist, below her ribs. His fingers moved around it, feeling for other problems.

She became more aware as the seconds passed, watching him. He found a scrape on her elbow and a knot forming on the back of her head. His fingers slid through her hair, carefully searching for signs of blood.

"You hit your head."

"Guess so. I think it'll stop spinning if I sit up."

She was going to whether or not he wanted it, so he decided to help her up. "Slowly."

She held on tight, gripping his arms as if he were the only thing holding her to Earth.

The MCC slung around a turn, and Tanner pulled her against his chest to protect her from being thrown about.

"Slow down," he yelled to his brother.

"Not until we lose the tail. I know they're back there."

"We'll never lose them in this," said Clay. "We're too slow. Let me out and I'll stop them."

"Alone?" asked Reid.

"Of course not. I'll bring a weapon. I'll slow them down and call you to pick me up when it's all done."

"Splitting up is a bad idea," said Tanner.

"So is getting caught with a hostage," said Clay.

It wasn't until then that Tanner realized there was someone in the MCC with them. He was unconscious and slumped over. His hands were cuffed behind him, and Gage watched him with an unwavering gaze.

"Roxanne hit him with a dart. He'll wake up soon," said Clay, "and when he does, we'll get him to talk."

Reid said, "Assuming we don't all get killed before then."

"Let me out here. I'll take out their tires and buy us some time."

"Do it," said Gage, never taking his eyes off their prisoner.

Reid hit the steering wheel in frustration and said, "Don't jump. I'm stopping."

The MCC slowed. Clay grabbed a bunch of gear and a toolbox, tossed them out the door, and jumped off before the wheels had completely stopped moving.

# Chapter Eighteen

Clay hit the ground running. He had only a couple of minutes to find what he needed and lay a trap. He readied his rifle as he searched for the toolbox, doing his best to ignore the pain in his ribs and shoulder.

It was dark out here, and as soon as the MCC disappeared over the next rise, it got even darker. He positioned his night vision goggles in place and went to work.

There was plenty of barbed-wire fencing to be had. It didn't take long to snip some of it free and lay it across the road. He tossed a handful of dust over it to help cover any shiny patches and then scouted for a good location to lie in wait.

The land sloped up slightly, then dipped down where water runoff had carved a shallow groove in the earth. Clay settled in that depression, which was angled perfectly to see any oncoming traffic.

Less than two minutes had passed since he'd jumped from the MCC, but that was all it had taken for the reinforcements to arrive. They weren't using their headlights, but Clay saw them all the same. Two men rode in a Jeep, speeding over the rutted road.

No way were they Ma and Pa Kettle out for a midnight drive.

The barbed wire was a few yards ahead of them. Clay

held his breath and sighted them through the night scope. He led the front tire, breathed, and fired.

The Jeep skidded, but he couldn't tell if it was because of his shot or because they'd spotted the wire and were trying to stop. He fired again, missing.

The wire clattered as it hit the bottom of the Jeep. The men kept driving. Clay could hear them shouting inside the vehicle, one screaming at the other, "Don't stop!"

*Shit.* They were going to get away.

Clay aimed again and took another shot, and this time, he heard the tire hiss as it blew out. The barbed wire must have gotten caught around one of the wheels, because their passage was ripping the fence apart, the wire singing as it broke free of each fence post. The aged wood splintered, marking their progress.

The Jeep slid to a dusty stop, and one man got out, weapon in hand. He scanned the area.

Clay froze. He really didn't want to kill this guy. Sure, these assholes had locked him and Gage in a room, and yes, they allegedly had Razor's friend held hostage, too, but a bullet in the head was a long way from a day in court, and Clay didn't like playing judge, jury, and executioner. He didn't sleep well as it was. He sure as hell didn't need more nightmares than he already had.

The man lifted his rifle. The barrel swung toward Clay as he searched. The deadly end lined up, pointing right at him.

Something inside Clay popped, as though a fuse had been blown. Rage poured into him like acid, and a low, feral growl rose from his chest. And then everything went black.

Roxanne's head throbbed and her side ached as though someone had clamped her in a vise for a few days. Other than bruises, a few scrapes, and a pounding headache, she seemed okay. Considering what could have happened, she was counting her blessings.

Tanner had wiped away the greasepaint on her face before taking care of his own. It didn't matter that she'd said she could do it. He seemed compelled to fuss over her. Whenever she pushed him away, he grew a bit angrier and more determined. Since she was too exhausted to argue, she finally gave in and let him fuss.

"I need to sit up," she told Tanner. He was crowding her, hovering over her, and keeping her body from sliding around as the MCC sped over the road.

"Not yet."

Vertigo grew between her ears until the spinning in her head was too much to ignore. "No, Tanner. Now. I'm going to be sick if I don't sit up."

His mouth tightened in frustration, but his big hands slid under her head and shoulders, and he eased her to a sitting position.

She kept her eyes shut tight, blocking out the motion of the world around her. Tanner's hands stayed on her, so warm and solid they became the center of her world.

Slowly, the vertigo eased, and as soon as she was sure she wouldn't vomit, she opened her eyes. He was staring down at her, concern marking his features. Lines that hadn't been there before formed around his mouth, and there was a deep wrinkle bisecting his forehead.

"I'm fine," she told him.

"You're not fine. You were shot."

"Only a little."

He cupped the side of her face, his touch gentle. "A little was more than enough. If I'd lost you . . ." His throat moved visibly as he swallowed back whatever else he might have said.

A warm comfort rose up inside her as she realized his words intimated that he had something to lose. In the concussed recesses of her head, she liked that idea. Sure, it was just the adrenaline and fear talking, but she liked the things they said. "You didn't lose me."

He nodded but remained silent. His fingers curled against her skin, stroking her and easing the last of her dizziness.

The man had a magical touch, and while she knew the time he'd spend touching her was fleeting, she was going to enjoy it for as long as she could.

"Help me up?" she asked.

Tanner stood and helped lift her to her feet. "Sit here. I don't want you walking around yet—not until we get your head looked at."

"My head is fine. Sore, but fine."

"Yeah, well, we're not taking any chances."

Rather than arguing with him over who was taking what chances with her body, she ignored his statement.

Gage was sitting next to the side door, his denim blue eyes fixed on something she couldn't see on the other side of the bathroom. The passenger seat was empty. "Where's Clay?"

"He's slowing down our tail," said Tanner.

"We're being followed?"

He frowned at her. "What's the last thing you remember?"

She remembered getting ready to go into the building. Everything past that was a blank. Whatever they'd done must have worked, because the men were free—at least she hoped so. Clay was smart. He was skilled. If anyone could evade capture on his own, Clay could.

"My head is fine," she told Tanner. "Just fill me in. Where are we headed?"

"Right now? Away."

"I want details."

"Fine. Stay put. I'll find out what our plan is."

He left, and Roxanne laid her head on her arms. The Formica table was cool beneath her skin, drawing away some of the remaining heat of battle. Her whole body was buzzing, and she couldn't seem to slow her racing heart.

At least they'd rescued the men. Now all she had to do was rescue Jake.

Tanner came back, his face grim. "We have one of their men. We're going to find a place to stop soon so we can question him, but the MCC isn't exactly built for stealth. It's going to be hard to disappear."

They had a prisoner? Someone who might have seen Jake?

Roxanne pushed herself to her feet and tried to shove Tanner out of her way. He was too big to budge, and he grabbed her arms. "Whoa. Where are you going?"

"To talk to him. He might know where Jake is."

"You're in no shape to be interrogating someone. And right now, he's still unconscious, so sit down before you fall down."

She sat, but she pulled out her phone. They had to find someplace to stop so they could get the man to talk.

"Did you find Clay?" Mira asked upon answering the phone.

"Yes. He's fine."

"I want to talk to him."

"He's working, but I'll have him call you back. In the meantime, I was hoping you could help. We need a place to hide the mobile command center. We're being followed and need to lie low. Got any ideas?"

"Hang on." Keys clicked on the other end of the line. "There's a ranch not far from you that's gone through foreclosure. It's vacant. There's a lockbox on the gate, and the code is one five four eight."

"How do you know that?"

"I hacked into the MLS system. The bank's selling it, and the info sheet says real estate agents can show it whenever they like since no one lives there. It's got a nice big outbuilding with an oversized door. Unless it's full of crap, the MCC will fit."

"Thanks, Mira. You're the best."

"You can thank me by getting Clay to call me. He's been . . . under the weather. I'm worried about him."

"I'll have him call as soon as I see him. Cross my heart."

Mira gave her the directions, which Roxanne entered

into her phone's GPS. "Give this to Reid. Tell him to go here and we can hide."

Tanner gave her a skeptical look but did as she asked. A few minutes later, they were safely hidden inside a run-down outbuilding, sharing space with a rusted truck with no front axle.

Reid turned off the engine. The silence was nearly overwhelming.

Roxanne was so tired. The blow to her head and shot to her body armor had made her sore, but they'd done more than that. She felt demoralized and worn out. Jake was still out there, and their only lead was an unconscious man who'd tried to kill them.

That didn't bode well for Jake's safety.

She was his only hope, and it was time to buck up and come through. He deserved no less, no matter how tired she was. At least she was breathing free air.

Roxanne stood slowly, conscious of Tanner's concern. He held her arms, ready to catch her if she passed out. Which she refused to do. There was too much work left for her to take a concussion break.

"Let me pass," she said.

"I think this is a bad idea. You're not at the top of your game, and this guy's going to see it. You can't interrogate from a position of power."

"Then I'll interrogate him another way."

"How?"

"I don't know. I'll appeal to his compassion. Jake's my family. This guy probably has a family, too, and will get where I'm coming from."

"It won't work."

"You don't know that until I try."

"This is a bad idea, Razor. We may get only one shot at him. If you screw it up, you'll never forgive yourself."

"He's right," said Reid, who'd come back to join them. "Do you have any experience with this kind of thing?"

"Questioning people? Not if I've done my job. Their fingers in the cookie jar tend to speak loudly enough."

"Chances are this could get ugly," said Tanner.

"I don't care. Jake is my family. I'm doing this."

Tanner and his brother shared some silent guy-speak over her head. Then he sighed. "Okay, but I'm going on record that this is a bad idea."

"Noted," she snapped. "Now let me pass."

She moved toward the front of the MCC and could now see the man they'd taken captive. He was young—maybe midtwenties. He had a lean face and a body straining with muscles under his camouflaged uniform. His hands were cuffed behind his back with plastic ties, and he was duct-taped to the seat at his ankles and around his torso. Another strip of duct tape covered his mouth.

Roxanne gave the three men a hard stare. "Back off. I'm doing this."

Gage stepped back, leaning his hip and shoulder against the wall. Tanner and Reid crossed their arms over their chests and took on identical, protective poses.

She stepped up to the man who looked like a soldier and ripped the tape from his mouth. His eyes popped open, and he let out a snarl of pain. A cut on his lip reopened and bled over his mouth.

"What's your name?"

He glared at her and said nothing.

"No one's coming for you, and we're not letting you go. Either you play ball, or things are going to get unpleasant. Now tell me, who do you work for?"

He scrunched up his mouth and spat blood at her. She jumped back, dodging the spray. Before she'd landed, Tanner had lunged forward and backhanded the man across the face.

She glared at him for the interference, but the sudden movement had made her dizzy, and she was sure her look lacked the heat she'd intended.

Roxanne ripped a small strip of duct tape from the roll

and taped his wound shut so he'd have no more ammunition. "Do that again, and you'll be bleeding from more places than just your mouth."

"You won't do shit to me," he said. "You can barely stand."

She was not going to give either Tanner or this man the satisfaction of being right. She wasn't weak. She would be as strong as she needed to be for as long as she needed to be to see Jake home.

"You're right," she said, settling the heel of her boot against his balls. "I could lose my balance at any moment, so you'd better talk fast."

He paled for a moment, then gathered himself again and looked away from her as if dismissing her.

Roxanne put some pressure on his crotch—just enough to get his attention. "Jake Staite. Where is he?"

"You'll never find him."

"So you do know where he is."

"Dead," spat the young man. "We used him for target practice when we found out he'd broken the rules and spilled his guts. You should have heard him scream. He was such a fucking pussy. He died a traitor and a coward."

His words crashed over Roxanne, chilling her. She started to shake as the images he'd put into her head bloomed to life. It didn't matter that he was lying. The thoughts were in her now, tearing down her little-remaining strength and crushing her hope.

"That's enough," said Tanner. "If he's going to lie, we should just kill him now."

"I'm not done with him yet," said Roxanne. Despite her resolve to be a stone-cold bitch, her voice wavered. She was cracking. She had to get out of here before it was too late.

"I'll do it," said Gage, his voice low and quiet. His gaze was fixed on the prisoner, unblinking and unwavering.

"Do what?" asked Reid. "Kill him?"

"Get answers. Leave. I need to be alone with him."

Something about the way he said it sent a chill down Roxanne's spine.

"I don't know if that's a good idea," said Tanner.

Reid shook his head. "No. He's right. We'll give Gage a shot. If he can't get answers out of the dick, then we'll kill him."

Roxanne let them usher her out of the MCC. She was shaking so hard, she could barely get down the stairs. All she could think about was Jake and what he must have gone through. Even if he was still alive—which she had to believe—he had to deal with heartless bastards like the man inside. And because she'd been so swept up in her own life, with the move and with starting over, out from under her parents' shadow, she hadn't even seen his cry for help.

Weeks had passed in which she could have been looking for him. He was out there, hoping she'd save him, and she'd been picking out paint and furniture.

If he was dead, it was her fault for not having acted faster.

Tears stung her eyes, but she held them back. Crying would only make her head hurt worse, making her more useless.

"That prick was lying to you," said Tanner. His eyes were blazing with anger, but his hands were gentle on her arms, giving her comfort and anchoring her.

"I know. I also know I shouldn't have let it upset me so much."

Reid's voice was low so it couldn't be overheard behind the closed door of the MCC. "We're not going to kill him. You know that, right? I just said it to scare him."

"Of course we're not going to kill him. For all we know, he's a victim the same way Jake is."

"That man who attacked you at the storage facility," said Tanner, "he was fucked in the head, not playing with a full deck. This guy seemed lucid."

"It doesn't matter," she told him. "We'll make him help us, and then we'll turn him over to the authorities."

"Which ones?" asked Reid. "The police? The feds?"

She turned around, taking herself out of Tanner's grasp. While she missed his touch, she needed to prove to herself she could stand on her own two feet. What she'd been through tonight wasn't going to keep her from finding Jake. "If what Jake said in his journal was true, then the military needs to be involved. They need to know what's happening to their soldiers."

"Do we even know for sure what that is?"

"No, but Jake will know. And when we find where they're holding him, I'm sure we'll also find all kinds of incriminating evidence."

They fell silent. Tanner paced like a caged animal. Reid stayed by the door, watching for signs that they'd been found. Roxanne watched the door, hoping Gage would walk through and tell her he'd learned where Jake was.

As close as she was, all she could hear was the low rumble of Gage's voice broken up by a whole lot of silence.

If this didn't work, she was out of ideas.


Clay had no idea where he was. It was dark. He was outside, sitting on the ground, but he couldn't remember how he got here.

Confusion fogged his brain, and he looked around, desperate for some sign of where he was.

He felt the familiar weight of his rifle in his hands and looked down. Sticky, dark splotches coated his fingers.

A man lay unmoving at his feet. Clay scrambled to his side, rolling him onto his back. He was a stranger—one whose pants were shiny with fresh blood.

Clay felt for a pulse. There was none. He was still warm, though. He hadn't been dead long.

A wind slid over the ground, cooling the blood on his hands. He could smell cattle nearby.

His head was pounding, and his stomach twisted with nausea. It took a force of will, but he pushed himself to his feet and surveyed the area.

A Jeep sat with the passenger door open. One of its tires was blown, and a strand of barbed wire was tangled around one wheel. The engine was running, but the headlights were off. The dome light shone on the interior, showing another man slumped dead over the steering wheel. His body armor hadn't done him any good against a headshot. Blood and pulpy bits of bone and brain splattered the side window. The bulletproof glass had withstood the blow, but it had only kept the round from busting out through the window.

Clay's stomach rebelled and he had to gulp down deep breaths to keep from puking on his boots.

As he looked away, he caught sight of another vehicle ten yards down the gravel road. Its headlights were on. He couldn't see if anyone was inside.

He raised his rifle and slowly approached from the side. As he got close, he saw a man's hand sprawled on the ground. The rest of his body was hidden by the SUV.

He tried to speak—to tell the man to put his other hand where Clay could see it—but his throat was tight and dry, and no words came out.

An image shattered against the inside of his skull, nearly driving him to his knees with the pain. He gritted his teeth and gripped his weapon tight, waiting for it to pass. He could do nothing else. The agony was overwhelming. With every beat of his heart, he saw a fragmented flash. First, a man fired at him. The muzzle flash of Clay's rifle spewed out like fire. A man appeared. He was bald, with a nose too big for his face. On his right sleeve was a patch sporting a red saber and words he couldn't read. Then Clay had a knife in his hands, and that knife was covered in blood.

Another throbbing pulse of pain hit him, and all the images vanished, as if they'd never been there.

Clay dragged in a deep breath, struggling to get enough oxygen. A wave of dizziness careened into him, and he locked his knees to keep from crumpling to the ground.

Finally, after what seemed like minutes, his vision returned and the man was still lying in the same spot. Only now Clay knew what the rest of him would look like. He'd be shaved bald. His nose would be too big for his face, and he'd be wearing a patch with a red saber on it on his right sleeve.

Slowly, Clay moved forward, compelled to see if he was right even as he prayed he was wrong. He'd never seen that man's face before—only just now in his head.

He cleared the bumper of the SUV and looked down. The man stared up at the sky with unblinking, blue eyes. He was bald. His nose was too big for his face. He wore that saber patch. His throat had been split open to his spine.

Clay had done it. He didn't remember doing it, but that changed nothing. He'd killed these men, and he couldn't remember a thing. Which left only one question.

How many other men did he not remember killing?

# Chapter Nineteen

"None of our men are reporting in," said General Bower. "We must assume that means they've been eliminated."

Dr. Stynger's bright red lips pursed in annoyance. "All of this fuss for one man? I thought you were supposed to vet our recruits to avoid this type of problem."

"I did. Jake Staite has no living family. No girlfriend. How was I to know that this woman would move heaven and earth to find him? Or that she would have the resources to be effective?"

Her pale green gaze caught his and held. "You were supposed to know because it's your job to know."

Nelson swallowed, trying to hide his apprehension. She was starting to look at him differently—the way she looked at her subjects. He had to sleep sometime, and he didn't want her getting any ideas. "What do you want me to do?" he asked.

She cocked her head to the side. Her neck was so skinny. It wouldn't take any effort at all to break it. Maybe that was the best choice—kill her before she could hurt him. But then what would he do? She was his meal ticket. A few more years doing this job, and he could have the retirement he should have had from the US military—the one they'd robbed him of because of one little mistake. One single dead soldier and his career was over. They hadn't cared that it was an accident.

"Our options are dwindling by the moment," she said. "We can kill him and remove all traces of evidence from his body that he was ever here, but that won't be easy. Fire or acid are the only options."

"How will they know it's him if they can't ID the body?"

"That is a problem. Which leaves our other option."

"Which is?" he asked.

"We finish his transition now. We use him to draw this woman out, and we eliminate her as a threat."

"He's not ready. He hasn't even finished the psychological conditioning yet."

"I've been toying with a new method. Something from Dr. Leeson's journal. He stated that it was fast and effective."

"Then why haven't you used it before?"

"Because it also has a fifty percent fatality rate. It's hard enough to find our subjects. Killing them needlessly seemed wasteful."

"If it works, then what?"

"He'll be complete and under our control."

"And if it doesn't work?"

"He'll be dead." She rose from her desk and picked up the worn leather-bound journal. Her tone became distracted, as though she were already working in her mind. She waved a bony hand as she passed him. "I suggest you procure a vat of acid, just in case."

It had been too quiet for too long inside the MCC. Tanner kept close tabs on Roxanne, watching her for signs that the blow to her head or side had been more serious than she let on. If he had to, he'd drag her to a hospital kicking and screaming.

He went to the door where Reid was standing guard. "How much longer do we wait?"

"As long as it takes," said Reid.

"I'm worried about Razor. I think she needs to see a doctor."

"She's tough. She's been through worse than this."

Anger uncurled inside Tanner, both at the thought of Roxanne suffering as well as how flippant Reid was being about it. "How can you say that so casually?"

Reid looked away from the road and met Tanner's gaze. He was angry, too. His voice shook with it. "Because I'm not fucking her. Not sleeping with your coworkers tends to give you clarity of thought. You should try it."

"I'm not going to talk to you about this. It was a mistake to even ask for you to come—"

"Well, I'm here, so deal."

Reid's phone vibrated. He read the text message. "Clay says we're clear. He has wheels and will meet us back at the motel."

"We should get moving, then."

A ragged, strangled scream shook the walls of the MCC. Both men raced toward the noise, but Roxanne got there first. She ripped the door open and jumped up the stairs. Tanner was right behind her.

The prisoner was on the floor, tape still clinging to his body. Gage was over him, pressing rhythmically on his chest. He bent and breathed into the man's mouth.

"What happened?" asked Roxanne.

Tanner pushed past her and took over chest compressions.

Gage breathed into the man's mouth again. "Seizure."

"Did you do this to him?" demanded Reid.

"No. Drive to a hospital."

"I'll get the door," said Roxanne; then she left.

Tanner met Gage's gaze between breaths. "What did he say?"

"Not much."

"Did he know where Jake was?"

Gage nodded.

"Did he tell you?"

"He said Dr. Stynger has him, and when she's done with him, he'll kill us all."

Roxanne had jumped aboard in time to hear that, which was something Tanner had hoped to avoid.

"I'm sure he was just blowing smoke up your ass," said Tanner, hoping to keep Roxanne from jumping to conclusions.

"No," said Gage. "He wasn't."

They kept working on him for forty minutes as Reid drove toward the nearest hospital, which was more than an hour away. Tanner had unintentionally broken at least two of his ribs, and he still hadn't taken a single breath on his own.

"We're twenty minutes away from a hospital," said Roxanne. "How's he doing?"

"Dead," said Gage; then he breathed into the man's mouth again.

Her voice was strained with fear. "He can't be. He's the only one who can get us to Jake."

Tanner was drenched in sweat, and his upper body burned from keeping up the exertion of CPR. He knew his efforts were futile, but he kept pumping the man's heart, anyway. He couldn't stand to let her down, even though he knew it was inevitable. "I'm sorry, Razor. I think Gage is right."

"You're tired. Let me take a turn."

Tanner backed away to give her room. Her jaw was set and her posture determined. If she could bring him back to life through sheer force of will, he'd be up and walking around before they reached the hospital.

They kept working on him, and Tanner had to lock his fingers together to keep from reaching for her. This man was their only lead, and as soon as she accepted that he was gone, she was going to be devastated.

"We'll find another way," he promised her, hoping to ease the blow. "This man is not the only one who knew where Jake is."

"Don't talk like he's dead. I'm not giving up yet."

"When we get there," said Reid, "I'll stay and answer questions. You three need to meet up with Clay and keep looking. I'm sure the police will be involved and it'll take a while. We can't all be trapped there."

"It'll look like we're running," said Tanner.

"I'll cover for you. You'll have to be questioned, but at least I can buy you some more time to look for Jake."

"I'll stay, too," said Gage between breaths.

Reid let out an amused grunt. "They're going to have fun getting answers out of you."

Gage shrugged.

Tanner moved to the front where only Reid could hear him. "Maybe we all should stay. It's going to look like we're covering something up."

"We could be here for hours. Days. Do you really think Razor is going to hang out that long?"

"Maybe she should. This is getting way too dangerous."

"Welcome to the job."

"Gage and I can go look for Jake. You and Razor can stay."

Reid shot his brother a scalding look. "You know damn well she won't go for that. She'll slip off when we're not looking and be out there alone. Is that what you want?"

He was right. Roxanne would do whatever it took to find Jake. If Tanner wasn't there to watch her back, it wouldn't stop her. "I'll stay with her."

Reid nodded. "We'll try to keep your names out of it. Work fast, though. I don't know how long we'll be able to hold them off."

They pulled up to the emergency room doors, and Reid ran in and got help. It didn't take long for the hospital staff to take over and load him onto a gurney.

Roxanne hid in the bathroom, while Tanner stayed in front and drove off as soon as everyone went inside. The police would be here soon, and they needed to be gone before that happened.

She slid into the passenger seat, and even with only his peripheral vision, he could see her slumped, defeated posture.

He wanted to reach over and comfort her, but the space was too wide. He gripped the wheel tighter, instead. "We're going back to the motel to get my truck. Clay is going to meet up with us there. We'll retrace our steps and find someplace to start looking again."

"I'm going to call Payton and see if they got any leads from the man who attacked us at the storage unit."

"Let me know what you find out."

She nodded, but he could tell from her lack of enthusiasm that she didn't have any more hope than he did that the news would be good.


Jake woke to pain. It throbbed through his veins like ice, freezing him from the inside out. He was shivering, and he couldn't figure out where he was. A huge sun glowed overhead, sending spikes of agony through his eyes. Tears streamed down his temples. He was lying down. His arms and legs wouldn't move. He could feel cold metal buckles against his skin.

A gloved hand moved the sun, and he realized it was some kind of light, like the one at the dentist's office. People gathered around his bed, surgical masks hiding their faces.

He tried to speak, but there was something in his mouth—in his throat. He could feel the plastic tube against his teeth. They'd shoved it down his throat.

Panic tore at him, compelling him to fight for his freedom.

"He's awake," said a man.

"It's too soon," replied a woman. He knew that voice. He hated that voice. "Sedate him."

"He's already had too much."

Irritation tightened her words. "I'll do it myself. Then we'll turn him over. We're running out of time."

Seconds later, lethargy fell over him, washing away his panic. His eyes closed, and his will to fight disappeared.

Payton couldn't eat—not after what he'd learned today—so he had General Robert Norwood meet him at home. He didn't trust the man enough to take him down to his secure basement where he was certain no bugs or parabolic mics could pick up their conversation. No one knew about his hidey-hole, and he liked it that way.

"Wine?" he offered as Bob sank onto his couch with a sigh of weariness.

"Whiskey."

Payton nodded and fetched them each a drink. They were both going to need it.

Bob leaned back. "We picked up Sergeant Evans today."

The name didn't ring a bell. "Sergeant Evans?"

"The soldier in the hospital. Or at least he used to be a soldier. He left around the same time Jake Staite did. They were in the same unit."

Payton's stomach sank a bit lower. "I got his medical records. There were several chemicals in his system they couldn't identify."

"I'm assuming you could."

He nodded, emptied his glass, and poured another. He waited for the burn to subside before he spoke. "They're not identical to the Threshold Project, but close enough that I'm convinced."

"Convinced of what? Exactly?"

"Norma Stynger is still alive."

"So you're sure."

"Between Staite's journal and the chemicals in Evans's system, I think it foolish to ignore the obvious."

"Damn it, Payton! Haven't we ruined enough lives? We haven't even finished cleaning up our mess, and now someone else is adding to it."

"There's more," said Payton.

"Hell," spat Bob. "Might as well pile it all on. I won't be sleeping for a week, anyway."

"It seems that Clay Marshall is degrading. Fast."

Bob scrubbed his face with his hands, suddenly seeming ten years older. "I had high hopes for that boy. He was such a fighter, even back then."

"I'm going to continue to monitor him, but the signs are bad."

"I'll take care of it," said Bob. "You shouldn't have to deal with someone you've gotten so close to."

"No. He's my responsibility. If he has to be stopped, I'll be the one to do it. I owe him at least that much."

"Hell, we owe him more than that, but a quick, easy death before he can hurt someone he loves is all we have to offer, it seems." He got up and poured himself another glass. "While we're at it, I've got my own bad news to share. Adam Brink has disappeared, but not before he found another three people on the List and abducted them."

"Any idea where he took them?"

Bob shook his head. He had more gray hair now than a year ago, but then, so did Payton. They were getting old. It was time for them to be retiring from this business to let the next generation take over and do a better job. But they'd screwed that up. The next generation had been their victim, and neither one of them could justify the selfishness of walking away. "None. He's got to have resources. No one man could do what he does and leave no trace."

Weariness weighed down on Payton. He let out a long sigh, wishing he could take back his mistakes—at least the big ones. "We need to address the most immediate problems first. Starting with finding and eliminating Stynger."

"Don't you have people searching for Staite?"

"I do, but it's not going well. And now there's a body in a morgue in New Mexico that is going to raise a lot of questions."

"Why's that?"

"One of my men was questioning him when he just . . . died. Gage didn't do anything to him."

"Are you sure?" asked Bob. "Things can get hairy in the heat of the moment."

"Not with Gage. That man is as calm and methodical as they come. He's one of the few successes the Threshold Project had."

"So far. When they turn, they turn fast."

"You don't have to remind me. I live with these people. I'm careful."

"So why are you worried about this body?"

"Because if he has the drugs in his system that I think he will, it's not going to take long for someone to connect the dots. The last thing we need is a multistate investigation. Media coverage. We don't want to do anything to trigger the memories of the few that have been lucky enough to find normal lives."

"I agree. I'll take care of getting the body."

"How?"

"Let me worry about that. You need to figure out what you want me to with the body once I have it."

Payton was tempted to have him burn it, but who knows what they might be able to learn from it. "Bring it back. I'll convince Dr. Vaughn to do an autopsy."

"Can you trust him?"

"Her. She's the only doctor I do trust. She owes me. She'll do what I ask."

Norwood's shoulder sagged. "We're doing a shitty job, Payton. We're too old for this. We need help."

"And just who would you like to ask for that help? Who can we trust not to handle things even worse than we have? At least we've protected some of them."

"It's not enough. What if I told you I think we need a task force—a specialized unit that can fully devote itself to dealing with the shit storm we created?"

"I'd say you've had too much to drink. Where the hell

are we going to find people who can deal with the things we've done?"

"Under your nose."

Payton stilled in the act of taking a drink. He stared at Bob for a long time, resisting the immediate knee-jerk reaction that had him rejecting the notion. "You mean the Edge."

"Yeah. I do. Many of them are ours, anyway. Why not contract them to find Stynger and bring her down along with anyone else she's poisoned along the way?"

"What about their memories? I'm trying to protect them—give them someplace, some chance at a normal life." That was the only thing Payton had to offer many of the people he'd hurt. It seemed vicious and cruel to rip that away from them.

"Their lives will never be normal. We saw to that. But what we can give them is a chance to set things right, to stop any more people from being hurt the way we hurt them."

Payton hated the idea. It was reasonable. Practical. But there was one part he just couldn't stomach—one part that left him lying awake at night in a cold sweat. "We'll have to tell them the truth."

Bob nodded, his face grim. "Fucking sucks, doesn't it? Sloane will probably never speak to me again."

That was the least that would happen. Lives would be torn apart. There was no doubt in his mind that some of those who learned the truth would take their own lives. Especially if they remembered. "Sloane wasn't a victim. You stopped that from happening. The others were."

"She won't care. Nor should she. We fucked up big-time. Sooner or later, we're going to have to own up to it."

"Publicly?"

"No. That's way too dangerous. Let the sleepers sleep. But the ones here, at the Edge—we'll bring them in. Tell the truth. Take the heat." He emptied his glass. "And then we'll cut them loose to take some control over their lives."

Payton eyed his drink, his stomach twisting. "You mean vengeance."

Bob shrugged. "A little of that, too."

"We'll be targets," Payton pointed out. Part of him didn't mind the idea. There was something comforting about the thought of letting go—of no longer keeping so many secrets. The weight on his shoulders would be gone. He'd be free.

"We've always been targets. The sad truth is that we're getting too old to dodge the bullets for much longer. Our mistakes can't outlive us. We have to make this right before it's too late."

The general was right. Payton hated it, but he knew it was true. It was time to own up to his mistakes and admit what he'd done to the people he'd grown to love despite his best efforts to remain emotionally distant.

Payton pulled in a deep breath, but it did little to steady his nerves. "I'll talk to Bella. Just give me a bit more time."

"We don't have much left, Payton. You take too long and it'll be too late."

# Chapter Twenty

Roxanne and Tanner had been waiting for two hours, and Clay still had not shown up. He wasn't answering his cell phone, either.

She was worried. "It's not like Clay to be a no-show."

Tanner peered through a gap in the motel room curtains. "He'll be here. Maybe he thought he was being followed and had to take a long way around."

She checked her phone for the thousandth time—no texts or voice mails from anyone. "How do you think it's going for Reid and Gage?"

"I imagine the police are having trouble getting much out of either of them. I'm sure we'll hear from them soon."

"They'll need a ride."

"Reid will call. Or he'll rent a car. Don't worry about them."

She sprang from the bed and started pacing. "I have to do something. This waiting is killing me."

She hadn't heard him cross the room. His hands settled on her shoulders, making her jump. She spun around, knocking his hands away. "Sorry. I'm a bit jumpy."

"It's understandable. You've been through a lot these past few days."

"Not as much as Jake's been through."

Her phone rang, and she nearly jumped out of her skin.

It took her shaking fingers three tries to answer the call. "Hello?"

"It's Clay."

"Are you okay? Where are you?"

"I'm fine. I'll be there in a couple of hours."

"Hours? Where are you?"

"I had to find a different ride. They were going to be looking for this one."

"Please tell me you didn't steal a car."

"Okay."

"Okay? That's all you're going to say?"

"Listen, Razor. It's been a shitty day, so can we just skip the lecture?"

"Sorry. Just get here as soon as you can."

"I will. And you'll be glad to know I think I have an idea of how we can find these fuckers."

"Really? How?"

"Not on the phone. I think I covered all my bases, but I'm not taking any chances. They could hear me."

Roxanne had no idea what to say to that. "Uh. Okay. I guess we'll see you soon, then?"

"Two hours. If I'm not there by then, then I was wrong." He hung up, leaving her wondering what in heaven's name he meant.

Tanner watched her as she hung up the phone with shaking fingers. His gaze was intent. "Well?"

"Clay is fine. He should be here in two hours. He said he might have a way of finding the people who took Jake."

"How?"

"He didn't say. He was worried they might hear him."

"He thinks our phones are tapped?"

She shrugged, and sore muscles screamed in protest. Her head still throbbed, but it was localized now to the spot she'd hit, rather than a pounding through her whole skull. "Maybe. We should assume they are."

Tanner nodded as he pulled out his phone. "I'll text Reid and warn him."

His fingers flew over the buttons, more nimble than they should have been, given the size of his hands. She watched the movement, remembering just how those fingers had felt on her skin, pinching her nipples and sliding between her thighs.

Her body warmed, and some of the shivers faded, leaving her feeling stronger and less fragile.

He tucked his phone in his pocket, unaware that she'd been watching him.

"You look tired. Maybe you should try to get some rest." His concern for her was genuine, shining in his blue eyes as the lines around them deepened.

Just seeing him eased some of the tension behind her eyes. He was so strong and solid. She knew deep down that if she fell, he'd be right there to catch her. It had been a long time since she'd put that much faith in anyone—since she was a kid. She wasn't sure she wanted to trust him quite that much. The last time she had, she'd been betrayed by the people who were supposed to love her the most.

"I am tired, but I can't sleep," she said.

He nodded in understanding and slid his hand over her hair. His touch lingered at her neck, his fingers stroking her bare skin.

Her whole body responded to his touch, lighting up like Christmas. Exhaustion faded, and worry dissolved more with every second. She loved how he could do that to her— how he could make the rest of the world disappear with so little effort.

"Just lie down. Give your body time to rest. I promise it'll make you feel better."

She knew what would make her feel better, and as thinly stretched as she was—as important as it was for her to hold it together—she wasn't above using Tanner to get it.

Roxanne stepped closer until their bodies were touching from knees to chest. His heat sank through her clothes, making warmth pool in her blood. He tensed but didn't back away. His jaw bulged, his lips tightened, and his eyes scrunched closed.

"Roxanne." She couldn't tell if he'd meant her name as a warning or a plea.

She dragged the pad of her thumb over his bottom lip, hoping to relax him. His lips parted, and a low groan of need vibrated against her breasts. He grabbed her wrist and stared down at her with an expression she'd never seen before. There was a fierce, almost predatory challenge in his eyes, while at the same time, he seemed uncertain.

"We can't do this," he whispered.

"I think we proved before that we can. Quite well."

His nostrils flared, and he sucked in a deep breath. "You're injured. We're risking our jobs."

"I'm fine, and no one has to know."

"Reid will know. He always knows."

"He already caught us. If he's going to tell Bella, then there's nothing we can do to stop him. We may as well enjoy ourselves before the ax falls."

He closed his eyes as if to gather his self-control. "You were hurt today. As much as I want you, I can't be the kind of asshole who would risk hurting you more."

She wanted him. He wanted her, too. She could see it in the way his muscles clenched and the stain of lust darkening his cheeks. She could smell his heated skin. His fears were unfounded, and right now, she needed his touch to distract her from the waiting and the danger that Jake faced with every passing minute. Two hours of fear felt like a lifetime, but two hours in Tanner's arms would pass in a heartbeat of pleasure.

Rather than give up, she pressed a kiss against his neck and felt the cords there tighten. "I think you should kiss me and make me better."

His chest rumbled, and his hands gripped her hips, tugging her forward. She felt his erection against her abdomen, and her body melted, becoming soft and hot. The need to have him inside her again swelled, shoving out all else.

Roxanne slid her hands to his waistband and tugged the button free. Tanner grabbed her hands, holding them captive. He stared down at her for a long moment, his eyes roaming her face. "Promise me you'll tell me if I hurt you."

"You won't."

"Promise me, or I walk out that door right now and wait outside."

"I promise." She'd say anything to have him.

He lowered his head and kissed her, his lips barely grazing hers. It wasn't enough. She wanted more—all of him.

She flicked her tongue out, tasting his mouth. He went still, except for a fine vibration that radiated out from his clenched muscles.

Roxanne slipped one of her hands free and pulled his head down, gripping his neck tightly so he wouldn't pull away. She took her time kissing him, delving inside his mouth to taste him. Slowly, he gave in, yielding to her onslaught.

She felt every shift as he lost the battle with himself. First, his breathing sped, and she could feel the hard pounding of his heartbeat against her breasts. Then, his muscles unclenched, and a sinuous power took over. His arms snaked around her body, caressing her as they went. He held her against him and leaned her back so he could control the kiss.

With anyone else, she would have worried she'd fall, but this was Tanner. He was rock solid and as steady as they came. She'd trust him with her life.

Roxanne's head spun. She couldn't get enough oxygen. Her heart was beating hard, and her whole body was alive and tingling. Sweat beaded on her skin in a futile effort to cool her down. Everywhere Tanner's hands passed, they left shivers in their wake.

She gripped his shoulders to try to steady herself, but he didn't give her time. His big, hot hands slid under her shirt, lifting it. She didn't even stop to think; she simply lifted her arms, letting him strip the garment off over her head.

His eyes darkened as he stared down at her. He traced one finger along the lacy edge of her bra, following the curve of her breast.

Her nipples hardened, and her breasts seemed to swell. Her bra became too tight, the fabric too rough. She needed his hands on her, his lips. She'd never been with a man who made her body sing with only his mouth the way Tanner did.

She unfastened her bra and flung it aside, then shoved his shirt up so she could rub herself against his bare chest. Tanner took the hint and stripped out of his shirt.

He was glorious. Hard, mouthwatering contours tempted her fingers to touch. She pressed her palms against him and closed her eyes, reveling in the feel of his body. No other man had ever turned her on like this with just the sight of him, but as breathtaking as he looked, the man inside was even more beautiful. He cared more for her comfort than his own pleasure. He worried about her. He'd risked his life for hers more than once. Maybe it was all part of the job for him, but the combination of kick-ass warrior and gentle protector was getting to her, tearing down defenses she hadn't even known were there.

She could love a man like him if she let herself. It wouldn't even be a long fall. The question was, would Tanner fall with her, or was what they had limited to the here and now?

Those thoughts were too heavy for her to deal with right now. She was already stretched thin, to the point of snapping in two. Any more pressure, and even the hope of something good would be destroyed.

She couldn't let that happen. She had to take what he was willing to offer and not be greedy. Men like Tanner came along only once in a lifetime, and she was going to enjoy him while she could.

Roxanne kissed him while her fingers played over his chest and abs. Her hands skimmed his rigid contours, sliding down until his jeans barred her path.

That simply wasn't going to do. She wanted all of him—as much as she could get.

She sank to her knees, drawing his zipper down as she

went. He towered over her, his chest pumping with each fast breath, his jaw tight. His eyes held hers as she peeled his clothes down and stroked him with her tongue.

His whole body went tight as if she'd sent an electric current up his spine. He sucked in a deep breath and threw his head back.

A heady rush of power flooded her as she witnessed his pleasure. She'd done that to him, and she was only getting started.


Tanner struggled to retain one coherent thought amidst the flood of pleasure sweeping through him: *Don't hurt her.*

She wasn't making it easy. Her hot mouth slid over his cock, sucking and licking just the way he liked. Her grip was firm, her clever fingers stroking him as her mouth moved. She wasn't shy or timid. She wasn't afraid of hurting him. He wished he could say the same.

Sweat beaded up on his spine. His legs shook. He fought the urge to hold her head and thrust into her mouth, knowing his grip would press against the knot on her skull. Instead, he clenched his fists and stood there, letting her do what she wanted.

He was swiftly spiraling out of control—nearing that space where rational thought ceased to exist and he'd forget all his good intentions. He was seconds away from climax, and he wasn't sure he'd be able to resist touching her while he came. The only part of her he could reach was her wounded head.

No way was he going to do that to her.

Tanner stepped back, pulling himself from her mouth. His cock was shiny, thick, and dark from her attention. She eyed it like she was starving for another taste, and in that second, he nearly gave in.

He shook with the effort of resisting her as he pulled her to her feet. "Does it hurt to lie down?" he asked.

"No."

"Then do it."

She offered him a hot smile that he felt all the way to his toes; then she sat on the bed.

Tanner knelt in front of her and unlaced her boots. His fingers trembled, but he managed to get the ties open and pulled them from her feet. Her pants were next, and he kept his focus on the job, refusing to look at any bit of bare skin until he was done. Once he had her naked, he kissed his way up her legs, parting them as he went. Small bruises marred her knees, which he paid special attention to, planting light kisses so he wouldn't hurt her.

She shivered and scraped her fingernails over his scalp as if searching for hair she could tug on.

The inside of her thighs was magically soft. He didn't know how she could be so tough while hiding so much softness. It was like a treasure no one else could see, and Tanner knew the secret.

His hands splayed over her thighs, pressing them wide. The contrast of his rough hands on her perfect skin drove him crazy, and he had to consciously keep his fingers from tightening on her, leaving marks of possession.

She opened to him, revealing her sex. It was flushed and slick with arousal. "I haven't even touched you yet, and you're ready for me."

"Sucking your cock turned me on."

Lust, pure and powerful, slammed into him at her words. Need took over, as instincts dominated thought. He didn't care about careful anymore. All he wanted to do was drive them over the edge so many times, they wouldn't even remember what it felt like not to be falling.

Tanner let out a growl as his mouth covered her. She bucked off the bed, but he pushed her back down and held her hips still while he explored. Her taste went to his head, clouding his thoughts even more. She was sweet and hot, making the sexiest noises he'd ever heard. Her fingers cupped his head, clenching and opening as he pushed her higher.

Her clit was swollen, and every time he flicked over it, she let out another high-pitched gasp. He pushed two fingers inside her, and her thighs tensed, shaking as her orgasm neared. She held her breath and tightened around his fingers. All he could think about what how good that contraction was going to feel on his cock once he got inside her.

A fine tremor started at her core and vibrated out through her limbs. She let out a long, breathless cry of release and dug her fingernails into his scalp.

Tanner nearly lost his load just witnessing her pleasure. He waited until the last flutter had passed before he moved away and shoved his jeans off. He was poised, ready to slide inside her when he remembered the condom. With a violent curse for his stupidity, he grabbed one and covered himself.

"Glad one of us is thinking," she panted.

What he was thinking was that he could have been naked inside her right now. He'd never done that with a woman before, and despite how irresponsible it would have been, he would have enjoyed the hell out of it, at least until it was over.

He came back to her and saw the dark, angry bruise on her side where the bullet had struck. Something inside him seized up. He froze, realizing how close she'd come to dying tonight.

That thought gave him the control he needed to slow down. He leaned over her, kissing the bruise. She grabbed his ears and tugged on them.

He smiled down at her. "You certainly don't have any trouble communicating in bed, do you?"

She smiled back. "I'd really like you to fuck me right now."

"That's pretty clear."

Her thigh slid over his, grazing him with that magically soft skin. She pushed him back onto the bed and straddled his body. There was a look of conquest on her face, and a wicked grin on her mouth as she gripped his erection and eased down onto it. Tight heat enveloped him as she sank down, working to take all of him.

She let out a rough sigh and braced her hand on his ribs. The curve of her waist and the flare of her hips drove him wild. The way her breasts moved as she arched her back was almost more than he could take. Not even the bruise detracted from her beauty.

She was glowing with perspiration, flushed with arousal. Her blond hair, which had come loose, was wild about her face. Her eyes were closed in concentration, and the sleek muscles in her thighs and arms flexed as she rode him.

Tanner watched, refusing to miss a thing. He knew it would hasten his release, but he couldn't stop himself from enjoying every moment with her.

He cupped her breasts, feeling her tight nipple rub against his palm. She gripped his wrists and sped up the pace. He could see her heart pounding in the hollow of her throat, and feel her muscles tighten as she worked herself toward another climax.

Tanner sat up, cradling her body against his. He helped her move, hitting the spot that made her breath catch in her throat. His own orgasm was barreling down on him, but he gritted his teeth and held back.

He caught her mouth with his. He had to kiss her again and swallow her cries of pleasure as she came. Her tongue mated with his, he sucked her bottom lip. Her rhythm sped up and her breath shot out in short, hard gasps.

Pressure built at the base of his spine. He wasn't going to be able to hold back much longer. He wrapped his arm around her hips, angling them so he could hit the spot she liked on every stroke. Her cries guided his way, rising up like music he longed to hear over and over. His lips covered hers, drinking in the sound.

Roxanne let out a small whimper, then screamed into his mouth as the first wave of her climax hit.

Tanner lost control. His body took over as his orgasm tore through him, choking the breath from his chest. Semen pumped out of him with every liquid clench of her body. Her spasms dragged out his pleasure until he was sure it would kill him. Lights flashed in his eyes, and the last pulse rippled out of him.

He flopped back onto the bed, bringing Roxanne with him. He gulped down air, trying to refill his starved lungs. Her heart beat against his ribs, and her breath spilled out over his chest. She was limp and boneless, lying over him like a blanket, seemingly in no hurry to move.

He would have stayed like this for hours if not for the condom. But reality was a thing best not ignored, so he rolled her over and pulled his cock out of her body. She made a weak noise of protest but let him go.

His legs barely worked as he dealt with the condom and stumbled back to bed. She lay sprawled across the sheets, too beautiful for words—the kind of woman a man never tired of looking at.

That was what his folks had had. Dad never once strayed from Mom. He'd never even had eyes for another woman. He'd looked at Mom as if she were the only woman on the face of the planet until the day he'd died. From the time Tanner hit puberty, Dad always said that when he found the right woman, he'd know to stop looking. There wouldn't be any question.

Tanner stared down at Roxanne. He couldn't imagine looking at anyone else. He didn't know her well enough to get ahead of himself, but one thing was certain. When he did find the right one, she'd be the kind of person who spoke her mind. She'd be the kind of person who would drop everything to help someone in need. She'd be the kind of person who would courageously put her life on the line for another. In essence, she'd be a lot like Roxanne.

There'd been a time in his life when thoughts like that would have scared him shitless, but a lot had happened in the last few months. He realized how fleeting life really was. He'd focused on his job for so long that he'd almost lost the ability to see anything else.

He was seeing Roxanne now, and a welcoming warmth began to uncurl inside him. He wasn't sure what it was, but for the first time since Dad and Brody died, he felt as if he were waking up. The shambling stupor that he'd been living through fell away, and he actually saw a future for himself. He didn't know what it would hold, but that hardly mattered. His life wasn't over. He'd lost a lot, but not everything. He still had Mom and Reid. And for now, he had Roxanne. That was a hell of a lot more than most people ever got.

She was asleep when he came back, snuggled into the pillows. He pulled the sheet up over her body, partly to help himself focus, but mostly because the air in here was chilly. As sweaty as they'd gotten, it wouldn't take long for her to cool down.

Unless he heated things up again.

That sounded like the best idea mankind had ever had, until he remembered that he'd just used his last condom. As close as he'd come to unprotected sex only a few minutes ago, he didn't think it was wise to test his self-control.

She lay on her side, resting her head on her hands. The hard metal of her bracelet seemed to be cutting into her skin, so he eased her hand out from under her cheek and flipped open the tiny latch that held it shut. It sprung open, revealing three pale, parallel scars on her wrist—the kind made in a suicide attempt.

Shock hit him hard, and he sucked in a breath. Roxanne's golden eyes popped open, and she snatched her wrist away from him, cradling it against her body in a protective gesture. "I didn't want you to see that."

He couldn't imagine her ever having been the kind of person who would give up. It just didn't sit right in his view of her, like an extra piece to an already-completed puzzle. He didn't know what to do with the information, so he sat there, staring.

She let out a long sigh of frustration and turned away from him.

Like hell he was letting this drop. He moved around the bed and sat on the other side, forcing her to face him. "Why?"

"Why what? Why didn't I want you to see the scars, or why did I try to kill myself?"

"Either. Both."

"I didn't want you to see the scars because I didn't want you looking at me like this."

"Like what?"

"With shock. Disappointment. Pity."

"You tried to kill yourself. How am I supposed to look at you?"

She sat up, gloriously naked and flushed with rage. "No, I didn't. I hide the scars because that's the first thing everyone thinks. My life sucked sometimes, but I'd never take the easy way out. I'm not a coward, and I hate seeing everyone look at me as though I am. I saved *myself*. I killed that fucker."

Confusion rattled through him. She'd killed someone? He grabbed her shoulders. "Slow down. What are you talking about?"

Roxanne looked away from him and pulled the sheet up over her chest. "I was kidnapped for ransom when I was fourteen. He told my parents he wanted ten million dollars to let me go."

That was a shitload of money, even for rich people. "But he lied, didn't he? He got the money and didn't let you go."

"No. He would have let me go. My parents refused to pay it. My dad actually bargained with him." Hurt shone in her eyes, but not a single tear fell. "I heard the whole thing. Dad said they could have another kid. That it would be more cost-effective to raise a new child to adulthood than it would be to get me back. As if I were some kind of investment, and letting me go was cutting his losses on a bad deal." She hugged her knees. "Dad said I was worth no more than three percent of his net worth."

Rage swam in Tanner's belly, making larger and larger circles until he was shaking with the spread of anger that filled him. How could a father say that? Even if it was a lie? "You're fucking kidding me."

She shook her head. "The kidnapper cut me, trying to convince Dad to change his mind. He didn't. I don't think he believed I was his biological daughter, and he hated me for that—for being proof of Mom's cheating. That's where the scars came from."

He couldn't imagine that kind of evil, treating a child like a commodity—even if she wasn't his child. If her dad hadn't already been dead, Tanner would have had a hard time not killing him for the crime of being a heartless monster.

Roxanne drew in a deep breath. "I knew I was on my own. No one was coming to save me. When the kidnapper was in the middle of throwing a fit over Dad's refusal to give him the money, I swiped the knife. When he came back, I stabbed him." Her eyes took on a distant look. "I didn't mean to kill him. I just wanted to get away. But I hit an artery in his thigh, and he died in minutes."

Tanner needed to hold her. He reached for her to pull her into his arms, but she shied away. "Don't. I don't want your pity." She snapped the cuff back in place, turned over, and shoved a cold wall of air between them.

"I don't pity you, Roxanne. I admire your bravery. Those are battle scars—signs of courage. You're the one who's hiding them as if they're shameful."

"The kids at school didn't see them that way. Did you ever wonder where I got the nickname Razor?"

He could see the other kids taunting her, mocking her for the scars. "Kids can be cruel. If you didn't like the name, why keep it?"

"To remind me of what I'd done."

"You were punishing yourself."

"No one else would. I had to do something."

"It was self-defense, Roxanne. That man deserved what he got."

"I'm not so sure. I've often wondered what drove him to do something so drastic. Was it drugs? Greed? Or did he have a sick kid at home who needed medical care? He didn't have a police record. No one knew who he was. No one claimed the body. To this day, I still don't know why he did it."

"It doesn't matter why. He made the choice to abduct a child. That automatically makes him guilty."

"I don't want to talk about this anymore. I just want to sleep," she said. "Please, leave me alone."

There was nothing he could do to take back what she'd suffered. He had no real claim to any relationship with her. They weren't even dating. If he'd been her boyfriend, he would at least have felt he had the right to push the issue. But the truth was, they had no future. Their jobs prohibited it.

If it had just been him, he would have walked away from the job without blinking, but it wasn't just him. He had to think about his family. They needed him right now, and he couldn't shirk that duty. He had to keep this job.

He stared down at Roxanne, aching to do something to ease her suffering. But all he could offer her was the rest she needed so that she wouldn't crumble under the strain of searching for Jake. So that's what he did. He got up and left her alone, hating every second of it.

Tanner grabbed a shower and got dressed. Clay was going to be here in about an hour, and he was planning on standing guard so she could get some sleep. Whatever the man's plan was, Tanner hoped it was a good one, because he didn't know how much longer he could stand to watch Roxanne hurt.

# Chapter Twenty-one

Jake opened his eyes, snapping awake in an instant. He had no idea where he was or how he'd gotten here. He was standing, wearing a backless hospital gown and looking into the aging face of Dr. Stynger. Her bright red lips burned his eyes, as did the light she was using to stab his retinas.

She clicked the penlight off. "Excellent. How do you feel?"

He wanted to shout some smart-ass remark at her, but, instead, he found himself taking a mental inventory of his body. He was sore, as if he'd had the hardest workout of his life two days ago and had been shoved in a coffin for his muscles to freeze in place. His head hurt, but that was nothing new. He wasn't nauseated, which was nice. "Fine."

"Good. Do you know who I am?" she asked.

*Evil bitch from hell.* "Dr. Stynger."

"See?" she said, turning to someone behind her. "I told you he'd survive."

Bower stepped up and clapped a hand on Jake's shoulder as if he gave a shit. "I'm glad you made it."

Jake barely resisted the urge to shrug the other man's hand away. He had no idea what he'd survived, but their worry seemed genuine.

He looked around the room he was in. It was small and

brightly lit. Medical equipment surrounded a gurney at his side. There were blue linens crumpled on a tray, dotted with blood. His? Probably.

Dr. Stynger stripped off her latex gloves with a snap and turned to Bower. "The next forty-eight hours will be crucial. If he makes it that long, he has an eighty percent survival rate."

"And what's my rate now, Doc?"

Her pale green eyes met his, and something in his mind opened up, desperate for her to speak and fill the void. She smiled as if she'd heard his thoughts. "Flip a coin."

He forced his sore shoulder to lift in a negligent shrug. "I've faced worse."

Her smile widened, and she walked to the door.

Bower was right on her heels. "Sit tight and rest here. We'll be back in a few minutes and run some more tests."

"What kind of tests? What did you do to me?"

"All in good time," said the doctor. "If you want to find out, I suggest you focus on staying alive. You shouldn't sleep for at least twenty hours. Thirty is better."

They shut the door on their way out, leaving him alone with her ominous warning.

Jake stripped off the gown, searching for signs of what they'd done to him. There were abrasions on his wrists and ankles. He had a bruise on the back of his hand where an IV had been. A patch on the back of his head had been shaved, and he felt an incision that had been stitched closed. He pressed around the area, but he couldn't tell what they'd done. He didn't know if they'd removed something, or put something in. Maybe they were just taking a peek inside, though he had no idea why anyone would want to do that.

He went to the sink and gulped down some water. His stomach woke up as though he hadn't eaten in a week. Maybe he hadn't. He had no way to tell how long he'd been asleep.

The door burst open and Jordyn rushed in, shutting it

behind her. She saw he was naked, and her frantic movement stalled out for a moment.

Jake covered his crotch with his hands. "Uh. Sorry."

A blush crept up her face, lending her pale skin a bit of color, but she otherwise ignored his nudity. "We have to hurry. Here, put these on." She tossed him a sack filled with clothes.

"Do you know what's going on?"

"Yes, but there's no time to explain. Please, Jake. Just dress. We have less than two minutes to get you out of the building before the security codes reset."

Out? He didn't need to be told twice if that was the prize. He pulled on the pants and shoved his feet into too-small boots. The shirt could wait. "I need to get the others. Moss, Mac, and Evans."

"There's no time for that."

"I can't leave them here."

She glanced nervously at the door as if expecting company. "You don't have a choice. There's simply no time. Please, Jake."

He considered digging in his heels for a split second before he realized this might be his one chance to save them. If he was free, he could get help. He'd come back for them— heavily armed.

Jake nodded. "Let's go."

She flew out the door and raced down the hall at a dead run. Jake's body was stiff, but he managed to keep up with her and not lose the unlaced boots.

They took a couple of turns and came to a dead end that housed an elevator. Jordyn swiped her ID card through a slot, then pressed the card into his hands, along with a set of keys.

Her hair was a mess, and there were dark circles under her eyes. Her lips, normally a dark pink, were pale and dry. A blue vein in her temple pounded fast. He didn't know what she'd done to make this possible, but it was clear the stress was taking its toll.

She drew in his gaze, and he couldn't help but stare as she gave him orders. "Go to level seven. Take a right. When the blue stripe of paint on the wall ends, take a left. My card will get you out through the door. These are the keys to the last car in row B. Drive west and don't stop until you're sure no one has followed you."

"You're not coming with me?"

"I can't. I'm sorry. You'll have to stay in hiding. Mother will search for you now that she's invested so much time, effort, and money."

"Come with me. I can't leave you here."

"Eventually she'll get bored, move on to a new experiment, and stop looking for you. If I go, she'll never stop searching. You have to go alone."

The elevator let out a muted ding as it reached their floor.

"I can't leave you here," said Jake.

A flash of yearning crossed her face before she hid it. "I'll be fine."

"I'll come back for you and the others," he promised. "I won't leave you here with that monster."

"She's my mother."

"She's a heartless bitch. She'll kill you for helping me."

Jordyn's eyes shimmered with tears. "She'll only make me *wish* I were dead. I'll survive it. I always do."

The doors hissed open. She grabbed his arm and pushed him inside, then pressed the button for level seven. Her slender fingers shook, and Jake wanted to pull her into his arms and comfort her. There was no time.

He was going to find Dr. Stynger and kill the bitch. He was going to find her and choke her with his bare hands, breaking her skinny neck. "I'm coming back for you. We'll storm this place and stop her."

She held up her hand, and tears slipped from her pale eyes. "Good-bye."

The doors slid shut. For a moment, he considered going back and tossing her over his shoulder. She might fight him, but at least he'd save her ass. Then he realized that his two minutes were nearly gone. She'd risked a lot to give him those two minutes, and he wasn't going to recklessly toss her gift aside. This might be his one and only chance to rescue her and the men.

Once he was free, he'd gather up an entire army to come back and clean this place out. Jordyn was tough. She'd been in her mother's grip for years. She could hold out long enough for him to gather some men and weapons. He'd come back and save her and make sure she got a fucking medal for her bravery.

Norma Stynger watched the cameras as S-eleven-sixteen got in one of her cars and drove away. His escape was Jordyn's doing, but then Norma was counting on her daughter's predicable weaknesses.

"How did you get Jordyn to do it?" asked General Bower. "I figured she'd be too afraid of you to defy you."

"My daughter is defective. Despite my best efforts, she makes decisions based on emotions rather than logic. It's a trait that makes her easy to manipulate."

"But she has to know what this will cost her. She'll end up right back in the white room again."

Norma sighed in disappointment. "I refuse to give up on her. One day she'll realize I only want her to succeed."

"I still don't know how you did it."

"I sent a memo to research team A that the subject was to be scheduled for an autopsy."

"But he's still alive."

Norma nodded. "I knew Jordyn had become attached to him and that she would help him escape if she thought his life was at risk."

S-eleven-sixteen was hers now. All she had to do was follow him and he'd lead her right to Roxanne Haught and the missing journal. Once that was destroyed and the subject was restrained once again, there would be no evidence floating about, unaccounted for. Her investors would be appeased, and the research could continue.

"Will he do it?"

"Of course. He'll do whatever I tell him to do now."

"He didn't seem to remember what you told him."

"If he had, he would have tried to kill me. At least until I triggered him." Norma entered a code on her cell phone. The alarm sounded inside the compound—a bit of theater to add to the realism of his daring escape.

"Are you sure he's under control?" asked the general. "He could go to the police."

"No, he can't," she said, her confidence unshakable. She trusted her mentor's notes implicitly, and while the procedure was risky, it appeared to be working as promised.

"Why not?"

"Because I told him not to. His orders are to steal a phone and call me as soon as possible."

"Orders won't control a man like Staite."

Norma sighed, tired of the general's endless skepticism. "Go and find Jordyn so we can deal with her punishment. She'll be expecting you."


Roxanne dressed as fast as she could in the little motel bathroom. Clay had arrived, and Tanner said he'd stall him outside while she put herself back together.

The sleep she'd managed to get had been much needed. While she wasn't fully alert, she felt better than she had only a couple of hours ago—in every way except one.

Tanner knew what she'd done. Would it change the way he looked at her, now that he knew she was a killer? Or even worse, a victim? The last thing she wanted from him was pity.

She pressed a cold washcloth to her face, but it did little to ease her heated skin. She wasn't sure if it was from the shame burning within her, or from remembering his touch, his kisses. He'd worn her out, making her boneless with pleasure, and yet she hadn't had enough. Not even close.

The question was, had he had enough of her? Fucking a killer wasn't exactly something most guys enjoyed, and the ones who did were not the kind of men she wanted to be with.

Once they found Jake, she probably wouldn't see him again. For now, he was assigned to babysitting her, but once that assignment was over, they'd go their separate ways. She'd have her missions; he'd have his. Chances were, their lives would not intersect, especially if Bella heard that they'd slept together.

Roxanne wouldn't lie about it, but she wasn't going to flaunt it, either. She knew it was against the rules, but some things were worth the risk, and Tanner was definitely in that category.

Even if he wasn't repulsed by her, she knew they couldn't date openly, like a normal couple. That was just a girlish fantasy.

Unless she quit her job.

She tried to picture it—doing something else. She could go back to school and get any degree she wanted. She could start her own business. But what about the friends she'd made at the Edge? And what could she possibly do that would give her the same thrills and sense of satisfaction as catching the bad guys?

She was meant for this work. She loved it. And even if she started her own security company, it wouldn't be the same. It would take years for her to build a client list, and thanks to the non-compete clause in her contract, she couldn't be hired out by any of the Edge's clients.

She could move, but she couldn't see either her or Tanner doing the long-distance relationship thing, so what would she gain?

It was best to accept the fleeting nature of their liaison and enjoy it while it lasted. Unfortunately for any other men she might meet, she'd always judge them against Tanner. He was kind, honorable, and sexy as hell. Most men wouldn't even be able to come close.

That was going to have to be a problem for another day. Right now, she was up to her nose in problems, and needed to focus.

Forgoing makeup and sweeping her hair into a simple ponytail, she straightened her rumpled clothes and went to face the men.

Clay sat on the bed, slumped against the headboard. He was pale, almost gray. Both his eyes were black, and a cut on his cheek was red and swollen. If she hadn't known better, she would have thought something had scared him. He looked up at her as she came out of the bathroom. "Hey, Razor. How are you feeling?"

"I should be asking you the same thing. You look like hell."

"It's been a rough day. For all of us. At least I didn't get shot."

"I'm fine," she assured him. "Just bruised."

"And concussed, most likely," said Tanner.

Her gaze strayed to him. He was standing with his feet braced and his arms crossed over his broad chest. His blue eyes seemed to darken as he stared. There were no obvious signs of revulsion, just his usual speculative interest.

She wanted to kiss him again. She wanted to feel his hands on her skin, feel him filling her until she thought she'd burst from the pleasure.

Roxanne swallowed and looked away. She couldn't see him and not want him, which was going to make things awkward if she didn't find some self-control. "Can we focus on the job?"

"Right," said Clay. "I stole a car from one of the guys who followed us, and I found what I think is a tracking device. I pried it out of the glove box, hit a hardware store, and wrapped the sucker up in steel wool before shoving it in a thermos."

"Where is it?"

"I left it in the car in case my efforts weren't good enough. It could be a listening device, but since it was in a car . . ." He trailed off, shrugging.

"You think that if we take it out of the thermos, they can track the signal."

"Right," said Clay. "I figure we set up a trap and see if we can lure in someone who knows where Jake is."

Tanner shook his head. "I'm afraid that's not going to work."

"Why not?" asked Roxanne.

"Payton called while you were in the shower. I answered your phone, since it might be important. It was."

"What did he say?"

"The soldier who attacked you at the storage facility—the one who went to the hospital—they questioned him."

"But that's a good thing," said Roxanne.

"Not for him. You know that seizure the guy we captured had? It wasn't a seizure. He was poisoned."

She took a step forward, angry at Tanner's accusation. "No. Gage would never have done that to him. He'd never kill a man in cold blood like that."

Tanner held up his hands. "Gage didn't do it. Someone else did."

"How? There was no one else there."

"There was some kind of capsule in his body. Payton isn't sure exactly how it works, but apparently he's seen it before."

"Seen what before?"

"He said they used to put these poison capsules in spies so they could kill themselves if they were captured and tortured for information."

Shock exploded in her chest, making it hard to breathe. Her voice came out in a low whisper. "You're saying that the guy with Gage killed himself?"

"It's possible."

Clay had been silent until now, staring sightlessly at the

rumpled bed. He lifted his head, and the look on his face was a disturbing mix of fear and anger. "Where was it?"

"Where was what?"

"The capsule. They found it, right?"

Tanner nodded. "At the base of the skull. Why?"

"Because someone who was bound to a chair would have had a hard time reaching that spot, and you wouldn't want it to be too easy to trigger. You wouldn't want the thing to burst accidentally when you were getting your head bashed in a fight."

"What are you saying, Clay?" she asked.

"You said that your friend Jake was recruited into what he thought was some kind of secret special forces group, right?"

"Right."

"And that he wasn't alone? There were more men with him?"

"Yes."

"If I was building a secret army of badasses for some nefarious purpose, I'd want a way to control the men."

Tanner's body went still. "You think the poison is the control. Anyone steps out of line and they die."

Clay nodded. "It would be pretty fucking effective, don't you think? I'd sure as hell think twice before trying anything."

Roxanne sank to the bed, struggling to keep herself from going to all the dark places this line of thought opened up. "How would they—whoever they are—have known that one of their men was going to talk?"

Tanner stepped closer but didn't touch her. She wished he would. To hell with what Clay thought. She needed his comfort right now—she needed to know he didn't hate her for what she's done. If these people were willing to kill their own men, Jake was in even more danger than she'd thought, and she wasn't sure she could face that alone.

"With the technology we have today," said Clay, "who knows? Mira would have some ideas, but I'd really rather not ask her to think about it. It's pretty dark shit. And she's squeamish."

"Both men died while being questioned," said Tanner. "Maybe it's activated by a key word or phrase. They wouldn't want it to respond to adrenaline or body temperature, since that could kill someone accidentally."

"My guess is that it's activated remotely," said Clay. "Or it goes off if someone is out of touch for too long. Maybe there's some kind of reset switch that has to be triggered every few hours or days. If one of the men goes missing for too long, it's activated."

She couldn't stand to hear them talk anymore. Her stomach turned sour, and she started to shake. For all she knew, Jake had one of those things inside him right now. He could be walking around with a ticking time bomb in his head.

Roxanne lurched from the bed and moved away. There was nowhere to go in the small room, but she had to move, had to do something. "We can't set a trap," she told them as she paced. "We could kill another man if we do. Maybe more than one."

"These men aren't innocent," said Clay. "We've seen them in action."

"Jake is innocent. What if the rest of them started out the same way? They could be good men who were turned into something else. We can't just keep killing them off in the hopes that one of them will give us information before he dies."

"Razor's right," said Tanner. "We need to find out how the poison thing works. Maybe we can block the signal or remove it before it's activated."

He'd called her Razor, not Roxanne as he had when they'd been together earlier, before he knew about the scars. She tried not to read anything into it. She knew they had to keep their feelings hidden, but she missed the sound of her name coming from his lips.

"I'll call Payton," said Clay. "Maybe he can find someone to analyze it and create countermeasures."

Roxanne's phone rang, making her jump. She closed her eyes and took a long, deep breath before she pulled it from her pocket. She didn't recognize the number.

"Hello?"

"Rox? Is that you?" The voice filled the line, sounding like a chorus of angels.

Tears welled up in Roxanne's eyes, and relief at the sound of his voice clamped her throat closed for a moment. Seconds ticked by; yet she couldn't find the breath to utter even a single word.

"Rox? Are you there? It's Jake. I'm in big trouble. I need you."

# Chapter Twenty-two

Tanner saw the color drain from Roxanne's face. Her hand shook as she gripped the phone so tight her knuckles turned white. He crossed the room, resisting the urge to snatch it from her grasp and snarl at the person on the other end—the one who'd clearly upset her.

She looked up at him, her golden eyes full of tears and pleading for help.

He took it as permission to put his nose directly into her business.

Tanner eased the phone from her hand. "Who is this?" he snapped.

"Jake. Who the hell are you?"

Surprise flickered through him for a moment before he regained his wits. He pressed the button to activate the speaker phone. "My name is Tanner. I'm a friend of Razor's."

"Let me talk to her."

"I'm right here, Jake," she said, her voice faint. She cleared her throat. "Where are you? Are you okay?"

"I don't have a lot of time. I stole this phone so they can't trace it, but I don't want to talk long. They may be keeping tabs on your calls."

"Who?"

"Not now. Just listen. I need your help. I need to find . . ." A strangling sound filled the line.

"Jake? What's going on?"

When he spoke, he sounded out of breath. "I'm all fucked up, Rox."

"Where are you? I'll come get you."

"I don't know if they're following me."

"I don't care. I'm not alone. I'll be safe."

Jake hesitated, but finally said, "Do you remember that vacation we took with my mom?"

"Yes."

"Do you remember the place where we got those banana pancakes?"

A sad smile touched her mouth and tears spilled from her eyes. "Yes, in—"

"No. Don't say it. Just meet me there."

"When?"

"Tomorrow. The same time we were there before. Do you remember?"

"I do. I'll be there, Jake."

"Come armed. Bring your friends. Bring—" He gasped as if in pain.

"Jake? Are you hurt?" asked Tanner.

"No. Just my fucking head. They cut my head open, Rox."

"Oh God," breathed Roxanne. She covered her mouth with her hand and choked back a sob.

Tanner took over. "Listen to me very carefully, Jake. It's possible they put a device inside you that can poison you. We don't know how it's triggered, but we're going to find out, okay. Until then, don't say anything to anyone. What you say could kill you."

"Could?"

"All we know is that two men who may have connections to Dr. Stynger died while being questioned."

"I understand. Gotta go." He hung up.

Roxanne turned away, and although her anguished cry was quiet, he heard it all the same.

Tanner pocketed her phone and stepped up behind her.

He cupped her shoulders, hoping to offer some sliver of comfort. She turned, folding into his embrace and hiding her face against his chest.

His heart broke open. He stroked her hair and her back. He held her tight, telling her without words that he was here. He wouldn't leave her.

Clay regarded them for a moment before he stood. "I'm going to grab a soda," he said as he walked out.

"Shhh," Tanner whispered against her hair. "We won't let anything happen to Jake. We'll find him. We'll get him help."

She sniffed and looked up at him. Her nose was red and her eyes were bloodshot, but she was still the most beautiful woman he'd ever seen. Her pain grated against him, making him want to lash out at whoever had hurt her friend.

"I'm so glad he's alive. I just hope we're not too late."

"Of course we're not. We're going to find him, Roxanne. I'm going to make it happen."

She wiped her eyes and gave him a lopsided smile. "I almost believe you when you look all fierce like that."

"It's not just a look, honey. I *am* all fierce, especially when someone is fucking with the friend of someone I care about."

She cupped his cheek. Her slender fingers sent sensation rioting down his spine. Part of him hated that she could make him respond so easily, but the rest of him reveled in the feeling. He'd never had a woman go to his head like she did. It was as if his whole world rotated around her and stopped spinning when she suffered.

He was going to fix it. He was going to find Jake and get that damn thing out of his head before it killed him.

And then what? Roxanne would kiss him in thanks, and they'd go their separate ways?

He didn't want that. He wanted her to stick around, to be part of his life. But if he did that, he'd lose his job and his family would suffer. They'd already suffered enough because of him. He couldn't put his own selfish needs before them. Not again.

It was best not to think about the future. He needed to focus on right now, on finding Jake and getting him home safe and sound without a dose of cyanide in his brain.

"Where are we meeting him?" Tanner asked.

"It's a little town near the highway, a few miles over the Texas border. We went there when I was thirteen. My mom and dad had gone to Europe for vacation, so Jake's mom took us on a little road trip. We stopped there for dinner." She gave him a sad smile. "I'd never had pancakes for dinner before. I was so enthralled by the idea that Jake teased me about it for years."

For a moment, Tanner envied Jake's relationship with her. It ran deep, shaping her whole life. There was a tie between them that couldn't be severed, and Tanner found himself wishing for that same thing.

Selfish.

He shoved the thought from his mind and forced himself to consider their options. "We need a plan to extract him safely. We'll have to assume he's being followed. They could even be listening to him."

"I'll see if Payton can send some more people our way."

"Good. We'll take all the help we can get. And we'll need them to figure out how to neutralize that device in his head."

She straightened her shoulders, wiped her eyes, and stepped back. Tanner let her go, though he already missed the heat of her skin and the feel of her body against his.

"I'll talk to Mira. Maybe she can come up with something."

"You do that. I'll fill Clay in and see if he can add any intel from his encounter with their men. He's had more interaction with them than any of us. He might know their tactics to help us plan for contingencies."

She met his gaze, her eyes glowing with relief. "Thank you. I don't know what I'd do without you."

Tanner said nothing, because the only words that came to mind were to tell her she'd never have to find out. That was a foolish, unrealistic notion, and he wasn't going to lie to either of them like that.


Jake tried to dial 911, but his fingers wouldn't move. He'd meant to ask Rox to bring police, but he hadn't been able to get the words out.

It was the pain in his head. It kept distracting him, pounding as if someone were hitting him with a ball-peen hammer.

He checked his rearview mirror. No one was behind him. The road stretched out for miles, dark in both directions.

Weariness tugged at him, but he wasn't going to take a chance that what Dr. Stynger had said was a lie. He didn't doubt for a second that she'd do something dangerous to him, that she'd risk his life for her own purposes—whatever the hell those were.

*I suggest you focus on staying alive. You shouldn't sleep for at least twenty hours. Thirty is better.*

He checked the clock and made a note of the time. He'd sleep once he saw Rox again. Once he was sure that a whole pile of armed men were on their way to rescue Jordyn.

He tried not to think about what her aid would cost her. She was brave as hell, and he was going to see to it that he got to tell her so to her face.

If he called the police now, they could move in and get her out of there. They could rescue Evans, Moss, and Mac. He ordered his hand to move, to pick up the phone, but it wouldn't listen. His fingers refused to budge from the steering wheel.

Fuck! What the hell had they done to him?

He tried to remember. There was a brief flash of lights and people behind masks, and then a bomb of pain detonated inside his skull. His vision went black and he slammed on the brakes, skidding to a stop.

Jake let go of the memory like it was a live wire and, slowly, the pain eased, allowing him to breathe again. The

spots across his vision faded, and he saw he was sitting in
the middle of the highway, sweating and shaking.

He let off the brake and moved the car off the road. He
knew he had to keep moving, but if he drove now, he'd kill
himself before he ever got to see Rox again.

The phone rang. He answered it, praying it was Rox with
good news.

"Do you know who this is?" asked the woman on the
line.

Every cell in Jake's body stood at attention at the sound
of Dr. Stynger's voice. "Yes, ma'am."

"Good. Tell me where you're meeting Ms. Haught."

No. He couldn't do that. It would put Rox in danger. He
tried to keep his lips clamped shut, but the words spilled out
of him, giving her every detail he could remember.

"Excellent." Her praise filled him with a buoyant sense
of joy. "Now, when I hang up, I want you to forget I called.
You never heard from me. Carry on as if we never spoke.
Understand?"

"Yes, ma'am."

The line went dead and Jake stared at the phone in his
hand, wondering why he'd picked it up. His emotions were
all over the place, jumbled together in an indistinguishable
pile of joy, fear, loathing and anticipation. He couldn't seem
to control them.

Whatever they'd done, it was too late to stop. He'd find
help and get himself fixed. All he had to do was hold himself together long enough to reach Rox. She was smart, capable. Thanks to her job, she knew a ton of badass men who
would do anything for her. He couldn't think straight, but
she could do the thinking for him. He just had to reach her.

Jake eased the car back onto the highway and started
driving.

# Chapter Twenty-three

The diner had aged since the last time Roxanne had been here. The neon sign flickered wearily, and the red paint had faded to a dismal pink. Several windows were fogged, their seals long broken. A few cars were scattered in the parking lot.

Roxanne and Tanner sat in his truck, three-quarters of a mile away, parked at the side of the road. She handed the binoculars to him. "What do you think?"

They'd driven the rest of the night to get here. The sun was up, but just barely, casting a searing light over the small town. There wasn't much here: a gas station, a mechanic's shop, a barn that had been converted into an antique shop, and the diner. The rest of the buildings and homes were to the south, out of sight.

"I think there are way too many places where a sniper could hide."

She scanned the rocky hills in the distance dotted with clumps of brush. "You're right. I'm going in alone."

"Like hell you are. We have all day to secure the perimeter. When *we* go in, it'll be safe."

"Jake wouldn't have told anyone where we were meeting. He wouldn't have risked my safety like that. I'm sure he'll come alone."

"I'm sure he'll *think* he's alone. They could follow him.

For all we know that thing in his head contains a tracking device. The best we can do is keep watch on the roads coming in and make sure that when he comes, he isn't followed."

"Payton said that the police released Gage and Reid and they're headed our way. I guess he had a friend—some general—talk to the police and vouch for them."

"How many more people is he sending?"

"That's it. Everyone else is on mission."

Tanner's mouth tightened in frustration. "It's going to be a hell of a job to secure this situation with only five men."

"We just need to get him and get out."

"I don't like it. They've had him for so long. How is it that he's just now able to escape?"

"Maybe the timing was bad before, or he was too weak. He said in his journal that the drugs were making him sick."

He took her hand, threading his fingers through her thinner ones. He wouldn't touch her like this if he was repulsed by her past, would he?

His calluses rubbed against her skin, reminding her of just how it felt to have his hands gliding over her body. His gaze was intense and his expression grim. "He also said he thought these people were brainwashing the men. What if the same thing happened to him?"

Denial rose up in her, swift and hot. "No. It didn't. He's too tough for that."

He stroked the back of her hand. "We have to be prepared for the worst. I know he's your friend, but you can't trust him. Not until we're sure."

"I *am* sure. He sounded like himself on the phone. Worried and scared, but not like some kind of mind-controlled zombie."

"I want to believe, too, but that's not smart. We have to stay safe ourselves or we won't be able to help him out of whatever mess he's in. Even if they mind-fucked him, we can save him. We just have to live long enough to do it."

Tanner was right. It wasn't going to help Jake for her to

shove her head in the sand and ignore the grim possibility that Jake could be compromised.

She gripped his hand tighter. "Okay. We'll do it your way. Whatever it takes to save him."

Tanner leaned forward and kissed her cheek, then offered her a smile. "He's lucky to have you, you know that?"

"And I'm lucky to have you. I would have thrown a fit if any of the others had tried to tell me Jake was lying to me."

His expression shifted, becoming thoughtful, almost sad. The sparkle that was normally twinkling in his eyes was gone, making him look grim and worried. "Let me go in alone and meet Jake. You can stay back and secure the perimeter."

"He doesn't know you. It needs to be me."

"No, it doesn't. He'll understand why I didn't want you in harm's way. He cares about you."

"Does that mean you care about me, too?"

His finger slid over her jaw, his touch so gentle it made her shiver. "Yeah, I do. I know it puts us in an awkward position, since we're working together, but I can't help how I feel. I don't want you to get hurt."

There was a lot more than one way to get hurt. From where she was sitting, Tanner had just as much power to tear her apart as any bad guy. In the few days they'd been together, she'd grown to care for him—a lot more than she should. Their relationship was nothing more than an adrenaline-fueled fling, or so she'd thought. Now she wasn't so sure.

The idea of anything bad happening to him made her panic. It was more than simply her concern for a coworker. It was deeper than that—much deeper than she cared to admit.

With Jake on his way, possibly tailed by bad guys, the last place her head should have been was on her feelings for some man, but she couldn't help it. She couldn't sacrifice one man she cared about for the sake of another.

"You can come with me," she told him, "but I'm going,

too. Jake's been through hell, and after all the years he was there for me, the least I owe him is my presence."

He pulled away from her, retreating to his side of the truck. His jaw was bulging with frustration, and his mouth was tight with anger. "Will you at least wear a vest?"

"Of course. We both will." Not that it would protect either of them from headshots some sniper might deal out.

He nodded once. "I hope Jake knows how lucky he is."

"I'm the lucky one," she said, conviction ringing in her words. "When you meet him, you'll see."

Her phone buzzed with a text. She read it. "Clay is here. He's going to scout inside the diner and then report back."

Tanner peered through the binoculars. "He just pulled in."

"Is he as good as he seems?" asked Tanner.

"Better. I'd trust him with my life."

"Good, because if he doesn't do his job right, that's what it might cost you."


Tanner was nervous. Usually before a mission, he went into a calm, relaxed state in which his senses heightened and his body reacted with little thought or effort. He'd been trained well, and he was confident that training would get him through just about anything.

None of his training had prepared him for walking into a likely trap with a woman he had feelings for.

He was stupid to have agreed to let her come. She would have been safer doing surveillance or guarding the road. But no, she had to come along and be here to meet her friend.

At least she hadn't balked at Tanner's tagging along. If she had, he might have had to resort to more extreme measures—ones that she would probably never forgive him for.

Jake had walked in a few minutes ago. They'd let him, holding back to see if there was any movement near the diner. Roxanne was impatient, wanting to rush in, but she'd held back, letting the others determine when it was safe.

After no signs of anyone following him, and no sightings of backup, they finally moved in.

Roxanne gripped Tanner's hand tight enough to drive the blood from his skin. She was shaking, and he had to keep pulling her back so she didn't draw attention by running. He set a slow, steady pace up to the door and across the tiled diner floor.

Jake sat at a booth in the back, near the rear exit. He looked like hell. He was gaunt and sallow. Several days' growth of beard lined his jaw, and his hair made him look like he'd just climbed out of bed. His eyes were shiny and red, as if he were fevered. Needle tracks marched up and down both arms. The fact that he didn't even try to hide them spoke volumes about his state of mind.

Tanner kept Roxanne hidden by his body as much as possible as they approached. He didn't want her taking another bullet if he snapped and went for a gun.

"Jake?" said Tanner as he neared.

The man's head jerked up, and his eyes narrowed in suspicion. A second later Roxanne stepped around him, and Jake's expression melted into a mess of happy relief and terrified anguish.

She pulled away, rushing up to Jake and hugging him.

"Razor," said Tanner in warning. "Back away."

She nodded and extracted herself from Jake, stepping back. "Sorry. I'm just so happy to see you."

Tanner kept his eyes on the man's hands. Clay, Reid, and Gage were outside, guarding their exit, but in here, they were on their own. "Come on. We need to go now."

Jake's expression went cold, and he sat down. "I'm not going anywhere until I'm sure."

"Sure of what, Jake?" asked Roxanne.

"Sure he's not with them."

"He's not. He's with me."

Jake shook his head. "I don't trust him. I don't trust anyone but you."

"*I* trust him."

Tanner used the comm unit in his ear to ask the men outside, "Any sign of movement?"

"None," said Reid.

"We're clear here, too," said Clay.

"Clear," echoed Gage in a deep, quiet voice.

Roxanne sat down and took Jake's hands. A waitress came up and asked, "What can I getcha to drink?"

"Nothing," said Tanner.

Jake didn't look up. "Coffee."

"Water."

She left, scowling at Tanner. He didn't care. "We need to go."

Jake ignored him. "Rox, how many men did you bring?"

"Don't answer that, Razor."

"He's right, Jake. We need to go. They could have followed you here."

"They didn't. I was careful. I wouldn't risk your life like that."

"You look sick. We need to get you to a doctor."

"No!" he shouted, his voice radiating out so that an older couple a few booths over gave him an odd look. He lowered his voice. "No. No doctors. I've had enough of them to last me a lifetime."

"Fine by me," said Tanner. "We'll go wherever you want, but we're doing it now."

Jake held his head as if it hurt. "Make him leave, Rox. I can't deal with him right now."

"I'm not going anywhere."

Roxanne's tone was gentle but firm. "He's here to protect me. We know those people did things to you. He's just here to make sure that you're still the man I know and love."

Tanner's gut clenched hearing her tell another man she loved him. He wanted her to love him, damn it.

The thought made all the others go quiet for a brief moment. Now was not the time to be thinking about love. Now was the time to be thinking about bullets ripping through Roxanne's head if he didn't get her out of here.

The waitress came back with their drinks. "What else can I getcha?"

"Nothing right now," said Tanner, still on his feet.

His scowl drove her away. He pulled a five from his wallet and tossed it down to cover the cost of the coffee. "Razor, we need to go."

She looked up at him with anger glowing in her golden eyes. Her voice dripped venom. "Back off, Tanner. Give us two minutes, okay? Can't you see he's hurting? There's no one here. It's safe."

She wasn't going to relent. She cared more about Jake's delicate feelings than she did about her own damn life.

Frustrated, he turned, scanning the diner for signs of danger. There were only a few people here—the elderly couple they'd interrupted and a young family with two small kids. The waitress didn't seem to pose a threat, and the cook behind the wall was busy over the grill. If there was anyone else here, he couldn't see them, but he was nervous, feeling that hair-raising, in-the-sights kind of feeling that he knew meant danger.

"Are you sure he's not one of them?" he heard Jake ask in a whisper.

"I swear," said Roxanne. "He's one of the good guys. Please, we need to go before anyone finds us. That thing they put in your head could allow them to track you."

Jake let out a low moan of pain. "I have to get it out. It's killing me."

"I know. We'll take care of it. But the less you talk, the safer it will be. Remember what we told you about those other two men?"

"Oh God. I'm going to be sick."

Tanner turned just in time to see Jake sprint by, running for the bathroom. He wasn't about to leave Roxanne's side and follow after him, since this could be a trick—a distraction. Clay had checked the bathrooms earlier, but that had been almost an hour ago. They'd kept tabs on it. Everyone who'd gone in had come out, but something here wasn't right.

Roxanne rushed past him, hot on Jake's heels. He grabbed her arm to stop her.

She tried to jerk her arm away, but he held firm. "Let me go," she warned under her breath. "I need to check on him."

"No. I'll do it. You stay here."

Tanner stalked into the men's room to find Jake hunched over a toilet, puking. They were alone. There were no doors or windows in here, no way out, no way for someone to sneak in. He checked all the stalls, looked into the trash can, under the sinks. There were no explosive devices or any other signs of danger.

Jake's misery wasn't an act. The retching sounds were real, as was his shaking body. The incision on the back of his head in the center of a shaved patch was as obvious as it was sinister. Someone had done that to him. Someone had cut him open against his will. Whoever had done it was going to pay.

Feeling like an ass for doubting the man, Tanner grabbed a wad of paper towels and wet them in the sink. Once the vomiting stopped, he handed them to Jake. "Here. Clean up. We need to go."

Reid's voice sounded in his ear. "I see movement. On the roof."

Roxanne was out there alone.

Fear took hold of Tanner. He raced to the door, but when he pushed it, it didn't budge. He twisted the dead bolt to unlock it, but the knob spun uselessly. Someone had tampered with it.

From above, a deafening boom shook the building. There was a huge crash, like a mountain had fallen on top of them, and people in the diner started screaming.

"Get down!" Roxanne gave that order, her voice ringing with command. "Under the tables."

As relieved as he was to hear that she was still alive, the million things that could be happening to her ran through his mind, sending him into a panic he could barely control.

"Chopper," said Gage, his steady voice lending Tanner some much-needed calm.

He barreled his shoulder against the door, but it didn't budge.

"I see it," said Clay. "It's headed right for us. Where the fuck did they hide it?"

He pulled out his pistol and fired at the lock. Wood flew back at him, biting his skin.

"What the hell is happening?" asked Jake. "You did this, didn't you? You locked us in here."

Tanner didn't waste time arguing. He shoved at the door with his foot, but it held firm.

Jake slammed into his back, knocking them both into a wall. A moment of shock trickled through Tanner, but then he regained his wits. Jake thought he'd been betrayed, but Tanner didn't have time to sit down and discuss it with him. Roxanne was out there alone.

Tanner turned, grabbed the thin man, and flung him across to the far side of the room. He went right back to the door, but even a solid blow from his boot did no good.

Right outside the door, three rounds went off. Roxanne's gun? He couldn't tell. "Talk to me! What's going on?"

Reid was out of breath when he responded. "They blew a hole in the roof. There's one guy inside. That's all I saw."

Another shot was fired, but this one sounded different, with a hollow ring.

"Razor's down!" shouted Clay.

"Chopper's over the diner," added Gage, his voice calm. "I'm out of range. Moving in."

Rage exploded inside Tanner. He fired at the lock again, barely waiting for the bullet to land before he slammed into the door. It flew open.

Ten feet away, a man covered from head to toe in gray

had Roxanne unconscious and draped over one arm. In the other was an odd-looking rifle.

The man lifted the rifle and fired. Something hit Tanner in the thigh, but he ignored it. He aimed his weapon. He had to be careful so he wouldn't hit Roxanne. Before he'd lined up his sights, his vision wavered and a swell of dizziness hit him hard.

Jake flew past Tanner in a blur, flying through the air. He let out an enraged scream as he barreled into the man in gray.

The man, Roxanne, and Jake all swayed to the side. Tanner stared in confusion as his head fogged up. How were they moving sideways? He couldn't figure it out.

He tried to find a shot, but his arm was too heavy to hold up. He took a step forward and stumbled. His vision narrowed, and he finally realized he'd been drugged.

Tanner looked down and saw the dart sticking out of his thigh. Tranquilizer? Poison? He couldn't tell. He didn't care. All he cared about was getting Roxanne back.

Jake punched the man in gray. The pile of people lifted up, and Tanner realized they were suspended from some kind of line.

"Gage, do you have the shot?" asked Reid.

"Negative."

Tanner shambled forward and fell to his knees. His body wouldn't listen. He couldn't move.

"Tanner's down," said Clay.

"I'm almost there." Reid sounded scared, which was something Tanner wasn't used to hearing. He tried to tell his brother that he was fine, that he needed to worry about Roxanne, but his mouth wouldn't respond to his demands.

The man in gray had his arm wrapped around Jake's throat, choking him while they rose up and out of the hole in the roof. Jake was fighting back, but every blow was weaker and less effective than the last.

"Hang on, Tanner. Don't you fucking give up."

Tanner struggled to remain conscious. He fell to his side. His weapon clattered uselessly to the floor. His eyes wouldn't focus, but he could see well enough to watch Roxanne be hoisted toward the helicopter as it flew away.

*Roxanne.* His mind screamed her name, but no sound escaped his lips—just a weak puff of air.

She was gone, and then everything else disappeared along with her.

# Chapter Twenty-four

Roxanne woke up with a jolt, her heart racing. She gasped, trying to suck in enough oxygen to feed her starved lungs. Panic seized her muscles and narrowed her vision so it felt like she was looking through a straw.

She moved to push herself up from her bed, only to realize she wasn't on a bed. She was sitting in a chair, and her arms wouldn't move.

Her panic deepened, churning her thoughts until nothing made sense.

*Don't move, little girl. We just want to cut you a little. Daddy's going to pay big to get his baby girl back in once piece.*

A low moan breached her lips as the memory hit her. It wasn't real. She was a grown woman. Her kidnapper was dead. He couldn't be here.

Her wrists throbbed, and there was little feeling in her cold fingers.

*Hold real still or you'll bleed to death.*

This wasn't happening. Her mind was playing tricks on her. She was in control. She just had to get a grip.

Roxanne forced her breathing to slow, despite her aching lungs. Her tunnel vision expanded, and she could see black strips of tape binding her wrists to the chair.

She wasn't losing her mind. She wasn't back in that

moldy basement, praying Daddy would give the man what he wanted.

She tried to still her churning thoughts and separate her memories from reality.

There was a man at her side, pressing a bit of gauze against her arm. A syringe was in his other hand. It was empty. He'd injected her with something.

Fear enveloped her, and she fought against her bonds, letting out a feral scream.

"Easy," said the man. "You'll be fine. The stimulant will counter the tranquilizer. It's a bitch to wake up to, but it won't kill you."

She had to calm down and figure out where she was, who this man was, and what he wanted. Forcing herself to take slow, deep breaths, she looked around to survey her surroundings.

It wasn't a basement. She was inside a large, open building. It was old and run-down. The ceiling stretched thirty feet overhead, revealing beams and a network of wire, conduit, and ductwork. Dirty windows high above let in searing light, adding to the stifling heat inside. Dusty, abandoned workbenches sat in neat rows near one wall. There was a large open space on the opposite side, and the concrete was discolored and dotted with rusted spots, as if some kind of large machinery had once sat there.

It was a factory of some kind, she guessed—one that hadn't been used in years. But how did she get here?

Her memory began to re-form, pushing to the front of her mind, sifting through and discarding the distant past. She'd been in that diner with Jake and Tanner. She'd finally found him, but he didn't look good. She hadn't seen him so scrawny since his preteen years, and never before had he looked so sickly. He'd always been strong and healthy. She'd had a hard time holding back her tears, but she'd done so out of respect for him. Jake hated seeing her cry.

As soon as she broke the seal on her memory, the rest of it flooded into her, filling in the gray spots with vivid color.

She felt the heat and power of an explosion. A man appeared from the rooftop. She'd tried to get the civilians out of harm's way, but they sat there, too shocked to move.

Roxanne lifted her weapon and fired, but her aim was off by inches. He fired back, hitting her. She fell into blackness.

Tranquilizer? That must have been what hit her. She certainly didn't have any throbbing gunshot wounds—just a slight ache in her thigh where she'd been hit.

The man turned away from a small table and faced her. He looked to be in his late forties with a salt-and-pepper flat top and frigid blue eyes. He was dressed in fatigues, marked by shiny stars and an emblem she couldn't recognize—a red sword on a field of black.

"Where am I? Who are you?" she demanded.

"I'm General Bower."

"Why am I here?"

He crouched down, putting himself on eye level with her. His face was tanned, and the sun had left its mark in deep lines around his eyes and across his forehead. "We want the diary. It wasn't on you, so you're going to tell me where it is."

Feigning ignorance seemed to be the safest course of action. "I don't know what you're talking about."

He stood, pulled his arm back, and slapped her across the face. The blow stunned her, and she nearly fell backward in the chair. Only his rough hands pushing down on her arms kept her from toppling.

Roxanne's ears rang, and a stinging ache radiated down her neck. She tasted the coppery tinge of blood in her mouth and felt a small cut her teeth had made along the inside of her lip.

Bower crouched down again, exactly where he'd been before. His expression hadn't changed. He wasn't mad. He wasn't upset. He didn't even seem frustrated. He'd simply hit her and gone on as if nothing had happened. "Let's try this again. Jake Staite sent you his diary. Where is it?"

She hesitated, weighing her options a little more carefully this time. "It's locked in a high-security vault, under twenty-four-hour surveillance."

He nodded. "That's better. I respect honesty. In fact, I think I should be completely honest with you."

Something about the way he said it made the hair on the back of Roxanne's neck lift in fear.

He covered her hand with his, and she couldn't help the immediate surge of revulsion she felt. "I have your boyfriend," said Bower.

"Tanner?" She craned her neck, stretching the limits of her bindings in an effort to see him. He was nowhere to be found.

Bower's eyebrows lifted in surprise. "Oh. I see. So Jake isn't your sweetheart. It's the other man—the one who hesitated when he should have taken the shot on my man. Tanner could have saved you, you know. One shot and you'd be with your honey right now, all safe and sound." He smirked as if that had amused him. "Actually, I was talking about Staite. He's here. He's waiting for the doctor so she can put on the final touches."

Trepidation vibrated through her body, chilling her. She didn't want to ask, but the compulsion was too great. "What did you do to him?"

"We're making him better. Stronger. Faster. Obedient. I think you'll like the change, at least for a little while."

"I'll give you the journal. Just let him go."

"You know, I think that's a fine idea. We'll have your boyfriend go and fetch it, then bring it here."

She couldn't ask Tanner or anyone else to risk their lives for her like that. "No. Let me go get it."

"Do I look that stupid? We're not letting you go anywhere. You're part of the show."

"What show?"

"Our investors are watching. We can't leave them bored without some form of entertainment. That would be bad manners."

He wasn't making any sense. She could tell he was toying with her, but she couldn't figure out his angle. "What do you mean?"

"Does he love you?"

Her confusion deepened. "Who?"

"Staite."

"He's like family. I'll do anything to save him."

"That's so sweet. And fortunate. You'll be the perfect test."

"I don't understand. Just tell me what you want to let Jake go."

"Oh, we're going to let Jake go, all right. We're going to let him out of his cage, and he's going to come down here and kill you. Once our investors see that our protocol works, the money will pour in like rain."

"I have money. I'll give it all to you if you let us go."

He leaned down so he was in her face, his hot breath shoving its way up her nose. "Sweetheart, I know who you are. You have millions, which is cute, but not nearly enough. We're looking for bigger fish. You're worth far more to us dead than alive."

# Chapter Twenty-five

"**W**ake the fuck up," shouted Reid.

Like all those years back at home, Tanner obeyed his brother's order and opened his eyes. For a second, he thought he might be late for the bus; then he realized how stupid that was. It had been years since he'd been in school.

Reid's face hovered over his, concern and fury mingling into a fierce mask. "Can you sit up?"

Confusion plagued him. Of course he could sit up. What kind of a crazy question was that? He tried to push himself upright, but his arms were too wobbly to support his weight.

What the hell had happened? Had they gone drinking last night? That didn't sound right. Reid never hung out with him like that. But the feeling in his head was the same. The bitter taste in the back of his throat, the pounding headache, the lethargy—it sure as hell felt like a hangover.

"Wake up, Tanner. Don't you do this to me." Reid roughly patted Tanner's cheek, and it wasn't until then that he realized his eyes had closed again.

"Do what?" Even the sound of his own voice was too loud.

Reid lowered his voice, as if he didn't want others to hear. "Razor needs you to wake up."

Razor? Roxanne.

Everything slammed back into his brain: the diner, Jake, the explosion, the man in gray flying off with Roxanne.

Fear for her shoved his eyelids up and gave his limbs the strength to move. He sat up and gritted his teeth through the wave of dizziness that hit him. "Where is she?"

Reid's expression was grim. "They took her. Jake, too. They used her earpiece to communicate with us. They'll only talk to you."

"Why?"

"How the fuck should I know?"

"It's a stall tactic," said Clay.

Tanner swiveled his head, tracking where the voice had come from. They were in the back of the MCC, though he couldn't remember how he got here. Clay was sitting at the table where Tanner had made love to Roxanne the first time.

She was gone. It had been his job to keep her safe, and he'd let her down.

He was always letting down the people he loved.

As the truth hit him, he pushed it away, unable to deal with the implications of his feelings. He couldn't love her right now, not when she was out there, in danger. He had to stay focused and think logically. She needed him right now, and no amount of love was going to save her. Only cunning and a shitload of bullets could do that.

"What do you mean a stall tactic?" asked Reid.

Clay looked up from his laptop. "They knew Tanner was hit with the tranq. They knew it would take him a few hours to wake up, giving them plenty of time to get away and regroup."

"Where?" Tanner struggled to his feet, forcing his legs to accept his weight. The MCC was moving. He could feel the vibrations of the tires under his feet.

Reid held on to Tanner's arm, keeping him steady. "We don't know. They wanted a phone number to contact, so I gave them mine. They'll call us."

"Did you call the police?"

"After what just happened at that diner? Do you really want to spend the next two days stuck in an interrogation room, answering questions? I've spent enough time that way lately, thank you."

Reid was right. Tanner wasn't thinking clearly yet. And he still wasn't convinced that whoever had the funding and organization to pull off something like what they'd done to Jake wasn't also in the business of buying off law enforcement. It was clear they were willing to drug people against their will. Bribing a few cops didn't seem like that big of a deal in comparison.

"They want the journal," said Tanner. "We need to get it."

"Payton's on the way with it. He made a copy, but he's bringing the original."

Clay poured a cup of coffee from the built-in coffeemaker and handed it to Tanner. "Drink this. It'll help flush that shit out of your system."

Tanner drank. It burned his mouth a little, but he didn't care. He needed to be thinking clearly. Roxanne was at stake.

"I don't like it," said Clay. "They've got to know that we'll copy the journal. The leak is sprung. The only way to stop it is to take out everyone who came in contact with the information."

"There's no way they can control something like that now. The cat is out of the bag."

"You don't get it," said Tanner. "You don't have to kill everyone involved—just enough of us that the rest of us are too scared to talk."

Clay shook his head. "They'll come after all of us. Mark my words. We either take them out and expose them for what they are, or they'll hunt every last one of us down."

"Wait a minute." Reid held up his hands. "Listen to yourselves. We're not going to storm in and mow people down. We're not at war."

"The fuck we're not," said Tanner. "They have Roxanne. I'll do whatever it takes to get her back."

Reid's brows rose; then his eyes narrowed as he studied Tanner in silence. That scrutinizing look was no good. His brother was far too perceptive for his own good.

"And Jake," added Clay. "If we don't get him out, Razor will be right back out there, looking for him."

A cell phone rang, and Reid answered it. He listened for a moment, then handed the phone to Tanner. "It's them."

Clay jumped up and went to the computer console toward the front. Tanner pulled in a deep breath and took the phone. "Hello?"

"Hey, lover," said a man. "I've got your sweet, hot thing here. Say hi, sweet, hot thing."

Roxanne's voice was rough and weak, but she was alive. Tanner's soul shouted in relief. "Don't come, Tanner. He'll kill—"

"None of that," said the man, coming back on the line. "We want the journal."

"I don't have it, but I will."

"Sooner is better than later. Your sweetheart doesn't have much time."

"Don't you fucking hurt her, or I'll kill you," growled Tanner.

"Threats? Really? How smart is that when you're all the way over there and I'm all the way over here? With her." There was the sound of a hard slap and Roxanne let out a gasp of pain.

Tanner's blood pressure shot up. He wanted to crawl through the phone and kill this bastard with his bare hands. Only the realization that his words could get her killed helped rein him in.

When he spoke, his voice barely sounded human. "Take me. Let her go. I'll even play nice and let you do whatever you want without a fight. You can put one of those fucking poison pills in my head. I don't care."

"You're not our type," said the man, "but that's sweet of you to offer."

"I'll be whatever type you want. Just let her go."

"Here's how it's going to work, lover boy. You're going to come alone with the diary to a location of my choosing. I'll have men there to meet you. You come here and we'll talk. If anyone comes with you, she dies. If anyone follows you, she dies. We find a single bug or tracking device on you, she dies. Get the pattern here?"

"I understand."

"Good. We get the diary and any copies of it you made, and you get the girl."

"What about Jake?"

"I have a feeling you won't want him anymore."

"Why? What have you done to him?"

"Two hours," said the man. "Have the diary in two hours or the deal's off and you'll never hear from me or your woman again."

# Chapter Twenty-six

Tanner thanked God that Payton was loaded and had his own plane. Tanner made it to the rendezvous point with only two minutes to spare. The diary was tucked inside a briefcase Payton had sworn was clean of surveillance devices.

Tanner was sure he was lying.

The field was in the middle of nowhere, with nothing but grass, cows, and oil pumps to hide behind. Pumps churned away, sucking oil out from deep wells. The sun blazed down, making him sweat beneath the armored tactical vest. He'd come without weapons and stripped himself of all tracking that he knew of, including the dog tags he'd been given by the Edge.

That didn't mean there weren't any devices on him. It just meant he didn't know where they were. Plausible deniability, he guessed.

Dust snaked in a path behind a black van in the distance. He'd had to hike in here on foot, letting his cell phone's GPS guide him to the indicated coordinates. The van pulled up beside him, and the back door slid open.

A stony-faced man sat inside, pointing a rifle at Tanner's gut. "Open the case."

Tanner did as he was directed, scanning the inside of the van for what he was up against. There were four men, all armed and holding weapons like they knew how to use them. "Where's Roxanne?"

"You'll see her soon enough."

"No one gets the journal until I know she's alive."

The man reached for a phone, and without taking his eyes off Tanner, dialed a single number. "He wants to know she's alive." There was a long pause; then the man tossed him the phone.

Tanner caught it and brought it to his ear. "Roxanne?"

On the other end, he could hear someone talking nearby. A man. "Lover boy wants to know you're alive. Scream for him, honey."

A gurgling scream of pain filled his ear, making his stomach drop with a jolt. That was Roxanne's voice, and whatever that bastard was doing to her was torturing her.

"Stop!" shouted Tanner.

The screams died off into gasping pants for air. The man said into the phone, "Are you convinced she's alive, or do you need more proof?"

"Don't you fucking touch her again," he warned. "I'm coming."

"Give the phone back."

Tanner flung it back at the man with the rifle, unable to control his rage.

They were hurting her, and there wasn't a damn thing he could do to stop it—not from here. He had to get to her and get her out of there.

The man with the rifle showed no flicker of emotion. "Strip."

"What?" asked Tanner.

"Your clothes. Take them off." He tossed a set of what looked like hospital scrubs onto the ground at Tanner's feet. "Put these on."

Apparently, they thought he might be bugged, too.

Fine. He'd do what it took to get to Roxanne, even if it meant going into combat naked.

He made quick work of the change of clothes. A second

man stepped out of the van with a two-foot-long electronic device that looked similar to the ones used by airport security. "Hold your arms out and spread your legs while I scan you."

Once again, Tanner did what he was told and held still for the scan. Of course, the rifle barrel pointed his way made him a hell of a lot more compliant than he felt.

"He's clean," said the scanner.

The first man nodded to the case. "Bring the book. Nothing else. Get in."

Tanner grabbed the case.

"No. Just the book."

Tanner opened the case and removed the notebook.

The man with the scanner swiped it over the journal. When it didn't set off any alarms, Tanner let out a sigh of relief.

"Put this on your head." They tossed him a black pillowcase.

He pulled the hood over his head, blinding himself, then tucked the journal in the back of his waistband so his hands were free if he needed them. These guys weren't fucking around, and they weren't taking any chances. In the end, it didn't matter if Tanner was outclassed. He was getting in that van one way or another.

Payton had a bad feeling about this whole situation. He stood in the back of the MCC, trying to look relaxed and hopeful even though his stomach churned with anxiety. Razor was out there alone, almost certainly in the hands of Norma Stynger. Payton had been willing to kill the woman because she had no conscience and would not be stopped. Apparently, even death couldn't stop her.

He began to pace, caught himself, and covered his action by pretending as though he'd meant to cross the cramped space. He hovered behind Reid, scanning the screen.

"He hasn't moved," said Reid. "I tried to call his cell, but he's not answering."

Payton slid a comm unit on. "Does anyone have eyes on Tanner?"

Clay's voice came through the headset. "We couldn't get that close without being seen."

"Something isn't right." Payton could feel it in his bones.

Reid pushed the chair back and stood. "I'm going out there."

"No. You're not thinking clearly. Let the others handle this."

Anguish burned in his blue eyes. "He's my brother. I can't lose him, too."

Payton clapped a hand on Reid's shoulder. "You aren't going to lose him." Into the microphone, he said, "Gage, move in. Clay, cover him. I want to know what the hell is going on."

Reid collapsed back into his seat in frustration.

What he wouldn't have given for a satellite of his own right now. Sure, Bob could probably pull some strings and get one, but it would take hours to get the approval and re-task it. They didn't have that kind of time. And that was the kind of thing that made people ask questions—questions that had the potential to ruin a lot of lives.

"He's gone," said Gage, his voice barely audible.

Reid went pale and began to tremble. "What do you mean *gone*?"

"His clothes are here. He's not."

Payton pulled in a silent breath. He couldn't let Reid see how upset this news left him. "Gage, pull back. Reid, access Mira's tracking system, and see if he's still wearing his ID tags."

"I already did. They haven't moved. He's gone." Reid pounded his hand on the built-in desk. "Fuck."

Payton pushed Reid aside and accessed the code to the tracking device he'd hidden in the case. It was stationary, too.

Reid was right. Tanner was gone, and they had no way to find him.

# Chapter Twenty-seven

Roxanne was bleeding. That was the first thing that registered with Tanner as they led him inside the defunct factory. They'd bound her to a chair. Her head hung limply to one side, revealing a trail of blood leaking from the corner of her swollen mouth. She had a dark bruise on her cheek, and a cut just below her swollen eye.

Fury swelled in his heart and pulsed out into his limbs. His hands curled into fists so tight his knuckles popped. Whoever had done that was going to pay.

An older man stood near her, his hips propped against a workbench. His thick arms were crossed over his chest, revealing a pistol on his belt. His salt-and-pepper hair was cut flat across the top, and he regarded Tanner with the same concern one would give a moth.

"I'm General Bower. You must be Tanner."

The name rang a bell. He was the one who'd recruited Jake, fooling him into thinking he worked for some secret military unit.

No way was that man a general. He had the air of a man comfortable with power, but there was no honor in him, no humility. His cold eyes fixed on Tanner, and his head tilted to the side as if he were studying him. Maybe he was sizing Tanner up, or maybe he was looking for new recruits.

Tanner kept his voice light and conversational, despite his desire to do bodily harm to the man. "I don't recognize the uniform. What branch?"

Bower's face darkened with either anger or embarrassment—Tanner couldn't tell which, and he really didn't care. The fact was that the comment got to him, which showed a weakness—maybe one Tanner could exploit.

"Where's the diary?" asked Bower.

Tanner pulled it from his waistband and started walking forward. All he had to do was get his hands on that gun. There were three of Bower's men here—including the two men who'd walked him inside—but Tanner was well trained and highly motivated. If he got that gun, three-against-one were not bad odds.

"Stop right there," ordered the man with an air of command.

Tanner kept walking, the journal stretched out in offering. "I thought you wanted it."

Bower drew his weapon and pointed it at Roxanne. "I said stop."

This time, Tanner did as he was told. He didn't doubt for a second that Bower would pull the trigger. Any man who would willingly kidnap and torture a woman wouldn't think twice about killing her. After all, she was a witness—one they'd probably already planned to eliminate.

At the sound of his voice, Roxanne's eyes opened and her head rolled around toward him. "Tanner?"

Hearing her speak sent a wave of relief shooting through him. He tried not to let it show, but his emotions were running hot, and his poker face was long gone. "I'm here. I'm going to get you out of here. Just hang on."

Bower smiled like he'd just heard some kind of inside joke. That only served to confirm Tanner's suspicions.

"Open the book."

Tanner did.

The man saw Jake's writing and nodded. "Toss it here."

"Let her go first."

"About that. There's been a change in plans. We're keeping her."

Tanner had to choke back the enraged comment that came to mind. He had to keep his cool here. Some anger was good—it would make him strong, fast—but too much would cloud his focus. "That's not the deal we had."

"I'm changing the deal. We need her for this one little thing. I'd tell you that I'd give her back to you when we were done with her, but I doubt you're going to want her. Or what's left of her."

"Let her go," Tanner said, his tone a bit more demanding than he'd intended. "I'll stay in her place."

Roxanne's eyes opened and she stared at him, her chin trembling. Tears spilled down her cheeks, mixing with the blood. "No. You can't."

He squared his shoulders, letting his love for her make him strong. "I can and I will."

Roxanne felt like she was going to burst with relief and fear all at the same time. Tanner had offered to trade his life for hers—without hesitation or reservation. No bargaining or conditions. Not even her own parents had been willing to do the same. How could a man she'd known for such a short time care about her enough to risk his life to save her? Even as the question rattled through her mind, confusing her, she knew without a doubt that he'd do the same for anyone. He was as selfless as he was brave, and she was as humbled by his choice as she was horrified.

He stood there, tall and proud, his body shaking with rage. But when he looked at her, there was gentleness there, concern. He gave her hope that they'd make it out of here alive, whereas before, she'd had none.

In that moment, seeing him facing a demon for her, her heart broke open and wept, because she knew without a doubt that she loved him. She also knew that she would never get the chance to show him that love, because the probability of both of them making it out of this alive was low.

She couldn't let him do it. She couldn't let him sacrifice himself for her. If it hadn't been for her, he'd never have been in this situation. He'd be safe and sound, at home with his family, where he belonged. And his family couldn't stand to lose someone else again so soon. They'd already lost so much.

Roxanne caught Bower's eye. "If you send him away, I'll cooperate."

"Roxanne, no!" shouted Tanner.

Bower's bushy brows went up. "Is that so? You know, that's tempting, but I think lover boy here will have something to say about your generous offer."

"Go, Tanner. Before you can't."

His blue eyes blazed with defiance, and he snarled at Bower. "I'm leaving here with her. There's a whole team of people backing me up. If you think they're going to sit by while you toy with us, you're fucked in the head."

"Watch your tone with me, boy. Do you really think I didn't know about your little mercenary company? Do I look stupid to you? They'll never find us. I stripped you of everything that could lead them here. And even if by some miracle they do find this place, they won't get here in time, so just sit back, relax, and enjoy the show." He nodded to one of the men behind Tanner.

The man pulled a stun gun at the same time Tanner started moving. His body spun around as he confronted the threat, but it was too late. The gun went off. The leads stuck and current sizzled along the wires, letting out a crackling sound that made the hair on the back of her neck rise. Tanner toppled to the ground, groaning as his body seized up.

Roxanne tried to lunge from her seat before she realized she was held in place, unable to help him. "Stop it!" she shouted, knowing her screams would do no good.

The second man, the one without the stun gun, came up

behind Tanner and landed a hard kick to the back of his head. Tanner stopped twitching and lay terribly still.

Roxanne bit back a sob of anguish. She frantically searched for a sign that he was okay but saw none. Tears blurred her vision, making it impossible for her to tell if he was still breathing.

Bower stalked forward, his face grim. "Did you kill him?"

One of the men leaned down and checked his pulse. "No, sir."

"Good. We'll add him to the show for the investors. Leave him there and go upstairs. Staite should be ready by now, and we don't want to be anywhere near that man once he's triggered."

She didn't know what he meant by that. None of this made any sense, but she couldn't think clearly enough to figure it out. The drugs they'd given her were playing havoc with her body, making her head spin. All she knew was that they were leaving, and she had to find a way to get to Tanner and get him out of here before she lost the man she loved.

Jake had no idea where he was, but he wasn't alone. The small room was dark except for the brilliant blue glare of a video screen. He couldn't remember how he got here, which was happening to him a lot recently. At least he recognized Bower's face, which was smug enough to tell Jake he was in trouble. He wished he could remember why.

The blank screen was too close. He blinked at the light, trying to force his eyes to adjust. His head felt like it weighed fifty pounds, and it ached as though someone had taken a hammer to it. "Where am I?"

Bower patted his cheek in mock affection. "Glad you're back among us, Staite. We missed you."

Confusion swayed inside his head as he struggled to figure out what was going on.

Back among them? Had he been gone?

In the time it took for his heart to beat once, his escape came rushing back in fragments. Jordyn's help. His bat-out-of-hell drive that took him miles out of his way, just so he could be sure he wasn't followed. Rox's meeting him at that dingy little diner that had made her so happy when she was a kid.

*Rox.*

"Where is she?" demanded Jake, fear settling in through his pores. He tried to stand, only to find he was cuffed to a chair, his hands bound behind him and his ankles locked in place. The chains jingled, mocking him as he struggled against them.

"Who?" asked Bower, grinning.

"You know who. Don't fucking play dumb with me."

Bower's face tightened in fury. "Watch your mouth, boy. You're nothing more than a damn lab rat right now, so don't go getting all uppity with me. I have permission to put you down if things don't go well."

Bower wasn't making any sense—or Jake was still too foggy to find any. The one thing he knew for sure was that he was being held against his will, and it was his duty to escape. He'd done it once. He could do it again.

His brain churned for a means of freeing himself, but nothing presented itself. The chair was metal. He might be able to smash it apart, but that would take time. Bower was armed and would shoot him before he'd have the chance. He tested his bonds, making his wrists burn as the skin split against the metal cuffs. "Where is Rox?"

"Safe. For now."

"If you've hurt her, I'll—"

"What? What will you do? Your ass is mine now, which means you'll do exactly what I say when I say it. Including putting a bullet in the pretty little blonde's head. We'll see how much attitude you have then."

Jake reeled in shock for a moment. Bower was serious. He actually thought Jake would shoot Rox. "The only one I'm going to shoot is you," he snarled.

Bower let out a bark of laughter. "The doc will call in any second, and once she does, you'll be too brain-dead to watch me gloat at your stupidity. Your mind will be hers." He leaned closer until he was only inches from Jake's face. His voice was quiet but full of smug satisfaction. "But I want you to see what you'll become. I want you to know what's waiting for you on the other side of the doc's little brain scrub."

He turned toward one of the SABERs—a man Jake recognized from the underground facility. "Jenson?"

"Sir?" The man stepped forward and saluted, which turned Jake's stomach.

"Do you like pain?"

"No, sir."

"Do you want to shoot yourself?"

"No, sir."

"Well, I want you to. Shoot yourself."

Jenson pulled his weapon. "Where, sir?"

Bower looked at Jake. "What do you think? Hand? Foot? Nothing lethal. We need him."

"Fuck off," said Jake, trying to cover his growing fear.

Jenson didn't even look worried. He simply stood there, calmly waiting for orders, seemingly willing to put a bullet wherever Bower told him.

Bower shrugged as if his decision didn't matter. "Your foot."

Without hesitation, Jenson aimed and fired a round into the middle of his shoe. His cry of pain was instantaneous, and he went down. The gun fell to the floor, and he clutched at his wound.

"See?" said Bower. "That's you in a few minutes. You won't want to put a bullet in the sweet blonde, but you will. Dr. Stynger is going to reach in and give that brain of yours a good twist, and once she does, you'll do whatever we say."

"You're a fucking liar."

Bower gave Jake a smug smirk. "She's already started

the process. Why the hell do you think you didn't go straight to the cops when you escaped?"

Jake stilled and some of his rage fell away, leaving a greasy smear of anxiety behind. He had meant to call the cops. He'd meant to tell Rox to use her connections and call in the feds, too. He'd tried to tell her, but the words wouldn't come out. And then he'd forgotten all about it, as if the thought had never even entered his mind.

Bower grinned. "I see you're starting to get it."

Jenson groaned in pain.

Bower waved a hand at the second SABER. "Take him out to the van and patch him up, then come back here."

"Yes, sir."

The two men left, Jenson hobbling on one foot and leaving behind a trail of blood.

Bower grabbed the back of Jake's chair and slid him across the floor toward a window. He twisted open the cracked vertical blinds, giving him a view below.

The room he was in was up high, hovering over some kind of factory. This small room must have been some kind of supervisor's office, positioned so he could oversee his workforce. In the open area below sat Roxanne, bound to a chair. She was bleeding, and he could see her struggles to escape even thirty feet overhead. As if sensing his presence, she turned and looked up at him.

Shock widened her eyes and made her go pale. Her mouth formed his name, but he couldn't hear her.

Jake moved to go to her, but he was trapped in place. "Rox! I'm coming."

Bower laughed. "And when you do, she's going to die."

"Shut the fuck up," Jake snarled.

He couldn't let Bower get to him. He had to stay calm and focused. Rox needed him. So did the man lying unmoving on the floor near her feet. It was her coworker, Tanner. From here, he looked dead.

Jake couldn't look away. "Did you kill him?"

"Maybe. But if not, you'll finish the job."

"There is nothing you can do that would make me hurt an innocent." He lurched against his bonds. Pain streaked from his wrists up his arms. Blood dripped from his fingertips. He could feel the metal cuffs grating against his wrist bones, but he didn't care.

There was an electronic beep behind him; then Dr. Stynger's voice filled the small room. "General, the investors are ready. It's time."

Bower closed the blinds, blocking out the sight of Rox's tearstained face. "Don't worry," he said as he maneuvered Jake's chair around so he could see the screen. "You'll see her again soon enough."

Dr. Stynger's face filled the screen, her red lips searing into his skull. She backed away, and behind her, he could see the forms of several men. They stood in deep shadows, but Jake could just make out the square shoulders and clean lines of the suits they wore.

"Who are they?" asked Jake. "Do they know you've been holding people against their will? Torturing them?"

Bower put a hand on Jake's shoulder and leaned close to his ear. "That's what they pay us for, son. Now, just sit nice and quiet, and this will all be over before you know it."

Dr. Stynger sat in a chair and smoothed her skirt over her bony legs. "Tell me, Jake, when was the last time you climbed a crooked oak tree?"

The words stung his brain like a thousand wasps, buzzing and filling his head with razor-sharp wings. When the noise stopped, emotion fell away, along with his thoughts of Rox and his buddies being held prisoner. His mind felt calm. Clean. Ready to be filled. He stared at the woman in front of him, watching her mouth in the hope that she might say something.

He loved her voice. He ached for her to fill his mind with it—to give him purpose.

"That's good." She smiled, and a hot glow of satisfaction suffused him, making him whole. She turned her head to speak to the men behind her. "The trigger phrase is unique to each subject, and until I tell him differently, my voice is the only one that will activate him. Of course, that control can be transferred to another, but I'm the only one who can do so."

She turned back around, and Jake held his breath, waiting to hear her speak again.

"There are people who are trying to hurt me. You don't want that, do you?"

"No, ma'am."

"Good. They're there, where you are. They must be stopped."

"Yes, ma'am."

"You hate them, don't you?"

Hatred welled up inside him, seething with the need to be set free. He was going to find the assholes who'd threatened the woman, and he would stop them. Anger rang through his voice until it shook. "Yes, ma'am."

"The general is going to give you a gun. He's going to show you these people. You are then going to kill them. Do you understand?"

"Yes, ma'am." Anticipation tingled down his arms and legs until the need to move was a driving force. He needed to feel that weapon in his hand, to feel it buck as it fired round after round into the enemy.

She turned away again, speaking to the men behind her. "As you can see, the subject is easily controlled. There's no concern for who his targets are, and no thought. He's a weapon eager to be used as you see fit."

Jake didn't know who she was talking about, but it didn't matter. All that mattered was getting free so he could do his job.

"Release him, General."

Bower unlocked the cuffs. Jake stretched his hands to work the feeling back into them and wiped his bloody fingers on his pants. He didn't want to risk the gun slipping inside his grip—not when Dr. Stynger's life was at stake.

Jake held his hand out for the weapon. The butt of the

gun filled his palm, and another hot rush of satisfaction shuddered through him.

He looked at the screen again, hoping for another few words from her mouth. Her bright red lips curled in a smile. "Welcome to the team, Jake."

# Chapter Twenty-eight

"**T**anner! Wake up!"

The panic in Roxanne's voice rang inside Tanner's head. A spike of adrenaline made his body start moving before his eyes were even open. He staggered to his feet, searching for the threat.

His head throbbed, and the room seemed too bright. His eyes burned, and tears flooded his vision. The room tilted, and it wasn't until he was falling that he realized how dizzy he was. His knee bashed into the concrete floor as he landed.

"Tanner? Look at me."

He lifted his head slowly, following the sound of her voice. The room was still spinning, but she was there, spinning right along with it.

She was still bound to the chair, so he crawled across the floor to her side.

She let out a relieved sob. "Thank God. I thought you might be dead. He kicked you so hard."

"I'll be fine." As soon as the damn spinning stopped. He closed his eyes. They weren't doing him much good, anyway.

His fingers found the duct tape binding her arms. He ripped it, working through several layers that had held her tight. One arm was free, and his fingers bumped hers as she worked to speed up the process on the other arm.

Her voice was quiet, but fervent. "I think Jake is here. They said something about triggering him. Do you think that means they're going to shoot him?"

Tanner's dizziness eased, and he opened his eyes to see if he could handle the reduced spin. "No. It sounds like they think he'll be the weapon."

"He'd never hurt us."

"We're not going to stick around long enough to find out. We need to get backup here. Fast. Where's your phone?"

She patted her pants with her free hand. "It's gone."

"I don't suppose you're wearing any of those fancy ID tags, are you?"

"They're on my keys."

Which, from the defeated look on her face, she didn't have. "That's okay. We'll manage."

The tape finally gave way on her left arm, and she bent over to work on her ankles. "Can you get that? I'm going to find a weapon."

She nodded, and Tanner eased to his feet, holding on to the chair for balance. His dizziness was getting better, but not nearly fast enough for his liking.

He wobbled to the nearest workbench and started searching for a cast-off wrench or hammer—anything he could use as a weapon.

The place was clean. Only dust, cobwebs, and rust remained. He couldn't even find a single screw or pencil left behind.

Footsteps sounded from overhead. A second later, he saw a set of vertical blinds open in a window high above. Bower stood there, a video camera in hand. He nodded to Tanner, giving him a mocking salute.

He raced back to Roxanne's side and started helping her free her legs. "Someone's coming."

Before they got her second ankle free, Jake descended the metal staircase. His face was blank. He was bleeding from his wrists but was seemingly unconcerned by it. In one bloody hand he held a gun.

"Jake!" cried Roxanne. "You're safe."

Jake didn't so much as bat an eyelash. He was cold. Silent. Like he was dead inside.

Something was terribly wrong.

Jake's finger moved to the trigger. A man trained with weapons did that only when he was ready to fire.

A sinking dread pooled in Tanner's stomach as he realized what was about to happen. Whatever they'd done to Jake had changed him. He wasn't Roxanne's friend anymore—not even close.

Tanner didn't waste time warning Roxanne. He simply looped an arm around her waist and picked her up. The chair dangled from her leg, bumping against his calves as he ran to the nearest workbench. He shoved it sideways and dropped Roxanne behind it while he slid into place next to her.

The gun fired, and a round went through the metal table a few inches from Roxanne's shoulder.

"Jake!" she screamed. "What are you doing? It's me!"

Two more rounds ripped through the metal, each one getting closer to hitting her.

"I don't think that's Jake."

They couldn't stay here. The flimsy concealment of the workbench was only a fleeting measure. A few more steps and Jake would be able to lean over and fire that weapon right into their skulls.

"Get free," he ordered her. "I'm going to distract him." He knew she'd argue, so he didn't wait around to hear it. Instead, he exploded out from behind the bench and charged Jake.

The weapon barked. Pain bloomed against his ribs, stealing his mind for a split second. It registered that he'd been hit, but there was no fear. Only screaming anger and a determination to stop Jake before he could put a bullet in Roxanne. He ignored the pain and crouched, gathering speed, closing the last few feet before Jake had time to get off another round.

Tanner pushed the gun high as he crashed into Jake,

slamming him down onto the concrete. They hit hard, skidding a few feet. Tanner kept control of Jake's hand and tried to pound it against the hard floor, but the man was strong. Freakishly strong. As skinny as he was, even with Tanner's weight on top of him, he managed to buck his hips and lift them both off the floor. He rolled until he was on top, gaining combat advantage. His weapon arm inched down, and the barrel of that gun got closer to Tanner's head with every passing second.

He used both his hands now, putting all his strength into controlling Jake's arm, hoping to keep the weapon aimed away from both Roxanne and himself.

Jake bared his teeth and shoved his free hand under Tanner's chin. He pressed up, wrenching Tanner's head back, grinding it into the concrete.

Pain seared his skull, throbbing in time to the bullet hole in his side. The dizziness returned with a vengeance, canting his world on its side. Something in the back of his neck popped. His vision wavered. The heel of Jake's hand dug into his throat, choking off his air.

Between black blobs, Tanner saw Roxanne appear above them. She held a metal chair over her head, biting her bottom lip in anguish at what she was about to do. A second later, the chair came whizzing down at them. She smashed it across Jake's back. Tanner felt the jolt, but Jake bore the brunt of it. He rolled away. The gun fell from his hand and scraped across the floor. Tanner's vision started to clear as he sucked in gulps of oxygen, but not fast enough to see where the weapon had gone. He pushed himself up, trying to right the spinning room.

Every revolution of his world showed him that Jake was only a few feet away, on all fours. He shook his head as if to clear it. Blood slid down under his ear and dripped from his chin.

Tanner didn't dare wait for him to regain his senses. He could barely stand, but he had no choice. Roxanne was already following up, chair in hand to whack him again.

He searched for the gun, but his focus was off, and all the gray concrete and black shadows ran together. He couldn't tell what was what.

"Jake, it's me," said Roxanne. "You don't want to hurt me. You need to fight whatever they did to you."

A low, rumbling growl emanated from Jake's chest. He pushed up to his knees, and his gaze fixed on her. His cold expression promised death.

Her voice was quiet and hollow with grief. "You know me. I'm your friend. I love you."

What Tanner wouldn't have given to hear her say those words to him. The need struck him out of the blue, making his thoughts reel for a moment before he gathered his focus once again.

"Get back!" he shouted at Roxanne. Jake was too strong for her. He'd kill her if he got his hands on her.

Tanner wasn't going to let it happen. He wasn't going to lose her. He took a sloppy step forward, lost his balance, and crashed to the floor. His poor body registered the pain, but there was so much pounding through him, it hardly seemed to matter.

He heard metal scrape over concrete. The gun. It was nearby.

He followed the sound, using his hands rather than his eyes to search for the weapon. It was their best chance at surviving this, and while he hated the idea of shooting Jake, he'd rather Roxanne never speak to him again than see her lying in a casket.

His hands hit something hard and warm. The weapon. The barrel was heated from firing.

Tanner gripped the gun, rejoicing in the feel of the hard steel in his palm. His vision still sucked, and the dizziness was going to make getting an accurate shot a crapshoot, but the noise of the weapon alone would draw Jake's attention away from Roxanne.

Jake was on his feet, his head down, his hands poised to strike, his body coiled to spring toward her. Roxanne backed away, batting at him with the chair to keep him at a distance. He angled his approach, forcing her to move to the left. She bumped into a workbench, and it funneled her toward a corner. Jake had trapped her.

Three seconds from now, he'd have her cornered, and that chair would do her no good.

Fear and anger coalesced inside his gut, allowing him to shrug off the effects of his injuries for a moment. Adrenaline poured through his veins, making his heart beat hard and fast. His senses sharpened and the pain dulled until he could feel the trickle of blood from his side and the chill of the bloody fabric clinging to his ribs, but the burning was a distant, inconsequential memory. The dizziness still plagued him, but the spin of the room had slowed so that it no longer made him queasy.

Jake closed the distance. Roxanne hit the wall and looked around for a means of escape. To her credit, she stayed calm, and when she saw no place to go, she went on the offensive. The chair flew at Jake's head. At the same time, she went low, executing a sweeping kick that knocked him off his feet.

He went down. Roxanne vaulted the workbench and ran toward Tanner.

Tanner stayed on the floor, knowing that if he tried to stand, it would only make his aim that much shakier.

Before she made it three steps, Jake launched himself at her, grabbing hold of her legs. She fell, barely catching herself before her head hit the concrete.

Tanner tried to find a shot, but they were too close together, and his whole world was on a merry-go-round.

Jake grabbed her ankles and dragged her over the floor. She flipped onto her back, raising her hands to fend off his attacks.

Tanner lifted the barrel and fired into the air.

Jake's head snapped up, and his gaze met Tanner's. Then it went to the weapon that wobbled visibly in Tanner's grip.

Jake smiled. "She's first. You're next."

Roxanne slammed her fist into his jaw. It didn't even

slow him down. She was too close to the ground to maneuver and give her blows the momentum they needed. He ignored her punches and kicks, smashing her down with the weight of his body.

He grabbed her head in his hands, and Tanner knew what came next. One swift twist, the snap of delicate bones, and she'd be dead.

Rage boiled through him, coming out in a roar of defiance. He knew what he was doing was dangerous. He knew he risked shooting her. They were so close together, wriggling around, it was hard to tell where their bodies met.

Tanner pulled in a steadying breath, and when the world swung back around, he aimed and fired.

Jake yelled in pain, clutching his thigh. Roxanne scrambled out from under him, backing away like a crab toward Tanner.

Jake pushed awkwardly to his feet and limped toward them.

He aimed again, this time for the man's chest. He wasn't wearing body armor. It was a killing blow.

"Don't kill him," she pleaded.

Tanner hesitated. He didn't want to kill this man, but he didn't want to ask Roxanne to do it, either. And it was becoming increasingly obvious that one of them was going to have to kill him to stop him.

Blood soaked Jake's pants. His gait was slow and shambling. Milliseconds drifted by as indecision and guilt weighed him down.

Roxanne grabbed Tanner's arm and helped him to his feet. She shoved her shoulder under him, helping him stay upright. They backed up. Tanner kept the gun aimed at Jake.

Above, staring through that office window was Bower, camera in hand.

There was a purpose to all of this—a sinister one that Tanner couldn't let go unchecked.

"I'm sorry," he whispered to Roxanne; then he fired the gun at Jake.

# Chapter Twenty-nine

Roxanne realized that Tanner was going to shoot Jake again, but she was too late to stop it. She reached for the weapon, but it fired, bucking in Tanner's big hands.

Jake toppled to the ground, letting out a bellow of pain and rage. She hesitated only a moment before rushing to his side. As soon as she got within reach, he grabbed for her, snarling in fury.

She jumped back, avoiding his hands, her heart breaking for her friend.

Tanner fired again. Roxanne yelped in surprise, expecting to see Jake's chest burst open. Instead, glass shattered and fell to the floor in a waterfall of sparkling shards.

She looked up and saw the office window above broken out.

"He's coming for us," said Tanner, grabbing her arm. "We have to go."

"We can't leave Jake here."

"I know." He handed her the gun. "Cover me."

She didn't know what he meant until he moved toward Jake, his face grim.

"I'm sorry to have to do this to you, but it's the only choice."

Both of Jake's legs were bleeding—one calf and one thigh. Blood soaked his pants and coated his hands. His movements were clumsy, but his ferocity was complete. He snarled at Tanner, swiping at him in an effort to reach some part of his body.

Tanner wasn't too steady on his feet, and he kept blinking as though trying to clear something from his eyes.

Jake lunged forward, taking a firm grip on Tanner's leg. Immediately, Tanner went down to one knee, slamming his elbow against Jake's head. Jake was stunned, and his fingers slipped on Tanner's leg. He hit Jake again, and this time, Jake collapsed, unconscious.

Roxanne saw movement from the corner of her eye. It was Bower, hurrying down the steps. His gun was raised, pointed right at Tanner's broad back.

She fired, hitting Bower's shoulder. He reeled back, catching himself on the stair railing. He fired back, and she felt her clothes tug against her skin as the bullet ripped through them.

She steadied her weapon and fired again, this time hitting his chest. He screamed as he went down.

Roxanne raced to him, keeping the weapon ready. He was wheezing. Blood pooled on the fabric of his shirt.

She pinned him down under her foot. "Tell me what you did to Jake. Tell me how to undo it."

"He's . . . ours."

She shifted her foot until it was against the wound and exerted pressure. He let out a sickening cry of pain and went deathly pale. "Tell me how to undo it."

"Can't undo. He's—" His words stopped cold, and his whole body started to shake like he was having a seizure.

Roxanne recoiled from the sight, and by the time she'd taken two steps, Bower had gone still. He was dead.

She'd failed. Jake was free, but he wasn't the same. Whatever these people had done had changed him, and she prayed to God they'd find a way to change it back.

Grief and regret made her go cold. Her hands shook, and she had to struggle to turn around and look at Jake, knowing how deeply she'd failed him.

"Time to go," said Tanner as he flung Jake over his shoulder. She could see the struggle it was to stay on his feet, but there was no time to wait for him to recover. They had to get out of here.

"There are more armed men outside," he told her. "At least four."

She released the magazine from the gun and counted the rounds she had left. "Five left." Not enough.

Despite her revulsion, she went to Bower's body and retrieved his weapon. It was nearly full, so it went in the back of her waistband, just in case. She grabbed up his phone and dialed Reid.

She didn't wait for him to talk but simply said, "We need an extraction for three."

"Where?"

"I don't know. Some kind of factory. Can you trace this phone to a cell tower?"

Tanner said, "Tell them we're south of the meeting point. Maybe five miles."

She did.

"Is the situation under control?" asked Reid.

"No, there are armed guards outside. At least four. I don't know if they called for backup, so expect company."

Tanner had moved to a door and checked to make sure it was locked. He leaned against it, swaying slightly from side to side. He was in bad shape. So was Jake.

She lowered her voice. "We've got injuries."

"How bad?"

Her throat tightened with worry, cutting off her ability to speak. She swallowed, trying not to think of what could happen to the two men she loved. "One is unconscious."

Fear filled Reid's voice. "Tanner?"

"No. Jake."

She heard a low breath of relief, and then words of reassurance. "Hold tight, Razor. We're on the way."

\*       \*       \*

Tanner propped his weight against the door and listened for the sound of men approaching. Reid and the others weren't going to make it in time. Tanner was dizzy as hell, and bleeding, though not as badly as Jake was. He didn't dare set the other man down long enough to patch him up, because he knew their only real chance was to run. He could barely hold his own head up, and there was no way Roxanne could hold off four men armed with combat rifles with two partially loaded pistols. If he put Jake down, he wasn't sure he'd be strong enough to pick him back up again.

Roxanne scanned the room, watching the shadowy corridors at the back of the factory. Even with the blood streaking her chin and the bruises on her face and throat, she was still the most beautiful woman he'd ever laid eyes on.

He loved her. It didn't matter that he wasn't supposed to because they worked together, or that she was so far out of his league it was laughable. All that mattered was that when he looked at her, his heart swelled and his whole world felt right. The little bit of time they'd had together wasn't nearly enough. He wanted more.

Not that it mattered what he wanted. He'd shot her best friend—twice. That wasn't the kind of thing a woman simply overlooked.

There was a good chance they wouldn't make it out of this alive, and his desire to tell her how he felt burned his throat. He held back only because telling her would be a selfish thing to do. She was already dealing with enough. She didn't need him heaping a bunch of emotional garbage onto the pile.

Something thudded at the rear of the building—then again.

"They're battering the door in."

She nodded. "Can you make it up the stairs? I can probably take at least one of them out from up there before they see us."

The thought of hauling Jake up all those stairs seemed impossible, but he'd find a way. "I can make it."

He kept one hand on Jake's back, and another on the railing. Each step seemed to sway out from under his feet, so he closed his eyes and felt his way as fast as he could.

Roxanne was right behind him.

He hurried into the office, hearing glass crunch under his feet. She followed him in and closed the door. Easing her way to the gaping opening in the glass, she peered down, weapon ready to fire.

Tanner laid Jake on the conference table and ripped off a couple of strips from his shirt to put some pressure on the wounds. It wasn't much, but it would at least help slow the bleeding.

His pulse was steady, but faster than it should have been. Tanner didn't know if that was because of loss of blood, or if it was something else. Adrenaline? Drugs? There was no way to know until they got him some decent medical care.

If they got out.

Tanner slipped up to Roxanne's side and pulled the gun from the back of her jeans. She gave him a brief nod of encouragement, then looked pointedly down into the room.

There were seven men, all heavily armed and all wearing body armor.

"On three," she whispered so low he almost didn't hear it. "One, two, three."

They both fired, then ducked as a hail of bullets flew up at them, digging holes in the ceiling of the office.

"Stairs!" shouted one of them.

"We're not going to make it," said Roxanne.

She was right, but he refused to admit it out loud. "Yes, we will."

He went to the door and opened it. A short hall led to the steps. It was narrow. They could come down it only one at a time. "We'll take them on here."

Another volley of gunfire exploded below. Tanner saw the first man's head and let loose. The shooter went down, but another took his place. He ducked back inside the office, hiding just inside the door. He wasn't sure if the wall would stop the bullets or not, but it was all he had.

Behind him, Roxanne fired her weapon through the window.

Bullets shredded the office door, sending shards of wood flying toward Tanner's face.

He went low, taking two quick shots. One of them missed, and he was greeted with another barrage of rapid fire. Something stung his thigh, and he knew he'd been hit.

"I'm out!" she shouted.

He tossed her his gun and unceremoniously turned the table on its side, dumping Jake onto the floor. He rolled it across the doorway, drawing more gunfire.

Roxanne took slow, measured shots. And then they stopped. "That's it. We're out of ammo and trapped."

Like hell. Tanner wasn't going to let it end like this.

He picked up one of the chairs and lobbed it through the opening. Then he did the same with another, and another. Below, someone grunted in pain, but he didn't dare look to see who it was or how many of them were left.

Roxanne followed suit, flinging chairs until there were none left.

He went to the desk. "Help me with this."

They shoved the heavy metal desk over the floor, pushing it to the door.

A huge boom exploded below. The floor shook with the force of it. Gunfire picked up, and then slowed to a stop.

"Razor! Tanner!" It was Reid's voice.

Roxanne rushed to the window and peeked around the edge. "Here."

Reid and Clay were below, as were several bleeding bodies. A moment later, Gage appeared from the back. "Clear," he said.

"Check the stairs," warned Tanner.

Clay jogged across the room and a minute later, there was a knock on the table. "It's safe."

They moved the desk and rolled the table away.

"Is he dead?" asked Clay.

Roxanne seemed on the verge of tears. "No, but he's in bad shape."

"Life flight is on the way. Payton is outside to guide them in. You don't look so good yourself," he said to Tanner.

"I'm fine. A few stitches and I'll be as good as new."

The need to comfort her pounded inside him, screaming for release. He was shaking like crazy and weaving on his feet, but he had to be near her. Tanner took a tentative step toward Roxanne.

She stepped away, holding her hand up to ward him off.

Tanner's world seemed to shrink and go darker in that moment. He knew that hurting Jake would hurt her, too, but until now, he hadn't realized how much.

She bent down to Jake and took his hand in hers. Tears pooled in her eyes. "He'll need to be restrained. He's not . . . himself."

Clay stared at Jake, his expression grim. "I understand."

# Chapter Thirty

Payton made arrangements to have them taken to a private hospital. They were separated, and none of the staff would answer Roxanne's questions about either Tanner or Jake. They cited privacy laws, but she didn't give a shit about that. She needed to know they were safe and that they were being taken care of.

Wearing only her flimsy hospital gown, she removed her IV and went out to search for some answers. Payton was standing outside her door. For the first time in her life, he looked slightly rumpled. His tie was loose, and his shirt had lost some of its starch. His face was pale, and there were lines around his eyes and mouth that she couldn't remember being there before.

"How are they?" she asked.

"Tanner will recover. He's got a hell of a concussion, but they're monitoring him. The bullet wounds were patched up, and he'll be as good as new in no time."

Relief stole her breath, and she had to grab the wall to steady herself.

Tanner was going to be okay. The words ran through her head, chiming like bells. He was going to be okay.

She had to swallow twice before she could speak. "And Jake?"

"He's alive."

"That's it? That doesn't sound good. Where is he?"

He regarded her with a steady stare. "You can't see him."

"He's my best friend. I'm the only family he has. Of course I'm going to see him. Pull whatever strings you need to, but you get me into his room."

"I'm sorry. That's not possible."

"Why not?"

He looked up and down the hall, then stepped forward, took her arm, and guided her back into her room. His voice was low, his tone solemn. "The things that were done to him—the doctors don't know if they can undo them."

"What do you mean?"

"They removed the device that was surgically implanted. There's no risk he'll die of poison like the others."

"That's good, right?"

"Of course, but it's not enough. They gave him drugs we can't identify. They subjected him to psychological conditioning."

"What does that mean?"

"They fucked with his head. They brainwashed him. That's not the kind of thing that is easily reversed, and when it is, there are no guarantees that he'll ever be the same man he was before. We can't trust him, Razor. We can't let him free."

The implications of what he said sank in, leaving a cold chill in their wake. "You're going to lock him up? I just risked my life to free him. You can't do that to him."

"We have to. He's a danger to himself and others. He's a danger to you."

"No, he's not."

"We were able to learn that the last order he was given was to kill you and Tanner. Do you really want to risk your life like that? Will you risk Tanner's?"

The thought made her sick. If it involved just her, she'd take the risk, but she couldn't do that to Tanner. Even if he could take care of himself, he had a family to think about. "What can we do?"

"I know people—powerful people—who may be able to help him, but he'll have to go away."

The idea of locking him up, of keeping him prisoner, made her sick. He'd hardly been able to stand sitting in a classroom at school. She couldn't even imagine what it would be like for him to be locked away. "I want to see him."

Payton's voice was hard. "No. It's out of the question."

Roxanne leaned forward, going up on her toes. "Either you let me see him, or I'll find a way to see him without your help."

"You'll never find him."

"Do you really want to bet on that? You know me. You know what I can do. I have money, resources. I'll spend every waking hour working to free my friend. You know I will."

He closed his eyes and let out a searing curse under his breath. "Fine. I'll let you see him, but you can't get close. He's hard to restrain, and they just finished sewing up the wounds on his wrists from where he tried to free himself before."

She nodded. "I don't want him to hurt himself. I just want to talk to him. I'll be careful."

Payton sighed and led her to a room with two armed guards posted at the door. She didn't recognize the men. They were dressed in civilian clothing, but they had the look of servicemen. He showed them his ID, and one of the guards opened the door.

The room was dark. A bit of light streamed out from the bathroom where the door had been left ajar. Several monitors sat around the bed, casting a bit of blue light onto the pristine sheets. She could just make out Jake's shape on the bed.

"Jake?" she whispered, not wanting to startle him. "It's Roxanne."

He shifted on the bed, letting out a low moan.

"He's sedated," said Payton.

"I don't care. I want to talk to him."

She pushed the bathroom door wider to let in more light. It was enough to see his gaunt features and the bandages covering his skin. He was held to the bed with wide leather straps around his upper arms, legs, and torso. An IV ran into the backs of both his hands.

"Jake?" She stepped forward.

"That's far enough," said Payton. "He's awake."

"No, he's not. He's—"

Payton grabbed her arm and held her back.

Jake's eyes opened. "Come closer, sweetheart. Give me a kiss."

Payton's grip tightened. "She stays here."

Jake thrashed against his bonds, his body arching off the bed. His face turned bright red and sweat began to bead on his forehead. His voice was rough with fury. "Let me go. Now!"

That wasn't her friend—it wasn't the Jake she knew. "What have they done to you?"

Payton said, "They drugged him. He can't control himself right now. It's not his fault."

"Don't talk about me like I'm not here," seethed Jake. "I'm sick of doctors. I'm sick of drugs. Just let me go."

Her heart broke as she witnessed his pain and frustration. "I'm sorry, Jake. We have to get you better first."

His body went limp, and he closed his eyes. "You should have let me die, Rox. At least Tanner stopped me before I hurt you."

"I'm going to get you through this," she promised.

He tensed, his limbs jerking against the bonds. "You should kill me now."

Roxanne choked back a sob of grief. She didn't want him to see her cry. She needed to be strong for him. "No one is going to kill you. We're going to help you."

His dark eyes went frigid, and he sneered at her. "Either you kill me, or I'm going to fucking kill you, bitch."

Roxanne flinched and stepped back in shock, unable to

control herself. She barely recognized him. He was cold. Angry. A sinister gleam filled his eyes, and a wicked smile twisted his mouth.

"Jake," she breathed out, anguish crushing her.

"Stay here," ordered Payton. He went to a machine controlling the IV and entered a code. The medicine began to drip faster.

Jake thrashed the whole time, struggling to reach Payton. His teeth were bared, and the tendons in his neck stood out as he stretched as if he might be able to bite the man.

Payton came back to her. "We should go. He needs to rest."

"I can't leave him like this. He doesn't have anyone else."

"We'll take care of him. I promise."

Jake's body sagged on the bed, and he panted. His voice slurred, as if he were falling asleep. "I'm sorry, Rox. I can't . . . control myself. Please go. I want to hurt you so much. I want to feel your blood run over my fingers. I want to feel your heart stop beating as I choke you." He let out a low moan of agony. Tears slid down his cheeks. "Oh God, Rox. Please go."

Grief pounded at her as she turned and fled the room. She couldn't stand to make him suffer anymore. She'd already caused him so much pain by failing to find him sooner.

Her bare feet slapped against the floor. Payton was right behind her. "Razor, stop."

She couldn't. She had to get out of there.

Reid stood up from the chair where he'd been waiting and blocked her path. She ran into him, and he held her arms so she couldn't get free. She was too tired to fight him, too crushed to care about her pride. "Please," she begged him, "get me out of here. I can't stay and make him suffer. I want to leave." She wanted Tanner. She wanted to fall into his arms and have him hold her until this was all just a distant nightmare.

But that wasn't going to happen. Tanner had been hurt by all of this, too. He'd been beaten, shot. All because he had the bad luck of being assigned to babysit her. Every ounce of pain he'd suffered—every cut and scrape and bullet wound—was her fault.

Tanner had his family to think about. They needed him. She couldn't go running to him anymore. If she did, she could cost him his job on top of everything else. Their time together was over. She had to let him go the same way she had to let Jake go. She couldn't stand to hurt either one of them any longer.

Reid looked over her head, then nodded. She didn't care that he was talking about her to Payton like she wasn't there. "I want to leave."

"Okay, Razor. Whatever you want."

# Chapter Thirty-one

Tanner had to get out of here. His body was on the mend, but after five days of no contact from Roxanne, he knew where he stood. He'd tried to call her, but she never answered. Reid said she'd gone to some mountain cabin to recover.

Alone.

She hadn't come to see him while he recovered. She hadn't called. She hadn't even said good-bye. If he needed any more proof that she couldn't forgive him for hurting Jake, he didn't know what it was.

At least she was going to be okay. He kept reminding himself of that, trying to put as much positive spin on the shitty situation as he could.

He rolled up a T-shirt and shoved it in the duffel bag with the rest. As soon as he was packed up, he'd hit the road. A buddy of his up north had a construction job waiting for him. The pay wasn't as good as at the Edge, but he'd find a cheap hole to live in and send most of it back home. His family needed the cash, but they'd be better off without him hanging around to disappoint them.

Especially Reid. His brother hadn't been able to look him in the eye since he got out of the hospital. That didn't bode well for their already-strained relationship.

Mom came in with a basket of laundry. She'd lost weight

since the accident. Her clothes hung on her frame, making her appear more fragile. Her eyes were red from crying, though there wasn't a single sign of tears. Since Dad and Brody had died, she'd become a master of hiding her sorrow.

She set the basket down on his bed. "I wish you'd change your mind. It was so nice having you home again."

"I'm sure Reid would disagree."

Reid appeared in the bedroom doorway. "I'd disagree about what?"

Tanner sighed. He didn't want to get into this. Losing Roxanne was eating at his guts, twisting his insides until he knew he'd never feel right again. He just wanted to get out of here and go somewhere he could lick his wounds in peace. It might not be possible to get over a woman like her, but he was going to give it his best effort.

Mom hugged Reid. "Tell your brother you don't want him to go."

"Of course I don't. I was the one who nagged him to come back here in the first—"

"I'll send you money," said Tanner.

Mom waved her hand in annoyance. "I don't care about the money. We'll make do. I don't need you boys taking care of me."

Tanner sighed. He was tired of this argument, especially now that it was keeping him from moving on with his life. "Dad would have skinned us alive if we left you and Karen to deal with the bills on your own."

"Well, Dad isn't here," she said. "It's time the two of you started listening to me."

"We've always listened to you," said Reid.

"No, you're both too busy being jealous of each other to listen to anyone."

"What's that supposed to mean?" asked Tanner.

She turned to Tanner and poked a finger at his chest. "You were always jealous that Reid got all of your father's attention."

Mom was right there. Dad had always spent more time with Reid than with him. Tanner had just never stacked up with Dad, so he quit trying.

Next she jabbed her finger in Reid's chest. "You were always jealous of Tanner for being free to do what he wanted while your father had very specific expectations for you as his firstborn."

Tanner stood there in shock. He'd never thought about it like that, but Mom was right. Reid had never been allowed to do the things that Tanner had. Dad had always had plans for him. Tanner had always been jealous that he wasn't included, but he'd never once thought that Reid would have envied Tanner's freedom.

Reid rubbed the spot she'd poked and looked over Mom's head at Tanner. "Is that true?"

Tanner nodded. "You?"

Reid nodded.

Mom let out a loud sigh. "Oh, for heaven's sake. The two of you are really that boneheaded? You're grown men, and you never stopped to talk about it?"

"Not until just now," answered Tanner.

She shook her head and stalked out of the room, muttering about how she was cursed to always be surrounded by stubborn men.

Reid eyed the duffel bag. "So, you're leaving?"

"It's not working out, Reid. I couldn't even make it to one simple birthday party."

"Razor told me why. You were being followed."

He shrugged. "It doesn't matter why. I let Karen down. Millie's too young to know I missed it, but that won't last long. I don't want to do that to—"

"You did the right thing."

Tanner's hands stilled in shock as he rolled another shirt. "That's not what you thought at the time."

"I didn't know all the facts. Now I do."

Tanner shoved the shirt in with the rest and turned to face his brother. "This just isn't going to work. I'd rather leave now before Mom gets too used to the idea of having me—"

"Too late for that. And what about me? I kinda like the idea of having you around."

"How can you say that? You told me you'd wished I'd been the one to die instead of Brody."

Reid looked at the floor. "I know. I'm sorry. It's not true. When you went missing, I thought . . ." He cleared his throat and pulled in a deep breath. "I thought you were dead, too. I realized that losing you would have been just as devastating as losing Brody. I never should have thought otherwise."

Tanner wanted to believe it. He wanted to think that Reid's anger and grief had made him wish Tanner had died in Brody's place. But words were easy, and the only way to know for sure was to stick around. Maybe believing there was a chance Reid loved him was better than knowing for sure he didn't. If he walked away now, that hope could live on and sustain Tanner. Things would never be the same between them again, but at least they wouldn't be worse. "We're different men. We're never going to see things eye—"

"We both love our family. We both give a shit what happens to Brody's babies. We both care about Razor. I think that's common ground enough."

"I'll always be your little brother," said Tanner. "You'll never respect me enough for us to work together."

"Respect takes time, but you're racking up points faster than any man I've worked with. The last time we spent any real time together, you were a scrawny teenager. I guess it took me a while to see that you've changed."

"But have you? I saw the way you looked at me after you found out about me and Roxanne. You were ashamed."

He pushed his hands into his jeans pockets and gave Tanner a sheepish look. "I was jealous."

"Jealous?"

Reid shrugged. "She's a hell of a woman, and you had the guts to break the rules and grab what you wanted with both hands. I never will."

"Yeah, well a lot of good it did me. She won't take my calls or return any messages."

"I was there when she found out that it was too late for Jake. She was crushed. Give her some time."

Tanner zipped up the bag. He didn't want to go, but he still wasn't convinced it wasn't for the best. Indecision weighed on him, making him drag his feet.

"You're in love with her, aren't you?" asked Reid.

He couldn't meet his brother's gaze. He couldn't even open his mouth to answer. That would make his feeling too real—too frightening.

Tanner nodded. "Not that it matters. I nearly killed her best friend. That's not the kind of thing a woman gets over."

"You're wrong. I think she loves you, too."

"There's no way. She left the hospital without even saying good-bye."

"Because she loves you."

"Even you can't be stupid enough to believe that."

"I know what I saw. She loves you. And she's terrified."

"She's far too tough to be terrified."

"Except for Jake. She was scared as hell for him, right?"

Tanner nodded.

"And she loves him, right?"

She did.

"See a pattern?" asked Reid.

Tanner couldn't let himself believe it. His feelings for her were too raw, but at the same time, he couldn't walk away without knowing—without fighting. If there was even a chance . . .

Hope budded inside him, blooming more with every second. "Where is she?"

# Chapter Thirty-two

The knock on Roxanne's cabin door startled her. Her pulse leaped into a dead run, pounding in her veins. She grabbed the semiautomatic from the coffee table and parted the curtains enough to peer through the window.

Tanner stood there, his shoulders back, his chest out. Determination poured off him. He was a man on a mission, and she wasn't strong enough to resist him.

"Please go away," she called through the door.

"Not until we talk."

The sooner this started, the sooner it could be over. She had too much to do to spend her time arguing. Her plans were coming together. She just needed to retain her focus long enough to figure out the best plan of action—one that wasn't certain to get her killed.

With Tanner around, all she'd be able to think about would be the two of them. She couldn't be that selfish—not when the people who hurt Jake were still out there.

She tossed a throw over the papers littering the coffee table and unbolted the door. She'd forgotten to hide the scars on her wrist, but she couldn't bring herself to care. She was tired of hiding.

Her hand stayed on the wood, barring his path.

He looked battered. Bruises covered his jaw, and she could see the subtle outline of a bandage under his shirt.

She ached to reach out and touch him, just to make sure he was whole and safe, but she held back. If she touched him once, she might never let go.

She couldn't do that to him. Or to Jake.

His eyes roamed over her, sliding over every inch as if inspecting her for damage. She was left with mostly bruises and more anger than she knew how to handle.

"I'm coming in," he informed her.

That anger began to bubble, rising to the surface. "Like hell you are. I want to be alone."

"I don't care. You're hurt. You're angry. You need someone, and Jake isn't able to step in."

The mention of his name made tears gather in her eyes. "I don't need you."

He moved forward, but she didn't budge. He was so close, she could smell soap and the scent of his skin beneath. She breathed it in, and her tears receded as a sense of calm enveloped her.

The hard planes of his chest were only inches away. She ached to lean forward and lay her head over his heart, to listen to it beat, and to know for certain that he was safe and well.

"What if I said I need you?" he asked.

She looked up at him in shock. His expression was serious without a hint of teasing. "I wrote up my report for Bella. I told her how you saved my life and how you were going to be an asset to the team."

"That's not what I'm talking about. I'm talking about us, about how I feel about you."

Roxanne wasn't sure she wanted to know. Her emotions were already in overdrive. She was barely hanging on to her self-control as it was. Curling into a ball and crying her eyes out would have been so easy. Not giving in to the temptation took every bit of her willpower.

Still, he'd offered to trade his life for hers, and that meant more than he'd ever know. She owed him for that, and out of respect and love for him, she couldn't turn him away without at least listening.

She stepped back, letting him into the cabin.

It was small, cozy, and rustic. There was no TV or Internet connection. She couldn't even make cell phone calls unless she went into the town at the foot of the mountain. The isolation had given her time to think, and when she wasn't worrying about Jake or plotting how to take down the people who'd done this, she thought about Tanner.

She didn't want to love him. It was too much for her to deal with right now. She kept wishing that her feelings would go away, but instead of fading, they'd solidified into this unbreakable ribbon flowing inside her.

Tanner sat down, eyeing the bumps under the throw draped over her work. "Not your usual décor."

She ignored his thinly veiled interest. "I'm in the middle of something."

"I'm sure you are. Probably something illegal, something that will get you killed."

"I won't let it go," she said, anger making her voice louder than she'd intended.

He held up his hands. "Whoa. No one's asking you to. Bella's just as pissed as you are. She's putting together a task force to look into the people who hurt Jake and the men who were held hostage along with him. Payton's got some government bigwigs willing to help, too. We're going to shut these fuckers down. You should come help."

She didn't want to help someone else. She wanted to do it herself. She wanted to make sure that everyone involved suffered at least as much as Jake did. Thoughts of revenge swirled inside her, making it hard to think about anything else. "I don't work for Bella anymore. I resigned."

"I know. I talked to her. She said to tell you she shredded your resignation. Mine, too."

"You quit?"

"Almost. I thought I'd give it another shot. I was hoping you'd come back and shoot with me."

"What about her policy of not letting coworkers date?"

"Oh, she totally chewed me out about that. She said we

can't be on the same team, and she threatened to remove my manly parts if I hurt you."

Roxanne could imagine Bella doing just that, and it almost made her smile. "I like your manly parts."

"So do I. Which is why I don't plan on hurting you. That, and the fact that I care too much about you to ever hurt you."

She believed him. The look on his face was too sincere, too earnest for her not to. But that changed nothing. She loved him, which was why she had to be careful. "I can't be around anyone right now. For all I know, those people will send someone else after me now that Jake failed to kill me."

"Join the club. He was ordered to kill me, too—remember? There's strength in numbers. Unless you want to spend the rest of your life hiding."

"I'm not hiding."

"You are. I don't blame you. Things are shitty. You're in pain. The instinct is to run off alone and suffer in solitude. I get that. But there's one problem."

"What?"

"I don't want you to suffer. And I sure as hell don't want you to suffer alone. I love you, Roxanne."

He didn't. He couldn't. She hadn't done anything to deserve his love. "You're just saying that to get me to go back."

He took her hand and tugged her down onto the couch. She should have resisted, but the thought occurred to her too late. "No, I'm saying it because I love you."

Tears stung her eyes, breaking down her anger. She didn't want to lose that defense around her heart, not now when it ached so horribly. "I'm not safe to be around."

"Bullshit. Besides, even if you are dangerous, you're worth the risk."

She shook her head. "Don't say that. I can't lose anyone else. You have to go."

"Not unless you can look me in the eye and tell me you don't love me. Tell me you hate me for failing to save Jake."

She had to find a way to lie to him, to send him away where he'd be safe. The chances of her surviving her plan of attack were slim. She couldn't bring anyone else along with her.

Roxanne straightened her shoulders, gathered her resolve, and looked him right in the eyes. "I . . ."

He waited silently. A hint of insecurity wrinkled his brow. He was so handsome, even with the bruises. Those were marks of courage and bravery, and without them, she would be dead right now. Jake would have been completely lost to the enemy. At least now he had a fighting chance.

She grasped onto that idea, clinging to it like a lifeline. Jake had a chance because of Tanner. Maybe it wasn't a great chance, but it was something. He was a fighter. If anyone could come back from what he'd been through, it was Jake.

Tanner had made that possible. She couldn't let him think otherwise; not when he already carried so much guilt over his brother's death. She loved him too much to do that to him.

She could live without her job, but she wasn't sure she could keep going without Tanner. He was her edge—her rock. "I don't hate you," she whispered. "I could never hate you. I love you."

A slow smile spread across his face. "For once I'm glad my brother was right."

She held up her hand to stop him before he got carried away. "It doesn't change anything. I'm too dangerous to be around. You can't take chances with your life. Your family needs you."

His smile faded. "What about you? What about what you need?"

"I'll be fine so long as I know you're safe."

He ripped the throw from the table, revealing what she'd hidden beneath. There were sketches of explosive devices, names and phone numbers of people who could supply her with weapons and explosives. She had a map of the area near Dry Valley, and satellite images showing possible locations for the kind of facility Jake had described in his journal.

"You call this fine? You're planning a one-woman invasion of a compound you can't even locate. You won't even make it past the perimeter guards."

"I'll find a way in."

He shook his head. "This isn't the way to get revenge. Getting yourself killed isn't going to help Jake or anyone else these people have hurt. It's not going to save the people they continue to hurt. You need help. Let me help you."

"You think it's a suicide mission, and yet you want to help me? What about your family?"

"If we do this together, neither of us has to die. Come back with me. Help us work with the authorities to bring these people down the right way—the way that will keep them down forever."

Roxanne looked at her plans, knowing they'd get her killed. Her anger had made her careless, sloppy. All she'd cared about was payback. But Tanner was here now, offering a voice of reason and sanity. She loved him, and that love shone bright inside her, revealing how sick and ugly her need for revenge had become.

Justice—that was what Jake deserved. He'd want her to make sure no one else got hurt.

He'd want her to be happy.

She stacked up her plans and maps and handed them to Tanner. "Take these before I change my mind."

He shoved the folder behind his back, out of her reach. "Does that mean you'll come back?"

"How could I refuse when the man I love is the one asking?"

He cupped the side of her face, his fingers gentle. His eyes fixed on hers, holding her stare. "You and I make a great team. Together, there's nothing we can't do. You'll see."

She felt the strength of his conviction swell inside her,

dampening her anger and grief. The power he had over her was almost magical, sending doubt and worry flying away. She could see his love for her glowing in his blue eyes, so pure and bright she knew it would never fade. It gave her hope that things would work out—that Jake would recover, that justice would be served, and that she and Tanner would have a long, happy future together.

"I believe you," she told him.

He leaned forward and gave her a delicious grin that made her toes curl in her shoes. His lips met hers, giving her a kiss that was over far too soon. A deep, hot longing swirled in her belly. She'd never get tired of that feeling, or the heated look of desire he was giving her now.

Her future stretched out in front of her, flickering with promise. And Tanner would be there, right by her side the whole way.

He pulled her closer, his smile widening. His mouth covered hers in a deep, hot kiss, and her body responded in a swift, liquid rush. She clung to his strong, solid shoulders and knew in that instant that he would always be there for her, as she would be for him.

"Do we have to go back right now?" she asked against his mouth.

He pulled back enough to stare into her eyes. "You're not having second thoughts, are you?"

She shook her head. "Not a chance. But we're alone. No bullets are flying. No one's trying to kill us. I thought it might be nice to take advantage of the situation. You know, like normal people."

His gaze caressed her face, and she swore she could see his love for her shining in his eyes. If she'd needed any proof that what he'd said was true, she had it now.

"We'll go back tomorrow," he said as he slid his finger over her bottom lip, making her shiver in response. "Or maybe the day after."

Turn the page for a sneak preview of
Shannon's next novel of the Sentinel Wars,

# DYING WISH

Coming in March 2012 from Signet Eclipse.

And don't miss Shannon's original e-novella
of the Sentinel Wars,

# BOUND BY VENGEANCE

On sale in February 2012.

*Missouri*
*April 2*

Jackie Patton was dressed to kill, and if one more of those burly, tattooed Theronai warriors tried to grope her, she was going to do just that.

Her red power suit was far too dressy for the occasion, but it made her feel better, almost normal. The thought sent hysterical laughter bubbling up from deep inside her. Normal was such a distant concept that she couldn't even remember what it felt like.

Two years. That's all the demons had stolen from her. She could never get them back, but she was free now, and determined to live that way.

She smoothed her hands over her suit jacket, ignoring the way they trembled. What little she had was already packed. She'd regained access to her bank accounts. Her house was gone—foreclosed and sold at auction—but she'd find another. She had enough money to live on while she found a job, and despite the tight job market, her résumé was impressive. A good position was just around the corner. She could feel it.

All she had to do now was let Joseph, the leader of this

place—this compound—know she was leaving. Today. Right now.

Jackie went to the door of her suite, hesitating with her hand on the knob. She was safe here. There were no demons roaming the halls, no monsters lurking around the corner. But there were men out there. Suffering. Desperate. Dying.

She'd been told she could save one. All she had to do was give up her life and dive into this world of monsters and magic.

They said it like it was no big deal, like she'd gain as much from this bizarre union as the man she chose. Not true. She was free now. There was no way in hell she was giving up that freedom after having lost it for two years. She wouldn't tie herself to any man. Not now, not while she was still broken and barely holding it together.

*Don't think about that now. If you do, you won't leave your suite today. Again.*

Jackie sucked in a long, deep breath and focused on her task. Simple. Fast. She'd be on the road within the hour.

That thought calmed her, and gave her room to breathe. She could do this. She had to. No one else could do it for her.

She grabbed what was left of her self-confidence and gathered it around herself like a cloak, holding it close. There had been a time when she could have faced a crowd and spoken to them without breaking a sweat, but those days were long behind her. Now, simply leaving her suite made her shake with nerves.

She was a different person now, not the powerful, confident corporate executive she'd once been. She was a refugee.

No, a survivor. That sounded better. Stronger.

She left her suite, feeling moderately less miserable. She had almost made it to Joseph's office when she rounded a corner and came face-to-face with one of the giant warriors who called themselves Theronai. As he towered over her, nearly seven feet tall, his gaunt body seemed to grow taller by the second. A shaggy growth of dark beard covered his wide jaw, and his amber eyes, shadowed with fatigue, lit up with the realization of who she was.

Jackie's heart squeezed hard, flooding her body with adrenaline. Survival instincts honed in the caves where she'd been held captive kicked in. She went still, hoping he'd pass by and leave her in peace as Joseph had ordered all of his men to do. But this man didn't pass. He slowed, coming to a stop only a few feet in front of her.

"You're the one," he said, his voice ragged, as if he'd been screaming for days.

"I'm late for a meeting," she lied.

His long arm reached for her, and she jerked back. "Let me touch you. Let me see if it's true."

Panic exploded in her chest, but she was used to that. She'd learned the hard way to hide her fear and terror, and now that skill rose easily, allowing her to speak.

"Leave me alone," she warned, trying to make her tone as stern as possible. It was a complete bluff. There was nothing she could do to defend herself against him. She was weak from her prolonged captivity, and even if she hadn't been, his overpowering strength was so obvious, it was laughable she'd even consider fighting him.

Angry desperation filled his gaze as he stared down at her. "I don't give a fuck about what you want. Grace is dying. If I claim you, we might be able to save her."

*Claim you.*

The words left her cold, and sent her careening back into the caves where she'd been held. The monsters who'd abducted her had treated her like a thing—a trough from which they fed with no more concern for her than they'd have for the discarded paper wrapper from a fast-food burger.

She couldn't do that again. She couldn't allow herself to be used or she'd be all used up, with nothing left of herself to salvage.

But what about Grace?

Jackie had heard rumors of Grace. She was a human

woman who'd sacrificed herself to save a Theronai warrior who'd become paralyzed. She'd taken on his injuries, freeing him, while she lay trapped and dying, her human body too weak to combat the poison that had caused his paralysis. No one had been able to save her. Not even the vampirelike healers these people called Sanguinar.

"Stay away," she warned, working hard to make her voice firm and unyielding. Sometimes that tone had worked to keep the smaller monsters away. For a while.

She backed up, holding her hands in front of her to push him away if he got too close.

His eyes shut as if he were waging some internal struggle. When he spoke, his voice was gentler, pleading. "I'm Torr. I'm not going to hurt you. But I need you. Grace needs you. You may be her only hope."

Jackie covered her ears before she could hear more. She didn't want to be anyone's only hope. All she wanted was to regain her life. "I can't. I'm sorry."

The man lurched forward and grabbed her arms. He moved so fast, she hadn't even seen it happen until it was too late. Violent, harsh vibrations battered her skin wherever he touched. It shook her bones and made her insides itch.

He stared down at the ring all the men like him wore on their left hands. A rioting swirl of colors erupted beneath the surface of the smooth, iridescent band. Jackie watched as his matching necklace did the same.

They called the jewelry luceria. Two pieces linked irrevocably together by magic she didn't care to understand. They were used to unite couples the way her sisters had been united to their husbands—to channel magic from the man into the woman. While that link allowed the women to do incredible things, Jackie wanted no part of it. This was not her world.

He took her hands in his and brought them to his throat, curling her fingers around his necklace. "Take it off. I need you to wear it."

The slippery band felt warm. A cascade of yellows and golds rushed out from her fingertips, flying along the smooth band.

"No. Leave me alone."

His lip curled up in a snarl. "I won't. I can't." His grip on her hands tightened until her fingers began to tingle from lack of blood.

"Please," she begged him. "Let me go."

The frantic desperation in his gaze grew until his eyes were fever bright. He backed her against a wall, pushing hard enough to knock the wind out of her. "Do it!"

Jackie couldn't bear to look at him and see his need. She knew he was in pain—all the men like him were—and she wanted to be the kind of person who would help, but she'd paid her dues. She'd been used for her blood, fed on for two years. She'd kept other women and children alive. Not all of them, but some. She couldn't let this man or any other use her now, not when she was finally free.

His body pressed against hers. She could feel the hard angles of bones and muscle, feel him vibrating with anger. She didn't like it.

Fear built inside her, but she was so used to it, she hardly noticed. Her fingers went numb and cold. She tried to shove him away with her body, but it was like trying to push a freight train uphill. He didn't budge an inch, and her efforts only seemed to anger him further.

"Stop fighting me. I told you I'm not going to hurt you."

"Then let me go."

He let go of her hands, wrapped his arms around her and lifted her off the floor. "We're going to go see Grace. Then you'll make the right choice."

*No.* Jackie didn't want that. She didn't want to witness any more suffering. She'd had her fill of watching the pain and torture of others.

She kicked him, landing a solid blow against his shins. He didn't even grunt. Instead, he tossed her over his shoulder. His bones dug into her stomach, and a wave of nausea crashed into her. She struggled not to puke over his back while she pounded at him with her fists.

"Put me down!"

A low, quiet voice came from behind them. "I suggest you do as the lady asks, Torr."

*Iain.* She'd know his voice anywhere. Calm. Steady. It slid over her, allowing a small sense of relief to settle in between the cracks of her panic.

Torr turned around and eased Jackie's feet to the floor. Her head spun, and she reached for the wall to steady herself. A hot, strong hand wrapped around her biceps, and she could tell by the vibration inside that touch that it wasn't Torr. It was steadier, stronger, more like the beat of a heart than the frenetic flapping of insect wings.

She looked up. Iain stared down at her, his face stoic. The warmth of his hand sank through her suit jacket, spreading up her arm and down into her chest. She stood there, too stunned to speak or move, simply staring and soaking up that warmth as if she'd been starved for it.

His black gaze slid down her body and back up again, as if searching for signs of injury. When he saw none, he looked right into her eyes. The contact was too direct. Too intimate.

Like the chicken she was, she dropped her line of sight until she was looking at his mouth. His top lip was thin, with a deep delineation at the center, while his bottom lip was full, almost pretty.

That thought shocked her enough that her gaze lowered to his jaw, which was wide and sturdy, and then down his throat, where she hoped to find nothing intriguing at all. The luceria around his neck shimmered as it vibrated in reaction to her nearness.

That sight set her straight and reminded her that he was not a man. At least not a human one. None of these men were. Then again, she wasn't human, either. Or so they said.

"Are you hurt?" he asked.

Pride forced her to look him in the eyes once more. She was not going to let anyone make her cower, not ever again.

There wasn't a single hint of desperation in his expression, and when his gaze met hers, it was blissfully empty of the same frantic hope she'd seen in so many others.

"I'm fine," she managed to squeak out.

Iain nodded and stepped forward, placing his wide body in front of her, so that she was safely out of Torr's reach. He paused for a second, his powerful body clenching as if in pain. Then he continued on as if nothing had happened. "You can't do this, Torr."

The loss of his touch left her feeling cold and shaky. It was ridiculous, of course, just a trick of her mind or some kind of illusion inflicted upon her by the luceria. At least he hadn't touched her bare skin. She'd learned that fabric muted the effects of contact with these men, and was never more grateful for long sleeves than she was right now. At least that's what she told herself, even as her hand covered the spot his had vacated, trying to hold in the heat he'd left behind.

Torr's voice came out pained, nearly a sob. "I have to claim her. She can save Grace."

"You don't know that," said Iain.

"You don't know she can't."

Iain's tone was conversational, without accusation. "This isn't how we do things. What would Grace say if she saw you throwing a woman around like that? Where is your honor?"

Torr's amber eyes filled with tears. "Grace deserves a chance to live."

"She made her choice. She saved your life. Don't cheapen her sacrifice by being an asshole."

"I can't watch her die."

"Then don't," said Iain, looking the taller man right in the eyes. "Leave. Come back when it's over."

Torr sneered and uttered through clenched teeth, "Abandon her to die?"

"She's in a coma. She doesn't know you're there."

Torr's jaw tightened. "What if you're wrong?"

"Then that's even more reason to leave. If she can some-how sense your suffering, do you really want to subject her to that?"

Torr gripped his head in his hands and bent over. A low moan, like that of a wounded animal, rose from his chest. "I can't do this, Iain. It's too much to ask. I have to save her."

Jackie tried not to listen. She'd already seen so much suffering. She didn't want to witness Grace's, too. It was selfish to wish for the bliss of ignorance, but she couldn't save everyone.

And that, in a nutshell, was why she had to leave.

"You've done everything you can," said Iain. "Let her go."

"Obviously you've never lost the woman you love," snarled Torr.

"Yes, I have. I know what it's like—the pain, the guilt. You'll get past it, eventually." His tone was devoid of emo-tion, as if he were stating facts from someone else's life.

Jackie almost wondered if he was lying, but something in her gut said he wasn't. Iain didn't look like the kind of man capable of love. He seemed too cold for that, too emotionless.

"There's no *getting past* something like this," Torr nearly shouted.

"You can't see a path forward now, but you will find one. Give yourself some time."

"You're a cold fucking bastard. You know that, Iain?"

"I know. And by the time you're over Grace, you will be, too. For that, I'm truly sorry."

Jackie stood there, unsure what to do. This conversation had nothing to do with her, and yet she couldn't bring her-self to slink away like a coward without thanking Iain for stopping Torr.

She backed up, well out of arm's reach. Torr stalked off, causing her to flinch as he passed by.

"I think he'll leave you alone now," said Iain. He didn't

move to touch her again, as so many men had. He stood still, just breathing, watching her with calm, black eyes.

He wasn't as tall as Torr, but still nearly a foot taller than she was. His broad shoulders seemed to fill the hallway. Even dressed in casual clothing, power emanated from him, radiating out in palpable waves. His arms and legs were thick with muscle, his chest layered with it. Faded jeans clung to his hips, the waistband tilted slightly with the weight of his sword, which she could not see but knew was there.

She could still remember the way her fingers had tingled at his touch the night he'd pulled her from her cage. Every Theronai here who managed to touch her had the same disconcerting effect, but with Iain, it had been different. She wasn't sure what it was about him that had the ability to straighten out her jumbled nerves, but whatever it was, she found herself soaking it up, hoping he wouldn't hurry off as he'd done so many times before during their infrequent, chance encounters.

She looked at the ground, uncertain of what to say. "Thank you. For stopping him. He's obviously not himself right now."

"It's polite of you to make excuses for him, but that's not going to help him in the long run. He needs to face facts. So do you."

Her spine straightened in indignation. She was the victim here. Who the hell was he to treat her as if she'd made some error in judgment? "Excuse me?"

"You heard me. You go traipsing around here, acting as if you're not a catalyst for violence."

"You think I asked for this? That I did it to myself? Torr was the one who went too far. I just left my room."

"That's all it takes. You're torturing these men, making them think they have a chance with you. If you had any sense at all, you'd pick one of them and get it over with."

One of *them*. Not one of *us*. She noticed the slight distinction and found it intriguing. Why wouldn't he count himself among the rest of the men? He still wore both parts of his luceria, which meant he was available.

Maybe it had something to do with the woman he'd loved and lost—the one whose death had left him a self-acknowledged cold bastard.

She forced herself to look him in the eyes while she lied, tipping her head back to make it possible. "I'll pick someone when and *if* I'm ready."

"Yeah? Well, let's hope that no one gets killed while you take your sweet time."

"It won't come to that."

"And just what are you going to do to stop it? These are big, armed warriors you're dealing with, not pansy-assed suits like the men you're used to."

How had he known? She hadn't told anyone about her former life. She didn't trust anyone enough to risk giving away more information than was necessary. "Did you check up on me?"

"I Googled you. I thought someone here should know who you really are, rather than daydreaming about who they want you to be."

"And?"

"And what?"

"Did you find a bunch of skeletons marching out of my closet?"

He crossed his arms over his chest, making his shirt stretch to contain his muscles. The tips of several bare branches of his tree tattoo peeked out from under the sleeve. "You're smart. Educated. A barracuda when it comes to business. People respected you. Feared you."

"You say that like it's a good thing."

"In our world, it is. Of course, I don't see any sign of the woman you used to be. All I see is a scared little girl who would rather hide than do the right thing."

"I've been through a lot these last two years," she grated out through clenched teeth.

"Who hasn't? Life's hard. Wear a fucking cup." With that, he turned on his heel and left her standing there.

Jackie watched him walk away, shaking with anger. And there was only one reason she would have been as infuriated by his words as she was: He was right. She was merely a shell of her former self, and she didn't like who she'd become. She didn't like being afraid all the time—not just of the monsters, but of the people who lived here. And of her future.

She gathered herself and marched the last few yards to Joseph's office. It was time to take back her life.

FIRST IN A BRAND-NEW SERIES FROM

# Shannon K. Butcher

# LIVING ON THE EDGE
*An Edge Novel*

After a devastating injury, Lucas Ramsay knows he's finished as a soldier. But when the general who saved his life asks him for a favor, he says yes. All Lucas has to do is keep the general's daughter from getting on a plane to Colombia—which is easier said than done...

Independent to the core, Sloane Gideon is a member of the Edge—a group of mercenaries for hire. But she's not on the clock for this mission. Her best friend is being held by a vicious drug lord, and Sloane must rescue her—no matter how many handsome ex-soldiers her father sends to dissuade her.

With little choice, Lucas tracks Sloane to Colombia—where she reluctantly allows him to aid her in her search. But as they grow closer to the target, they grow closer to each other. And before the battle is over, both will have to decide just what they are willing to fight for...

**Available wherever books are sold or at
penguin.com**

S0208